# Dragon Blood
## Sydney Newbern Book 2
### Helen Bell

# Table of Contents

# Chapter 1

I forced a smile as I approached table six. The man sitting there, a regular, was notorious for his rudeness. Today he seemed even crankier than usual.

"It's about time you got around to taking my order," he barked when I arrived.

"Sorry for the wait, Mr. Clark." I tried to keep my voice calm, summoning every ounce of patience I could muster. "We've been a little busy today. What can I get for you?"

He snorted and glared at me as if I'd just insulted his toupée. "Busy, huh? I saw you chatting with the cook. Looks like you've got plenty of time for that."

I clenched my jaw. *Yeah, asshole, that's how waitressing works—you take orders and give them to the cook. Which, believe it or not, involves communicating with them.*

Keeping my thoughts to myself, I repeated, "What can I get for you?"

"I'll have the usual. And tell the cook to get it right this time. Yesterday, my eggs were overcooked, and the toast was practically burnt."

"I'll make sure it's done right," I promised, even though Mr. Clark's usual order had always been prepared perfectly.

My smile dropped as I turned and headed for the kitchen. I pushed through the swinging doors and, with a frustrated sigh, handed the order to Jake, the cook.

Sympathy softened his features. "Mr. Clark giving you a hard time again?"

I slumped against the counter. "I swear to God, that man wouldn't know kindness if it smacked him in the face."

Jake started to prepare the order. "You're a saint for putting up with him. I'd have broken a plate over his head by now."

I chuckled, picturing the scene with relish. "Trust me, the thought has crossed my mind more than once, but I need this job too much to risk it. Can't have the boss mad at me for scaring away the customers."

Jake grinned, and I returned to the dining area to check on my other tables. Asher, another regular in his mid-twenties, signaled for the check.

When I got to his table, I set it down. "Here you go."

He reached for his jeans pocket, but hesitated before looking up at me with a shy smile.

"Hey, uh, I hope I'm not overstepping any boundaries, but I was wondering if you'd like to join me and some friends for a hike this weekend. We're planning on going to upstate New York and exploring some trails. Should be fun."

I tensed. His words triggered a buried memory—the fateful hike with Laurel, my college roommate. The man who had attacked us on a mountain trail had taken Laurel's life and turned mine into a nightmare, shattering my once sane, normal world. He locked me in a tiny room, where I woke up with the number 777 on my left palm, a countdown tattoo. The black ink was dark magic—so powerful that it'd given me cancer.

A shiver ran through my body as I remembered how scared I'd been of dying in that cell, all alone. Luckily for me, the king of the fae himself, Oberon, freed me without any explanation. He then vanished, and I had nowhere to go. My kidnapper had men watching my family around the clock. They'd kill my parents and sister if I ever tried to contact them. Fortunately, luck had been on my side again because I'd crossed paths with a vampire named Gideon. We made a deal: my blood in exchange for him curing my cancer. After he'd done it, I'd written him a goodbye note and flown to New York with a new ID.

Now the desire for revenge burned in me. More than anything, I wanted to track down the man who had ruined my life, make him remove the tattoo from my hand, and kill him. Only then would I be able to reunite with my family without worrying about their safety and get my life back. Problem was, I had no idea where he might be. But that wasn't going to stop me. *I will find him.*

"Sorry, I didn't mean to upset you." Asher's voice brought me back to the here and now. I gave him an apologetic smile. He seemed like a nice guy, but my life was too chaotic for dating. After politely turning him down, I dove back into the growing crowd.

When my shift finally ended, my feet were throbbing, and I was exhausted. All I wanted to do was get to my hotel room, kick off my shoes, take a hot shower, and collapse into bed. But instead, I had to meet Sarah, a potential roommate, at a nearby coffee shop. With my coat shielding me from the biting night cold, I walked out of the diner.

When I arrived, I stepped into the cozy interior and took a deep breath, praying that this meeting would go well. I scanned the room until I recognized Sarah from the picture she'd posted on a roommate-search site. She was sitting at a table in the corner with her laptop open. I approached her, the aroma of freshly brewed coffee and baked goods wafting through the air.

Noticing me, she grinned. "Hi, you must be Donna."

I smiled back and nodded at my fake name, the one printed on my new ID. We shook hands, and after I sat across from her, we ordered two cups of tea. The conversation flowed easily as we chatted about work, hobbies, and our preferences for cleanliness and organization. Sarah seemed friendly, and things were going well. Just as I was beginning to feel hopeful, Sarah's expression changed to one of apology.

"Oh, I just realized I forgot to ask you something important during our phone call. Do you have any references from previous roommates or landlords?"

I hesitated, feeling a knot form in my stomach. "No, I don't. I just moved out of my parents' house, and I'm staying with a friend until I find a place," I lied. Crashing on a friend's couch sounded like a more realistic temporary living situation for a waitress than a five-star luxury hotel in the city.

"I'm so sorry, Donna. I should've asked you before we met. Things have been incredibly hectic for me at work, and it completely slipped my mind. Look, I feel very positive about you, but after some bad experiences in the past, I've become more cautious, which is why references are important to me. I hope you understand."

My shoulders sagged as I nodded.

"I'm sorry to have wasted your time. I hope you find someone soon," she said.

"Thanks, good luck with your search, too."

I let out a heavy breath after leaving the coffee shop. Apartment hunting was hell. I'd spent the last week searching nonstop for affordable places outside the city and in low-income neighborhoods, only to see them snatched up before I could even schedule a viewing. The few apartments I'd managed to apply for were taken by others with more financial stability. After failing to find anything outside the city, I'd decided to look for a roommate to share the cost of renting a place in the city. However, that, too, had proven challenging. Sarah was the third potential roommate to reject me. The first had been worried that my occasional late-night returns from work would be too disruptive, and the second had been concerned about having a roommate who relied solely on a waitress's income. I was getting worried; if I didn't find a place to rent soon, I'd end up without a roof over my head.

Concerned thoughts about the future swirled in my mind as I headed to the subway. On my way, I passed by some sketchy alleys. Before my abduction, I hadn't believed in the supernatural, unlike my sister. Now, I knew there were far more dangerous creatures than human street criminals lurking in the shadows. Despite the creatures' supernatural powers, I wasn't defenseless. After Oberon had freed me, I discovered I was physically stronger and had martial arts skills I'd never trained in. These new abilities, I assumed, came from the rare dark magic on my hand.

As I continued walking, I kept my senses sharp. My foul mood made me hope that some vampire would attack me, just to release the pent-up anger and frustration that was simmering inside of me. However, the silver dagger in the inside pocket of my coat remained undisturbed all the way to my hotel.

Fatigue clung to my body as I stopped at the elevator bank in the lobby. A skinny guy, looking about two years younger than me, and a woman in her late forties stood in front of the polished brass doors. She held herself with an air of regal command, her gaze sweeping over me, a hint of disdain flickering across her face as she took in my waitress uniform beneath my open coat. To her, I was an unwelcome intrusion in her world of elite refinement.

As the elevator slid open, the three of us stepped inside. The woman's perfume enveloped the space with rich, floral notes of jasmine and rose. When the elevator doors closed, I could feel her eyes on me, probing and judging. It'd been a long, exhausting day with difficult customers, and my feet were killing me. I was in no mood for her disapproving and condescending gaze.

I turned to her. "Is there something I can help you with?" Her chin lifted in response, and her lips compressed. She said nothing, as if she didn't think I was worthy of acknowledgment.

The guy, however, looked amused. "My mother is just a curious person. She's probably wondering how someone like you can afford such an expensive hotel. Would you indulge her curiosity? Who's picking up the tab for your room? Got a sugar daddy? Maybe someone famous?"

The woman's head whipped toward her son. "Evan!"

I met his gaze. Instead of telling him it was none of his damn business, I decided to make him and his mother think twice before coming near me in the future by telling him the truth.

"Yes, he's very famous, but not in this world. He lives in the faerie realm. His name is Oberon, and he's the king of the fae." Evan's amusement turned to unease as I continued in a serious tone. "I made a deal with him while trapped in a supernatural prison in another dimension. He promised to bring my dead sister back to life, but only if I stayed away from Gideon, the vampire who had cured my cancer."

The woman took a step back, clutching her expensive purse and nudging her son away from me. The expression on her face made it clear she considered me not only unhinged, but also potentially dangerous.

I looked at her son. He seemed uncertain whether I was being serious or joking. To ensure he shared his mother's opinion of me, I continued, maintaining a straight face. "When I returned to our world from the supernatural prison, Oberon sent a common fae on his behalf. She arranged for me to receive an envelope with a plane ticket to New York, cash, and a new ID, so I could start over after leaving my vampire friend. I also got to see my dead sister alive again from a distance. Then, the nice common fae had a cab driver take me to this fancy hotel, where I had a room booked for three weeks. And that's how I ended up here. Oh, and if you're curious about—"

The elevator doors opened, and they both bolted like their asses were on fire. I leaned against the wall and smiled with satisfaction. Something told me they wouldn't bother me or ask such rude, personal questions again.

When I got to my opulent room, I took a long, hot shower. The water cascaded over me, its warmth soothing my tired muscles and easing the tension of the day. After I finished, I stepped out of the bathroom. A cloud of steam followed me, the scent of rose soap filling the air. I slipped into my pajamas and plopped down on the edge of the bed. I started to massage my aching feet, savoring the relief.

Then I looked at the black ink on my palm. The number 684 stared back at me. During the time I'd been in New York, the tattoo kept decreasing by one every twenty-four hours. Fourteen days had passed since the cab driver dropped me off at this hotel, took my cell phone, and gave me a new one with a different number.

Since that day, life at the hotel had settled into a steady routine. Aside from a few bizarre dreams about a vial containing dragon blood that jolted me awake with a hammering headache, things felt almost normal.

Knowing that the money in the envelope I'd received from the cab driver wouldn't last forever, I'd started looking for a job, which turned out to be a struggle. I'd hoped to land a waitressing position, but since I lacked experience in the service industry, no one was willing to hire me. Then, in a twist of fate, I found Marvin's diner. He was in a bind—two of his servers had just quit. Desperately needing a new waitress, he couldn't afford to be picky. After I got the job, I went apartment hunting, which didn't go very well. The pressure to find a place was mounting as I only had a week left at the hotel.

The next day, I tried not to dwell on my troubling circumstances as I got ready for work. When my shift was over, Veronica, one of the waitresses I worked with, caught me at the front door of the diner, and I wondered if it was to thank me again for helping her boyfriend, Nick.

Just the other day, he'd come by the diner to pick her up at the end of her shift. He'd waited outside while she put on her coat. As I was serving food, I spotted him through the diner window. Leaning against his Lamborghini, he seemed to get a call. He pulled his phone out of his jacket and answered it. Then, he popped a piece of gum into his mouth and started choking on it.

Luckily for him, my mom had taught me the Heimlich maneuver. I ran outside to help. With my new strength, I was extra careful not to break his ribs as I locked my arms from behind him and jerked my fist inward and upward hard. After the gum had flown out of his mouth, he'd thanked me over and over again for saving his life. So had his girlfriend.

I liked Veronica. Under other circumstances, we might have been good friends, but my new reality didn't allow for new friendships or socializing. Nothing about my life was normal now. Gloves had become my constant companions, hiding the countdown tattoo on my left hand.

Those who saw me every day thought I had a skin condition, unaware that the gloves served as a shield against a far more terrifying truth. I also had to lie about myself. I went by the name Donna, and my official story was that I'd just moved to the city after taking some time off from college to rethink my life choices. In the meantime, I was crashing at a friend's place and desperately needed an affordable apartment to rent.

"Last night, Nick asked how he could repay you for saving his life," Veronica said as we stood at the entrance to the diner. "I told him about your apartment-hunting frustration because his mother owns a rental unit in the city. It became available a week ago, so he hit her up on her cell this morning to vouch for you. After hearing how you had saved her only son's life, she was so grateful she agreed to give you a long-term lease if you like the place."

My eyes bugged out, and I drew in a breath. "No way, Veronica, this is amazing! I can't believe it! Oh my God, thank you!"

She waved a dismissive hand. "Don't mention it. Nick owes you big time. And don't forget, you covered my last three shifts so I could go on that vacation to the Bahamas with him. Helping you out is the least we can do."

"Where's the apartment?" I asked. When she named the neighborhood, my eyebrows went up and my excitement popped like a balloon. "I'm pretty sure that's way out of my price range."

"Yeah, it's a pricey area. That's why I didn't mention the apartment to you when it became available. But Nick told his mom you were going through a rough patch and asked if she'd lower the rent for you. She agreed right away."

"What's the new rent?" I asked and blinked in surprise at the number she said. It was a significant reduction for that neighborhood and within the income range of a waitress.

"And there's more good news." A broad grin spread across her lips. "She's giving you the first two months' rent free."

"Two months' rent free?" My voice reached a higher octave, but the enthusiasm in me quickly faded. It seemed too good to be true, and I grew suspicious. I'd always assumed Veronica was a regular human, but what if she was a Daywalker? Vampires were born with the same anatomy and characteristics as humans. During this phase, they were known as Daywalkers. The sun didn't harm them, and they ate, slept, breathed, and looked like humans. However, this state was temporary. Eventually, a Daywalker would undergo the Change, a process that stripped them of human-like traits, biological functions, and appearance. They'd then become a full-blown vampire, passing through three distinct stages of existence: Newborn, Adult, and Ancient.

If Veronica was a Daywalker, her intentions might not be innocent, and I could end up as the main course for her bloodthirsty vampire family. There was another unsettling possibility that she was a demon, a soul-sucking evil monster that looked human. In that case, whatever her intentions toward me were, they had to be bad. Then again, Veronica could indeed be a human—just not an innocent one. Maybe she knew about the existence of the Hidden World. This whole thing could be a trap to get me alone and vulnerable, then drain my blood to sell it to a vampire or offer me as a meal for a demon.

At that moment, I wished I had my sister's ability. She could sense what kind of creature someone was. I regretted dismissing all the books Zoey had read about supernatural creatures as nonsense and a waste of time. Her obsession with them, which I'd once considered ridiculous, now felt like a missed opportunity for practical knowledge.

"Would you look at that? Yummy..." Veronica said, shifting her gaze to a guy who had just entered the diner with his phone to his ear.

He chose a table in the middle of the room and gestured for us to take his order. Veronica held up a finger to indicate she'd be with him shortly then jotted down a phone number on her notepad, tore off the page, and handed it to me.

"Here's Nick's mom's digits. She's expecting your call," she said before heading over to the customer. I stared at the number for a moment and sighed. Maybe I was being overly paranoid. I slipped the paper in my pocket and left the diner.

The cold night clawed at my bones as I walked outside, the streets glistening from a recent rain. Halfway to the subway, an unsettling feeling of being followed crept over me. I paused and glanced over my shoulder, confirming my suspicion. A woman stood in the middle of the sidewalk, not far away, staring right at me. Holding a closed umbrella, she appeared to be in her mid-forties with natural, fair skin. Her long, brown hair was tied in a ponytail, and a white coat enveloped her body.

Who was she?

Confused, I stepped toward her, and a pack of rowdy guys passed by me, blocking my view of her. As they crossed the street, my line of sight cleared, but the spot where she'd been standing was now empty. I scanned the area, looking for her, but she was nowhere in sight. Where the hell had she gone? A raindrop splattered on my face, and the biting wind prompted me to resume my walk toward the subway. I pushed the strange incident out of my mind and shifted my focus to getting to my hotel room before I turned into a Popsicle.

When I arrived, despite my suspicions, I contacted Nick's mother and made an appointment to see the apartment. In my current situation, I couldn't afford to pass up what might be a legit offer.

The next day, after my shift was over, I changed out of my uniform and armed myself, preparing for the possibility Veronica wasn't an innocent human and had set up an ambush for me.

Before I left the hotel, I also took a BFB pill from a bottle I'd taken the day I left Gideon's house. BFB was the only thing that could protect your soul from a hungry demon. They were expensive, had side effects like sensitivity to sunlight, and contained dried vampire blood, which demons found repulsive. As long as you had BFB coursing through your veins, your soul was safe from them.

When I reached the apartment, I was greeted by a harmless-looking woman who introduced herself as an employee of Nick's mother. As she showed me around, my suspicions began to wane. The woman's demeanor remained professional, and at no point did she make any move to harm me. It seemed Veronica hadn't set me up after all. At the end of the tour, I felt relieved and happy. The apartment was everything I could have hoped for, with a washer and dryer, a spacious bedroom, windows in both the kitchen and living room, and an impressive view. Best of all, it came fully furnished.

After signing the lease, I gathered my belongings from the hotel room and made my way back to my new apartment. I unpacked and put everything in place. Then I sat on the couch and basked in the sweet feeling of having my own place. I wished Zoey and my parents could be here. They would have loved this place. Anger erupted in me as I thought about the person responsible for keeping me away from them.

With a job and a place to live, I could now focus on finding my kidnapper. I knew two things about him: what he looked like and that he was a powerful witch. Only someone truly skilled could have cast the spell that created the tattoo on my hand. I planned to use this information to track him down, hopefully before the tattoo reached zero. It wasn't much to go on, but it was a starting point.

I was set on getting revenge for what he'd done to me. When I finally found that bastard, I was going to pay a strong witch to help me lock him up in a cell as small as the one he'd put me in. I'd let him rot in there, enjoying every moment of his suffering before I ended his life. Picturing him getting what he deserved brought a smile to my face, and a spark of hope replaced my anger. I lingered on the thought until my mind drifted to Gideon in the silence of the room.

What was he doing right now? How had he reacted to the note I left him? Was he upset that I had gone? Did he even care? My hand moved up to where his teeth had sunk and drawn my blood the night I'd left his house. I closed my eyes as heat spread through my body. My nipples hardened, and I snapped my eyes open, angry at myself. I had to stop thinking about him. He was just a part of my past now, and that was it.

Hunger started to take over, and a quick trip to the kitchen reminded me I had an empty fridge. I slipped into my coat and went out to pick up some groceries. A few minutes later, I entered the bright interior of a grocery store and made my way to the bread and frozen meals at the end of the room.

I was moving down the aisle of crackers and cookies when, suddenly, a fog descended over my mind, making it difficult to think. A sense of detachment from my surroundings filled me as an inexplicable urge to abandon my shopping and leave the store consumed me. My own will ceased to exist. The feeling was familiar, and I realized what it was. Compulsion.

Two supernatural beings possessed the ability to mess with human minds. One was an Ancient vampire, a vampire over a thousand years old, and the other was an illusionist, a witch skilled in creating magical illusions and reading minds. Gideon and Audrey, an illusionist and his friend, had taught me how to protect my mind and soul from compulsion and mind tricks.

Despite my new ability, I was unable to resist the power that was controlling me. From the way my mind was being manipulated, I suspected whoever was behind this must be an Ancient vampire, not a witch. My current actions were not of my own volition. While illusion magic had the power to influence a person's decisions and actions, it couldn't impose the illusionist's will on them. Ancient vampires, on the other hand, had the ability to override free will with compulsion.

I glanced around the room. What puzzled me was that there was no one in front of me or in the store who looked suspicious. Eye contact was necessary for an Ancient vampire to compel a human. The only possible explanation I could think of was that the vampire controlling me had ordered my mind not to perceive their presence. Who the hell was doing this? What did they want? Alarmed, I found myself leaving the store. I hopped on the next train to an address in the city and arrived at an apartment on the fifth floor of an old building.

The front door was cracked open. Crap.

# Chapter 2

Under the influence of compulsion, I entered the apartment. I extracted the dagger from my boot and walked cautiously down the entrance hallway, my breath becoming a visible vapor. The lights were on, soft.

"Hello?" I said and was answered with silence. I advanced into the living room and stopped. My mouth dropped open at the scene in front of me. Papers and heavy books were floating around the room, the pages of the books were turning, and the words on the papers were dancing. The scent of incense and herbs hung heavy in the air. The window was open, the sheer curtains billowing inward. Near the coffee table, a girl lay on the floor with her eyes closed.

I slipped my weapon back into my boot and eased toward her, moving between the objects in the air. Lying on her back, dressed in black pants and a tight sweater, she looked to be in her early twenties. Her skin was ashen white, her lips tinged blue, and her short hair was disheveled. I knelt beside her and checked for a pulse. There was none.

The old Sydney, who had lived a sane, quiet life, would have been shocked and frightened and called the police immediately. But a lot had happened since my kidnapping. Now, seeing a body didn't faze me as much as it should have. I looked at the books and papers suspended in the air and assumed she'd been a witch. Her death wasn't a case for the human police.

The Hidden World had its own system of justice. Millions of years ago, in ancient Egypt, Herit, a mighty supernatural being whose true nature was a mystery, had established a system of justice to govern the supernatural creatures. Her laws forbade the use of dark magic, or anything related to it, and mandated that all vampires, demons, and witches ensure that their supernatural nature was not widely known by humans. To enforce these laws, Herit had created Ice Prison and the Watchers. They were magical beings whose job was to imprison any creature from the Hidden World who broke Herit's laws. I knew that each supernatural race was allowed to establish its own justice system, but I had no idea whether the witches had a police force, or if there was some kind of magical 911.

A cold breeze swept through the window, drawing my attention back to the dead girl. I scanned the living room, looking for anything that might tell me what had happened. It was clean and tidy, and there was no sign of a struggle or blood. As I stood up, I experienced another compulsion that drove me to a bedroom with a desk facing a window. It was cluttered with notebooks, books, pens, and crumpled balls of paper. A warm, amber glow emanated from a lamp, illuminating two small, round glass bottles sealed with cork stoppers. Another, smaller than the others, rested on the unmade bed.

With no control over my actions, I approached the bottles and drained the tasteless liquid from all three, then cursed aloud. What the hell had I just drunk? As the compulsion released its grip on my mind, I started sifting through the clutter on the desk for some answers. Just as I spotted a fortune teller's business card and a cell phone, I heard a beeping sound.

I turned to look at the digital alarm clock on the nightstand. Instead of the time, it displayed a warning: "Attention, Ivy, a Watcher is outside the building."

That was my cue to get the hell out of there. I slipped the cell phone and the fortune teller's business card into my purse and hurried to the front door, hoping I wouldn't be held back by any more compulsions. I made it to the elevator, and when the door opened, it revealed a tall man with dark brown skin, wearing a suit and a trench coat. His hair was neatly styled with the sides and back trimmed short and the top left slightly longer. The parting was on the left, and the hair was combed smoothly to the side. There was something odd about him. His eyes were empty and emotionless, like those of a robot. Was he a Watcher? I didn't have my gloves on, and his eyes went down to my tattoo. Damn it.

My heart raced. I tried to reassure myself that he could just be an ordinary human resident of the building. Avoiding eye contact, I moved to get into the elevator. He held the door open with his hand, blocking my way.

Glancing up at him, I caught a fleeting glimpse of his irises changing color from brown to a chilling blood red before returning to normal seconds later.

Any doubts I had about him being a Watcher vanished. He seemed bewildered, and I assumed it was because he was not supposed to arrest humans, even if they had dark magic on their hands. I decided to feign ignorance and act as any normal human would in this situation.

I cleared my throat. "Excuse me, sir, you're blocking my way."

Towering over me, he stood still for a few agonizing seconds, scrutinizing me. His head cocked to the side, the movement unnatural and mechanical. I braced myself for an interrogation about the tattoo, but instead, he stepped aside to let me pass.

"Of course, my apologies." His tone was polite. I entered the elevator, and he let go of the door, which closed after I pushed the button. Once enclosed within the confines of the elevator, I pressed my hand to my chest, releasing a sigh of relief. My heart returned to its normal rhythm after I left the building, but my mind was in chaos. Who had notified the Watcher of the girl's death? Had he come to her apartment to take her body so that humans wouldn't discover her? And what had caused her death? Was it murder? A spell gone wrong? A health problem?

When I reached my new home, my head felt like it was going to explode, and a bone-deep fatigue suddenly hit me. My mind became foggy, my eyelids growing heavy as I shuffled into the bedroom. I only wanted to rest for a short while, but the moment my head touched the pillow, sleep overcame me.

It wasn't until morning that a burning sensation jolted me awake as the winter sunlight streamed through the window and touched my skin. I hissed and twisted my face in pain while jumping out of bed.

"Damn BFB pills and their side effects," I grumbled as I stepped to the curtain and closed it. Since it was my day off, I decided to give in to my exhaustion and go back to bed. The next time I woke up, the clock read seven p.m.; I'd slept through the day. As I sat up in bed, stretching and rubbing the sleep from my eyes, I felt the strange fatigue finally dissipate.

Memories of recent events started to rush in. I couldn't help but speculate about the connection between the mysterious stuff I'd consumed and the subsequent onset of fatigue and loss of appetite. My stomach remained calm and quiet although I'd skipped dinner the night before. Despite these disturbing symptoms, I didn't believe the liquid in the bottles had been deadly, or I'd have been dead by now. However, this realization did little to alleviate my concerns.

The thought that someone out there had the power to control my mind even though I was immune to compulsion, or was at least supposed to be, scared the hell out of me. They could make me do whatever they wished, and I had no idea what their agenda was. Trying to track down the man who had kidnapped me would have to wait until I found out who had compelled me. I needed to know what their motives were, what I'd drunk, and why I'd been forced to go to a dead witch's apartment. Who had she been? What had happened to her?

After getting out of bed, I showered, brushed my teeth, and tossed on a pair of jeans and a cozy sweater. Then I fished out of my purse the cell phone and the fortune teller's business card I'd found in the witch's apartment.

I fired up the phone, hoping it'd provide some helpful insight. The good news? It was unlocked, no passcode to try to crack. The bad news? There wasn't much info on it. The phone belonged to the dead girl whose name had been Ivy. I'd figured as much from the warning on the alarm clock. I scrolled through the only ten photos on her phone. One showed her sitting on her bed, smiling at the camera, while the other nine were from a birthday party. She was celebrating with four girls, who seemed to be of different ages.

As I looked at Ivy, standing among them with the birthday cake on the table, my mind took a trip back to one of my birthdays. It'd been a cold, rainy night, and I was in my bedroom with Zoey. She was doing my hair and makeup for my birthday party. Wearing a brand-new dress, I wanted to look perfect for Jared, who was my boyfriend at the time.

He texted, saying he was on his way. When the doorbell rang, my heart raced with excitement. Zoey went downstairs to answer the door. As I took one last look in the hall mirror outside my room, I heard Zoey's angry voice downstairs.

"What the shit, Jared? Are you trying to kill her?" she exploded at him.

I trotted down the stairs to the living room where Zoey held the front door open. Jared was standing on the doorstep with a cupcake box. My parents and I joined the scene.

"Language, Zoey," my mother chided.

"Mom, he brought her a cupcake with edible gold dust. Gold!" Zoey's voice boomed through the room. My parents' expressions changed to sheer panic when they heard the word "gold."

"I'm sorry, I forgot she's allergic to it, okay? But it's not like it would've killed her or anything, right?" Jared said defensively.

"It's okay; I wouldn't have eaten it," I said, redirecting everyone's attention to me.

Admiration replaced the distress on my mother's face when she saw me, a hand flying to her chest. "Oh, honey, you look so beautiful."

Dad chimed in with compliments on my appearance, and I turned my expectant gaze to Jared. He glanced in my direction, but then his eyes settled back on Zoey, and my cheerful smile faded.

"Again, I'm really sorry... but you're not allergic to gold, right? Here, you can have it. It's yours." Zoey's lips pursed as she snatched the box from his hand.

"Thanks, but I hate cupcakes," she lied, marching to the kitchen and throwing the box in the trash.

"Son," my dad said to Jared, "I understand your intentions were good, but you must be more careful next time. Sydney could have had a severe allergic reaction from ingesting the gold and choked to death."

Jared had known about my allergy, but the jerk went ahead and bought me a cupcake with edible gold. I'd been so in love with him that it blinded me to his true motives. I'd given him the benefit of the doubt, believing that he'd simply made an innocent mistake. Now, it was clear to me that the cupcake had been meant for Zoey all along. Jared had bought it to try to win her affection, thinking she'd be willing to accept the cupcake because I couldn't, but his plan backfired.

After watching Zoey dispose of his gift, Jared turned to my dad and said, "It won't happen again, Mr. Newbern."

"Let's just forget about it, okay?" I told Jared, taking his hand and leading him into the living room. While we waited for my friends to arrive, I waved at my dress. "What do you think? You like it? It's new."

He screwed up his face in dissatisfaction. "Uh, sorry, I don't. I mean, yeah, the dress is hot, but on you? Not so much. It doesn't suit you, Syd. Only girls like Zoey can pull off dresses like this." He stopped when he saw my expression. "You're not gonna cry on me now, are you? I'm just being honest because I care about you."

He reached out to touch my cheek, but I moved my head away, holding back the tears that threatened to spill. "Oh, come on, Syd, don't make me out to be the bad guy here. What was I supposed to do? Lie to you? Look, if you wanna look better, maybe lose a pound or two and style your hair more like Zoey's."

"I like my hair just the way it is," I said through clenched teeth.

After my party ended and everyone went home, he apologized for his behavior. Despite his hurtful words, which made me feel ugly on what should have been a special day, I forgave him. It turned out to be the worst birthday ever, thanks to him. I should have dumped his sorry ass right then and there.

When my mind returned to the present, I realized I was clutching Ivy's cell phone in anger. Pushing Jared out of my mind, I loosened my grip, and my attention went back to the phone. I tapped on the only video file and hit play. The four-minute clip was from Ivy's birthday party. The four girls I'd seen in the photos sang "Happy Birthday" to her, ending with a cheery, "From your awesome sisters." Then each of them followed with a personal greeting until the video ended.

It looked like Ivy had been close to her sisters. I texted the video and Ivy's photos to myself in case I needed to show her or her sisters to someone as part of my investigation. Before I could check the contact list, her phone shut down and refused to turn back on even though its battery was at eighty-eight percent. I let out a frustrated groan. Damn it! I put the device down and picked up the business card, studying it. One side was black, the other was white and featured a stylized drawing of a hand with alchemy symbols and an eye in the center. The card identified its owner as "Madam Florence, Fortune Teller" and included a phone number. I looked her up on the internet and found a brief biography on her website, in which she claimed to have always been aware of her unique gift of seeing the future. She invited readers to visit her shop for a psychic reading. The old me would have scoffed at such a thing.

"No one can read your future; they're all con artists," I used to tell Zoey when she talked about this stuff. Now I knew they existed, and in the Hidden World, those humans were called Gifted. They were born with a supernatural gift, like fortune tellers and tea readers. That didn't mean there weren't plenty of frauds out there. Was Madam Florence a fake? Maybe, maybe not, but it didn't matter. I just needed to find out why her business card was in Ivy's apartment, nothing more.

Before going to Madam Florence's shop, I took another BFB in case she turned out to be a demon. Her shop was on a side street cluttered with an assortment of indie stores. I pushed open the door to the cozy shop with a neon crystal sign in the window. A fragrant current of air swept through the room, and the crystal wind chimes dangling from the ceiling made a musical sound.

The scent of incense sticks and sandalwood reached my nose. Tables and cases were crowded with antique occult items, gems set in rings and brooches, tarot cards, and dried herbs. Along one wall was a row of shelves containing pamphlets and old books with unusual and strange titles, such as *The Haunted Hair*, *When the Crystal Ball Is in Love*, and *The Seer's Crazy Handbook*. At the back of the store, a beaded curtain covered a doorway to the right of the counter. The place was empty of customers. I stepped to the counter, and the woman behind it greeted me with a welcoming smile. Her dark hair was short and parted down the middle. Her friendly face was lined with wrinkles that seemed to tell stories of wisdom and experience. A necklace with a large crystal pendant hung around her neck.

"Madam Florence?" I asked. She nodded, studying me. Her gaze fell on my tattoo. In my rush to get to her shop before it closed, I'd left my gloves at home. An intrigued look crossed her face.

Meeting my eyes again, she said, "Six hundred eighty-one. Pardon my bluntness, but that's an unconventional choice for a tattoo." There was a slight Eastern European accent in her voice.

"Yes, uh, it's the result of a drunken night."

The skepticism in her eyes indicated that she wasn't buying my lie. "Ah, the impulsive nature of young people, often leading them to act without considering the consequences. Dabbling in things they neither understand nor can control." Her response caught me off guard; did she know the tattoo was dark magic? Was she the real thing? A true fortune teller? At my silence, she added, "I apologize, I meant no disrespect. How may I assist you? Have you come to hear your fortune?"

I cleared my throat. "Uh, no, I'm actually here because I have some questions about someone named Ivy." I reached for my phone to show her Ivy's picture, but the woman stopped me.

Her eyes went back to the tattoo before she said, "I would be happy to answer any questions you may have. However, before we continue, would you indulge me by allowing me to read your future? I assure you, there will be no charge for this service," she said, her tone implying that refusal would mean the end of her cooperation.

"All right," I replied, figuring there was no harm in humoring her. She could be a real fortune teller, or she could be a fraud. Either way, hearing what she had to say would be interesting. A satisfied smile graced her face as she led me through the doorway with a beaded curtain revealing another room. The walls were covered with strange symbols and occult paraphernalia, and the soft glow of candlelight cast dancing shadows on them.

A round table draped in red linen occupied the center of the room. On the table lay a crystal ball, a deck of tarot cards arranged in an intricate pattern, and an old, weathered book of ancient runes. Mismatched chairs, each with its own character, surrounded the table. As I approached it, she turned to me.

"Before we begin, you need to understand something about my gift. It will save us unnecessary questions later. First, I have no control over what I see. My gift reveals whatever it chooses, glimpses of both past and future events. Second, when I look into my client's past or future, I see it only through their eyes, sometimes even sensing what they're feeling at that moment. However, I cannot read their thoughts. Is that clear?"

I nodded, and she sat down at the table. I took a seat across from her. She shuffled the tarot deck and asked me to draw five cards. I did, and she studied them in silence for a long moment then looked up at me, her expression grave.

"This doesn't look good," she remarked before adding, "Place your left palm on the table, please." I followed her instructions, and she reached for my hand, her fingers wrapping around mine as her eyes closed.

When she looked back at me, she said, "The tattoo holds dark magic, but you already know that, yes?" I remained silent, assuming it was just a random idea she'd thrown out. "You are familiar with the Hidden World and its creatures... Ah, I see I misjudged you.

"I feel your confusion, your fear, when you discover the number on your palm. You had nothing to do with it. Now you live with a very dangerous magic on your hand that counts down. Sickness or emotional exhaustion causes the number to decrease faster." My eyebrows shot up. The additional information was far too accurate to be made up.

She was Gifted.

# Chapter 3

Eyes closed, Madam Florence fell quiet, her hand holding mine. After a long silence, she spoke again, her voice heavy with concentration.

"Now I see your future. You're standing on a street, overwhelmed by a turbulence of emotions. You glance down at the number on your hand. It's zero." She stopped, her brows furrowing.

"And?" I asked, almost pleading for her to continue.

Her face contorted, as if she was expending a great deal of mental effort. "Oh, it's very, very bad."

"What? What's bad?" My mouth went dry as a shiver ran down my spine.

She carried on, her voice strained. "I sense a lot of bad energy. You're shaking your head from side to side as you repeat, 'No, no, no, no, no.'" Her breathing quickened, and she became still.

"Madam Florence? Are you all right?"

She stiffened and released my hand. Her eyes snapped open. Fear and shock covered her face. "You must stop the dark magic from completing its countdown. You can do it. Our futures are not set in stone."

"What did you see that frightened you?" I asked.

The lines on her forehead deepened as her lips pressed tight. "I have seen the face of unspeakable evil. You must be careful, for when the countdown ends, someone with evil intentions will come to you. Through your eyes, I saw that person standing nearby with a triumphant smile on their face as they excitedly declared, 'I did it. I did it.'"

"Who is this person? A male witch?" I asked, dread coiling in my abdomen.

"A strong spell binds my tongue. It doesn't allow me to reveal any more details about this individual," she replied. My head spun with confusion. I started to ask her questions, but she slammed her hand down on the table.

"This reading is over." The look on her face told me there was no point in trying to change her mind.

"All right," I relented after taking a moment to collect my thoughts. Upsetting her wouldn't be helpful, not when I needed her cooperation. Ivy was, after all, the reason I'd come to her shop.

As if reading my mind, she said, "As promised, I will answer your questions about the young illusionist, Ivy."

"Thank you," I said, then asked, "Why did she have your business card? Did you meet her in your shop?"

"Yes, I did. She wanted a psychic reading. A witch patron had recommended my services," she replied.

"No offense, but why would Ivy come to you for a reading? I'd imagine that witches have their own ways of seeing the future, like spells or visions."

"Magic can rarely be used to see into the future, and visions don't always come to a witch," she explained. "When Ivy walked into my shop, she seemed nervous, often looking over her shoulder with trepidation. Despite my assurances of her safety within these walls, her fear persisted. I led her into this room, and she confided that her parents and sisters had been murdered. She wanted to know if her future held a similar fate."

I was taken aback. Her sisters and parents had also been murdered?

"Did she know who killed them?" I asked.

Madam Florence shook her head. "When I gently pressed for more details and urged her to report the murders to the witch authorities, she said that coming to my shop was a mistake. Before she left, I gave her my card so she could contact me if she changed her mind about the psychic reading. You are her friend, yes? Tell me, has she sought the help of the proper authorities in this matter?"

"I don't know. She's dead," I said, and she offered her condolences.

I rose from my seat and thanked her for her time. As we returned to the shop's main room, the tinkling of wind chimes announced the arrival of a customer. Madam Florence greeted the guy at the entrance with a smile, which he returned with a polite nod as he tucked his hands into the pockets of his well-worn jeans.

My gaze traced over his athletic frame, taking in the open zippered hoodie and the gray shirt underneath, then moved up to his clean-shaven face framed by short, dark brown hair. His white skin was lightly tanned, and he appeared to be in his early twenties. He looked familiar, and I narrowed my eyes, trying to place where I'd seen him before.

As he approached us, his pale green eyes met mine, and I placed his face. He was the guy who had walked into the diner the other day, the one Veronica had pointed out as being hot, right before giving me the phone number of my new landlady.

He gave me a toothy grin with two dimples. "Yeah, I can see it on your face; you recognize me, don't you?"

"Are you following me?" My tone was sharp.

"Guilty as charged," he replied nonchalantly. His eyes closed as he inhaled deeply. "That rare dark magic on your hand. When it's not covered by gloves, I can smell its wonderful scent... which makes the disgusting stench of BFB in your blood a little more bearable."

He opened his eyes and looked at my alarmed expression. "Oops, sorry. I was being rude, right? Forgot the whole introduction thing, didn't I?" A chuckle escaped him. "Yeah, I get carried away sometimes. All right, let's hit the do-over button. Hi, I'm Eric, and I'm a demon."

Every muscle in my body tensed. My previous encounters with his kind hadn't been the most pleasant: one had eaten almost all of my soul, and the other had tried to steal my body to escape from Ice Prison. So, yeah, you could say I wouldn't be running the Demon Fan Club anytime soon.

I looked at Madam Florence. Without BFB, she was a sitting duck in his presence. I whipped out my dagger. It wouldn't kill him since only two things offed a demon: a bullet to the heart or failure to finish eating their victim's soul. It would, however, inflict a painful injury that would draw his attention away, giving Madam Florence a chance to escape.

Because demons needed eye contact to suck souls, I told her, "Close your eyes."

Shock showed on her face, which was understandable. I had the feeling it wasn't every day someone casually strolled into her shop and announced they were a demon.

"W-what?" Her voice trembled.

"Close your eyes," I repeated.

The soul sucker looked at my dagger. "Looks like someone skipped Demon Killing 101. Silver daggers? Not effective against us. All this drama is totally unnecessary." His stare moved to the frightened fortune teller. "Madam Florence, no need to close your eyes. To show Sydney that I come in peace, I'm not gonna eat your soul." He looked back at me. "Which, I gotta say, it's a real buzzkill, 'cause you know, killing is just so much fun, and her soul smells good."

"I have BFB pills in my purse that she can take right now," I lied. "Don't even think about tasting her soul."

"Oh, Miss Terrible Poker Face, let's not pretend you're carrying around those awful BFB pills in your purse," he said. "But don't worry, I'm not here for a soul snacking, remember?" He let out a sigh. "Now, about that dagger you're pointing at me. Do me a favor and put it away. Let's keep things simple between us: you play nice, I play nice. Got it?"

I maintained my grip on the knife. "What do you want from me? And how the hell do you know my name?"

He sauntered over to the door and swung it open, letting the cold air rush in. "You want answers? Well then, how about we take a little stroll down the street? Just you and me. And as an added bonus, you'll keep the big bad wolf—me—away from your psychic friend here." He held the door open, waiting for my decision. With him out of her shop, Madam Florence's soul would be safe.

I reluctantly put the dagger away. "Okay, I'll come with you." I looked at Madam Florence. "You'll be fine."

Still in shock, she mumbled something that resembled a faint, "Thank you."

As I left the store with the demon, he approached a black Mercedes parked at the curb, then lowered his face to talk to the driver.

"Wait here. I won't be long," he said. When he returned to me, I instinctively took a step back from him. Being in the presence of a demon gave me the creeps. Everything about his kind made my skin crawl.

He gestured for me to lead the way. "After you." I started moving in the direction of the subway, and he walked with me.

"How do you know my name? Why are you following me?" My voice was laced with a snarl.

"What? No small talk? Getting right to the point, huh?"

I sneered at him. "The less time I spend around demons, the happier I'll be."

Rather than taking offense, he looked amused. "Yeah, we're not exactly the best crowd to hang out with, especially for humans and witches. Oh man, witches are like a delicacy. Their souls, mmm, so delicious. Once I had this feast that included a witch's soul and"—I shot him an impatient glare, and he cleared his throat, giving me a mischievous grin—"sorry. I'll get to the point. The reason I've been following you is because I believe we can help each other.

"Now, before you dismiss me and go all..." He paused to clutch his chest in mock horror and mimic my voice with an exaggerated lilt. "Help a demon? Never. That would be so immoral." He finished and returned to his normal voice. "Just hear me out, okay?"

I rolled my eyes but didn't stop him. He continued as we crossed the street. "Given your knowledge of the Hidden World, I assume you're familiar with the vial containing stolen dragon blood." He paused for confirmation. I gave him a nod before he carried on, "And that my old man is desperate to get his hands on it."

My steps faltered. "Your father? Who is your father?"

"Oh, did I forget to mention in my introduction that my father is Damon, the demon king?"

I came to an abrupt stop. "You're his son? The demon king has more than one child?" I remembered Audrey had mentioned Damon had a daughter, Heather, but she hadn't said anything about a son.

"Yes, he has two children. The charming me, and Heather, my bitch sister."

I stared at him for a long time. Was he really the demon king's son? A prince? Or was he lying for the fun of it?

"Look, I don't have time for bullshit," I said.

His eyes suddenly darkened. "Are you saying you don't believe I'm a prince? How dare you not recognize my importance?" His lips curled as the muscles in his jaw tightened. I watched him, ready for an attack. A few tense seconds passed before an unexpected burst of laughter erupted from him.

"Kidding! Oh, you should've seen your face—so serious, so intense." When his laughter subsided, he said, "Don't sweat it; you could never insult me. You're human and I'm immortal. Your opinion of me is as insignificant as what those little sidewalk ants think of you. You might say that, to me, humans are," he shrugged, "well, nothing more than dirt on my shoe."

I shot him a contemptuous look. "Yet, here you are, needing me—one of those mere mortals—for something." He wouldn't have bothered with me if I wasn't crucial to whatever he was after.

He smacked his tongue. "Point taken. I do need you, which means I have to be on my best behavior around you because you have something called feelings and all that. Ugh, being nice is hard. All right, let's circle back to our little trust issue. I can prove my identity to you if you want."

"That won't be necessary. I couldn't care less who you are. Let's get back to my first two questions: what do you want from me? And how the hell do you know my name?"

"I know all about you, Sydney. I watched you ace every test Mayet threw at you. You remember her, right? The ancient leech who set you up to be kidnapped by a human?"

My stomach churned at the memory of those horrible tests. Along with several other girls, I'd been subjected to them to determine which one of us had the best chance of surviving in Ice Prison. After passing the tests, I'd been thrown into that place, trapped with Mayet. She'd helped the demon king find the Gifted humans he needed to free Serena, a demon with unique abilities, from Ice Prison.

Mayet had worn a necklace that contained a powerful stone called the Tara Stone, which glowed around Gifted humans and had revealed that I was one. I didn't possess cool powers like seeing glimpses of the future or sensing the true nature of supernatural beings. What made me Gifted was my body's ability to withstand the tattoo on my hand. Although it'd caused me cancer, it hadn't killed me instantly. The dark magic was so powerful that no ordinary human could survive carrying it for even a second.

The sound of a passing car pulled my attention back to the demon.

"Yeah, I remember that bitch," I answered him.

"Dear Old Dad tasked her with finding a Gifted human to free Serena," he said. "During that time, he only spoke to her when she had questions about the tests. He didn't bother with the mundane stuff, like watching the tests she gave the Gifted humans or finding out who came out on top. He didn't think it was worth his time, so he waited for Mayet to update him when the job was done and Serena was out of Ice Prison.

"You see, I'm not like him. Not to be involved in such operations? That would be a mistake, if you ask me. Which was why I watched all the Gifted humans take the tests and made sure to stay informed about what was going on in Ice Prison while you were there with Mayet. When word reached me that Oberon took down Serena and saved your ass, I became even more curious about you.

"A mere human with extraordinary dark magic on her hand, who survived Ice Prison and got the king of the fae himself to save her? I figured you must have some seriously impressive skills up your sleeve, skills I wanted to discover. I planned to keep tabs on you, but I lost track of your whereabouts after you returned to our dimension. Not for long, though.

"One of my minions saw you at the diner where you flip burgers or whatever. He spotted that fascinating tattoo on your hand when you took your gloves off for a minute during a break. After that, he couldn't stop yammering about your dark magic. So, I had my driver take me to the diner. And there you were, chatting with another waitress at the entrance."

I snorted. "Yeah, well, that was a waste of your time. I don't want anything to do with a demon." I turned a corner, quickening my pace, but he easily kept up.

"Great, 'cause I'm not in the market for a BFF. I do have something else to offer you, though," he said with a lopsided smile.

"And what would that be?"

"A deal. Seeing as you're human and all, I'm guessing you're eager to get rid of that beautiful dark magic on your hand. Am I right?" I nodded and he went on, "So here's the deal: I'll do you the favor of removing the tattoo from your hand if you find me the hidden vial that contains the dragon blood. Call it a gut feeling, but I have a hunch that you might succeed where all others have failed," he said.

I stopped short and turned to him. "What did you just say about the tattoo?"

"That I'll take it off your hand, provided you meet my condition, of course. I'm not in the business of doing favors for free."

I stared at him with wide eyes and raised eyebrows. "Let me make sure I understand this; are you saying you can remove my tattoo?"

"That is what I'm saying, yes."

Even though it sounded like a big, fat lie, I asked, "But how? You're not a witch. And even if you were, removing the tattoo is impossible by any stretch of the imagination." Gideon and Audrey had told me that dark magic like the one on my hand was so rare and powerful that no witch could ever remove it.

He shrugged. "Well, I can."

"Does that mean you know what the number is counting down to?"

"No. I have no idea, nor do I care."

I thought about his offer. In the wrong hands, the vial with the red dragon's stolen blood could unleash chaos. There were seven dragons of different colors known as Soul Reapers, one of which I'd met in Ice Prison. They maintained a specific balance between good and evil on Earth. Whenever it was disturbed, a magical list of names was created, detailing the good or evil beings that had to be killed to restore the balance. Nothing could keep you off their death list except consuming five drops of red dragon blood.

The demon king wanted to find the vial so he could gain more power and money by duplicating the dragon blood. Gideon was also looking for it but for different reasons. He was determined to destroy the blood to prevent Damon from getting his hands on it and threatening the balance of good and evil.

"Let's assume for a moment you're not feeding me a load of bull, which I highly doubt. Why the hell would I give a demon something that could potentially cause chaos in our world?" I asked.

"What I plan to do with the dragon blood won't lead to that at all. I want that vial for one simple reason: to make Dear Old Dad regret ever thinking my sister was superior to me. When he realizes I'm the one who managed to find the stolen dragon blood, he'll finally see how much he underestimated me. Oh, the look on his face will be priceless. As for my bitch sister? She'd be in the deepest pit of humiliation for letting our old man down.

"And let me make one thing crystal clear: you can bet your bottom dollar I'll never hand over that vial to him—I'd rather grow horns than do that. I intend to keep the stolen blood hidden away under constant surveillance.

"Every day, he'll be able to see it, tormented by the painful reality that it'll forever be out of his reach. And I'll make damn sure he knows the dragon blood in the vial is authentic, and that it was my handiwork that crushed his dream of using it to gain more power."

His phone chimed, and he pulled it out to look at the screen, seeming to read a message.

When his gaze shifted back to me, he said, "It's my driver. Got some urgent stuff to take care of, but before I go..." His attention returned to the phone, his thumb tapping away as he navigated the screen. Then, my cell rang with an incoming call. "That's my number. Make sure you save it."

"How the hell did you get mine?" I demanded, taking out my phone.

"Your friend, the waitress at the diner, was more than happy to give it to me after I asked nicely. You'd be surprised how persuasive I can be when I want something."

An annoyingly smug smile formed on his lips. And right as it did, the sleek black Mercedes from earlier pulled up beside him.

Before sliding into the car he said, "We'll pick up where we left off another time. In the meantime, consider my offer."

As I watched the Mercedes disappear into traffic, a teeny tiny spark of hope lit inside me. What if the demon wasn't lying? What if it was possible to remove the tattoo? After saving Eric's number, I felt the need to confide in someone about his tempting offer. And before I thought better of it, I dialed Gideon's number from memory.

However, as soon as the first ring began, I quickly hung up, regretting my impulsive decision. The deal I'd made with Oberon resurfaced in my mind. If I went back on my word to cut Gideon out of my life, there was no telling what Oberon might do to Zoey.

On the ride back to my apartment, my mind was filled with thoughts and theories about Ivy, Madam Florence's eerie prediction, and Eric's offer. When I got off at my stop, hunger took over as my appetite returned, and I remembered that my fridge was still empty. After picking up some groceries, I returned to my apartment. Clutching a grocery bag with both arms, I opened my door, and my grip on the bag slipped. A dozen eggs and a glass bottle of olive oil fell out, meeting a tragic end on the floor.

Yolks, whites, shells, and oil became instant decorations everywhere, not even my jeans and boots were spared. Cursing under my breath, I hurried inside, dropped my purse and the grocery bag on the kitchen counter, then returned to the mess to clean it up. When I was done, I peeled off my dirty clothes and went to the bathroom to wash up. After toweling off, I padded into the bedroom and got dressed. Sitting at the dressing table, facing the mirror, I brushed my damp hair and studied my reflection.

Since my life had taken a tumultuous turn, concerns like bad hair days or blemishes didn't bother me as much as they used to. I had more important things to worry about than my appearance. But now as I looked in the mirror, every little flaw caught my eye. Perhaps it was the looming prospect of my birthday tomorrow that heightened my self-scrutiny.

The memory of how unattractive and ugly Jared's words had made me feel on that awful birthday was seared into my brain. After our breakup, I'd sworn I would never let anyone make me feel that way again, including myself.

*Way to keep your promises*, I thought as I blew out a deep breath. I set the hairbrush down on the dresser and ran my fingers over my pale complexion. My hair didn't look any better—dull and dry. Dark circles marred the skin under my eyes, and my eyebrows were overdue for tweezing.

"You look the worst," I said to my reflection, overwhelmed by a deep sense of unattractiveness.

"Well, if you ask me, all I see is the most beautiful girl I've ever laid eyes on." A male voice came from the bedroom doorway.

I nearly jumped out of my skin as I let out a small yelp, turning to look at my bedroom doorway. When I saw who was standing there, leaning against the doorframe, I lost my breath.

"Gideon," I whispered.

# Chapter 4

"Wh-what are you doing here?" I asked, my heart pounding.

"You called; I came," he said simply.

I rose to my feet. "How did you get in? How long have you been here?" I hadn't even heard him enter the apartment or noticed him standing at the bedroom door.

A frown creased his forehead, etching a clear line of disapproval across his face. "Your front door was open. I was worried someone might have broken in, so I let myself inside. Glad to see everything's fine, but you should really be more careful about locking your front door. I could easily have been a burglar, or worse, a demon seeking dinner."

My stomach dropped as the gravity of the situation sank in. How could I have been so careless? In my haste to clean up the mess I'd made of the groceries, I'd forgotten to lock the door, leaving myself vulnerable. An icy tendril tickled my spine at the thought that anyone could have strolled into the apartment while I'd been defenseless in the shower. I was lucky Gideon had been the one who—wait.

"How'd you find me? And how did you know I called you? I have a new number," I said.

"After I read your note, I had to make sure no one had twisted your arm to write it and kidnapped you. I went to Audrey and explained the situation, then asked for her help. As concerned as I was for you, she agreed.

"I gave her something of yours so she could cast a locator spell. While not as accurate as a tracker, it still allowed me to narrow down your location. As for your new number, I compelled the receptionist at the hotel to give it to me."

"How long have you been in New York?" I asked.

"The last week." He eased closer to me, and my stomach fluttered. His scent, crisp and musky, bombarded my senses.

My gaze went to his lips, then up to his eyes, crystal clear blue. My heart hammered faster. Dressed in black jeans, a tight shirt, and a brown leather jacket, he was as gorgeous as I'd remembered. I was taking him in when the deal I'd made with Oberon came crashing back into my consciousness.

"You can't be here. You have to leave, right now." Urgency suffused my voice.

He didn't budge an inch. His arms only crossed over his chest, his expression demanding an explanation. I told him about Oberon, the deal I'd had to make, and the envelope containing a new identity and money.

Surprise flashed across his features as he processed the information, and after a weighted pause, he said, "So Oberon is the reason you left me that goodbye note? That's why you disappeared?"

"Yes, I had to keep my word to him for my sister's sake."

"Killing Serena was the second time he came to your rescue, wasn't it?"

"Yes."

He fell into a long silence, looking deep in thought, then said, "I'll handle Oberon."

"No, you can't. He'll think I broke our deal by coming to you."

Gideon shook his head. "He won't; I'll tell him I compelled you to reveal why you refuse to talk or see me."

"Okay," I said after a long moment.

I had more questions for him, but before I could speak again, he told me, "Don't forget to lock your front door after me." With those words, he was gone in a blur of motion, disappearing as suddenly as he'd appeared.

I stood there, staring at the space he'd occupied just seconds ago, trying to process that he'd been there. Was he back in my life? What was his plan for dealing with Oberon? Did he intend to confront him directly? If Gideon had a way to access Oberon's world, what could he do to get me out of the deal I'd made with him?

It'd been almost three weeks since I'd seen Gideon. I hated the rush of happiness that had coursed through me when he showed up in my bedroom, and the way my body had reacted to his presence. I had to remind myself that we'd never work as a couple. He was a creature of the night while I preferred the light of day; he would remain forever young while I would inevitably age.

A sudden, sharp pang of hunger pulled me out of my brooding thoughts like a claw digging into my insides. It was a stark reminder that I hadn't eaten anything all day. I headed to the kitchen to prepare a meal, making sure to lock the front door this time. Later, as I settled into bed, Gideon once again dominated my thoughts until I fell asleep.

When I awoke the next day, I reached for my cell phone on the nightstand, hoping to find a missed call or text from Gideon. There was none, and I wondered if his attempt to contact Oberon had been unsuccessful. My gaze then shifted to the date displayed on the screen, and a cloud of sadness descended over me.

"Happy birthday to me," I murmured to myself, the words filled with bitterness.

This year, there would be no surprise balloons or cake from Zoey, no phone calls from my parents and friends to wish me a happy birthday, and certainly no celebratory outing. The overwhelming sense of loneliness was inescapable.

With a heavy sigh, I slipped out of bed. It was nine a.m., and my shift at the diner didn't start until one in the afternoon. After applying a layer of sunscreen and donning a pair of sunglasses, I took the subway back to Ivy's neighborhood. Unlike last time, the door to her apartment was closed and locked. I knocked, not expecting anyone to respond, but to my surprise, a bald, wiry man opened the door.

"Yes? Can I help you?" There was a hint of annoyance in his tone.

I hesitated, considering the best way to approach the situation before opting for directness.

"Are you a witch?" I asked. I figured that if I was wrong, the worst that could happen was that he'd dismiss me as crazy and slam the door in my face. But his body tensed, indicating that my hunch had been correct.

"I'm a busy man, and I don't have time for nonsense." He tried to shut the door, but I stuck my boot in it.

"There was a body in this apartment two days ago. I have photographic evidence, and I won't hesitate to involve the human police if you don't tell me who you are and explain everything." I was hoping he wouldn't call my bluff.

His eyes turned white as he attempted to use illusion on me. In past encounters with illusionists trying to reach my soul, I'd often experienced a subtle pressure engulfing my body, but there were times, like now, when I didn't feel anything. That's why seeing the color change in his irises reassured me; it was an indicator that my mind had recognized his magic and blocked it from reaching my soul. Given my recent susceptibility to compulsion, I was relieved that I was still protected from illusion magic. He wrinkled his forehead.

I smiled. "Surprised? Yeah, I'm immune to your mind tricks. You won't get rid of me that easily." His lips curled in discontent.

"Look, I didn't know the dead girl," he began, his eyes returning to their normal brown. "I flew in from Los Angeles yesterday for an international magic convention that starts today. I needed a place to stay for the event, so a friend told me about this apartment." He paused, considering his next words. "The woman who rented it to the dead girl is human, and she cannot know what happened here. The illusionist's death, which has been ruled a homicide, isn't a matter for the human police, but for my kind.

"And before you ask, no, I don't know who's leading the investigation, or the cause of death. Since I'm not a family member, I don't have access to that information." He gestured toward the apartment. "You're welcome to come in if you want, but there's nothing left of the crime scene. The Watchers did their job and removed the body."

I thought about the weird dude I'd seen coming out of the elevator. He must have been the Watcher who took care of Ivy's body.

He continued, "They also collected all of the victim's belongings for the witch's investigators and then erased the dead witch from the landlady's mind. My friend told me she wouldn't be back in New York City until the end of the month, and the place would be empty. I took advantage of the situation, and now I'm here. That's it. Have I answered all your questions? Are we done now?" His voice carried an edge of impatience.

"Yes," I said and pulled my foot from the door. He slammed it in my face, leaving me with no new leads to pursue. So, I decided to talk to Ivy's neighbors to see if someone had known her and could share some details about her. I knocked on several doors, but no one answered.

The frustration of finding out nothing about Ivy and the sadness of being away from everyone I cared about on my birthday hung over me like a dark cloud until I arrived at the diner. It was bustling with hungry customers, which helped distract me from my gloomy thoughts. At eight p.m., I clocked out, put on my coat, and left the diner. As I walked down a side street on my way to the subway, a voice behind me called my name. I stopped and turned.

"Hello," greeted a striking man in a shiny silver suit. His skin, eyes, and hair were all a rich, dark brown. I took a cautious step back, eyeing him with suspicion.

"I'm sorry if I startled you," he apologized. "My name is Daelyn, and I have been sent by my king, Oberon. He wishes to inform you that you are no longer bound by your agreement to stay away from the night creature, Gideon."

Surprise broke over me. So Gideon had actually done it. He had somehow managed to free me from the deal I'd made.

I looked at the fae. Eager to uncover any information he might have, I launched into a series of questions. "Do you know why Oberon wanted to keep me away from Gideon? Or why he's helping me? Does he have any idea why I was kidnapped?"

"My deepest apologies, but I must leave," he cut me off. The cold wind ruffled his shoulder-length hair, revealing his pointed ears. Recognizing that further questioning would yield no answers, I saw no reason to press on.

"Goodbye," he said and walked away.

I was in a bad mood by the time I reached my building, but that changed when I stepped off the elevator and onto my floor. My breath caught in my throat as a jolt of electrifying excitement pulsed through me—all because of one vampire waiting outside my door.

With each step that brought me closer to Gideon, my heartbeat accelerated, pounding in my chest like a drum. His black hair was slicked back, and he wore a fancy suit that exuded elegance and luxury. Did he have a date tonight? As I reached my door, his rich scent of sandalwood and spice wafted toward me, making me take a deep breath. I tried to push aside the painful ache in my heart at the thought of him being on a date with some beautiful woman.

"I am now officially allowed to talk to you again," I announced. "How'd you get a meeting with the king of the fae?"

"I didn't. I sent him a message through one of his fae living in our world."

"What was the message?"

"That by using compulsion, I discovered he'd made a deal with you, one that interferes with my personal matters. I let him know that you were valuable to me because of the dark magic on your hand. And since it's pretty obvious he wants you alive, I also said that if he continued to meddle in my affairs by trying to keep you away from me, he'd have a seriously pissed-off vampire on his hands. And despite your value to me, I wouldn't hesitate to snap your neck out of spite. Something I will never do, of course, but Oberon has to believe otherwise."

"Do you think he'd tell you why he saved me if you asked him?"

He shook his head. "I can only speculate that the tattoo is the reason. Though, it doesn't explain why he'd want to keep us apart."

No, it did not. Since parting ways with Gideon, my life had become even more of a whirlwind of chaos filled with unanswered questions. I wanted to tell him about the events that had unfolded, the discovery of the dead witch, the compulsion that had led me to her apartment, and the proposal from the demon prince. However, when I opened my mouth, he silenced me with a wave of his hand.

"I didn't come here tonight to talk about Oberon," he said.

"Then let's talk about demons. I—"

"Or demons, or witches, or anything to do with the Hidden World."

"So why are you here?" I asked, but he held out his hand without answering, leaving me confused. "What's going on?"

"Trust me. And no more questions," he said. I took his hand, and he led me back to the elevator and outside the building. A chauffeur, clad in a black suit, stepped out of a Chevrolet Suburban. He extended a warm greeting with a polite nod as he opened the car door, welcoming us inside. A short, quiet ride later, we climbed out of the car. Gideon guided me into a designer clothing boutique. Still in my waitress outfit, I felt out of place, to say the least.

Impeccably dressed in a crisp white blouse and black pencil skirt, a tall woman greeted Gideon by name with a wide smile. We followed her into a spacious room where she showed me a beautiful, expensive-looking dress. I turned to Gideon and cast him a questioning, uncertain look.

"Try it on," he said. "You can choose a different dress if you'd like, but I think this one would look beautiful on you."

The woman handed me the navy satin dress with thin straps. Given my non-existent budget for such stores, I was about to tell her to take it back, but then I reconsidered. There was no harm in just trying it on, was there? I entered the fitting room and slipped into it, then checked my reflection in the mirror. The soft fabric caressed my body, down to my knees, and looked perfect in every detail.

I must have lingered a moment too long because the woman asked, "Is everything all right?"

"Yes," I said and stepped out. Gideon's face lit up with a slow, admiring smile as his eyes roamed over me.

"Just as I thought, it looks gorgeous on you," he said, his gaze hot and possessive. Despite myself, I felt my cheeks burning. I broke away from his intense stare to enter the fitting room, intending to remove the dress and return it.

"No." Gideon's voice stopped me. "Leave the dress on." He turned to the woman. "Could you please bring the coat and shoes?"

She nodded, and a short moment later, she returned with a stylish cream-colored belted coat and a pair of heels, both of which were undoubtedly way out of my budget as well. When she handed them to me, I shook my head. Trying on one expensive dress I couldn't afford was entertaining enough, anything more would be a waste of time.

"Thank you, but I won't—"

"The expenses have already been taken care of," Gideon interrupted me. "Put them on." His tone brooked no argument, but I was about to object anyway. Before I could, he added with finality, "Consider them a gift." This made me wonder if he'd somehow remembered it was my birthday.

I'd mentioned the date offhand during one of our training sessions, but that was a while ago. There was no way he'd remembered such a small detail. I was more inclined to believe he just wanted a night out, which happened to coincide with my birthday. And judging by his attire, I assumed we were going somewhere with a dress code. Showing up in my waitress uniform would be kinda inappropriate.

"Okay," I said and took the items from the woman's hand.

After I put on the shoes and coat, the woman placed my uniform in a bag, which Gideon grabbed before we walked back to the car. The chauffeur dropped us off at an upscale restaurant in midtown Manhattan. The hostess smiled at us and greeted Gideon by name. She took the bag with my belongings and our coats, then ushered us to a private room with a table for two and a window overlooking the city.

The light was soft and dim, creating a romantic atmosphere. We were left alone in the room, and Gideon placed his hand on the small of my back to guide me to the table. His intoxicating scent captivated my senses, and the mere touch of his hand sent a wave of goosebumps across my skin. My legs weakened in response to his proximity, and I inwardly chastised myself for my body's betrayal. I shouldn't feel this way about him.

He pulled out the chair for me. I sat down, and he gently pushed the chair back in. Then he moved across from me, took off his suit jacket, draped it over the back of the chair, and sat down. The white dress shirt he wore accentuated his muscular shoulders and arms.

"I know you must miss your family and friends, especially on a day like this," he said, his voice gentle. "However, I hope you can still find some joy in tonight's celebration. Happy birthday, Sydney."

I felt my lips curve into a wide smile. He *had* remembered! I couldn't believe it.

"Thank you," I said.

Something warm blossomed in my chest, dispelling the loneliness that had plagued me all day.

# Chapter 5

A waitress breezed into the room and placed a chilled bottle in an ice bucket next to Gideon. With a deft motion, she set a glass in front of him as well. Turning to me, she unfolded the menu and wine list. As I perused the offerings, my mind drifted to Zoey. Whenever we'd celebrated my birthday at a restaurant with Mom and Dad, she'd agonize over her choice, prompting my dad to instruct the waiter to surprise her.

Over time, ordering a surprise dish had become a family tradition for birthdays. Inspired by the memory, I decided to do the same. After ordering my main course and a glass of red wine, I requested a surprise appetizer. Since I couldn't be with my family on this birthday, it was a small way to feel connected to them. With a nod, the waitress collected the menus and left.

I turned my attention to Gideon and wondered what he was going to eat.

"Do they serve blood here?" I asked.

"Yes, they do. The establishment is vampire-owned and staffed by Daywalkers and my kind alike. Though the human clientele is largely unaware of this fact," he replied, then took the bottle from the bucket and poured a splash of crimson liquid into his glass.

When the waitress returned with my appetizer, shrimp bisque, I felt a twinge of disappointment. Seafood had never been a favorite. Yet as I sampled the shrimp, an unexpected burst of flavor delighted my taste buds. I could tell from the appetizer that this place was a culinary paradise.

Later, as I drank from my glass of wine, the waitress came back with the main course. I continued to enjoy the food while Gideon took slow sips from his glass, seeming to savor every drop of blood.

Curious about his kind, I asked, "Can vampires eat human food, or is it like poison to you?"

"It's not poisonous, but it's insipid to us and doesn't nourish our bodies," he replied, then asked, "How's the food?"

"Great," I said, closing my eyes as I appreciated the symphony of flavors in my mouth. "Mmm so good. I could eat like this every day." When I opened my eyes, I found Gideon staring at me, his blue gaze penetrating. The intensity of his stare made me shift in my seat and triggered a sense of déjà vu. Jared had hated it when I showed my enjoyment of food.

"Don't eat pizza," he used to tell me. "Carbs are bad for you; you'll get fat. You already had a big lunch. You don't want your dinner going straight to your thighs, do you? Look at Zoey. She has a flawless body, and it's because she cares about how she looks. Learn from her."

He'd always been overly critical of anything he perceived as a change in my figure, afraid I'd put on a few extra pounds. One day, I'd had enough of his lectures. I grabbed a large bagel, took a defiant bite, and glared at him.

"If you don't like what you see, find another girlfriend," I'd snapped.

He responded with his typical apology. "Syd, I'm sorry. I didn't mean to hurt you. I only said that because I care about you." Then he moved in for a hug, and despite the knot of resentment in my stomach, I'd found myself wrapping my arms around him and forgiving him, as always. Anger crashed over me at the memory.

"What's wrong?" Gideon asked.

I looked down at the carby dish on my plate. Was he also going to comment about the importance of watching my weight? He hadn't seemed to mind when I indulged in ice cream before, but the way he'd watched me eat just now made me wonder if I'd misjudged him. Was he exactly like Jared? Feeling uneasy under his gaze, I put the fork down on my plate and gently pushed it away.

"I'm full. Thank you for dinner. It was thoughtful of you. I'm ready to leave," I said. He leaned back in his seat and swirled the blood in his glass before taking a sip.

"We'll leave when you're really full. There's more food to come, including dessert. Relax, enjoy, and eat. And while you're at it, please share what's on your mind." His eyes drilled into mine. "Talk to me. What's bothering you?" I started to formulate a lie in my head, but then he added in a firm tone, "The truth, please."

I couldn't tell if it was the alcohol flowing through my veins or the persuasive tone in his voice, but words began to cascade from my mouth like a waterfall. I confessed the true reason for my reluctance to finish my meal. Then I delved into the details of my relationship with Jared, why he'd asked me out, my unwavering love for him, and even the painful sting of his rejection when I'd wanted to have sex with him for the first time. By the time I'd drained my fourth glass of wine, I realized I'd shared far more than I had intended.

Opting for sarcasm to ease my embarrassment, I said, "Nothing screams social grace quite like oversharing cringe-worthy personal details, right?"

He took another sip from his glass, his expression inscrutable. I'd have given anything to know what was going through his head right then. Rather than speculate, I decided to ask him point-blank.

"Gideon—"

"Exactly," he interrupted, his voice soft.

My brow furrowed. "What?"

"Gideon, not Jared," he clarified. "It appears you've mistaken me for the likes of imbecile boys. Let's set the record straight: I am not him. The reason I watched you while you were eating was because I, unlike that pathetic human boy, can appreciate true beauty. Now that we've got that sorted, no more nonsense about you feeling uncomfortable around me. And just so we're clear, if you ever offer yourself to me, you better believe I'll gladly accept the invitation."

I gazed at him, realizing that even though he was a vampire, he made me feel good. Happy. It'd been wrong of me to judge him based on Jared's actions. Gideon had never given me any reason to believe he was anything like him. Breaking the silence, the waitress entered the room with another bottle of blood for Gideon. He thanked her and finished what was left in his glass while I returned to my delicious meal, savoring every bite.

For the next two hours, I ate, drank, laughed, and felt like myself again. Thoughts of the tattoo, Eric, Ivy, and my uncertain future were banished from my mind, which allowed me to enjoy my birthday. When we finished at the restaurant and returned to my apartment, I surprised myself by inviting him in. Uninhibited due to the effects of the alcohol in my bloodstream, I took his hand and led him into my bedroom. I inched closer to him, standing in front of him. The light from the hallway cast its stream into the room.

I looked up at his handsome face. "Will you show me what it's like?"

He skimmed his finger along my jaw, a hint of a smile playing on his lips. "I'll show you anything you want, but you'll have to be more specific."

*No, no, no, no, do not ask for it*, a small voice cried in my head.

Too tipsy to listen to it, I said, "A Euphoric Bite." Audrey had told me Gideon was skilled at giving Euphoric Bites. Vampires had a substance in their fangs called Erasure. It was typically used to make mortals forget they had been bitten. However, in the right hands—or rather the right fangs—this substance could be transformed into something else entirely: sexual pleasure. If a vampire was skilled enough to cancel the memory-erasing effect of the Erasure fluid and turn it into an orgasm inducer while it was in the mortal's bloodstream, the result was known as a Euphoric Bite.

The corner of his lips tipped up. "Oh, I would love to give you a Euphoric Bite, but are you sure you want me to do it now?"

"Yes, I am dying to experience it," I said, unable to hide my enthusiasm.

"Would you let me take a few sips of your blood as well?" His voice was seductive and smooth.

My heart pounded in my chest at the thought of him drinking my blood again, sending a rush of excitement through me. "Yeah, sure. Do that too; I have no objections," I said as I moved my hair to the side of my neck.

He shook his head. "No, not the neck." He placed a hand on my waist and guided me backward toward the bed.

When my legs brushed the edge of the mattress, he said, "Sit down."

I perched on the bed, and he got down on his knees. His fingers worked the skirt of my dress up my legs, and he positioned himself between them. My body burned in sharp contrast to his cold touch. He gently pushed my upper body back onto the bed. His eyes gleamed gold in the bright moonlight that streamed through my bedroom window. He sank back farther on his calves, spreading my legs wider.

His fangs came down as he grabbed my ass and slid me forward to his mouth. His tongue flicked out to taste my skin. My breath locked in my throat, heat throbbing between my legs. Then he sank his teeth high into my inner thigh, right next to the lace edge of my wet panties.

He sucked my blood, and I moaned at the sharp, unexpected pleasure. It felt different than the last time he drank from me—better, more intense. Waves of sensation began to ripple through me. As they grew stronger, and I was about to burst into flames, he changed something about the way he drew my blood. It made me hold on and kept me on the edge. My body begged for release. I moaned as I whimpered his name, my voice pleading.

"Yes, that's what I wanna hear. Say my name louder, love, and let me hear your pleasure." His voice was low, his tone commanding.

He returned to sucking my blood, and once again he brought me close to a powerful orgasm. I screamed his name, and my voice mingled with his deep, satisfied rumble. He continued to work his magic on my body until I was close to climaxing again, and this time he let me come. Shuddering, I cried out his name again and again as I shattered into a million pieces.

A long moment passed before my thoughts could fully gather. I struggled to catch my breath. Still reeling from the intense experience, I managed a dazed murmur through heavy breathing.

"Wow... that... that was... that was... wow. Best birthday ever."

A lopsided smile hooked his mouth, and he licked my blood from his lips. "I'm glad you enjoyed it."

He stroked my leg, and for a while the only sound in the room was the rhythm of my breathing. When it returned to normal, tiredness swamped me, and I tried to stifle a yawn. He stood and swung my legs up onto the bed, then planted a light kiss on my mouth.

"Are you leaving?" Even as I asked, my eyes began to close.

"Yes. The first Euphoric Bite can sometimes cause drowsiness in humans. Don't fight it, allow yourself to sleep."

"Wait," I said through a yawn. "Let me walk you to the door. I'll lock it after you."

"No need. Stay in bed. Sweet dreams, love." He moved to the window. I watched him open it and disappear into the night just before sleep took complete control.

I woke up as the morning light filtered through the edges of the curtains. My eyes fluttered open, and a deep sense of relaxation flowed through my body. I stretched in bed until images of Gideon in a suit appeared in my mind. I rubbed my forehead. Had last night really happened or was it just a dream? Throwing back the covers, I glanced down. I was wearing a dress instead of my pajamas. Oh boy. The memories of last night came rushing back.

I rearranged my thoughts as I sat up. Spending my birthday with Gideon last night had been awesome. Everything about him made my heart race. I couldn't deny or fight my feelings anymore—I was falling hard for him, and that was bad, especially since I knew almost nothing about him.

Were his parents still alive? Did he have any brothers or sisters? Where had he grown up? When was his birthday? And what was the deal with his abilities being different from other vampires? He was an Adult vampire, yet he possessed traits and skills exclusive to Ancient vampires. His eyes turned gold instead of silver in response to intense emotions, and he had the power to compel.

I looked at the curtain. There was no cold air coming in, indicating that Gideon had closed the window after leaving my apartment—through a sixth-floor window, no less. Apparently, he could fly. Another surprising thing I hadn't known about him. It didn't help that he wasn't one to share things about himself. My life was already a tangled mess, and having my heart broken would only add more turmoil to the mix. It was the last complication I needed right now. Besides, after I finally killed the man who had kidnapped me and got rid of the tattoo, I wanted to live a normal life as much as possible. Dating a vampire would make that difficult.

I looked down at my thighs and touched the spot where his mouth had been. *Last night has to be a one-time thing*, I thought and dragged myself out of bed to start my day.

When my shift ended, I planned to head back to Ivy's building. Maybe this time I'd have better luck talking to her neighbors. But my plans took a turn when I received an unexpected text from Audrey, who had gotten my new number from Gideon. She was in the city for the magic convention and asked me if I could swing by her hotel room tonight, so I went to my apartment to change and took the subway to her hotel.

Shortly after, I got off the train and walked to Audrey's hotel. On the way, Gideon called. When I told him Audrey was in the city, which wasn't news to him, and that I was heading to meet her, I discerned a black

Mercedes following me. Was it Eric? I stopped and looked back, but the car drove off.

"Sydney? Are you still there?" Gideon's voice called from the other end.

"Yes, I'm here," I replied, then recounted the incident with the suspicious car, my encounter with the demon prince, and his offer.

"Eric approached you?" he asked, sounding surprised.

"Yes, have you crossed paths with him before? Do you know him? Or if a royal demon can remove my tattoo?"

"I've never heard of a royal demon being able to remove such powerful dark magic, but that doesn't necessarily mean he was lying. I'm gonna make some calls, see what Eric is up to. I'll talk to you later."

After putting my phone in my purse, I reached Audrey's hotel. Stepping inside, I realized I had no idea where Gideon was staying while he was in the city. I made a mental note to ask him about it later. When Audrey opened the door to her room, a wide smile brightened her face, and she pulled me into a warm hug. She looked as stunning as ever. Black skinny pants molded to her perfect body, paired with a loose-fitting blue blouse. Her lilac hair was loose and hung down her back.

"It's so good to see you again," I told her.

"We have a lot of catching up to do," she said, then offered me a drink. I politely declined, and we settled into two chairs by a large window overlooking the street below.

"I can't even tell you how relieved I was to find out you were safe and sound," Audrey said. "You know, right after Gideon read that note you left him, he rushed over to my apartment. In all the years I've known him, I've never seen him so scared."

My brow rose as my lips parted. "He was really that worried?" She nodded, and I added, "When I wrote him the goodbye note, it never occurred to me he'd assume something bad had happened to me."

"I think what frightened him was that he couldn't reach you. Your number was disconnected, and he was afraid you'd been kidnapped again by the man who had tattooed you. He was dead set on finding you and the man responsible. I was worried too and tried every locator spell I knew, but nothing gave your exact whereabouts."

"Then how'd he manage to find me?" I asked.

"My magic narrowed your location down to New York City, which made it a bit easier for him. As a vampire with the power to compel, he must've used it and his connections to find you."

Curiosity nagged at me. "He had my new number and knew where I was. Why did he wait for me to call him before making contact?"

A small wince registered on her face. "I'm the one to blame. After locating you, he called to say you were okay, and that it didn't seem like the man who had kidnapped you was involved in your sudden departure. There was a note of concern in his voice, though.

"When I asked him what was bothering him, he said you were staying in an expensive hotel, which seemed strange to him as he knew you couldn't afford it. He was afraid you might've been taken by a wealthy witch collector because of your tattoo. He needed to be certain you weren't being held in their hotel room and under a spell to do whatever you were told. His first instinct was to kick down the door and see if you were okay, but I advised him to hold off for a short while, reminding him that you didn't appear to be injured or in any distress when he saw you.

"I also floated the idea that maybe you wrote that note because, for whatever reason, you actually wanted some space from him. Then I suggested perhaps you'd reached out to an old rich friend to help you out, hence the five-star hotel. My speculations were enough to give him pause. He agreed it was best to wait before breaking down any doors or contacting you. He also put his search for the dragon blood on hold until he could be sure you weren't in trouble. I thought it was a good idea, and when he—" She stopped, looking as if she'd almost spilled something she shouldn't have.

I narrowed my eyes. "When he what?"

She bit her lip, conflict evident in her expression. After a moment's hesitation, she said, "Gideon will have my head for telling you this, but you're my friend too, and keeping it from you feels wrong."

"What does he not want me to know?" I braced myself for whatever she was about to reveal.

She crossed her legs and leaned back in her chair. "After a few days in New York City, Gideon's suspicion that some wealthy collector had kidnapped you turned out to be unfounded, so he relaxed a bit. But when he discovered no one would rent you an apartment and you couldn't find a roommate, he decided to take matters into his own hands. You remember the guy you saved from choking? The boyfriend of the waitress you work with?"

"Yes, Nick, Veronica's boyfriend." How did she know about that? Had Gideon seen me save him?

"Well, here's the thing—he wasn't really choking. Before Nick went to the diner to pick up his girlfriend, he was intercepted by Gideon, who compelled him. He handed Nick a pack of gum, took down his phone number, and instructed him that if he heard his voice on the phone, he'd pop a piece of gum in his mouth and be convinced he was choking on it."

The shock hit me like a ton of bricks. I'd once mentioned to Gideon that my mom taught Zoey and me the Heimlich maneuver. He'd known I'd try to help Nick.

"Why would he want me to think I saved Nick's life?" I asked.

"If Veronica came up to you one day and said her boyfriend's mother was willing to rent you an apartment in an upscale neighborhood for a remarkably low rent, wouldn't that strike you as peculiar?"

"Of course, it wouldn't have made any sense," I replied.

"That's why he needed you to believe you saved Nick's life—to make the apartment offer seem credible," she said.

"What about Nick's mother? Does she think I saved her son too, or did Gideon compel her to rent me the apartment?" My voice took on a sharp edge.

"The boyfriend doesn't have a mother. She passed away. He was raised by his rich father."

"She's dead?" My voice jumped a few octaves. "Then who the hell showed me the apartment? Who owns it?"

"The woman you met works for Gideon. She's from a company he hired to manage his many properties in New York City. He had her look for an available unit in one of his buildings near his penthouse. He told her to pretend to be Nick's mother and show you the apartment. After you called her, she gave him your phone number at his request."

"So that's how he really got my new number," I muttered.

As the full implications sank in, another realization struck me. "Wait a minute. Are you saying I'm renting an apartment in one of Gideon's buildings? That he's my actual landlord?"

"Yes, and his penthouse is just a few blocks from your apartment," she replied. I shook my head, my lips tightening as I thought about how he'd manipulated me and hidden the truth.

"I can't believe he did that," I said.

"Look, I know he'd be upset with me if he knew I told you, but I think you should talk to him about it anyway, straighten things out. And don't be mad at him. His heart was in the right place."

My anger subsided as I remembered the desperation and fear I'd experienced when I thought I'd soon have nowhere to live. If Gideon hadn't stepped in, I'd have been out on the cold streets.

"I suppose you're right," I said.

"What I don't get is why you left and came here. Why'd you write Gideon that note?" Audrey asked. "Did something happen between you two that made you want to get away from him?" I shook my head and explained my deal with Oberon, and then what Gideon had done in response.

"Oberon?" Audrey said, her tone ringing with surprise. "Damn, that's insane. From the stories I've heard, he's ruthless and arrogant, not giving a shit about humans or our world. What interest could he have in a human?"

I raised my left hand. "Maybe it's the dark magic that interests him."

"Yeah, could be. Speaking of which, that's actually why I asked you over. Last night at the magic convention, I spoke with an illusionist who had given a talk. Lily has an impressive knowledge of dark magic. I described your tattoo to her, mentioning the countdown and the two words I heard when I touched the number: "eternal gods." I asked for her take, but she said she'd have to see the tattoo for herself." Audrey pulled out her cell phone. "Mind if I text her to come see it now?"

"No, not at all, go ahead." Audrey sent the message and, seconds later, her phone buzzed.

She read the incoming text, then looked back at me, disappointment evident on her face. "She can't make it tonight. Do you have plans for tomorrow night?"

I shook my head. "No."

"Perfect, Lily's on a panel discussing the dangers of dark magic tomorrow night. We can catch her before it starts."

"Sounds like a plan. I'll be there," I said.

"And listen, about the whole Oberon thing, I've got someone in mind who can help you figure out what the king of the fae wants from you. He's an illusionist PI, and he's got a fae girlfriend. She might be able to help, too, as she's familiar with the royal fae. Fair warning, though, Ian Robinson's a real scumbag, but he's also top-notch at what he does. He's your best chance of uncovering Oberon's intentions toward you."

I drew my eyebrows together. "Ian Robinson?"

His name rang a bell, and it took me a moment to recall why. I'd crossed paths with him in the past, and our encounter was far from pleasant. The guy was a total jerk, and I told Audrey that.

She sighed. "Yeah, like I said, a real scumbag, but don't worry. Despite your history with him, he'll take your case free of charge. I saved his life once. He owes me, and it's time to cash in that favor.

"Actually, if you're up for a quick trip, I spotted him at the convention before you arrived and overheard him mentioning he's meeting a potential client tonight at a bar called Hell's Happy Hour, just a few blocks from here. He's probably there by now. Want to head over and have a chat with him?"

As much as the idea of seeing that sleazeball again turned my stomach, I'd take any help I could get, even if it meant tolerating a prick like Ian Robinson. On our way to the bar, I looped Audrey in on what had happened with the dead witch, Ivy. To my disappointment, she hadn't heard anything about her murder in the witch community and, like me, couldn't explain how someone had been able to compel me.

When we arrived at Hell's Happy Hour, we put aside our discussion about Ivy's death and the mysterious compulsions. The place wasn't overly crowded, with tables and seating areas tastefully filling the space. We chose a booth near the bar.

"Do you see Ian?" I asked, scanning the room.

"No, but he'll be here. Let's have a drink in the meantime."

A waitress came over to take our order. While we were waiting for Ian to show up, Audrey brought up Ice Prison and asked me about my time there. She was horrified to hear all the harrowing things I'd endured in that place.

"Thank God Gideon rescued you from Ice Prison," she said, then caught me off guard when she added, "How are things between the two of you?"

I cleared my throat. "What do you mean?"

Her eyebrow quirked. "Oh, you know exactly what I mean."

I took a long sip from my drink. My cheeks warmed as the image of him sucking blood from my thigh replayed in my mind. I felt them grow even warmer as memories of me screaming his name while having the best orgasm of my life surfaced.

"He gave me a Euphoric Bite," I confessed.

Her mouth formed a silent O, then she said, "Spill the tea."

"You were right about the bite; it was incredible, the most erotic and amazing experience I've ever had. Though, it will never happen again. I prefer things to be platonic between us."

"Yeah, I get it. It's Gideon, and God knows he's got his fair share of issues, but if you ask me, you should still give him a chance." She took a sip from her glass. "When he was looking for you, I saw a side of him I'd never seen before, a protective one. The fear on his face as he told me about his concern for your well-being made him look so vulnerable. I think his love for you is beautiful."

"His love for me? You think he loves me?" Where did this come from? I knew Gideon cared about me and wouldn't mind if we had sex, but there was a big difference between lust and love.

Audrey snorted. "Oh, come on, it's clear he's in love with you. He put everything important to him on hold to find you. Then, instead of just sending someone else, he flew all the way to another state to make sure you were okay."

My heart raced at the possibility that Gideon felt the same way I did, but then my brain kicked into gear, reminding me that being with him would be a bad idea.

"Even if he does have feelings for me," I said. "My life is too complicated right now to consider dating anyone, let alone an enigmatic vampire."

"Sounds like an excuse. You're lying to yourself. The question is why. Are you afraid of getting hurt again?"

The memory of the day Jared had revealed the real reason for being with me flooded back. Finding out he'd used me to get close to Zoey had shattered my heart into tiny pieces. The pain was unbearable. For weeks, I'd been reduced to a puddle of tears. Everything around me served as a painful reminder of him, of what we had once shared. I'd been a full-on wreck over him. My mother assured me time would heal my wounds, and to some extent, it had. But Jared had left a deep scar on my heart.

Audrey was right. Deep down, I feared experiencing that unbearable heartache again. Then I caught sight of a guy who looked familiar. He approached our booth, and I felt the blood drain from my face.

Sweet. Baby. Jesus.

"What? What is it? Ian's here?" Audrey said, glancing back at the crowd.

I raised my hand to shield my face from the guy's view. "No, worse. My ex."

# Chapter 6

Audrey's eyes boggled. "Your ex? Where?"

"Yes, Jared, at your three o'clock."

She shifted her gaze in that direction. "The skinny guy with the brown buzz cut, wearing a polo shirt and jeans?"

My hand remained on the side of my face as I confirmed, "Yes, that's him. He can't know I'm here. If he sees me, he'll tell my parents, and I can't let them get even the slightest hint of my whereabouts. Their lives would be in danger if they found me. The man who kidnapped me will make good on his threat and kill them."

She turned her head to face me in profile. "Your ex is not near us anymore. He took a seat at the bar and is flirting with the bartender."

"Would it be possible for you to change my appearance like you did before?"

She shook her head. "No, sorry. It's forbidden for a witch to use that kind of magic in the open with so many humans around."

"Then we gotta get out of here," I told her and sneaked a peek at Jared. A brunette wearing a black skirt and a strappy top walked up to him. She tapped him on the shoulder, and he turned around, sizing her up. A satisfied look appeared on his face just before she leaned in and kissed him.

"Yeah, let's go," Audrey said. "Before he sees you." When her gaze returned to Jared, her body tensed, and she drew a quick intake of breath.

"What's wrong?"

"Sydney, that woman your ex is with? She's a demon, and not just an average demon. She's royal. I can sense it."

I looked over at Jared again. The demon was still kissing him. When she pulled away, he started to cough. The woman leaned closer and whispered something in his ear. He nodded obediently and stood up, looking at her as if waiting for her next command. She took pleasure in the control she had over him; I could tell by the little upward curve of her lips. Taking his hand, she guided him toward the back exit. He staggered beside her as they made their way through the crowd.

I watched them, taking a long sip of my drink as I leaned back and relaxed in my seat. I mean, it wouldn't be the end of the world if I just let that demon have her way with Jared's rotten soul, would it? In fact, you could argue I'd be doing the world a favor. One less jerk to womankind was always a good thing in my book. I smiled to myself, enjoying the thought, until my damn conscience decided to crash the party. Annoyed, I groaned inwardly as I put down my drink.

"I have to go help him," I told Audrey. "Stay here. I'll be right back." Hopefully in one piece.

Audrey grabbed my arm and stopped me from getting up. "What do you think you are doing? She's a royal demon, Sydney."

"I'm aware of that. I have BFB in my blood, so she won't be snacking on my soul. I'll be fine."

She raised a skeptical eyebrow. "Do you also have a gun and perfect aim? Because if you miss her heart the first time, you won't get a second chance. Royal demons are like Ancient vampires. They're very powerful and strong, and she could beat you to death."

"I don't have a gun with me, just a dagger," I admitted. "But I'll make it work. I can't stand by and let her kill him."

She released her grip on my arm. "Fine, then I'll go with you. The demon just went out the back door with him, which leads to an alley. Let's just hope it's dark and empty of humans, so I can use my magic freely."

We paid for the drinks, went to the back door, and stepped into an alley with a single streetlamp. At the far end of it, Jared was kneeling on the ground with his back to us, looking up at the demon in front of him. His body shook as she stared down at him, feasting on his soul.

Gathering my courage, I shouted, "Hey! Get away from him!"

The demon's attention shifted to me, and Jared's body crumpled to the ground. She hissed in my direction and wrinkled her nose as if she'd caught a whiff of something unpleasant.

She snarled at me, her voice dripping with malice. "Don't rely on that filthy vampire blood coursing through your veins to shield your soul from me, human. It won't stay there forever, and I have all the time in the world." Her gaze moved to Audrey, her lips twisting into a sinister grin. "And you brought a witch. How delightful. It's been ages since I ate a witch's soul."

Except for Jared and me, the alley was devoid of human presence, and Audrey didn't hesitate to use her magic. She took a few steps in the demon's direction before stopping and whispering incantations. The soul sucker's face contorted in pain. Whatever spell Audrey was casting, it was working.

But then the demon screamed, "Ronan!" Her voice echoed down the alley. Audrey suddenly fell silent, and her breathing became erratic while she started to move toward the demon.

I hurried to her and grabbed her arm. "Audrey, no, what are you doing?" Her complexion drained of color.

She shoved my hand off her arm as she seemed to be looking at something, a strange determination in her eyes. "Don't touch me! You're keeping me from him!"

Him? Who was she talking about? Audrey reached the woman, walked past her, and continued toward the silhouette of a tall man emerging from the darkness behind the demon. The soul-sucker bitch wasn't alone. She had a companion, and he was feeding on Audrey's soul.

A vise grip of panic tightened around my chest. "No, Audrey, stop looking at him! Snap out of it!"

I rushed toward her, but the royal demon blocked my way, laughing. I lashed out with a powerful kick that sent her reeling backward. She recovered quickly, lunging at me in retaliation. I ducked and unleashed a blow to her stomach. With a growl, she grabbed a handful of my hair, eliciting a painful scream from me.

I managed to break free and continued to fight her. Possessing immense strength, she soon had me pinned against a wall, her forearm crushing into my neck. She looked at me as her lips pulled back in a grin.

"Calliope, I hate to be a buzzkill and ruin your little party, but that mortal you're playing with happens to be under my protection. Please keep your hands off her," a male voice said, and I registered Eric's presence near the back door of the bar.

She turned her head to him. "Since when do you protect *humans*?" Her voice was sharp.

"Funny, it's almost like you're convinced I owe you an explanation," Eric said, and the demon released her grip on my neck. I collapsed to the ground, dragging air into my aching lungs, the cold cement beneath me offering little comfort. As I lay on it, regaining my strength, I heard footsteps approaching, and a pair of black boots came into view. I looked up to see Eric.

"You really shouldn't be lying on the floor. It's still wet from the recent rain. You could catch a cold and die on me. You humans tend to do that, you know, die easily. Here, let's get you up." He held out his hand to me.

Ignoring his outstretched hand, I scrambled to my feet and quickly found Audrey and Jared with my eyes. They were both lying motionless on the ground.

"No, no, no, no," I muttered, rushing over to them.

My blood ran cold as I knelt beside Audrey's lifeless body. Tears stung my eyes, and a lump of grief and fury formed in my throat. Gritting my teeth, I rose to my feet and faced the two demons responsible for Audrey and Jared's deaths. I whipped out my dagger. Though I knew I couldn't kill them with it, the thought of making them suffer, of hearing them scream in pain, fueled my resolve.

Eric stepped between the demons and me, stopping my advance.

"I can't let you fight them. Don't get me wrong; normally, I'm all for a good spectacle of blood and slaughter, but"—a sigh—"I kinda need you to stay alive, and I'm afraid that you going up against two royal demons would only result in your blood being spilled. I can't have that. So, here's the plan: Calliope and Ronan will return your friends' souls to their bodies, and you'll keep breathing. Problem solved."

"What!" the two demons shouted, sounding bemused and outraged at the same time. Eric, who kept his focus on me, ignored their protest.

"They can bring back their souls even though they already ate them?" I asked.

"Yeah, if it's been less than two hours since they ate it. Your friends are not dead yet," Eric replied, then added, "And in case it crossed your mind, no, they won't turn into brain-craving zombies once they get their souls back.

"Pity, though, right? Wouldn't it be awesome if they did? Eating human brains, now that's a unique diet. Too bad zombies don't exist in real life." He paused before giving a single clap of his hands. "All right, enough chit-chat." He turned to the demons. "You two, regurgitate your dinner, so I can get back to my business. The night is short, and I still have some lives to ruin and people to piss off."

Calliope glared at Eric. "You're out of your mind if you think we're simply going to return their souls."

Ronan's face screwed in anger. "What do you think you're doing? Do our king and queen know you're protecting a human? Does Heather?"

"Duh, of course not. How could I ever carry out my brilliant plan to destroy them if they knew everything I was doing?" Eric said, then raised his hand, and the two demons froze like two sculptures. Their mouths hung open and wisps of fog poured from their mouths.

The two tendrils of white smoke swirled toward Audrey and Jared, then entered their nostrils. When Eric lowered his hand, the two demons fell to their knees. He turned back to me, his eyes glowing yellow before gradually fading to green.

My jaw slacked. Had he just controlled them? Did demons possess magical powers too? Or was it just Eric?

"Your friends got their souls back. They'll wake up in about fifteen minutes," Eric said, and I breathed a sigh of relief.

"Ronan and I will not be treated like lowly demons. Heather will help us tear you apart for what you've done to us," Calliope threatened. Eric looked at her expectantly, as if waiting for her to say more. When she didn't, he spoke.

"That's it? Just one threat? Come on, Calliope, where is the creativity? I was expecting something a little more... interesting. Maybe a promise to feed me to the rats after you've skinned me alive, or an evil laugh thrown in for dramatic effect." Shaking his head, he clucked his tongue. "I am very disappointed in you. I always thought you had more flair. Guess I was wrong." With a casual air, he pulled a pair of surgical gloves from his jacket and slipped them on. "I'd suggest you do better next time, but I'm afraid there won't be a next time for you two."

Before Calliope and Ronan could react, Eric had closed the distance between them, plunged his hands into their chests and pulled out their hearts. He then dropped their still-beating organs onto the cement. I gasped in horror at the sight. A grimace of pain distorted Ronan and Calliope's faces, their lips drawn tight in a silent scream.

They fell to the ground, and Ronan begged, "We're sorry, Your Highness, please, our hearts, it hurts, please."

Ignoring him, Eric began whistling as he took off his bloodied gloves and strolled over to the nearest dumpster. He disposed of the gloves and withdrew an object from his jacket. When he returned, I could see it was a gun with a silencer attached.

He looked down at the demons. "I don't think you've suffered nearly enough, but unfortunately, I don't have time for prolonged torture sessions," he said before taking aim and ending their misery with two precise shots into their beating hearts on the ground.

As if he hadn't just killed two demons in a gruesome way, he turned to me with a casual expression on his face.

"You know, you're pretty lucky I spotted you and the witch trailing Calliope."

I snorted at him with disdain, recalling the car that had followed me as I'd walked to Audrey's hotel.

"You mean I was lucky to have you stalking me, watching my every move."

"First of all," he tucked his gun back into his jacket, "why do you make it sound so bad? What's wrong with stalking? I'll have you know it is an art form. It builds character and is an excellent practice for honing your patience. Do you have any idea how much patience it takes to watch someone for days on end? Trust me; stalking you was as exciting as watching paint dry. And secondly, I stopped following you after we met at the fortune teller's shop."

"Yeah, right, I saw your black Mercedes earlier," I said.

"Oh, that. Yeah, that was my driver, not me, but don't worry, he won't be a problem anymore. I killed him after he disobeyed my direct order and kept following you. He became a tad too obsessed with your tattoo, thinking he could cut off your hand and sell the dark magic." He paused and glanced at my hands. "Smart move, hiding the tattoo with gloves to avoid unwanted attention."

I scoffed. "You expect me to believe it was pure coincidence that you happened to be in this very bar at the exact time I was attacked?"

"Hardly a coincidence. I'm the owner of Hell's Happy Hour, so naturally, I'm here quite often."

My eyebrows shot up. "You're the owner? This is a demon bar?"

"Not exactly. My bar is mostly populated by humans, but there are also witches who come here sometimes. Although, they have no idea it's owned by a fabulously awesome demon." A smirk teased his lips.

"Maybe it's because demons and awesome go together about as well as oil and water," I said.

"That's where you're mistaken. Awesomeness practically radiates from me. It's just part of my undeniable charm." A smug grin spread across his mouth.

I rolled my eyes and stepped over to Audrey and Jared. "Will they have any pain or side effects when they wake up?" I asked.

He walked up to me. "No pain, but there may be some side effects, such as fatigue and headache. They're going to wake up with no idea what has happened to them in the last forty minutes. It'll be like they just blinked. The witch may also not act like her usual self. In my experience, witches tend to get mischievous and pull pranks in the first few hours after waking up. If you suddenly find yourself in a conversation with a three-headed pig, don't blame the alcohol—it's your witch's magic at work.

"And here's a piece of advice: it's best not to tell them what happened to their souls. It could be quite a shock to them and lead to their death. You also need to remember where they were forty minutes ago. Like, if they were in the bathroom or something, make sure you put them there. Everything should look natural to them when they open their eyes. That'll save you the headache of answering their confused questions."

"I don't want him," I gave a small jerk of my head to Jared, "to see me when he regains consciousness. He doesn't know I'm here, and I'd like to keep it that way."

Without asking my reasons, he said, "I think I can help with that."

He bent down and searched Jared's jacket and pants pockets until he found his phone. Holding it, he lifted Jared's finger to unlock the device. A glimmer of light from the screen shined down on Eric's hand as he navigated the phone. From my vantage point, I had a clear view of the screen. He scrolled down the contact list until he reached the name, "Summer, girlfriend." He called her, raising the phone to his ear.

After a few seconds of waiting, he said, "Summer, hey, a good Samaritan here. Your boyfriend Jared? Yeah, he's not handling his drinks very well. In fact, he's currently having a pretty intimate conversation with the floor. I was hoping you could swing by this awesome, cool bar called Hell's Happy Hour to make sure he gets home safe." There was a pause before he spoke again. "Great. I'll text you the address."

After he sent the location to Summer, he put the phone back in Jared's jacket and stood up.

Unable to contain my anger, I blurted out, "God, I can't believe he has a girlfriend. He just locked lips with Calliope." What a cheating bastard!

Eric stared at me for a moment with a thoughtful expression. "Hmm, interesting."

"What's interesting?"

"The way your face scrunches up in disgust when you talk about the human. I was sure that look was reserved just for me. Who would have thought there were others out there capable of earning your deeper contempt than me?"

My hand fluttered to my chest in mock sarcasm. "Oh, I'm sorry, does that hurt your feelings? Knowing there are others I could despise even more? Don't worry, Eric; to me, you will always hold the title of the most arrogant jerk demon to ever walk the earth. That's a distinction no one can take away from you." Ignoring the amusement on his face, I nodded in Audrey and Jared's direction. "Can we focus on them now?"

He glanced at the back door of the bar. "I'll get some of my men to help you carry them back inside while I take care of the mess here." He gestured at the dead demons sprawled on the ground.

After a brief disappearance into the bar, he returned with two guys in tow. One of them helped me with Audrey and put her in the same booth we'd been sitting in before the attack. Her body was propped up against the side of the booth. The other man placed Jared at the bar, making it look like he'd had too much to drink and was dozing off with his head resting on the counter.

About forty minutes ago, Jared had only just walked into Hell's Happy Hour, so he'd be confused to suddenly find himself sitting at the bar. All I could do was hope his mind would fill in the blanks with some plausible explanation to rationalize the situation and forget about it. After Eric's men finished helping me, I waited for Audrey to regain consciousness, vibrating with tension.

Just a moment ago, her soul had been in the stomach of a demon, and I had to pretend it'd never happened. Otherwise, she might get suspicious and cast some kind of spell to force the truth out of me. I prayed my acting skills were up to the task. I took a few deep breaths, my heart pounding. When she opened her eyes a few minutes later, she looked around. I was not sure what to say. Damn it, what was the last thing her mind remembered from our conversation?

She shook her head as if to clear it. "Sorry, I had a strange headache for a second. Anyway, that sounds like an excuse. You're lying to yourself. The question is why. Are you afraid of getting hurt again?"

It took me a moment to recall she was talking about Gideon and my wish to stay platonic with him.

"I think so, yes," I answered honestly, then looked at Jared. Waking up, he raised his head and scanned the room while scratching his head.

"What is it? Ian's here?" Audrey asked, following my gaze.

"No, it's my ex," I said.

Surprise colored her face. "The skinny guy with the brown buzz cut, wearing a polo shirt and jeans, looking wasted?"

"Yes."

A girl approached Jared, and the look of panic that flashed across his features when he saw her told me it had to be Summer. The jerk thought he was about to meet Calliope and didn't expect his girlfriend to show up. Watching him squirm in his seat and trying to play it cool was satisfying. He kissed her, took her hand, and seemed to be in a hurry to leave the bar. *Yeah, I wonder why—cheater.*

"He really hurt you, didn't he?" Audrey said as she looked at Summer and Jared, her voice full of empathy. Her gaze returned to me. "You have to forget about him. Heartbreak is part of life, and you shouldn't let the fear of getting hurt keep you from giving Gideon a chance.

"Besides, dating a vampire comes with some perks—you don't have to worry about protection because there's no risk of STDs or unwanted pregnancy. Oh, and here's a fun fact: while vampires do have blood tears, their semen is normal."

"Audrey, I can't go out with someone I know nothing about, not even where they live."

"You're right. This is a—hold on, my phone just vibrated." She reached into her purse, nestled next to her thigh, and pulled out her cell. "Speaking of the devil, he just texted." She read Gideon's message then looked up from the screen. "He wants us to come to his place, like right now. Says it's urgent and that he can't go into any details over the phone." She put her cell back in her purse. "Come on, let's go see what's going on. I'll talk to Ian tomorrow." A big yawn escaped her mouth as she stood up. "Oh, wow, where did that come from? Sorry, I suddenly feel so tired. No idea why."

Just the side effects of helping me. A pang of guilt squeezed my chest. I pushed it away, not wanting Audrey to notice any signs of discomfort on my face and become suspicious.

"Okay, let's get out of here," I said.

A few minutes later, we were sitting in the back of an Uber on our way to Gideon's. I released a weary sigh. It seemed like my night, which I'd hoped was coming to an end, was just getting started.

# Chapter 7

As we entered the well-maintained lobby of a high-rise building, Gideon's doorman acknowledged Audrey with a polite nod. Then the security guard at the desk smiled at her.

"Miss Miller, it's a pleasure to have you back. Mr. Hawthorne has already informed us of your visit, so there's no need to sign in. Please feel free to use the private elevator on your right, which will take you directly to Mr. Hawthorne's penthouse."

After he gave us the PIN code to activate the elevator, Audrey thanked him then let out another yawn. She seemed to be on the verge of falling asleep right there, her eyelids beginning to droop.

"Sorry, you're gonna have to go up without me," she told me. "I don't know what's gotten into me. I'm so exhausted, and I feel like something took the edges off my senses. I'll Uber back to my hotel and get some rest. Tell Gideon I'll call him tomorrow, okay?"

I nodded. "Yeah, no problem. Go back to your room and get better."

After she left, I punched in the code to access Gideon's private elevator. Or, as the security guard had referred to him, Mr. Hawthorne's private elevator. As it turned out, Gideon had a last name. Would I learn more about him once I was in his apartment? I doubted there would be any family photos on display, but maybe I'd stumble upon other personal items that could provide some insight into his life.

The elevator doors slid open, revealing a box with mirrored walls and overhead lighting that cast a soft glow. I stepped inside, pressed the penthouse button, and the elevator began its ascent. When the doors opened, I walked into a foyer with a high ceiling. The pristine white marble floor gleamed beneath my feet, reflecting the soft ambient light from the modern crystal sconces adorning the crisp white walls. I walked past the round sofa in the center of the opulent foyer to the archway that opened into a spacious living room with a breathtaking view of the Hudson River.

As I admired it, the sound of voices from across the room to my left drew my attention. I turned to see two women, their immaculate pale white skin radiating an inhuman glow—vampires. They had their backs to me as they faced Gideon, who was sitting on a plush white couch.

"This is turning out to be quite a disappointment," one of the vampires said. She was a blonde, sporting an open top with spaghetti straps crisscrossing her back paired with a tight miniskirt.

Gideon opened his mouth to respond but closed it when he noticed me, his eyes registering surprise and bewilderment.

"Yes," her friend, also scantily clad, chimed in with a foreign accent I couldn't place. "We assumed after talking about Eric we'd move on to the fun part. Yet here you are, asking us to leave." She tossed her long dark hair over her shoulder with a flick of her head. Gideon rose to his feet and approached me in a flash of movement.

"Sydney, what are you doing..." He stopped, and his expression of confusion shifted to one of concern. "Are you hurt? Did something happen while you were with Audrey?" His reaction puzzled me. Why did he look taken aback to see me there, or think something bad had occurred?

"I'm fine. And Audrey was tired, so she went back to her hotel room. She'll talk to you tomorrow."

The blonde let out a derisive snort. "Don't tell me your Donor is the reason you want us to leave. You really prefer food to mind-blowing sex?"

In the blink of an eye, the dark-haired vampire appeared beside Gideon. "You know, you can have both." Her voice was a sultry purr. Her gaze moved to me then back to him before she added, "And if you don't mind sharing, I would love a taste of your human."

I glared at her. "And I would love to see you try, bitch."

Her eyes widened with rage and turned gold. Long, wide fangs popped out of her mouth. Crap, an Ancient. My hand shot to my dagger. Just as she was about to attack me, Gideon positioned himself in front of her, stopping her.

"You will not touch her if you value your existence, Katina." His voice cut through the air like a hot knife through butter.

She leveled a piercing stare at him. "Who do you think you're threatening? I am an Ancient, you fool."

"I never said killing you would be easy. Hell, I bet you'll even manage to land some brutal and painful blows. But let's be real—you can't defeat me. Being an Ancient has its advantages. However, it doesn't make you a skilled fighter. Now, me? I've had my fair share of fights, and you damn well know it. The way I see it, you have two choices. You can either stay for a lesson in pain, and trust me, I'm an excellent teacher. Or you can make the smart choice and walk out of here in one piece. Your call. Though if you choose to stay, don't say I didn't warn you."

Katina was silent, her jaw clenched and eyes narrowed into slits. The tension hung in the air, thick like a dense fog.

Breaking the silence, the blonde spoke. "All right, this is getting way too heavy for me. I came here for a good time, not to watch you two fight over a Donor. I'm outta here." She headed for the elevator.

"Wait for me," Katina barked, her accent thick. She then turned her gaze back to Gideon. "You and your Donor can rot in hell." She spat on the floor at Gideon's feet before joining her friend. When they left, I released a breath, feeling the tension drain from my muscles.

"Nice friends you've got," I said, sarcasm infusing my tone. My eyes wandered around the lavish living room. "And place," I added. The room had floor-to-ceiling windows, which I assumed were light-proof, and a terrace that encircled the entire apartment. To my right was an open kitchen with stainless steel appliances, white cabinets, and a sleek island.

What stood out to me was the stark contrast with his house in New Haven. While the decor there was sparse and simple, this place oozed luxury with its lavish furnishings and elegant design. Items that added a personal touch decorated his penthouse, such as vases, fresh flowers, and exquisite artwork gracing the walls. No picture frames with family photos, though.

I stepped toward the floor-to-ceiling windows, taking in every detail of the room. "This is where you live? Where you call home?"

"Yes," he answered.

Recalling what Audrey had revealed, I turned to him. "Were you ever planning on telling me you compelled Veronica's boyfriend to believe he was choking so I'd end up renting a unit in a building you own?" Disapproval dominated my voice.

A frown creased his forehead as he appeared to ponder how I'd obtained this information. A few seconds later, a dry smile tugged at the corners of his mouth, and understanding flashed across his features.

"Well, it looks like I didn't have to, thanks to Audrey." His tone was more sarcastic than angry. He closed the distance between us. "After I learned about your housing predicament, I took the necessary steps to solve it. Allowing you to spend the nights in a homeless shelter or on a dirty bench was never an option."

I let out a soft sigh as my eyes shifted to the stunning night view his living room offered, my anger waning.

When I returned my gaze to him, I said, "Why'd you ask Audrey and me to come over?"

His eyebrows squished together. "I did what?"

"Didn't you text Audrey to tell us to come over because you needed to talk to us?"

"No, I didn't."

"But the security guard in the lobby said you were expecting us."

He seemed to think for a moment. "Was Audrey with you when he said that?"

"Yes."

"And did you see the text I supposedly sent to Audrey?"

When I realized what he was implying, I cursed myself inwardly for my stupidity. The guard had been under Audrey's spell! Eric had warned me she wouldn't behave like her usual self for the first few hours after waking up. I should have been suspicious when she'd told me about Gideon's text.

"Damn it, she tricked me…"

"It's not like Audrey to pull something like that."

"She did it 'cause she wasn't herself," I said and told him what had happened with Eric and the royal demons at the bar. By the time I finished, his eyes glowed gold and his lip curled into a snarl.

"Demons," he spat out the word with palpable disgust. "I wouldn't be surprised if Eric masterminded the whole thing, letting his royal demons eat Audrey's soul to make you feel indebted to him. Considered a disappointment by his family, he is often underestimated by other demons due to his reputation as the less capable sibling.

"It would be unwise to underestimate him, though. Much like Heather, he possesses unique abilities of his own. And he is cunning, crafty, and smart, perhaps even more so than Heather. I have to uncover his true intentions toward you."

"He claims he wants the dragon blood to destroy Heather and the demon king," I said.

"Always take a demon's words with a grain of salt." Gideon's eyes returned to their usual shade of blue. "But Eric was right about one thing: you must keep what happened in the alley to yourself. Telling Audrey the truth could send her into shock and possibly kill her."

"I won't say a word," I said, then sighed, shaking my head. "I can't believe I fell for her trick and came over here. Too bad she didn't know you already had company." A spark of jealousy slipped into my tone at the word "company."

"The Ancient vampire, Katina, is an information broker, trading in valuable secrets. She has spies working for her, and they've been keeping an eye on some royal demons, gathering intel. I reached out to her, hoping she might have some useful insights about Eric or know what he's up to. She agreed to meet, but she didn't come alone." He paused before adding, "Even if you hadn't shown up, nothing would have happened between us. I need you to know that."

"It's okay; it's really none of my business." My tone came out a little harsher than I'd intended. I was crazy jealous, and I didn't like feeling like this. Not one bit. I reminded myself I had no right to be angry with him, even if he'd chosen to sleep with them. I cleared my throat. "I mean, you don't owe me any explanations. You can do whatever you want." I hoped my words sounded sincere, even though they left a bitter taste in my mouth.

He reached out and cradled my face with one hand, his piercing gaze burning with intense fire.

"Like this?" he whispered as his head dipped, and his lips brushed against mine before claiming them in a kiss. An electric thrill ran up my spine. His tongue slipped between my lips, and he took complete possession of my mouth. My eyes closed as he deepened the kiss. His hands moved to my waist, his tongue exploring, heat building inside me.

I pressed my body against him as I ran my fingers through his hair. I melted into him. My hands went down and fumbled with his shirt buttons. I wanted his naked body against mine. I let out a soft moan of protest as he pulled away. He ripped off his shirt and tossed it on the floor while he kicked off his boots. I followed suit and got rid of my coat, sweater, and shoes. Then, in one swift motion, he scooped me into his arms.

The next thing I knew I was in a bedroom, lying on a luxurious black bedspread covering a king-sized bed, the moonlight illuminating the dark room. Gideon hovered over me. Looking down, he stroked my face, my neck, my chest, then loosened the cup of my bra, exposing one breast. My chest rose and fell in a quick rhythm.

"So beautiful," he whispered, his eyes gleaming wild gold. His thumb and forefinger captured the sensitive nipple. I shuddered. His thumb rubbed over the nub then squeezed harder, his fingers plucking and pinching.

He moistened his lips, seeming to enjoy watching me. "Like this, do you?"

"Oh, God, yes!" I cried out.

The sensations shot right between my thighs. He lowered his mouth and flickered his tongue over my nipple, then encircled and sucked it. I arched against him, my whole body jerking in response. Lips still tugging at my nipple, he removed my bra and cupped my other breast to knead it. His thumb rubbed the underside of the nub until he moved his mouth to it. He grazed his teeth over the taut flesh before licking and sucking it. My hand clasped his hair as I moaned loudly, my body shaking.

When he lifted his head, it was to unzip my jeans and push them down, along with my panties, and then throw them away. I admired his body as he took off his pants and moved to lean over me. He bent his head to trace a path of kisses from my lips to my jaw to the hollow under my ear.

As he nuzzled it, he slid a hand between my thighs, slowly stroking the sensitive nub with his fingertip. The heat inside me burned higher with each stroke. While he continued his slow caress between my legs, his mouth trailed lower to lick the spot where my neck and shoulder met. He eased a finger inside me as his thumb swirled over the sensitive nub.

"So tight," he murmured. I took a deep, ragged breath as I gripped his shoulder, my nails digging into his skin. He inserted another finger inside, then increased the pace of his strokes until my body exploded in an exhilarating climax.

"Gideon!" I threw my head back and felt him kiss the side of my neck.

As my breathing slowed, he withdrew his two fingers and took them into his mouth.

"You taste so good," he said, his voice rough. Every cell in my body wanted him.

"I need you inside me, now."

He settled on top of me, and I felt his heavy erection, thick and hard, nudging against my stomach. He ducked his head to run the tip of his tongue along the seam of my lips. I wrapped my legs around his waist.

"Yes, open for me, love," he said. Then he covered his lips with mine for a slow and deep kiss as he positioned himself at my entrance. He brushed the head of his erection over my wet folds, up and down. I moaned his name. He pushed gently into me a few inches before he held still inside my body, giving me time to accept his size.

"Are you okay?" he asked.

I nodded. He pushed forward inch by inch, stretching me more and more, almost unbearably. My hands gripped his shoulders. He pulled back a couple of inches, then pushed a fraction deeper.

"Sorry, love, but this is going to hurt a little," I heard him say. Then he slid back before ramming deep inside me. I hissed as a searing pain burned through my body. He stopped and rested inside me, letting me recover. His eyes met mine, and he gently brushed my hair from my face.

As the pain began to ease, I rocked my body against him, and his head fell to my shoulder. He growled against it and began to move again, slowly filling me. His lips found mine, and he increased his movement. With each thrust, the tension grew and coiled inside me.

He broke the kiss and said, "Open your eyes. I want you to look at me when you come." I did as he'd asked, and my gaze locked onto the mesmerizing golden depths of his eyes. I clawed my fingers into his back as he moved faster and harder, sending pulses of ecstatic pleasure through my entire body until bliss exploded inside me. I cried out. A moment later, I heard him grunt as he reached his own climax, emptying himself into me.

When my ragged breathing returned to a somewhat normal pace, I said, "That was... that was... perfect."

He chuckled deep in his chest as he rolled over onto his back, taking me with him. My head rested on his still chest.

"Yes, it was," he said.

I wanted to stay awake in bed with him, to feel him close to me, but soon his hand, stroking my back in a soothing rhythm, lulled me into a deep sleep.

# Chapter 8

Waking up to a pitch-black room, I reached over and patted the bed, but it was empty. I drowsily rubbed my eyes and sat up.

"Gideon?" I called, but there was no answer. "Gideon?" I repeated, and the bedroom door swung open. Bright artificial light flooded in, revealing the bedroom, which I now realized was quite large. It included a sitting area to one side, a walk-in closet, and an en suite bathroom. The blinds on the floor-to-ceiling windows were closed, making it impossible to tell the time.

Gideon stepped closer and perched beside me on the bed, dressed in a black shirt and jeans.

I yawned. "Is it morning?"

"Yes, it's almost nine," he said. There was a faint taste of peppermint on his breath. I wanted to ask him when he'd woken up, but then he pulled me into a long kiss, and his cool touch reminded me he was a vampire. Nights were his active time, so he'd been wide awake during the hours I was lost in slumber.

"How are you feeling? Are you sore?" he asked.

"I'm fine, not sore." I leaned in for another kiss. Things had started to heat up when the phone in the back pocket of his jeans began to ring. He ignored it, but it wouldn't stop, so he reluctantly pulled away, muttering a curse at the interruption.

"Just a sec, I'll silence it."

"No, you should answer the call. It might be important."

He took out his phone, glanced at the caller ID, and put the device to his ear.

"Robin," he answered, his voice icy. After a short moment of silence, he said, "Yeah, I tried to reach you earlier." There was another pause before he continued, "Because I need to talk to you about Eric. A little birdie whispered to me that you two have been getting close lately... I agree, we should meet up. Text me the time and place."

After he hung up, I asked, "Who was that?"

"A demon who used to feed me information about Damon and Heather. She stopped after a while, fearing the consequences of being discovered. Now she runs a strip club in the city."

"What about Eric? Why didn't you get information about him? Doesn't he want you dead too?" I asked.

"Eric has spent his entire existence in Heather's shadow. His obsession with destroying her, and Damon, always took precedence. Whereas I was never significant enough to him to make his list of people he wanted dead or destroyed. That's why I didn't have to hire someone to spy on him."

"Who told you about Robin and Eric?" I asked.

"Katina. She didn't have much information about him and suggested I talk to Robin instead. Apparently, Robin and Eric have been seen together a few times in the last few weeks. She might have some insight into Eric's plans."

"Great, I'll come with you to the meeting," I said.

"No. It wouldn't be safe for you."

"I'll wear my gloves so my tattoo won't draw attention and take BFB before we meet her."

"That's not what I'm worried about."

"Then what is?"

"Having you with me when I meet Robin. That'd be a problem because I love you. If I slip up and give away my feelings for you through my behavior or expressions, Robin, or any demons she might bring with her, could report back to Damon. He would go to great lengths to hunt you down, using bounty hunters and every resource at his disposal. Then he'd kill you just to make me suffer. No demon can ever know the depth of my feelings for you, including Eric. Your safety depends on it."

I stared at him as my mind focused on the three significant words he'd said.

*I love you.*

I'd heard those three words before, from Jared, but when Gideon said them, they were filled with something... more. There was an undeniable sincerity in his voice that sent tingles of excitement down my spine. I loved him too. I just wished I knew more about him, like why the demon king hated him so much. Was it merely a rivalry between species, or was there more to it? I was about to ask him when the sound of ringing came from my jeans lying on the floor. Gideon got up to get my phone, but just as he handed it to me, the ringing stopped. The screen showed a missed call.

"It was Audrey," I said, unlocking my phone.

"Call her back, see if she's all right. Remember, don't mention the demon attack," he said, and his phone chimed. He read his text then updated me. "Robin will meet me at her strip club tonight."

"I get why you're worried about me tagging along, but there might be subtle nuances during the meeting that you could miss. A slight hesitation in her voice, a quick glance away, or a sudden change in posture often reveals more than words alone. That's why it's important for me to be there and hear what she has to say about Eric firsthand. Don't worry; we'll be careful around the demons. I'll play the part of the submissive Donor, and they won't suspect a thing," I said.

He rubbed a hand over his face. "You're not going to change your mind, are you?" I shook my head, and after a moment, he relented. "Okay, we'll meet Robin together. There are two bottles of BFB on the kitchen counter for you. And don't forget to wear your gloves to the meeting."

"I won't," I said. Remembering his nocturnal nature, I added, "You're probably tired; you should go to sleep. I'm gonna take a quick shower and start the day. Give me a call when you wake up."

Before he could change his mind about me coming with him to see Robin, I hopped out of bed and made my way to the bathroom. The questions about his past would have to wait. I slipped into the snail shower, a spiraling oasis of relaxation.

Back at my apartment, I changed into clean clothes and called Audrey. She didn't sound sick or tired, so I assumed the side effects had worn off. After she apologized for her behavior, chalking it up to an unexplained bout of illness, I turned the conversation to Ian. She told me she'd spoken to him an hour ago. He'd initially refused to help me, but a reminder of the favor he owed her changed his mind. He'd agreed to meet me despite his busy schedule, offering a slot at eleven o'clock, which was an hour away. Audrey also reminded me to stop by the magic convention so Lily could examine my tattoo. I assured her I'd be there before we hung up.

Then I looked up the address of Ian's office. My shift didn't start until two thirty, which gave me plenty of time to get to the appointment. Forty-five minutes later, I stood in the third-floor hallway of an office building, outside a frosted-glass door marked "IAN ROBINSON: PRIVATE INVESTIGATOR." Before I could knock, the door swung open and a furious woman stormed out, her eyes glowing silver. She pushed past me, nearly knocking me off balance. As I turned to watch her stomp down the hall toward the elevator, I heard an annoyed male voice behind me.

"I hate domestic cases involving unfaithful husbands. There's too much drama for my taste. If you can't handle the truth, don't hire me to uncover it." I turned to see Ian standing in the small outer office. A suit clung to his thin frame. His short brown hair was plastered back in a greasy mess by an overabundance of gel, and his light complexion was pitted with acne scars.

He gave me an irritated look. "And now I have to deal with a human who sent a vampire to steal from me."

He walked to the door of his office on the other side of the reception area. I scoffed at his back as I followed him into a medium-sized room. He sat behind a desk facing the door, and I had a mental image of myself grabbing him by the collar, yanking him out of his chair, and beating the crap out of him. His condescending attitude grated on my nerves, but I had to put up with it; he was supposed to be the best in his field, and I needed answers.

I took a deep breath to calm myself and said, "If I recall correctly—and I do—*you* were the one who stole from me. I merely took back what was mine."

Ian pursed his lips and motioned for me to sit down. His office was simple and unadorned. There were metal filing cabinets along one wall, a desk cluttered with stacks of papers and folders, and another desk occupied by Ian, with two guest chairs placed across from him. I stepped over to one of them and sat down.

"Audrey mentioned you needed my services," he said, "but she didn't provide any details. So, what can I do for you?" His tone made it clear he was obligated out of necessity.

I leaned back in my chair and talked about Oberon, recounting the times he'd saved me, first from my kidnapper and then from Serena in Ice Prison.

His brow furrowed. "You're saying the king of the fae intervened on your behalf not once, but twice?" I nodded, and he continued, "It's hard to believe a royal fae would concern himself with a mere mortal, but I see no reason for you to make this up."

I wasn't wearing my gloves, and his gaze caught the tattoo. If he was going to work on my case, he needed to know about the black ink on my hand; it might be important information for the investigation.

"Care to explain how you came to possess such rare dark magic on your hand?" he asked.

"The man who kidnapped me did this to me."

Ian looked impressed. "He must be a highly skilled witch. The number on your hand is the most powerful thing I've ever seen. Maybe you're not as ordinary a human as I first thought. The dark magic may be the reason for Oberon's interest in you."

"I am not looking for theories; I have plenty of those already," I snapped. "I'm looking for answers. I wanna know what Oberon's agenda is regarding me. Can you help me or not?"

He nodded. "I believe I can."

"I've told you about my encounter with Oberon. Is there anything else you need from me?"

"Just your phone number, so I can contact you if necessary. When I'm done with your case, Audrey and I will be even. Make sure she understands that."

Gritting my teeth, I swallowed a nasty curse and gave him my number, then took the subway to work.

After my shift ended and I changed out of my waitress uniform, I texted Audrey to let her know I was on my way to the magic convention. By the time I reached the address she'd given me, the sun was setting, its golden rays streaking through the gray and white clouds, painting the sky pink and coral.

I tucked my sunglasses into my bag as I approached Audrey, who was standing at the entrance of a large building. With no flags or banners associated with the convention, the massive rectangular metal and concrete structure sat on one side of a large parking lot.

"Lily's inside, waiting to see the tattoo," Audrey said.

"I also want to ask her about Ivy. Maybe she knew her parents or sisters."

"I already told her about Ivy and what happened to you with the compulsion incident, but like me, she had no explanation for it or knew Ivy. She hasn't heard about her murder either." At my sigh of disappointment, she added, "I'm sorry, I know it's frustrating."

"That's okay, at least you tried."

"Come on, let's go inside."

"Wait, am I allowed in? I'm human," I said.

"You're Lily's guest. No one would say no to the guest of a respected witch like her."

I looked hesitantly at the entrance. "What about my tattoo? I bet any witch in there will sense the dark magic, even with my gloves on. Won't that be a problem since this magic is illegal?"

"No, because you're human and the dark magic was done to you. You're the victim here," she said, turning to face the entrance. She whispered something that sounded like an ancient foreign language, and the doors opened. Staring at the doorway and the darkness beyond it, I didn't move. Audrey gestured with her head for me to enter.

I followed her into a dark hallway that led to a dimly lit lobby. Tall white candles floated around the room, bobbing and casting a wavering glow over the walls. Small glass tables with chairs were scattered about. As I watched the witches milling around in the lobby, a woman in a black gown came up to us.

She examined me from head to toe and then looked at Audrey. "Who is your human friend?"

"Lily's guest," Audrey answered.

"The one with the dark magic on her body?"

Audrey nodded, and we were granted entry to the main hall. As we moved toward it, the number of candles around us increased. The place grew brighter, and the sound of chatter filled the air. We maneuvered through the crowd and took the escalator to the second floor. There, Audrey led us to a woman in her forties with long, black hair. She was standing near a doorway, talking to a man in a T-shirt and jeans.

"Oh, there you are," she said to Audrey when we reached her. She looked at the man she'd been talking to. "I'm sorry, but we'll have to pick this up later."

After he entered the room in front of us, which held a podium and a long table, she turned her focus back to me.

"I'm Lily. Audrey told me about your situation. I must say I'm furious one of my kind used their powers to terrorize an innocent human. The practice of dark magic is a serious offense in our world. Rest assured, the Watchers will apprehend the individual responsible and hold them accountable for their actions." She looked down at the tattoo. "May I examine it more closely?"

I held out my left hand, and she took it, palm up.

Her eyes grew wide. "Such immense power..."

"Do you have any idea why it's counting down?" I asked.

She shook her head. "This is unlike anything I've ever seen." She brushed her fingers across the number and muttered, "Eternal gods."

"Do you know what it means?" I asked.

Lily released my hand. "I'm really sorry, but I don't have answers for you. Your tattoo is quite the enigma. I thought maybe a closer look would help me understand why it behaves the way it does, but I was wrong. However, I found something interesting I think you should know. After Audrey told me about you, I did some research and discovered there may be a way to get rid of the tattoo for good. According to a book I came across, demons with pure demon blood can separate powerful dark magic from its host."

So maybe Eric hadn't lied to me after all.

"Pure demon blood? That's new to me," Audrey said. "Who has that? Royal demons?"

A group of people walked by and entered the room near us, acknowledging Lily with a nod.

She smiled at them then answered Audrey, "My understanding of demon physiology and bloodlines is rather limited. Unfortunately, the book didn't provide any more information, so I'm afraid I don't have the answer." Her focus shifted to something over my shoulder. "But I think the illusionist over there might know more." She waved someone over. "Cole."

I turned, and my breath caught in my throat. A rush of nausea threatened to overwhelm me as my heart slammed against my ribs. My whole body trembled, and I almost fainted.

The man who had ruined my life—my kidnapper—was walking right toward us.

# Chapter 9

"**S**ydney? You don't look so good. What's wrong?" Audrey asked.

"It's... it's..." I struggled to find the words and tried to collect myself. "It's..." I started again, but fear, shock, and rage choked me.

Dressed in black pants and a button-down shirt, the monster stood there, looking exactly as I'd remembered him. The memory of those dark days locked in a tiny room flashed before my eyes. Fury pounded against my senses as my hands clenched into fists.

"You piece of shit!" I lunged at him, but my body went right through him like he was a ghost. I tumbled to the floor behind him. What the hell? He appeared oblivious to what had happened as he looked at Lily and Audrey, who stared at the scene in disbelief.

He frowned at Lily. "Is something wrong?" When he didn't get an answer, he followed her stunned gaze to where I was.

I pushed myself to my feet. "You bastard! You ruined my life!" But he stared past me, as if he didn't see me at all.

"Sydney, I think you're invisible to him," Audrey said, looking addled. "And it seems he can't hear you either."

The monster stiffened at Audrey's words. A crowd started to form around us, drawn by the commotion.

"Cole, what have you done? Why is she so upset? What's going on?" Lily demanded.

I gritted my teeth as my chest heaved with rapid, shallow breaths. "He's the one who kidnapped me and poisoned my body with dark magic!" I shouted, and the bastard winked out of existence. "No!" My eyes snapped to Lily. "Where did he go? Can you use magic to find him?"

"No, I'm sorry, I can't," Lily answered, then turned to the onlookers with a reassuring smile. "There's nothing to be concerned about; everything's fine." They hesitated for a moment before dispersing.

"What was he doing at the convention? Who is he? How do you know him? Why wasn't he able to see or hear me?" My voice wobbled with adrenaline and shock. Audrey put a hand on my shoulder to steady me.

"I met him here at the convention," Lily replied. "The one time we spoke, our discussion of dark magic revealed he had an impressive depth of knowledge on the subject. He seemed like a decent man. It's shocking to discover he's the one who abducted you."

"You have his description and his name. Give that to the Watchers. They'll find him, right?" I told Lily.

"Yes, I'll report him," she said, "but I have to be honest with you. When Cole used his magic to vanish, I sensed an immense, formidable power emanating from him. I wouldn't get your hopes up about the Watchers finding a witch like him. It seems like it wouldn't be hard for him to evade them."

Audrey chimed in, "She's right. He's very powerful, more than any witch I've known. At least you're safe from him. He can't see, hear, or even touch you."

"Yeah, but why is that? Is it because of a spell?" I asked, but neither of them had an explanation.

A man emerged from the room near us and reminded Lily that the panel was about to begin.

"I'll be right there," she told him, then turned back to me. "I'm truly sorry for everything you've been through. I wish there was more I could do to help. I'll keep researching. If I come across anything useful, you'll be the first to know."

"Thank you," I said.

As Audrey watched Lily walk into the panel room, she said, "I can't wrap my head around the fact that the man who kidnapped you was here at the convention." When her gaze returned to me, her eyes rounded wide. "Whoa, Sydney. You're shaking like a leaf. Hey, it's gonna be all right, c'mere." She hugged me for support. "We'll find him."

Tears of shock and fear trickled down my cheeks. I wiped them away when my phone rang. After taking a few seconds to compose myself, I answered Gideon's call. He knew something was wrong the moment he heard my voice. I explained I was at the magic convention with Audrey and went over the whole incident with Cole.

After I answered his flurry of concerned questions, he noted a potential lead—we finally had the name of my kidnapper. Of course, it was possible that Cole wasn't his real name, but I clung to the hope it was, and that this new information could help find him. Before we ended the call, he told me he was coming to pick me up for the meeting with Robin.

I went outside to wait for him. Audrey decided to stay inside and mingle with the convention attendees, hoping to find someone who might have talked to or known Cole. When Gideon arrived, I had to reassure him again that Cole hadn't harmed me. Then I put on my gloves and climbed onto the back of his bike, wrapping my arms around him. Half an hour later, he parked on an empty street, dark and deserted, three blocks from Robin's strip club.

We dismounted from the bike, and while he called Robin to let her know of his arrival, I found myself watching him, a warm glow of love spreading around my heart. After he hung up, we started to walk toward the club, turning into a side street. While he gave me pointers on how to convincingly play the role of his Donor to Robin and the other demons, I decided to tell him how I felt.

"Gideon," I started, halting in my tracks.

My sudden stop caught him off guard, and he reached for the gun in his jacket. We were approaching a place teeming with demons, and I realized this was not the best time to pour my heart out, particularly since we had to hide our relationship from them. But there was no one around to hear or see us, and I needed him to know what he meant to me.

He flung a glance from side to side for any imminent threats.

"What's wrong?" he asked.

"Nothing. I just want to tell you I love you."

As his expression changed from alarmed to delighted, I spotted someone advancing toward us past his shoulder. Probably a demon sent to escort Gideon to Robin. Before I could draw Gideon's attention to the guy, he pulled me close and leaned in for a kiss. Since I was supposed to be nothing more than his Donor, I had to stop him.

Thinking on my feet, I punched him in the jaw then winced inwardly. Yeah, a simple slap would have sufficed, but it wasn't as if I'd had enough time to calculate my moves. He let go of me and raised a confused eyebrow as he rubbed his jaw.

"No offense, love, but you've got a rather unique way of showing affection. I would have settled for the old-fashioned way—a kiss."

"You can't feed on me now. We are in public. Someone might see us," I said, loud enough for the approaching man to hear. The puzzlement on Gideon's face deepened until I cast a meaningful glance over his shoulder.

With a flash of comprehension he said, "Yeah, you're right. I wasn't thinking clearly." He pivoted to face the man who now stood before us.

The stranger's lips twisted into a sneer. "I work for Robin. You Gideon Hawthorne?"

"I am," Gideon answered.

The man jerked his chin at me. "Who's the human, leech?"

"Just a snack for later. I doubt your kind keeps A-negative in the fridge, so I thought I'd bring my own." Even though I knew it was just an act, Gideon's distant, callous tone when referring to me was still hard to hear. I had to find the strength to feign indifference.

When we reached the strip club, the man led us to its back door and down a dark hallway. The music faded to a muffled pulse and was gone after we'd climbed to the second floor. There, he guided us into a room with a glass wall overlooking the club's narrow stages, where women danced in nothing but G-strings.

"Thank you, Norman. You can go now," said a woman with velvety fair skin sitting on a red leather couch in the middle of the room. The man nodded and stepped out, closing the door behind him and leaving the three of us alone in the room. She stood, passed a black round table, and walked over to Gideon. Her blue dress had a cleavage that exposed half of her ample breasts and hugged her voluptuous body tightly.

"Hello, Gideon." She smiled at him then pinched her nose and sniffed the air. Her brown eyes darted to me before returning to Gideon. "You brought a human and protected her soul with BFB. She must be very special to you."

He shrugged. "If you count her ability to satisfy my need for blood as special, then yeah, I guess she is. I brought Little Miss A-Negative so I'll have something to eat when we're done here. As for giving her BFB, I can't feed on a dead Donor, can I?" His voice was frosty.

"True," she said. Her eyes flickered to my gloved hands before she resumed speaking. "You know it's not safe for me to be seen with you. My staff is loyal, and they won't breathe a word to Heather about this meeting. However, I do expect to be compensated for my time. Five grand would be a fair amount."

"Two grand," Gideon countered firmly. "Non-negotiable."

After a brief silence, she said, "Fine."

"I'll wire the money tomorrow," he said.

She gave a nod, then asked, "What do you want to know?"

"I hear you've been spending some time with Eric. What's that all about?"

She smoothed a hand over her honey-colored hair and glanced at my hands again before answering, "He recently discovered we have common interests. We both hate Heather, and he wants to destroy her and our king. I have no doubt he'll succeed. Eric is not just a pretty face. He's smart, and when he becomes our new king, he'll remember who was on his side and helped him. Who knows, I might even end up being the new queen. Why the sudden interest in Eric?"

"Cut the bullshit, Robin. You know why. I saw the way you looked at her hands." Gideon nodded at me. "Eric clued you in on her dark magic. I want details."

She grinned. "Yes, I know about your human's tattoo, but not from Eric. His driver—James, I think his name was—shared the intel. We spent a few nights together, and yesterday, he showed me a picture he'd taken of your human. He mentioned he'd driven Eric to meet her. While he was busy talking to her, James caught a glimpse of the tattoo and recognized the number as rare dark magic.

"He thought the ink must hold significant powers, given Eric's investment of his precious time with the human. So, James planned to kidnap the human, cut off the hand with the tattoo, and sell the dark magic to a collector for a substantial sum of money. The human's safety was clearly important to Eric, which offered me an opportunity to prove my loyalty to him. I warned him of his driver's plan and, as I expected, Eric was pleased with me.

"He even let me tag along when he killed James." Her lips curled into a satisfied grin. "When I saw your human, I recognized her from the picture James showed me and knew she was not a regular Donor. Her blood is spiced with dark magic, which must be a delectable cocktail for you. Interestingly, you don't look sick. I suppose human blood mixed with dark magic does not have the same destructive effect on vampires as the blood of my kind."

The corner of her mouth lifted into a taunting, crooked smile as she continued. "You know, I can't help but wonder what the mighty Herit would've said if she knew her own son was drinking blood mixed with dark magic. Wasn't she the one who vehemently denounced it as the source of all evil?"

The words "her own son" echoed in my mind. Then my brain short-circuited, leaving me in a state of bewildered shock. Gideon was Herit's son? As in, the Great Herit? The one the Memphis Warriors worshiped? The one who had brought the Original Rulers to their knees? The one who had created the Watchers and Ice Prison?

"I'm not here to discuss my mother," Gideon said sharply. "Let's get back to Eric. Did he tell you anything about the human or her dark magic?"

She hesitated. "No, nothing."

"If I find out you're lying to me, I'll make sure Heather hears all about our little chat."

Her lips tightened into a hard line. "I'm not lying. Eric wouldn't give me any answers about your human or her tattoo. And that's the whole truth." She checked the time. "I have another meeting in ten minutes. Can we wrap this up?"

"Just one more thing. Did Eric mention Oberon regarding the human?" Gideon asked.

She shook her head. "No, I don't remember your brother's name coming up when I met with Eric."

Another bolt of surprise shot through me. Oberon was Gideon's brother? What the hell was going on? Was Gideon even a vampire? What was he?

After we exited the strip club, my mind was reeling. Astonishment rendered me speechless, and my thoughts swirled in a chaotic jumble. Gideon, who seemed to sense my need to process the new revelations about him, remained silent as well. When we reached his penthouse and entered his living room, he broke the silence between us.

"I know you're probably feeling confused, and your head is spinning with all the questions you want to ask me. Before we get to that, though, let me tell you my story first."

He gestured for me to sit down on the couch and joined me.

# Chapter 10

"My story begins in ancient Egypt, five thousand years ago," he said. "I was born human, just like you."

I interrupted him. "But you said you were one hundred and sixty-five years old. And you were born human, not a Daywalker?"

"I was born human to human parents, and I came into this world five thousand years ago, but I've lived one hundred and sixty-five years. I know it doesn't make sense right now, but it'll all become clear soon. As I was saying, I was born in ancient Egypt, a time when human sacrifice was part of the rituals to honor the gods. It was also a time when demons, vampires, and witches coexisted openly with humans, and there were no Watchers or Ice Prison.

"When a famine struck the land and supernatural killings escalated, due to the starvation of the warriors who had protected humans from them, Pharaoh, an ancient Egyptian ruler and a human, believed the gods were punishing his people. He reasoned that sacrificing two pure and innocent human lives, like newborn babies, instead of one adult life at the next ritual would appease the gods. They would then end the famine and protect his people from supernatural beings.

"Impoverished farming women about to give birth were ordered to leave their husbands and live in a large mud-brick house by the Nile. It was within those walls that Damon and I were born."

"Damon? You mean the demon king?" I asked. Gideon nodded, and my jaw dropped like a stone. "He was born human too? Is he your twin?"

"He was born human too, yes, but we're not twins. We were born to different mothers with no family ties. Damon and I are not related by blood," Gideon clarified, then continued the story. "After our births, the Pharaoh and the High Priest got what they needed, two newborn babies to sacrifice to the gods.

"We were then taken to a tent while the other women were allowed to return to their families. On the night we were to be sacrificed, someone snuck into our tent and stole us. Our savior was the woman whose blood had spawned the vampire race. Her name was Herit."

I blinked at him. "The Great Herit? She was a vampire?"

He shook his head. "No, she wasn't a vampire; she was a royal fae—the queen of the fae, in fact."

I dragged my hands down my face, struggling to wrap my brain around this. Herit was the freaking fae queen, which explained her immense power.

Gideon went on, "Long before Herit knew about the existence of our world, she lived in the faerie realm with the king and their only child, Oberon. Herit had a close friend named Eldrin, a powerful royal fae who harbored a secret love for her. A magic expert, he was a scientist and had an insatiable appetite for exploring alternate dimensions, a passion that led him to discover our world.

"After two brief visits here, he shared his findings with Herit, knowing her curious nature would be intrigued by the prospect of exploring this new planet with him. However, Herit hesitated, reminding him of her royal responsibilities and inability to just pick up and leave her kingdom. Eldrin eased her concerns by explaining that time passed much more slowly on Earth, which meant she could spend long periods of time here while only seconds passed in her kingdom.

"With her concerns addressed, Herit agreed to accompany Eldrin. But before they could begin their journey to the new world, Eldrin had to make sure Herit's body could adapt to the unfamiliar environment and withstand the diseases present on Earth. He ran a series of tests on her blood in his lab. The results showed that Earth's sun posed a significant threat to Herit's well-being, and her appearance, much like Eldrin's, could strike deep fear into the hearts of Earth's inhabitants, leading to their deaths.

"To solve this problem, a protective vessel was needed to shield Herit from Earth's sun and to keep her and Eldrin's true forms from harming the people of the new world. After much experimentation in his lab, Eldrin successfully concocted a potion that would generate a second skin over their bodies.

"This barrier would not only shield Herit from Earth's sun, but would also transform their appearance to resemble Earth's creatures, hiding their true form while retaining their magical abilities. Which was important as removing the vessel would require their magic. The first time Herit and Eldrin visited was about two million years ago, during the Stone Age.

"Herit assumed they were on an expedition to study the new world and its inhabitants. However, Eldrin had a hidden agenda he kept from her, one she never agreed to. He had taken a sample of Herit's blood from his lab and brought it to Earth for experimentation. As they explored the new world, Eldrin discreetly selected thousands of its inhabitants and placed them under a spell to ensure their obedience. He divided these individuals into two groups. One group received his blood, while the other got Herit's blood.

"He'd planned to monitor the effects of their blood on the humans, but Herit, unaware of his secret experiment, decided to return to their own world after just a few days. He tried to persuade her to stay, but his efforts were in vain. Upon their return to the faerie realm, Eldrin's experiment notes tumbled out of his bag, catching Herit's eye before he could pick them up. She grabbed the notes and demanded an explanation, which forced him to confess to the secret experiment.

"Herit was furious with him. Her anger diminished, though, when she discovered she'd left her bag behind. It contained a bottle of fae food, a container of fae water, and a magical fae stone known on Earth as the Tara Stone. She realized she'd been just as irresponsible as him. As soon as she could, Herit returned with Eldrin to our world to see the consequences of their actions.

"While only a short time had elapsed in the faerie realm, countless millennia had passed on Earth by the time they arrived here, landing them in 3000 BC. The results of their interference were plain to see. New species, mortal and immortal, now roamed the earth, their presence casting an ominous pall of fear over the land. The streets were strewn with lifeless bodies, and chaos reigned as the supernatural beings terrorized the human population.

"Eldrin's analysis of hair samples from the new species led to two discoveries. One, that immortals on Earth could look at royal fae without succumbing to death, and two, that the fae blood, food, and water had slowly mutated those who had consumed it. While the initial changes to their bodies were minimal, as these mutated mortals continued to reproduce over generations, they evolved into immortals and humans with magical powers.

"Demons descended from the group that drank Eldrin's blood, while vampires descended from the group that took Herit's blood. The lineage that led to witches evolved from the mortals who ate fae food. And those who consumed fae water were transformed into a unique species known as Goldeneye.

"These extraordinary beings produced tears of pure gold, infused with power as great as the Tara Stone. Their tears made them a target, and for centuries, they were hunted to extinction. Here and there, over the years, some have claimed to have encountered these creatures, but there has never been any real evidence to support their stories."

I opened my mouth to ask about the girl I'd seen when Oberon freed me from my captivity. She'd been in the cell next to mine. Golden tears streamed down her cheeks as she warned me not to look at Oberon because humans died from a single glance at royal fae, unlike common ones who weren't dangerous to look at. After I'd been freed, I discovered a strange enchantment at work; whenever I'd attempted to mention that girl or anything about golden tears, I found myself expressing a craving for ice cream instead. Since I could feel this spell taking effect as the words "ice cream" began to bubble to the surface, I closed my mouth.

Gideon took notice. "What is it? What were you going to say?" Answering his question was pointless. The spell would just twist my words into a desire for an ice-cream break or something.

"Nothing, forget it, go on," I said. "Tell me what happened during Eldrin and Herit's second visit here."

"While Eldrin was busy studying the new species," Gideon went on, "Herit wandered through the city until she came upon a mud-brick hut housing a group of human women. Inside, she saw two women giving birth. Herit used her magic to translate the human language they were speaking and learned the grim fate that awaited their unborn babies—Damon and me.

"Horrified, she later stole us from the tent in which we had been placed. Eldrin tried to dissuade her from taking us to the faerie world and raising us there. He reminded her it was fatal for humans to look at royal fae, but she told him there was a way around it."

"What might that be? Give you their blood?" I asked.

"No, that would only have caused mutations, not the immediate immortality we needed to protect us from their true form. Herit had another idea. In the faerie world, fae royalty who struggle to conceive have the option to adopt and imbue the adopted baby with some of their DNA, essentially making the baby biologically their own.

"Herit suggested they do the same with Damon and me, believing fae DNA would protect us like immortality. She didn't know what the outcome would be, though, as it'd never been attempted with babies who were not fae. However, she was determined to try anyway, as it was better than us being sacrificed."

My brow furrowed. "Wait, how does this fae DNA injection work? Can any fae transfer their DNA to others?"

He leaned against the back of the couch. "No, the ability to transfer DNA is exclusive to powerful royal fae, and even then, they can only do it once. That's why Herit needed Eldrin's cooperation; she couldn't give her DNA to both of us. At first, Eldrin was against it, but his love for her eventually swayed him to agree, not realizing it might expose a deep secret he'd been hiding from everyone.

"After Herit shifted one baby from her arm to his, Eldrin intertwined his essence with Damon's, and Herit wove her DNA through mine. Our bodies changed in a matter of seconds. We were no longer human, though not exactly fae either. My appearance changed to resemble Herit's. My eyes turned blue like hers and my skin became lighter and paler, while Damon's features became similar to Eldrin's.

"Herit cast a spell to remove her vessel, testing whether their DNA would provide protection for us against her true form. Her solution proved successful; we didn't die, but her relief was fleeting. As she held us both in her arms, she sensed something was not right with Damon. She asked Eldrin what was wrong with him. Anticipating that she'd eventually uncover the truth, he confessed to his secret practice of dark magic—a capital crime in the faerie world.

"This kind of magic is addictive to fae, who can feed off the energy emitted by dark spells. It's not poisonous or dangerous to them, but once a fae tastes it, they crave more and more. Eldrin became addicted, and his DNA was tainted with dark magic that made Damon different from me. Eldrin didn't disclose everything to Herit, though. What he left out of his confession was that he'd stolen the Forbidden Stone, the primordial source of dark magic.

"It was unearthed from the depths of one of the fae forests by the first king of the faerie realm. The Forbidden Stone is capable of creating the most powerful dark spells. It holds so much power that if mortals look at it, they die. If immortals touch it, their souls are corrupted. The stone is also a threat to worlds made of ordinary magic, such as the faerie realm. You see, their land, their forests, their water, their food, all contain ordinary magic. Except for the Forbidden Stone, which is pure dark magic.

"After the king found the stone, he was unaware of the danger it posed, and his people used it to craft dark enchantments, which they documented in books. Soon the king discovered the devastating effects of dark magic on ordinary magic. Prolonged use or sudden excessive casting of these spells in a short period of time could wipe out the fae world. While it has no adverse effect on the caster aside from addiction, dark magic literally eats away at the fabric of worlds with ordinary magic like a ravenous bacteria. If not stopped in time, it'll consume everything in its path, leaving nothing but a void. So in response, the king took decisive actions. He destroyed the books of dark magic spells, locked the indestructible stone away in a magic-protected vault, and outlawed dark magic."

I stopped him. "If all the books were destroyed, how could Eldrin explain to Herit where his dark spells came from without revealing he had the stone? Why not just tell her he'd stolen it?"

"Eldrin didn't want anyone to know he had the stone. He was worried someone, including Herit, might try to steal it from him for their own gain, so he lied to her. He said the dark spells came from a book he'd found on one of the planets he'd explored," he replied.

"What drove him to steal the stone? Wasn't he aware using its dark magic could unravel the very foundation of his world?" I asked.

"As a scientist, he'd always been curious about the stone and the great power it possessed. He also doubted the claims that it was dangerous to their world, so he dedicated himself to obtaining the stone. After years of searching, he finally discovered a spell that could bypass the magical protection of the vault, where the stone was kept. Just weeks before Herit's first journey to Earth, he broke into the vault, stole the stone, and replaced it with a perfect replica, leaving no one the wiser."

"Smart of him, using a replica," I said. As I placed a couch cushion behind my back and leaned against it, a question occurred to me. "Herit is a powerful royal fae, so couldn't she have sensed something was wrong with Eldrin, just as she did with Damon?"

"Eldrin, being a magic expert, knew how to hide the stain dark magic had left on his soul from her and everyone else."

"What happened after Herit heard Eldrin's confession?" I asked.

"She demanded to know more about the new species created from his blood. He told her his limited research had revealed a clear difference between the demons and other species in terms of emotions. The demons exhibited a distinct lack of remorse and compassion. This worried Herit. She feared that Damon, who received Eldrin's DNA tainted with pure dark magic, might grow up to be even more sinful than the other demons.

"After she shared her concerns, Eldrin promised to stop practicing dark magic and help her raise Damon to be good. She believed he'd stop and agreed to let him help. Then she told him she had to clean up the mess they'd made on Earth and asked him to go back to their world with Damon and me. She entrusted him with the task of looking after us until she could restore order here and reunite with Damon and me upon her return.

"After he left with us, she began searching for the leaders of the creatures her blood had created. When she met with the Original Rulers, they laughed at her and tried to kill her, but royal fae are skilled warriors and immensely powerful. Herit fought and defeated them, then ordered the other new species to follow her rules. The witches and demons refused, and the Big War broke out. Despite having only a small army, Herit emerged victorious.

"She stayed in our world for a few more years to train the female vampires who fought with her in the war."

I crossed my legs. "You mean the Memphis Warriors?" They were an all-female organization of vampire warriors, and after the war had ended, they settled in Memphis in ancient Egypt.

He nodded. "Yes. During these years, Herit built Ice Prison and created the Watchers. Once order was restored, she returned to her world. Though only a short span of time had passed in the faerie realm, much had happened there. Whispers of Eldrin's infatuation with the queen had reached the king's ears. Suspecting infidelity, he confronted Eldrin at his home.

"Eldrin led him to believe he and the queen were lovers, hoping Herit's husband would leave her and she'd turn to him for comfort. The king, convinced of his wife's betrayal, was enraged. As he let loose a storm of curses at Eldrin, he heard the sound of babies crying from the study. He burst into the room and discovered us along with dark spells written on various parchments.

"After Eldrin explained what Damon and I were doing in his study, the king's rage intensified upon learning Herit and Eldrin had put their DNA into mortal babies. He was also convinced Herit was dabbling in dark magic with Eldrin, a notion Eldrin denied, but the king refused to believe him. When Herit returned, he wouldn't even listen to her and had his guards throw her and Eldrin into separate cells for their supposed crime of using dark magic.

"Oberon believed in his mother's innocence and demanded her release, but his father, the king, wouldn't budge. Meanwhile, Eldrin, who had managed to hide the Forbidden Stone in his clothes before his imprisonment, utilized its power to break free. He headed to court with the intention of killing the king."

"How do you kill a royal fae?" I asked.

"Only a knife known as the Death Dagger has the power to sever a fae's life force. Like the Forbidden Stone, the dagger was secured in a vault. When Eldrin took the stone, he also stole the Death Dagger. Armed with it, he killed the king and unleashed a torrent of dark spells to fight his way through the king's many guards and free Herit from her cell.

"Herit was shocked to learn he'd stolen the stone and was appalled when he told her he'd killed the king for imprisoning them. She screamed at him to leave her alone. After he left, the ground beneath her feet began to shake. Eldrin's dark magic, which he'd used to escape his cell and kill the king's guards, was seeping into their world and destroying it. The tremors grew stronger by the second, toppling trees and tearing gaping cracks in the ground.

"Amid the chaos of sinkholes swallowing fleeing figures, structures crumbling to rubble, and flames consuming everything in their path, she ran back to court to search for Damon and me. She found Oberon kneeling by his father's dead body. Herit revealed to him the extent of Eldrin's betrayal, and Oberon vowed to avenge his father's death. He wanted to kill Eldrin and get back what he'd stolen, but Herit stopped him. She reminded him he now assumed the role of king and had a sacred duty to their people.

"They needed a new planet. As the son of two powerful royal fae, Oberon possessed enormous power and the ability to build worlds, like his mother. While the desire for vengeance seethed within him, he knew his mother was right. He had to act fast and create a new faerie world to save his people. Herit assured her son she'd help him as soon as she found Damon and me, so she could take us with her to the new faerie world.

"After a guard told her Eldrin had kidnapped us from the palace, Herit did exactly what she'd convinced Oberon not to do: she rushed to Eldrin's house to kill him. But her plan failed. When she broke into his residence to look for the Death Dagger and Damon and me, Eldrin caught her. She demanded he give us back. He refused, telling her he'd only reveal our location if she agreed to return to Earth and raise us there with him."

I frowned. "Wait, what was he planning to eat on Earth? Can human food sustain fae?"

"It can sustain common fae, but not royals. Before Eldrin and Herit made their second journey to our world, Eldrin, not wanting to carry fae food or water again, had discovered a way for their vessels to capture light energy and convert it into nourishment for their bodies, just as plants use sunlight for photosynthesis."

"Interesting," I said with a thoughtful nod. Then I asked, "So how did Herit respond to Eldrin's terms?"

"Unwilling to abandon us, she reluctantly agreed to go with him. Before drinking the potion that generated the second skin, she went back to Oberon and told him what had happened. Oberon couldn't talk her into leaving us with Eldrin and joining him in the new faerie world. She said goodbye and returned to Earth with Eldrin, Damon, and me. The year was 1830.

"Herit was pleased to see that the Watchers had done a good job of maintaining order. The humans were oblivious to the existence of supernatural creatures, and there were no piles of corpses everywhere. Eldrin and Herit settled in the land of America. They chose local names for us, Damon and Gideon, and after living together for some time, Eldrin declared his love for her. Herit, however, didn't reciprocate, a rejection that infuriated him. Bitter and resentful, he left and never returned.

"Though finally free of his controlling presence, Herit couldn't go with us to the new faerie world, where she belonged. Before leaving, Eldrin had threatened to kill us if she ever went there. To ensure her compliance, he had cast a dark spell that would allow him to know if Herit ever left Earth."

"What a jerk. Why'd he care where she was?" I asked as a rumble of thunder rolled through the living room.

"He wanted to punish her for not loving him back. Despite Herit's formidable magical abilities, she had to obey Eldrin's will. The dark magic gave him power over her. She couldn't break his spell, which forced her to stay in our world. So, she continued to raise Damon and me on Earth.

"Her true nature was hidden by her vessel, making her powers undetectable to those in the Hidden World. Presenting herself as Herit Hawthorne, a widowed mother of two, she made sure Damon and I had as normal a childhood as possible. It was important to her we fit in. Her only deviation from conventional parenting was that she taught us fighting skills at an early age as she wanted us to be a warrior like her."

"Did you and Damon know you had fae DNA when you were kids?"

"No, Herit held off on revealing our true nature until she felt we were ready to know."

"How'd she manage to keep the truth from you? Were you a regular Daywalker before your Change? Did you eat, drink, and breathe like humans? And what about Damon? Are demons like Daywalkers before they become full-blown soul suckers? Can they live on human food?" I asked.

"Demons, like vampires, stop aging at a certain point, but the similarities end there. They're born demons and must always feed on souls to survive. When they become immortal, they don't go through the same transformation as vampires because they're already demons.

"Damon was unique. He was born a human. Eldrin's DNA didn't make him a demon right away. It changed his body, yes, but it still functioned like a human's until he stopped aging, attained immortality, and had to feed on souls. As for myself, my physiology was also similar to that of a human before I became immortal, so I guess you could say I was like a regular Daywalker.

"Thinking we were humans, we remained unaware of the existence of the Hidden World until we reached the age of fifteen. That's when Herit felt we should know the truth. She told us about the Hidden World and its creatures, and how they came to be. She explained Eldrin's dark magic and the Forbidden Stone, recounting how it had brought about the destruction of the faerie realm. She also spoke about Oberon.

"She explained that he was our brother, and that he'd created a new faerie world where time flowed similarly to our dimension, unlike their previous world. Then she told us about where we came from and about the day we received fae DNA. We also discovered that when we turned twenty-five, Damon would become a demon, and I, a vampire. She emphasized our difference from other vampires and demons, explaining that our DNA made us superior to them in every way."

"Daywalkers cannot predict when their Change will occur," I interrupted, perplexed. "So how did Herit know when you'd become immortal, or that you'd be superior to the others? It wasn't like other mortals had received fae DNA before you."

"She knew because Eldrin had told her so after running tests on our blood samples," Gideon replied. His expression clouded as he continued, "Damon's behavior took a dark turn after the day we found out what we really were. He stopped acknowledging Herit as his mother and began calling her by her name. He constantly expressed his desire to see Eldrin, considering him to be his true parent and blaming Herit for his departure.

"His aggression escalated during our routine sparring sessions, accompanied by disturbing signs of psychopathic tendencies, including the cruel killing of stray animals. Herit harbored a deep-seated fear that Damon would succumb to the malevolence within him. She dreaded the day of his twenty-fifth birthday. In her attempts to guide him, she told him that once he became a demon, he'd have to consume corrupt souls like those of murderers and rapists.

"However, Damon refused to promise her he wouldn't hurt innocent humans. He continued to rebel, accusing her of playing favorites with me since, like Oberon, I was her biological son, her flesh and blood. She denied favoring me and insisted she loved him as much as she loved me, but her words fell on deaf ears."

"Why didn't she just use her magic to make him do what she wanted?" I asked as rain began to slide down the glass of the floor-to-ceiling windows.

"Magic doesn't work like that," he explained. "It's not a wish-granting power. Casting spells requires deep knowledge and years of practice, and even then, many spells have dangerous side effects, strict conditions, or may not work as intended. Much like witches, royal fae face similar limitations. Their powers may be immense, almost godlike, but that doesn't mean every royal fae can easily wield their magic, especially on worlds unlike their own. On Earth, because their power is so vast, it's harder for them to control and predict the effects of their magic. Their spells can have fatal results, from vicious side effects that backfire on the caster to catastrophic environmental damage, such as massive earthquakes.

"Though Herit was talented with her magic, she had to learn to use it with meticulous care in our world. She managed to safely create Ice Prison and the Watchers, but there were still many spells she didn't know how to cast without endangering our world, herself, or weaker beings like Damon and me. That's why her magic couldn't help her deal with Damon, and as time passed, things got worse. His anger grew into a raging inferno. He came to hate me with a passion, resenting the fact that Herit's DNA made me her biological son while he wasn't.

"When we turned nineteen, a mysterious illness struck Herit, robbing her of her strength day by day. I searched every nook and cranny for the cause of her illness and how to cure her but came up empty-handed. As her condition worsened over time, Damon took sick pleasure in her suffering. The twisted bastard did everything in his power to weaken her further.

"One night, I went to check on her, and when I opened the door to her bedroom..." Gideon's eyes flared gold as he gritted his teeth, his jaw clenching before he spat out the words, "I found Damon beating her up. My mother lay there helpless on the floor as he kicked her again and again. But she endured his beatings without so much as a whimper, afraid I'd hear her and hurt him.

"Seeing her like that, something inside me snapped. I was consumed by a blind rage, wanting nothing more than to see him dead. I grabbed him and threw his body across the room. We fought until I finally managed to pin him to the floor, my hands wrapped tightly around his throat. He was seconds away from blacking out when my mother, who was battered and bruised, begged me not to kill him.

"Only for her sake did I ease the pressure on his throat. He owed her his life, and I made it clear to him, ordering him to thank her for that and to apologize for putting her through hell. He refused, but his attitude changed as my hands tightened around his neck again. When his apology finally sounded sincere enough, I released him. He struggled to get up, and I could tell by the way he held onto his side that he had broken ribs. With what little strength she had left, my mother tried to help him, but he yanked her hand away.

"He managed to stand up on his own and limped out of the room. It was the last time she saw him. He took his things and never came back. As time went by, her health continued to deteriorate. Doctors tried to heal her, but nothing helped. I stayed by her side day and night, despite her protests. She wanted me to meet a Daywalker and start my own family before I became a vampire and it'd be too late for me, but I refused to leave her while she was sick.

"When she sensed her end was near, she had me promise her I would not kill Damon once she was gone. I was furious that she'd still protect him after all the crap he'd put her through. But for her sake, I gave her my word that I wouldn't end his miserable existence. Then, she turned her attention to my upcoming Change.

"She gave me a comprehensive rundown, warning me of the dangers of sunlight and the UV virus. Since the Hidden World can be a dangerous place for a Newborn vampire, she advised me to be vigilant against its creatures, especially the demons, the enemies of my kind. She stressed that as a

Newborn, trust was a luxury I could not afford to give freely, except to the queen of the Memphis Warriors, Lucilla, who had always been loyal to her."

The name brought back a flood of bad memories. A few of her warriors had kidnapped me, locked me in a room, and then dragged me onto a stage in front of hundreds of Memphis Warriors. Lucilla was there too, ready to execute me. Fortunately, Gideon had arrived and saved my life.

Gideon's voice pulled me out of my thoughts. "When I went to check on her the next day, I opened the bedroom door to find her bed empty, the sheets undisturbed. I searched the house, but she wasn't there either. I looked everywhere for her, leaving no stone unturned in my desperate attempt to find her." He paused, his gaze drifting to the rain falling outside the windows. His expression grew somber, a dark cloud of sadness settling over his features. When he looked back at me, he continued, "Maybe she just wanted to spare me the pain of witnessing her last moments.

"I eventually gave up on ever finding her and had to face reality. She was dead... somewhere. After mourning her death, I immersed myself in studying the vampire world: its rules, politics, and customs. A few days before my Change, I received an unexpected visitor. Lucilla herself appeared on my doorstep. She told me that sometime around the time my mother's health began to fail, my mother had sent her a letter, which came as a surprise to Lucilla as it'd been ages since she'd last heard from her.

"In that letter, Herit revealed she had a son, who was a Daywalker and different from other vampires. She asked her to travel to the New World and introduce herself to me a few days before my Change. She wanted her to take me under her wing and guide me through my early years as a vampire."

Curious, I asked, "Did Lucilla know Herit was a royal fae? Or that her blood created the vampire species?"

"No, she kept those truths closely guarded. Herit carried a heavy burden of guilt for what she and Eldrin had done to our world. She never spoke a word of her past or her true identity to anyone. However, in the Hidden World, some know the story," he replied.

"Yeah, and Robin is one of them."

He nodded. "She served Heather closely for many years, so she heard the story."

I furrowed my brow. "Didn't Lucilla demand to know what Herit was?"

"Lucilla and her warrior saw Herit as their goddess, so questioning her was unacceptable," he answered.

"Then Lucilla must have felt immensely honored to receive a letter from Herit," I said.

"Yes, and her commitment to Herit was unwavering. Lucilla agreed to do whatever she was told without question. This included dropping everything and traveling across the ocean to meet me before my twenty-fifth birthday. She dedicated her time to assisting me. During my Change, she was by my side day and night, providing me with fresh human blood whenever I needed it and teaching me how to control my bloodlust. When the time came to choose between joining the vampire society or living as an Outsider, I chose the latter."

"Why?" I wondered. Outsiders didn't have obligations like paying taxes or following the vampires' laws, but they were left unprotected, and crimes against them went unpunished.

"Because I refused to submit to their laws and customs. Lucilla, who is also an Outsider, supported my decision and stayed with me for the next few years, helping me adjust to my new life as a vampire and an Outsider."

"What about Damon? Do you know what happened to him after your fight in the house?" I asked.

"After Lucilla returned to her warriors, rumors spread of a new demon king, more powerful than any before. I knew it had to be Damon. Whispers among the demons suggested a mere sip of his blood held the power to transform them into better versions of themselves, stronger and faster. Those he chose to drink his blood rose to the esteemed status of royal demons. As for his queen, Eve, he amplified her power beyond all others by granting her an even greater portion of his blood."

"When was the first time you saw him after the incident with your mother?" I asked.

"It was a few years later, when he tried to kill me—the first of many attempts to come," he replied, then leaned forward and put his elbows on his knees, anger mingled with bitterness showing on his face. "Which doesn't make the promise I made to my mother any easier to keep."

He fell silent, and I looked at him with a newfound understanding. Now I knew why Damon was so bent on ending his life, and why Gideon was no ordinary vampire. I took off my gloves and placed a comforting hand on his shoulder. He took it and kissed my palm tenderly.

The ring of my phone broke the silence in the room. I fished my cell out of my purse and saw Audrey's name flashing on the screen. Gideon asked me to put her on speaker to hear if there were any updates on Cole. Disappointment filled me when she told us she couldn't find anyone else at the convention who had interacted with Cole or knew Ivy.

I thanked her for her efforts, and after I hung up, Gideon wanted to know who Ivy was. I went over the episode in her apartment. He was upset I hadn't told him about it sooner, but I reminded him that I'd tried to on my birthday. Then I showed him the photos from her cell phone. When he saw the picture of her sitting alone on her bed and smiling at the camera, his expression changed, as if he'd noticed something.

"What is it?" I asked.

"We need to find the dead witch's lover."

# Chapter 11

I scrolled through Ivy's pictures again, looking for anyone who could be identified as a romantic partner but found none.

"Her lover is not in the pictures," Gideon told me.

"Then how do you know there is one?"

"Look at her left wrist in the photos where she's sitting on the bed," he said. "She's wearing a half-heart charm on a black rope bracelet. See what is engraved on it?"

Struggling to make out the engraved words, I zoomed in on the photo. "It says, 'I love you more.'"

"If you look closely, you can also see a velvet bracelet box and a rose between the pillows on the bed. My guess is her Newborn vampire lover took the picture after giving her the bracelet and rose."

"You're right, she was romantically involved with someone, but how do you know that person was a vampire?" I asked.

"The pictures of the dead witch show she had visible hair loss, pale skin, and brittle fingernails—classic signs of anemia in humans. A vampire drank from her, and he'd clearly never heard of S pills, which would've healed her and prevented anemia. I'm guessing her lover didn't have anyone to educate and guide him about our world," he said.

"Maybe the anemia wasn't caused by a vampire," I argued. "Maybe Ivy was vegan."

He shook his head. "Her condition was caused by a vampire feeding on her repeatedly. In every picture, she wears a turtle shirt or scarf around her neck, no doubt to hide bite marks, another indication that her lover was a Newborn. Some of them lack healing properties in their saliva, which explains why her puncture wounds didn't heal quickly."

"Okay, now that we know she had a Newborn lover, how in the world do we track them down?" I asked.

He gestured to my phone. "Look at the shirt hanging over the back of the chair by the bed."

I enlarged the photo again and spotted the clothing. "It's a man's shirt, and it looks like it has a star with the letter *C* in the center."

"That's Cynric's company logo. He's a two-thousand-year-old vampire. He runs an auction service staffed by vampires. His employees are required to wear shirts with his logo during work hours."

I connected the dots. "So, Ivy's boyfriend works for this Cynric guy. We gotta talk to him or one of his employees to find the boyfriend."

Gideon pulled out his cell phone and exchanged texts with someone, then turned his attention back to me.

"I've just been informed Cynric is holding an exclusive auction of rare magical artifacts in an hour. I have the address and an invitation. Come on, let's go."

Forty minutes later, Gideon pulled up next to a row of luxury cars parked outside an old two-story building. I got off the bike and surveyed our surroundings. We were in the middle of nowhere, and the sole source of light came from inside the old building. After putting on my gloves and handing Gideon my two daggers, as weapons were not allowed in the auction, I glanced around the flat land.

"You sure this is the right place?"

"Yes, that's the auction house." He nodded at the old building, the only structure in the vast expanse. "And it's heavily guarded to protect the valuable items up for auction," he added, disarming himself as well.

When we reached the entrance, Gideon took out his phone to show the guard his invitation. As expected, humans were not allowed in unless they served as vampire snacks, so once again I had to play Gideon's Donor. The vampire attitude toward humans pissed me off, but I suppressed my irritation as we passed through security.

We walked into the large main room. The space was filled with display cases featuring all sorts of items like thick old books, katana swords, amulets, and ancient-looking jewelry. The bidders moved slowly around the room, studying the various items.

In one corner of the room stood two stoic employees with a star and the letter *C* on their shirts. Had one of them been Ivy's boyfriend?

"We don't know what Ivy's boyfriend looks like," I pointed out to Gideon.

"Cynric might know, but let's talk to the employees first." He indicated with his head to the two staff members in the corner. As we set off toward them, a male vampire intercepted us.

"Sorry, sir," he said. "Donors are not allowed in the exhibition room. The human can wait for you in the bidding room upstairs." Gideon bobbed his head, and the man walked away.

"I'll try to get some information from the staff here, then meet you upstairs, and we'll look for Cynric," Gideon told me.

I nodded and went upstairs, passing a few humans before entering the bidding room, which contained six rows of chairs. Except for a guy wearing a shirt with Cynric's company logo and sweeping the floor near the podium, the room was empty. I approached him, intending to ask about the vampire who had been Ivy's boyfriend.

When I got halfway to him, an accented male voice behind me said, "Who do you belong to, lovely?"

I turned to see a tall man in a suit, with ivory vampiric skin and a wolfish grin, his black hair brushing his collar and tucked behind his ears. Two women flanked him, also vampires.

He looked over my shoulder. "Leave," he ordered the employee. The guy scurried away, leaving me with the intimidating trio.

"I should leave too," I said, not liking where this was going.

The man revealed his teeth in another smile. "What's the hurry, lovely? Why don't you let me show you around?"

I maintained my distance. "No, thanks." My voice was steadier than my nerves. I refused to show weakness or fear.

The vampire on his right, in an elegant red dress and sporting a sleek bob-cut hairstyle, let out a chuckle. "Poor thing. Did you really think it was a request?"

My gaze shifted to her. "Actually, I was thinking how I could evade this little situation without getting pieces of your brain and blood on my shirt and pants. Unfortunately, I didn't bring a change of clothes with me."

I wouldn't have provoked them if I thought there was a chance they would let me go. However, it was clear they wanted blood—particularly mine. I had no weapons on me, but I wasn't exactly without resources. My eyes went down to the women's stilettos. As I'd learned in the past, heels could be turned into effective weapons against vampires.

The undead in the scarlet dress fixed me with a venomous glare. "Oh, you are so dead."

An ironic snort escaped my lips. "Says the one without a heartbeat."

She extended her fangs, which glinted in the light of the room. She moved closer, scanning my form as she seemed to consider the most effective way to inflict pain. Irritation began to gnaw at me, undermining my composure.

"Why don't you get out of my way?" I demanded. If they were going to attack me anyway, there was no point in being polite.

"I don't think so," she spat, lunging at me to sink her teeth into my neck. I twisted out of her grasp and snapped my leg out, shattering her knee with a loud crack. A growl of pain erupted from her, and her murderous gaze intensified as she focused on me again.

I gave her a mocking smile. "Poor thing. Did you really think it was a request?" She prepared to attack again, but the man's voice stopped her.

"Don't," he ordered. Confusion appeared on her face, but she obeyed without arguing, staying in her place. "That was surprising," he said as he looked at me. "The way you handled Marsha... I must admit, it increased my desire to taste your blood."

In an instant, he was two inches from me, his presence exuding an aura of predatory menace. I raised my arm to strike, but with lightning reflexes, he caught my wrist, his grip like an iron clamp. I struggled to free my hand, but my efforts were futile. Within seconds, I was pinned to the wall, my back pressed against the cold surface. His strength was staggering. I squirmed and writhed as his tongue darted out, moistening his lips hungrily.

"Cynric, you've had your fun, now release the breather. Don't be stupid. You don't know who she belongs to. There are influential and important bidders downstairs who might not like someone touching their toys," his companion in the black dress said.

So this was Cynric. That explained his strength.

"Yes, you're right," he said, then asked me again, "Who do you belong to?" Before I could respond, a sharp, clipped voice cut through the air.

"She is mine," Gideon declared, his figure filling the doorway. Cynric, still holding me, turned his head toward the door.

"Mr. Hawthorne," he said. "What a pleasant and unexpected surprise. You have a very lovely Donor. Would you mind if I had a quick taste, just a sip?"

"I don't share." Gideon's tone was saturated with venom.

Cynric released me and said, "Possessive, are we? Come now, Mr. Hawthorne, there's no need to get so worked up over a mere Donor. I just wanted a little taste, but please accept my sincerest apologies. You know you're always welcome at my events."

"Yeah, me and my money," Gideon said.

Cynric shrugged off Gideon's remark, then said, "The auction will start soon. If you have any questions, don't hesitate to ask me or my staff."

"I do have one. Where can I find Logan Moore?" Gideon said.

Cynric's eyebrows scrunched together. "Logan Moore?"

"Yes, he worked for you. One of your employees mentioned he recently resigned. Did Logan happen to mention where he lives?" Gideon asked.

Cynric looked at the vampire in the black dress. "Are you familiar with an employee by the name of Logan Moore?"

She nodded and told Gideon, "I have no idea where he lives. He was paid daily in cash and kept his personal life private, sharing almost nothing. The only detail I know is that he has a witch lover named Ivy. I was sorry to see him go; he was a good employee, never late and always reliable."

"Any chance you have a photo of him?" Gideon asked her.

As bidders began to enter the room, signaling the start of the auction, the woman told Gideon she didn't have a picture of Logan. She did, however, provide him with a detailed description of Logan: his height, build, hair, and eye color. Cynric then excused himself to take his place at the auction podium, and the woman joined him. After they walked away, an employee approached Gideon. She had an air of tension about her.

Her eyes darted around the room before she leaned in and whispered to Gideon, "I saw you talking to Daniel and Charles downstairs. I know where Logan is. Follow me."

She pivoted and strode toward the door. We trailed behind her until she stopped near a yellow Mini Cooper outside the building.

She turned to Gideon. "Why're you looking for Logan?"

"We need to talk to him. Where is he?" Gideon said.

She fumbled with her hands. "I'm his friend. He's…" She cleared her throat. "He's in trouble. If I take you to where he's hiding, will you help him?"

"I can try," Gideon told her.

Satisfied with his answer, she agreed to take us to him and got into her car. We walked to Gideon's bike and followed her until we pulled into the empty lot of an abandoned factory warehouse. Broken windows marred its facade, and stained walls bore the scars of time and neglect. The murky light of distant streetlamps cast long, distorted shadows, and the chirping of crickets was the only sound that broke the silence of the night.

Was Logan in this building? What kind of trouble was he in? Was he running from someone? Was Ivy's killer after him?

She got out of her car, and my mind cleared to form one thought: I might get some answers about Ivy's murder and the potions I'd drunk.

"He's inside," she said, leading us to the entrance of the abandoned building. When we reached the rusty metal door and she began to slide it open, Gideon's eyes narrowed in suspicion. Suddenly, he threw himself in front of me and wrapped his arms around my shoulders as a volley of gunfire shattered the air. Shielding me, his body jolted as a series of bullets hit his back.

He held me until the gunfire died down. Then he scooped me into his arms and moved in a blur to the yellow Mini Cooper. Behind its sturdy frame, he laid me down and ran his hands over my body, searching for wounds.

He made a sound of relief. "Good, you're unharmed." His features then hardened. "Goddamn it, she set a trap for us."

Still shaken by the near-death experience, it took me a moment to regain my composure.

"What makes you so sure she's involved?" I asked.

"The deep fear in her eyes just before she opened the door was unmistakable. She knew what was about to happen," he explained, and I noticed he was dragging his words. His complexion appeared paler, too.

Blood dripped from his back. Alarm bells started ringing in my head. This was bad. This was really, really bad. The bullets should have popped out of his wounds by now.

My voice trembled with concern as I asked, "Why aren't you healing?"

He drew out his dagger, wincing in pain at the movement. "The bullets are silver, which prevents my body from expelling them and healing me." I responded with a sudden intake of breath, and he tried to calm me down. "I'll be fine. Our attacker deliberately missed my heart. Their goal was to incapacitate me, not kill me." He straightened. "I hear men approaching. Stay here, they're carrying guns."

He was gone before I could say, "Yes, with silver bullets!" and stop him.

Crouching low, I peeked around the back of the car and unsheathed the silver dagger Gideon had given me back after leaving the auction. Six vampires circled him with their fangs bared. As I rushed in his direction to help him, he sprang into action, moving with incredible speed despite his injuries. He sidestepped the first vampire that came at him and delivered a powerful kick that knocked him off balance. As he grabbed the vampire's head and snapped his neck, another lunged at him, and in a matter of seconds, that attacker met the same fate.

The other four charged at him. In a blur of movement, Gideon plunged his dagger into the heart of the nearest vampire. With his free hand, he grabbed another knife from his coat and hurled it at a second vampire, striking her in the heart. After retrieving his dagger from her chest, he killed two more attackers while deftly dodging their gunfire, weaving and ducking with precision as his long coat billowed around him. By the time I reached Gideon's side, all six vampires lay dead on the ground. However, the intense fight had taken its toll, and he sank to his knees.

"Gideon!" I cried.

More vampires emerged from the warehouse. He tried to rise but faltered, his limbs trembling with exhaustion. I stood guard beside him. As the first vampire leaped at me, I pivoted and executed a spinning back kick that caught him square in the chest, sending him flying backward into the vampire behind him. Two more rushed me simultaneously. I ducked under a wild haymaker from the one on the left, then drove an uppercut into the solar plexus of the one on the right. As he doubled over, I grabbed his collar and threw him into his partner. Then I dropped low to the ground to avoid another vampire's blow and swept my leg in a wide arc, knocking the attacker's feet out from under him.

He fell hard, and when his head hit the concrete, I drove my dagger into his heart. Straightening up, I noticed two vampires closing in on Gideon, who could barely move, his face contorted in pain. I darted toward him and intercepted one of the vampires with a strong kick to the groin. As he let out a guttural growl, I pierced his heart with my dagger. He collapsed, and I quickly threw out my leg for a kick to keep the other vampire from reaching Gideon. Not giving him a chance to recover from my strike, I stabbed my knife into his heart with a swift upward thrust before another horde of vampires came to attack. I continued to slash, kick, and kill every undead that approached Gideon until I felt a shift in the air behind me just before a syringe was jammed into the side of my neck. The world spun around me, and within seconds, I was knocked unconscious.

When I regained consciousness, my entire body ached. I eased up into a sitting position and rubbed my throbbing head, glancing around. With my hands ungloved, I was locked in a cage the size of a small shipping container, with metal bars and a heavy padlock securing the door. Panic gripped my heart, the cage bringing back vivid flashbacks of the tiny room Cole had kept me in.

Beads of sweat trickled down my forehead as my heart pounded in my chest. I took deep, calming breaths. As the panic inside me receded, I rose slowly on unsteady feet and my gaze met an identical metal cage across from mine. Inside it, facing me, Gideon's motionless form slumped against the bars, his legs outstretched in front of him.

His wrists were tightly bound, secured by heavy chains dangling from rings bolted to the wall behind his cage. His head hung limply to one side, his eyes closed and his skin ashen. A cold fear settled in my bones as I hurried to the door of my cage and gripped the bars with both hands.

"Gideon!"

He didn't respond. I jiggled the padlock, but its construction resisted my efforts. With nothing on me to pick or break it, not even a dagger, frustration surged through me. I fumbled in my jacket pockets, and my fingers brushed against the familiar shape of my cell phone. With a flicker of hope, I pulled it out, only to be met with the crushing disappointment of no service.

I scanned the room outside of my cage, searching for any means of escape or clue to our whereabouts. A purse sat on a chair in the middle of the filthy room. Whose was it? Several wrought-iron lanterns were scattered across the floor, their flames dancing in the moonlight streaming through the broken windows.

It looked like we were in the abandoned factory. I sighed in helplessness. Nothing useful was within reach. I shook the bars, afraid for Gideon. The thought of him being dead was almost unbearable. A rhythmic clatter of footsteps echoed through the room, and Logan's friend—if she was even his friend—emerged from the shadows. She made her way toward the purse.

"Who are you? Why did you bring us here? What do you want?" I demanded.

She paused, her gaze shifting from the purse to me. "I wasn't the one who put you in those cages. My instructions were to lure you here. That's all. The opportunity presented itself when I happened to overhear him," she nodded toward Gideon, "asking about Logan. The truth is, I've never met him, but I had to make up a lie to get you here, so I told you he was in trouble. Sorry, it was nothing personal. She would've killed me if I hadn't brought you here."

My forehead pinched together. "She?"

"I don't know her name." The vampire's voice was tight with fear. "She approached me at the auction. I'd never seen her before. That woman threatened to cut off my head if I didn't do what she said, which was to trick your friend into coming here. She has my wallet and my home address. I had no choice. She's got one thousand years on me."

My confusion grew. Who the hell could this Ancient vampire be? A sudden flutter of wings startled the vampire, her head jerking toward the broken windows. Three pigeons swooped in and landed on the floor.

She grabbed the purse, took out her cell phone, and said, "I gotta go."

"No, please don't leave," I said, hoping I might convince her to free us.

"Sorry, I can't help you. I have my own problems. I'm in so much trouble for leaving the auction. I gotta call my superior and come up with an excuse as to why I had to leave during work hours. Then I'm outta here."

As she turned and walked away, my peripheral vision detected a shift that drew my focus to Gideon's cage. He was coming to, his eyes fluttering open. He looked at his restraints then strained against his bonds. A spike of worry for him shot through me when he tried to move and his eyes squeezed shut, his face contorted in a grimace.

"Gideon? Are you okay?" I asked, and the sound of heels clicking on the floor reached my ears.

"No. He's anything but okay. He's in excruciating pain," a female voice said. I turned and saw Katina, the Ancient vampire I'd met in Gideon's apartment. She approached my cage. Black pants were molded to her legs, a burgundy jacket draped over a tight shirt.

"You?" I spat in contempt.

She smiled. "Silver bullets inflict a searing, burning pain on vampires. Some would even say it's worse than hurting our eyes."

My glare intensified. "God, you are a vindictive bitch."

She chuckled and strolled over to Gideon's cage, then swung it open and moved closer to him.

"Nobody disrespects me and gets away with it," she said.

Gideon, his face pale and drawn, raised his head with a slow, labored movement. His half-lidded eyes met hers.

"You got me. Good for you. Go ahead, have your fun, do your worst, but do you really need the human? She's nothing, a mere mortal, incapable of challenging you. Let her go." His voice, strained and raspy, carried the weight of pain with every word.

"Your Donor stays here, and I intend to make full use of the special abilities I acquired when I became an Ancient," she told him. A vampire's power grew with age, which made the Ancients exceptionally strong. Some even developed unique abilities like flying or empathy.

As I wondered what power she'd gained, Gideon warned, "Sydney, she can read minds. Block her from your head."

She scoffed. "The thoughts and emotions of mortals are of no interest to me. But yours, Gideon, have long fascinated me. Your mind is an impenetrable fortress, its secrets tantalizingly out of reach. What do you hide from the world? Whatever it is, I suspect it must be valuable information I could sell." She crouched down beside him. "Now that you are so weak, it will prove effortless to breach those walls and reveal everything to me."

Gideon tried to resist as she placed her fingers on his temples, but the silver bullets rendered his efforts futile.

"I feel deep fear," she murmured. "What is it, I wonder, that could cause such fear in you?" A wide smile curved over her red lips. "Is it the prospect of your existence being extinguished that sends shivers down your spine?" Gideon remained silent, his expression unreadable. "Okay, if you refuse to willingly reveal your fears, I will take a journey into the depths of your mind where the answers I seek are to be found." She gazed at him for a moment, then said, "Stop your pathetic attempts to block me. It's pointless in your current state."

A tense silence hung in the air for a long moment. Then, with a sudden hardening of her features, she rose, letting out a scornful huff. "Your fear is for that Donor's life? Not for your own existence? You are such a disappointment, a poor excuse for a vampire."

She glided out of his cage, moved close to mine, and reached her hand out to grab my left wrist. My arm was caught between the metal bars, and I twisted it to free myself from her grip as she examined the tattoo.

She turned to Gideon. "Or is it the powerful dark magic on her hand that you really want to protect?"

"Katina, I am right here," Gideon said, his voice filled with desperation. "Take your revenge on me. Inflict whatever pain you wish, but I beg you, let her go."

She arched a disdainful eyebrow at him. "You beg?" She stepped back into his cell. "Your weakness is disgusting. You'll pay for the way you treated me. I'll make you suffer." Bending down beside him again, she grabbed his hair and forced his head up to meet her gaze. "Your mind is an open book to me now, and I've already read what you tried to hide from me. I know that your deepest fear is losing the human to death."

"Get away from him!" I screamed.

Gideon's eyes blazed gold, his gaze locked with hers. "If you harm her, I—"

She released his hair, her lips slanting into a cruel smirk. "You what? Have you seen yourself? You can't do anything." Turning away from him, she strode out of his cell. "My original plan was to make you suffer with a silver dagger I brought with me until you apologized for your disrespectful behavior, then kill you and use the human as a test subject for a new product I purchased a few nights ago.

"But now I have a much better idea. I'll let you live, so you can watch your Donor die." Standing near the bars of my cage, she reached into her jacket pocket and drew out a small organza bag. She emptied its contents into her palm, revealing a shimmering green powder. "The witch who sold me this claimed it has the power to quickly extinguish human life, and then, for a short time, turn their blood into a potent elixir that amplifies a vampire's powers upon consumption."

"No, don't do this. I will do whatever you want," Gideon pleaded.

She laughed and blew the pile of green dust in my direction. I recoiled, coughing as the substance coated my face.

She looked at Gideon. "If she doesn't drink a few drops of my Ancient blood in the next five minutes to heal her lungs, your deepest fear will come true. It's unfortunate that despite being a great warrior, you are completely powerless to make this happen. Such a funny twist of fate, don't you think? I'm going to revel in the sight of your Donor slowly suffocating before your very eyes. The torment of not being able to save her will haunt you forever, a punishment far more agonizing than any physical torture."

A sudden weakness swept through my legs, and I fell to my knees. Terror clawed at me as I felt something blocking my airway. I panicked and grabbed my neck.

"NO!" Gideon roared, fangs exploding from his mouth. Pure rage burned in his golden eyes, which seemed to infuse his body with power. He strained at the shackles around his wrists, the sharp metal biting deep into his flesh, exposing bone.

Gritting his teeth with unwavering determination, he continued to tear at his bonds. I watched in horror as his left arm was ripped from his shoulder, blood gushing out. Yet he appeared impervious to pain. Eyes fixated on Katina, whose face turned into a mask of disbelief, his lips drew back in a savage grimace. The shackle around his right wrist gave way under the pressure and snapped open. With a single arm, he pounced on Katina like a wild tiger.

Fighting to stay conscious, I crumpled to the floor. My vision began to blur and my lungs screamed for air. Lifting my head with effort, I saw two figures locked in battle until everything started to fade. Seconds ticked away like a countdown as the life drained from my body. Was this the end? I thought about my parents and Zoey. Would I ever see their faces again?

The grip of fear tightened around me. I fought to keep my eyes open, to cling to life, until I could no longer resist. My eyes closed and the encroaching blackness overtook me. A cold hand cupped the back of my head, lifting it, and something wet brushed against my lips.

"Open your mouth, love. Drink the blood." I heard Gideon's trembling voice as a distant echo in the fading realm of consciousness. Then silence enveloped me. I felt myself slip out of my body and float in the cage. I saw Gideon kneeling next to me. Katina lay near him with a silver dagger lodged in her heart. He was pressing her slashed wrist to my pallid lips, blood pulsing from it. I wanted to open my mouth and drink the red liquid; I wanted to be saved, to live, but it was too late for me.

I guessed he no longer heard my heartbeat as he pulled Katina's wrist away from my mouth and cradled my motionless body with one arm. A crimson tear escaped his eye and traced a path down his cheek before landing on my forehead. I watched as he faded into the background, then the cage, then the entire room.

This was not how I had imagined I would die.

# Chapter 12

I was dead, or so it seemed. My mind was still functioning, but I had no physical form. By some inexplicable force, I'd been plucked from the cage and transported back in time to a specific memory: the conversation I'd had with my sister on Christmas night during my freshman year of college. Stripped of my corporeal form, I hovered in my parents' living room near the fragrant evergreen branches on the mantle, watching my past self and Zoey. We lingered in the living room after my parents had retired for the night, chatting over hot cups of tea as snowflakes drifted against the window.

"I love Christmas movies, especially the ones with spooky ghosts," Zoey said, taking a sip from her cup. "I know you're a skeptic when it comes to the existence of witches or vampires, but what about ghosts? You can't tell me you've never entertained the idea."

"Nope," I replied. "When we die, that's it. No ghosts, no spectral hauntings, just the silence of non-existence."

*Yeah, well, you might want to reconsider that*, I thought.

As Zoey delved into the topic of ghosts, dead me drifted toward her. Would she be able to sense me? The calm I felt as I floated through my parents' living room surprised me. I should have been freaked out by this surreal situation, but I wasn't. Instead, confusion filled me. What was I? Some kind of ghost trapped in the past?

Everything in the room suddenly froze when I moved again, as if time had stopped. Silence fell over the house. My sister and my past self were stilled like two statues. The front door swung open with a snap, and a towering silhouette manifested on the threshold. They glided into the house with ethereal grace, a black hooded cloak obscuring the figure's face. They approached me and reached out to touch my arm.

My parents' living room dissolved into blackness. After what seemed like a few seconds, I started to feel the presence of arms and legs and then my whole body. I opened my eyes and found myself lying on a couch. The face of a middle-aged woman came into view, hovering over mine.

"Back from the dead," she whispered in amazement.

"Her heart... It's beating again." I heard Gideon's voice.

"Gideon?" I said. He materialized beside me on the bed, and before I could process his sudden presence, I was wrapped in the warmth and comfort of his arms. I hugged him back, holding him tightly until the memory of his injuries reemerged, and I pulled away.

"The silver bullets," I murmured, scanning his body for wounds. His missing arm had regenerated, and his wounds seemed to have healed, but he still looked paler, his veins like visible threads beneath the surface, and his eyes dull and sunken.

"Are out of my body," he reassured me.

"He's going to be fine," said the woman. She had the kind of eyes that knew things, as if she could easily see someone's truth. "He's a vampire. They heal quickly, especially the stronger ones. There's nothing unusual here. But you, now you're truly extraordinary. Coming back from the dead."

I turned to Gideon, and my eyebrows drew together. "Where are we?"

"You are in my house. I'm Mariana, an illusionist and friend of Audrey's mother," the woman introduced herself. "Gideon came to me because I specialize in life and death spells. He showed up at my door with you, looking so weak. He begged me to heal you and collapsed as soon as he put you on my sofa. I removed the silver bullets from his body, but there was nothing I could do for you.

"You see, as long as a person's soul is still in our world after leaving the body, magic can bring that soul back, even though the body no longer has any detectable heartbeat or brain activity. But once the soul leaves our world for the afterlife, there's no magic, dark or regular, that can return it to the body. After Gideon recovered, I told him your soul had left this world. You were beyond saving. Mad with grief, he wouldn't accept the immutable limits and expected miracles from me. I am a mere witch, not God."

Gideon reached out and caressed my cheek. "What matters now is that she's back." His voice was raw with emotion.

"But it was not my doing. There was a powerful force behind it. Do you know what brought you back from the dead?" she asked me.

The word "dead" echoed in my mind. The realization that I'd been a corpse just a moment ago began to sink in. The whole situation was seriously messed up, beyond anything I could have ever imagined. I touched my face, then looked down at my arms and legs and found no visible signs of physical damage or anything amiss.

"What's wrong? Are you feeling sick?" Gideon asked.

I shook my head. "No, I'm just a little overwhelmed by everything."

"Understandable, given your extraordinary experience," Mariana said. Then she disappeared into the kitchen and reappeared with a glass of water. After she offered it to me, I told them what had happened to me while I'd been dead.

Mariana looked at Gideon. "You mentioned Oberon saved Sydney in the past. The figure with the cloak she saw could be the king of the fae. He's the only one I can think of who might have the power to bring back souls from the afterlife."

"Yes, it's possible," Gideon agreed.

"If it's him, why save me again? What does he want from me?" I said.

"Good questions," Mariana told me, and her eyes dropped to my left hand. "It seems that mystery tends to follow you."

The tattoo! Had my death affected it? I turned my left palm up and drew a shocked breath when I saw the black ink.

"While you were dead, the number kept dropping. It stopped when you opened your eyes," Gideon said.

"Oh, God," I whispered, my eyes fixed on the number 503 on my palm, a wave of panic sweeping over me. It'd plummeted from 678 to 503.

Gideon touched my cheek. "Hey, look at me." His voice was soft, a soothing balm to my racing heart. The fear that had gripped me receded under Gideon's calming gaze. "I know it's alarming, but at least the number has stopped decreasing. We still have five hundred three days to figure out how to remove the tattoo."

"Yes, you're right," I said, then asked Mariana, "Could the tattoo be the reason I came back from the dead?" I wondered if my recent resurrection was a one-time fluke or an ongoing benefit of my tattoo, a kind of get-out-of-death-free card etched into my hand.

"Frankly, anything is possible in your case, so I don't know. I understand that you may be frustrated, but for now, focus on the small victories, like the fact that you're not dead," she replied.

Gideon asked her, "Are you sure your stash of magic books doesn't have anything about dark magic tattoos that count down? Or how this kind of rare magic might affect Sydney?"

She shook her head. "As I told Audrey after she sent me the photo of the black ink, I searched every conceivable source, ancient texts, grimoires, and even the most obscure corners of the internet, but nothing came up that could explain the purpose or behavior of the tattoo's dark magic."

I glanced at the windows of the living room. It was still night outside. "How long have I been... well, dead?"

"About an hour," Gideon answered.

"An hour? Felt more like a few minutes," I said, then noticed the subtle tremor in Gideon's hand.

Mariana saw it too and told him, "The silver bullets have taken a heavy toll on your body. The healing process has been remarkable, but your body is still in a weakened state. You must drink a substantial amount of blood to regain your full strength and resilience. Unfortunately, I don't keep bottles of blood in my fridge." Her tone was apologetic.

"That's okay. I'll drink when I get home," Gideon said and thanked her for her time and help.

We headed back to the city in the yellow Mini Cooper that belonged to the girl who had set us up. After I'd died in the cage, Gideon, unable to ride his bike while holding me or fly due to his condition, carjacked her as she was getting ready to leave, kicking her out.

Back at Gideon's penthouse, I was glad to see that he'd stocked his fridge with human food. While I prepared a meal for myself, Gideon drank two bottles of blood. With each crimson gulp, his trembling hands steadied, his skin regained its lost vibrancy, and his eyes blazed with vitality. Shortly after I finished eating, my cell phone rang. When I answered it, Audrey's voice came from the other end.

"Oh, finally! I've been trying to reach you, but it kept bouncing straight to voicemail."

"What's up?" I asked.

"There has been a development in Ivy's murder case. A suspect, a male witch, has been brought in for questioning."

"By who? A witch cop?" I said.

"Yes, witches have their own system of law enforcement. Criminal suspects are held in facilities owned and run by our police. We don't have our own prisons, though, so if a witch gets busted and found guilty, the Watchers will send them to Ice Prison," she explained.

"What if the suspect in Ivy's murder was human?" I asked.

"They would still be tried by a witch court. If found guilty, we use magic to punish them according to the crime committed. Since humans can't go to Ice Prison, a severe punishment might be something like a spell that will cause endless physical pain for years while medical tests show nothing. However, in the event of an acquittal, the human would be released, and a spell cast by a highly skilled witch would erase their memory of the entire ordeal.

"Anyway, I know a cop who works closely with the detective assigned to Ivy's case. This cop, Craig, told me Ivy's parents had been found stabbed to death in their home not long ago. Then, one by one, her sisters met the same fate. Worried she might be the next target, the detective offered Ivy protection. She refused without explanation, and now she's dead too."

"Would it be possible for Gideon and me to speak with the suspect?" I asked.

"Yes, Craig has always had a thing for me, so it was easy to convince him to give us a few minutes with the suspect they brought in. You can go see him now. I'll meet you there."

I wrote down the address she gave me then hung up and filled Gideon in.

"We should get moving," he said, and we left his apartment.

When we reached the location Audrey had given me, we found her standing near a bunker, accompanied by a man in a trench coat.

"This is Craig," Audrey said, gesturing to the man beside her.

"You have ten minutes with the suspect," Craig said curtly.

"We'll keep it brief," Gideon told him.

Following Craig, we descended the stairs into the depths of the bunker and entered a large room. From there we walked down a long hallway, and he unlocked the second door on the left. We stepped into a windowless room. In the center sat a restrained man, his hands tied behind the chair and his feet cuffed separately to the front of the chair.

"This is Tyler, the witch we've brought in for questioning," Craig said.

Audrey sent Craig a grateful smile, her eyes twinkling with appreciation. "I owe you one."

Craig nodded once, his expression stern. "Ten minutes, and not a second more." With that, he closed the door behind him, leaving us alone with Tyler.

Tyler's gaze moved from Gideon to Audrey and then to me. "A vampire, an illusionist, and a human? What is this? The beginning of a bad joke? Who the hell are you?"

Audrey turned to us. "Tyler was brought in based on a statement from Ivy's neighbor. He lives across the hall from her and is also a witch. According to his account, he heard noises about a week before Ivy's death, and when he looked through the peephole, he saw a man matching Tyler's description standing outside Ivy's door, demanding that she open it and threatening her."

Tyler rolled his eyes as his lips pursed. "For heaven's sake, not this again! How many times do I have to explain myself? I never threatened Ivy! And I had nothing to do with her death or the deaths of her sisters!"

Gideon looked at Audrey, ignoring Tyler's outburst. "What was the cause of Ivy's death?"

"Poisoning. A lethal toxin was detected in her bloodstream," Audrey replied.

Gideon came closer to Tyler, crossing his arms over his chest. "What was your relationship with the dead witch?"

Tyler's face softened. "We were close friends. When her parents were murdered, I stood by her side and offered whatever comfort I could. Then, as if fate wasn't cruel enough, her older sister was killed. That's when she began to withdraw. She made up excuses to avoid our usual hangouts, stopped returning my calls, and no longer dropped by to say hello.

"When I heard another one of her sisters had died, I went to her place to check on her. She looked terrified, asking me to leave. I respected her wishes, but I was worried about her. I contacted Piper, a mutual friend of ours, and she told me Ivy had also pushed her away. I was pissed off that Ivy had shut us out like that.

"After my talk with Piper, I returned to Ivy's apartment to try to find out why someone was targeting her and to protect her from them. I knew she was alone; I didn't see her vampire boyfriend's car outside her building. I warned her that if she didn't open the door, she'd die.

"Her nosy neighbor misinterpreted my words. He thought I was threatening her, but I meant she'd end up dead because of the killer, not because of me. It wasn't safe for her to be in her apartment alone. If she had opened the door, I would've protected her. I was even willing to move in with her until the cops caught the killer."

"Yeah, somehow, I don't think her lover would've been too happy about this arrangement," Gideon said.

"What can you tell us about the boyfriend, Logan?" I asked Tyler.

He shrugged. "I don't know much about him. They met in a coffee shop and their connection was undeniable. Like Ivy, he lost his parents too. They weren't murdered though; their hatred of their vampire nature drove them to expose themselves to the sun and let the UV virus kill them."

A chill crept up my back as I imagined the agony they must have endured. It was a terrible way to die. Vampires could only catch one disease: the UV virus, contracted from exposure to the sun. It progressed in stages, and death was slow and extremely painful.

"Ivy kept Logan a secret from her sisters 'cause she didn't think they would have approved of her being with a vampire," he continued. "Which is not surprising as she was a very private person; she never talked about her sisters, her parents, or her past." He exhaled a long breath. "Now that I come to think about it, I realize I didn't really know her." A veil of sadness fell over his face, and a deep-seated intuition told me Tyler was not the killer.

"Do you have any pictures of Piper or Logan?" I asked him.

"Yes, we took a few group selfies in the past, but the photos are on my phone," he replied.

Audrey looked at Gideon and me. "Before we head out, I'll have Craig return his phone so he can show them to us."

Gideon nodded and then asked Tyler, "When'd you hear about Ivy's death?"

A somber expression darkened his face as he seemed to recall that day. "At work. The last time I spoke to Ivy was the night she wouldn't open the door to me. Then Piper showed up at my workplace a week later and told me the bad news about Ivy's murder. Man, her death hit me like a punch in the gut."

Audrey stepped away from the door and moved toward Tyler, stopping in front of him. "Do you have Logan's phone number, or Piper's?"

"I don't have the vampire's number. I would've given you Piper's, but it'd be a waste of your time. She's a super suspicious person and doesn't answer calls from unfamiliar numbers. She also recently blocked my number and refuses to talk to me. I wish I knew why."

"Where can we find her or Logan?" I asked.

"I have no idea where the vampire is," he replied, "but I can tell you where Piper is if you promise to protect her from the killer. I'm afraid she might be next. I had a very vivid dream that a faceless figure murdered her, and since then I haven't been able to shake the feeling that it might be more than just a dream."

"We'll do our best," Audrey said.

The door opened and Craig stepped in. "Time's up."

"Just one more minute, I swear," Audrey told him.

Craig sighed. After a short silence, he said with a look of discontent on his face, "Okay, but hurry up."

Audrey nodded and moved her gaze to Tyler. "Where can we find her?"

"First off, I have to confess something I'm not proud of," Tyler said. "I cast a tracking spell on her favorite earrings without her knowledge. It's an outright violation of her privacy and trust, I get that, but I did it for her own protection.

"I needed to know Piper's whereabouts at all times, in case she was kidnapped by Ivy's killer. I know my plan wasn't foolproof. Earrings can be taken off, but given my terrible skills at casting tracking spells on people, Piper's earrings were the most viable option. She always wears them. They're her favorite."

"All right, confession time is over. Check her location," Gideon ordered him, impatience in his voice.

Tyler's eyes closed, his lips murmuring what seemed to be an incantation. When he opened his eyes, surprise crossed his face.

"She's in a place called," he cleared his throat, "Black Whip."

# Chapter 13

Black Whip was a private club for people who took sexual pleasure in physical pain. As far as Tyler knew, Piper wasn't into BDSM. So, either someone was keeping some naughty secrets, or her earrings had been stolen. According to Audrey, who had asked about the place, it wasn't owned by supernatural beings, suggesting that the employees were probably humans unaware of the existence of the Hidden World.

When Gideon, Audrey, and I arrived at the building that housed the private club, Gideon used compulsion to let us in. A spectrum of red dominated the club's interior, a seductive symphony of scarlet that enveloped the walls, the furniture, and the soft glow of the lights. In the reception area, a beautiful woman in a form-fitting dress sat behind a burgundy-colored desk. Assuming we were new members, she gave us an overview of what the club had to offer. She explained that the place boasted ten soundproof sanctuaries designed to explore one's desires and fantasies. She also went over the rules and regulations of the place. Although cell phones were strictly forbidden there, Gideon's compulsion ensured that we could keep them.

A few minutes later, an elegantly dressed man approached and introduced himself. He led us to an empty waiting room. Wine-colored curtains covering the windows blocked out the world outside. The man gestured to the red chairs lining the wall for us to sit. He told us someone would arrive soon to show us the various rooms, but Audrey used her magic to make sure we would not be disturbed and our presence would be forgotten.

To save time, I suggested we split up to search for Piper. Gideon and Audrey agreed, and we all left the waiting room, each heading in different directions. After I turned the first corner and stepped into an open doorway leading to a hallway, a girl in her twenties caught my eye. She had earrings that resembled the ones Piper wore in Tyler's photo. It wasn't her, but she looked familiar. As I tried to place her, she entered the second door on the right. I followed her into the room, and when she turned to face me, a spark of recognition struck me. It was Summer, Jared's girlfriend. She'd come to Eric's bar the night the demons had eaten Audrey and my ex's souls.

She scrunched up her eyebrows. "What the hell? Who are you?" Up close, her earrings looked identical to Piper's. The jewelry had to be hers. Was this girl a friend of Piper? Did she know where she was?

"I'm sorry to bother you, especially in here, but I need to ask you a few questions. It will only take a minute," I said. Then it dawned on me that Jared could be here with her. Crap! I glanced around the dimly lit room.

"Who're you looking for?" she asked as my eyes fell on the large glass window to our left. It was a one-way mirror. My brow rose when I realized the guy on the other side was Jared. Shirtless, he was sitting with his wrists tied behind his back, a black blindfold covering his eyes. Electrodes were attached to his fingers, under his fingernails, and to his nipples. His legs and arms were bound with ropes. Next to him was a woman wearing a tight black latex catsuit and holding a device. Each time she pressed the button, there was a buzzing sound and Jared moaned in pleasure.

"I had no idea he was into that." Surprise leaked into my voice.

"Yeah, neither did I," Summer said. "I found out yesterday when he confessed he liked being watched while someone hurt him and suggested we go to this place. Are you his ex or something?"

"Yes," I answered and walked over to the glass window. Behind it sat the guy I'd once loved. Then despised. Now he provoked nothing in me.

My attention went back to Summer. She deserved to hear about Jared's infidelity. "I'm sorry to tell you this, but I saw Jared cheating on you before you picked him up from a bar called Hell's Happy Hour."

I expected shock, anger, denial. Instead, she shrugged indifferently. "Yeah, well, not a surprise. All men cheat." After a brief pause, her eyes sharpened with curiosity. "Your questions, are they about Jared and me?"

"No, they're about your earrings."

Her brow lifted slightly. "Oh, okay." She reached up, her fingers brushing the delicate, diamond-encrusted ballet slipper charm. "Pretty, aren't they?" She smiled. "What do you wanna know?"

It was possible that she had stolen the jewelry. Not wanting to sound accusatory and risk her becoming defensive or uncooperative, I chose my words carefully.

"I came here because I'm looking for someone named Piper. She has earrings just like yours, so I thought maybe you got them from her and could help me find her."

"Piper?" she repeated, a frown creasing her forehead. "I don't know anyone by that name. And I didn't steal these earrings, if that's what you think." Her voice was calm, not offended. "Actually, there's a rather unusual story about how I got 'em." She seemed to hesitate before asking, "Are you familiar with the Hidden World?"

I nodded. "Yes, and its creatures." A tingle of alarm crept down my neck and shoulders when I added, "Please don't tell me you're a demon."

She twisted her features as if I'd uttered the vilest insult. "God, no! I'm not a demon. I'm a witch. Which is relevant to how I ended up with these expensive beauties." She gestured to her earrings. "It all started a few nights ago when I went to a bar with some friends. The drinks were flowing, and eventually, nature called. On my way to the bathroom, I bumped into this cute vamp. We started talking, and he invited me to join him at his table. After a few margaritas, he surprised me with an unexpected offer. He said he'd pay me if I approached Jared, who was sitting across the room from us, and use my magic to uncover the nature of his connection to some dead girl named Ivy. I wasn't going to say no to easy money, so I agreed."

"What was the vampire's name?" I stopped her.

"Logan," she answered. Confusion threaded through me. Why would Ivy's vampire boyfriend think that my ex, a human, had some kind of connection to his dead girlfriend?

"So," Summer continued, "after I took the money, I went to Jared and cast a spell on him to ask him about Ivy. He remembered seeing her in a bar one night. She came over and sat down next to him with a drink in her hand. She introduced herself and asked him something, I don't remember what it was, then her expression changed. He said there was panic in her eyes.

"She claimed her drink had been poisoned, and she was going to die. Suddenly she pressed her hands to his temples and whispered something. He was too stunned to react, and then she disappeared into the crowded bar. He didn't think much of the whole thing, though. He assumed she was just a nutcase."

The newfound details before Ivy's death sent a train of questions through my mind. Why had she approached my ex of all people? Could he have been the last person to see her alive? Was he mixed up with some shady supernatural creatures?

"Does Jared know about the Hidden World? And about you being a witch?" I asked.

Summer shook her head. "He has no idea that witches, vampires, and demons exist."

"Jared told you Ivy touched his temples. Do you think it was some kind of spell she put on him?" I asked.

"Yes. She used a complicated spell to implant a message into his mind," Summer answered. "Logan offered me extra money if I could uncover the contents of the message. I was game to try, but I warned him it'd take time. That's when he came up with the idea for me to fake date Jared while I tried to get the message out of his brain. Before I agreed to his plan, I made it crystal clear to him that I wanted half the money upfront, regardless of whether or not I could get Ivy's message from Jared's head. Compensation for my time was non-negotiable. Since he didn't have enough cash in his wallet that night to cover half of what I asked for, he gave me the earrings, which he had kept in his car. He said he'd withdraw the rest of the money if I was successful with Ivy's message."

"And were you?" I asked.

"No luck so far, and it's not for lack of trying. We've only known each other for a few days, but I moved in with him yesterday so I could have constant access to his mind. I've spent hours trying to unlock the message in his head."

I raised an eyebrow in surprise. "Was he okay with moving in together after only a few dates?"

"I'm sure he wouldn't have been if I hadn't cast a spell on him. He likes me a lot, but obviously, it was way too soon for him to even consider that kind of commitment. Which is why I had to use magic. Love potions aren't really my specialty, so whipping one up to make him fall madly in love with me was not on the table. I had to get creative. Instead, I cast a spell that made him think we'd shared five great months together and were exclusive. Yeah, the spell wasn't perfect; he cheated. But as long as he's still with me and lets me touch his head, I don't care what he does in his free time. What bothers me, though, is that I keep failing with the message. That Ivy girl was seriously skilled. She knew how to lock down whatever she put in his head with some killer magic. I—"

The door to the room opened, and Audrey and Gideon walked in.

Summer looked at them. "Sorry, this room is already taken."

"It's all right. They're with me," I said to her. After making the introductions, I told Audrey and Gideon that Jared was in the other room, behind the one-way mirror. Then I filled them in on everything Summer had shared with me.

When I was done, Audrey asked her, "Do you know where we can find Logan? Where does he live?"

"I've never been to his place. We've only met a couple of times," she replied.

"What's his phone number?" Gideon asked her.

She gave him his number then said, "Are you gonna call him now?"

"No," he answered, and his gaze shifted to the glass window. "There's something else I need to do first." And just like that, he vanished from the room, only to materialize on the other side of the one-way mirror.

Gideon's sudden appearance startled the woman in the room. His eyes glowed bright emerald as he walked over to her and leaned in to whisper something in her ear. When he finished, her eyes glazed over, and in a trance-like state, she handed him the wireless remote control she was holding.

Then she said to Jared, "I'm needed elsewhere, but I'm leaving you in good hands. The person covering for me has gone over your list of likes and dislikes, so he'll know how to take good care of you."

I snapped to alertness after Gideon was left alone with my ex.

Jared got upset. "No, you can't just bail in the middle of our session! I paid for you, not some replacement." The corner of Gideon's lips curled into a wicked smirk as he looked down at the device in his hand.

"She's gone, but no need to worry. You heard her. I can take good care of you. Rest your mind; you're in for a world of pain and screaming. Here, let me demonstrate." Gideon pressed a button on the device.

Jared clenched his teeth in pain and yelled, "Eggplant! Eggplant! Eggplant!"

Gideon's eyebrow arched leisurely as he removed his finger from the button. "Your safe word is eggplant?" His tone dripped with mockery.

"You don't know my safe word?" Jared's voice was incredulous. "Ellie said you read my card. What's going on? And why do you sound like you're making fun of me? I specifically wrote on my card that I'm not into humiliation."

"Making fun of you?" Deep sarcasm clung to Gideon's words. "Never. Jacob—"

"Jared."

Ignoring the correction, Gideon continued, "We're going to play a game where I ask you questions. Only one rule in this game: you have to answer every question I ask. Otherwise, I'll make you scream—and not in a pleasant way. First question: did a girl named Ivy approach you while you were in a bar?"

"What in the world?" Jared's voice seethed with a combination of confusion and anger. "I don't know what the hell is going on, but we're done here." He squirmed in his seat, trying to free himself. "Take off my blindfold and untie me right now."

"Sorry, Jerry, not until we finish the game."

"Jared!"

"I'm waiting for my answer," Gideon said, but Jared refused to answer. "Looks like someone needs a reminder of the punishment for breaking my rule." Gideon pressed the button on the remote, causing Jared to scream.

When Gideon's finger lifted from the device, Jared quickly said, "Yes, some weird chick named Ivy approached me at a bar."

"What did she talk to you about?"

"I'm so gonna complain about you. This is *not* what I asked for. My girlfriend is in the observation room and—Aghhhhhh!" Gideon used the device again.

Watching Jared through the glass window, Summer said, "There's really no need to put him through that; has the vampire forgotten that he can just compel the truth out of him?"

A smile danced on Audrey's lips. "Oh, he most certainly has not."

Gideon's finger left the button. "Jimmy, my patience is beginning to wear thin."

"Jared."

Once again, Gideon disregarded the correction and went on, "Will I be getting an answer anytime soon, or do you need another reminder of what happens when you don't follow my rule?"

"No, no, no. I'll answer. I was sitting in a booth, drinking alone, a little buzzed, and she came over with her drink, acting really weird, but she had nice tits, so I didn't mind. She introduced herself. I thought she was going to invite me to her place next, but instead, she said she'd approached me 'cause she was looking for Sydney, which surprised me. The only Sydney I knew was my annoying, stupid ex, Sydney Newbern—" Jared gave a loud cry of pain as he was electrified again.

Gideon's eyes darkened to a dangerous degree. "Call her annoying or stupid again, and the next thing you'll be doing is screaming the word "eggplant" on repeat. Is that understood?" Jared nodded vigorously before Gideon asked in a tight voice, "What happened after Ivy told you she was looking for Sydney?"

It took Jared a moment to collect himself. "I was a bit confused as I hadn't spoken to my ex in ages. To make sure that chick was talking about her, I asked if she'd meant Sydney Newbern—Aghhhhhh!" When Gideon withdrew his finger from the button, Jared whined, "What was that for? I was answering you!"

Irritation flashed over Gideon's face. "I don't like her name coming out of your mouth. Don't ever say it again."

"You're batshit crazy," Jared said.

"Glad you've noticed. Feel like finding out what happens when a crazy person's patience snaps?"

"N-n-no, please, don't hurt me."

"Then go on."

Jared took a deep breath before speaking again, "I was waiting for her to answer me when suddenly her breathing became ragged and she was mumbling some weird shit about her drink being poisoned and her dying, sounding like a real lunatic. She touched my head with shaking hands and started whispering gibberish. I was too shocked to pull away from her touch.

"I swear to God, it was the weirdest thing that ever happened to me. I felt dizzy, my vision blurred, and I couldn't move my body. After her gibberish, she switched to English and said, 'Only for the one you're in love with,' then took her hands off me. My head was throbbing like a bitch. I closed my eyes. When I opened them, I felt better and could move again, but she was no longer in her seat or at the bar."

Gideon looked in the mirror, signaling us to join him.

The three of us entered the room, and Gideon turned to Audrey, "Do you think you can get the information out of his head?"

"What's going on? Who else is in the room? Who are you talking to?" Jared demanded.

"I don't know. I'll try," Audrey told Gideon, then used magic to put Jared to sleep. As his eyelids closed and he began to snore, Audrey placed her palms on his head and chanted unintelligible words. The air around us crackled with energy. She seemed to be in deep concentration. Her face then contorted in discomfort as she stopped in mid-word.

Concerned, I placed a hand on her shoulder. Just as I asked about her well-being, the room around us dissolved into another, and Gideon, Jared, and Summer disappeared. I blinked a few times. As I took in the new surroundings, my confusion increased. On a desk in the room was a notebook with my sister's full name written on the cover. Next to it, an open laptop cast a soft glow, its screen displaying a selfie of her with some guy.

I looked at Audrey. "Um, did I fall asleep too? Is this some strange dream where I'm with you in what looks like my sister's dorm room?"

"It's not a dream," she said. Her features twisted into a frown of perplexity as she glanced around. "We gotta get out of here before someone comes in."

We hurried out of the room and down the stairs to the dormitory lobby, a loud chorus of voices filling my ears. The space was large and open with high ceilings, the walls covered with posters and flyers, advertising everything from campus events to local restaurants and bars. Three frat guys stopped near us and made a show of checking out Audrey.

She rolled her eyes at them. "In your dreams, boys. Keep moving."

After they set off in the direction of the basement, I turned to Audrey, "Okay, what's going on? Why are we in my sister's dormitory?"

"Ivy created a powerful magical barrier in Jared's head to prevent access to the message. Instead of trying to break through it, I employed a spell to communicate with the barrier itself."

"Communicate with the barrier? What does that mean?" I asked.

"The barrier Ivy put in Jared's head is magic unlike anything I've ever encountered. It's somehow sentient, has some kind of awareness. Ivy was no ordinary witch."

"When you touched Jared's head and did your witch thing, you looked like something was wrong. What was it?" I said.

"The experience of interacting with the barrier was unpleasant. It felt like a loud voice echoing in my head, which caused a little pain. The voice said I was not the intended recipient of the message in Jared's mind. So, I asked, 'Who was it meant for?' and I was zapped into your sister's dorm room."

"We," I corrected. "We got zapped."

"Yeah, because you touched me just as Ivy's magic teleported me here and... Sydney, are you with me?"

My attention had wandered across the room. "Zoey," I murmured.

My sister walked into the building, accompanied by a girl and a guy with a fraternity shirt under his jacket. I was overjoyed to see that Zoey's life was back on track, having re-enrolled in school after she'd dropped out.

"Your sister? Where?" Audrey asked, her eyes scanning the room before she said, "Oh, I see her. The gorgeous girl in the pink cardigan over there." She nodded in Zoey's direction.

My voice was thick with surprise as I asked, "How'd you know it was her?"

"She's supposed to be Gifted, right? You've mentioned it to me before. She's the only person here with the ability to sense the supernatural."

"Yeah, and if she gets close to you, she'll know you're a witch. She once told me that when a supernatural being was not too far away from her, she could see colors emanating from them, and they changed depending on the type of creature," I said and looked back at Zoey.

She waved goodbye to her friends and headed for the elevator where Audrey and I were standing. I tore my gaze from Zoey and turned my back to her, fighting the urge to give her a bone-crushing hug and tell her how much I missed her.

"Yeah, you're right, we have to be careful," Audrey said.

As we moved away from the crowd and into a secluded corner, the words Ivy had said to Jared while she touched his head flashed through my mind.

With an epiphany, I looked at Audrey. "The barrier took you to Zoey's dorm room after you asked who the message was for. And before Ivy let go of Jared, she said the message was only for the one he's in love with."

Audrey, catching on to my train of thought, made a face of disgust. "Ewww, I can't believe that shithead ex of yours is still mooning over your sister."

"Yeah, apparently his feelings for her haven't faded a bit, but I don't think Ivy was under the impression his heart belonged to Zoey when she sealed her spell with the words, "Only for the one you're in love with." Ivy didn't ask Jared about my sister, she asked him about me. It seems she approached him because she thought we were still together for some reason," I said.

Audrey nodded in agreement. "Yeah, and if she thought that, she'd naturally assume you were the one he was in love with. It looks like the message she put in his head was for you. Unfortunately, it won't be released until Jared hears or sees Zoey. That's how these kinds of spells work, even the powerful ones."

"There is no way I am getting her involved. We have to find another way to get the message out," I said.

"I hear you, but we don't have much of a choice. Zoey's voice is the key to unlocking whatever is in Jared's head. I know you're worried, but trust me, your sister will not be put in danger. We don't even need Zoey to have a long conversation with your ex. One word from her will be enough to get Ivy's message out."

After a moment, I sighed in resignation. "All right. How are we going to do that?"

"I have a plan, but we need to talk to Gideon first. Do you have your phone? Mine's in my purse, which is in Black Whip."

I reached into my jeans pocket, pulled out my cell phone, and checked it. "Damn it, my battery is dead."

Audrey's eyes flicked around the room, scanning the people's faces. Her gaze then settled on a guy deep in conversation on his cell phone. She whispered a few arcane words under her breath, and the guy's voice trailed off as his gaze shifted to Audrey. He walked over, ended the call, and handed her his phone.

She flashed him a smile. "Thank you."

The guy was unresponsive, his eyes fixed on Audrey, unblinking and empty. I used his phone to call Gideon and put him on speaker. Gideon was still in the room with Jared and Summer, trying to figure out where Ivy's magic had taken us, his attempts to reach me or Audrey on our phones having failed.

After we looped him in on what had happened, Audrey outlined her plan to unlock the message in Jared's mind.

# Chapter 14

The plan was simple. We'd call Zoey, and when she picked up, Jared, under Gideon's thrall, would remain silent in the background while he heard her voice, and Ivy's message would be unlocked. Then we'd hang up, and Zoey, who would probably assume it'd been some random misdial, would go about her daily business. Before we called my sister, Gideon placed his phone on speaker and woke Jared from his slumber. My ex mumbled something, sounding puzzled.

Gideon ordered him to shut up, then intoned, "You will give your full attention to the voice you're about to hear." Two rings later, my sister's voice reached my ears.

"Hello?" When she didn't get an answer, she repeated in a firm tone, "Hello? Who is—" Zoey's voice was cut off, and I assumed Gideon had hung up. There was a tense silence, broken only by the sound of heavy breathing. Jared then recited a cryptic series of numbers.

When he stopped, I turned to Audrey. "What could these numbers mean?"

Audrey mirrored my confusion. "I have no idea."

"Wait, there's more," Summer said. "Jared's drawing something in the air with his finger."

"Search for a pen and paper," Gideon told Summer.

"Get my purse in the observation room. I keep a notebook and pen in it," Audrey said.

In less than a heartbeat, sounds of movement and paper rustling came through the line.

A few minutes later, Gideon said, "He drew a triangle with a crescent moon in the middle."

"Why would a witch I had never met leave me a cryptic message? What the hell was she trying to tell me?" Bewilderment laced my tone.

Gideon's voice came through the phone, cool and authoritative. "We'll figure out the meaning of the numbers and the symbol later. Right now, I need you both on the first available flight to New York. Text me the flight number, if you can. I'll be waiting for you when you land."

"Whoa, why am I feeling nauseous? I think I'm gonna puke." I heard Jared complain.

Summer's voice cut in, clearly directed at Gideon. "It's okay, I got him. You go ahead."

Gideon took us off the speaker. "We'll talk later," he said before hanging up.

Audrey and I hopped on the first flight to JFK without showing IDs or tickets, thanks to her magic. When we landed in New York, Gideon was waiting for us at arrivals. He handed Audrey her purse before draping my coat over my shoulders. Not missing the lingering kiss on my lips, she shot me a sly look that conveyed her approval just before her phone rang. She fished it out of her purse.

"Yes," she answered and a few seconds later said, "Wait, wait, Willow, slow down. Who got hurt?" Her face sharpened. After several minutes of listening, she ended the call with, "Okay, I'm on my way to you. Don't touch anything in the meantime."

She put her phone back in her purse and explained, "A witch I met at the convention is in a real jam and needs my help. She tried out a new spell, and it has gone totally haywire. Now she's freaking out in her hotel room with no clue what to do. Guess she didn't know who else to turn to, so it looks like it's up to me to clean up this mess." A sigh escaped her lips. "Sorry, but I need to get over there right away."

I nodded. "Yeah, sure, go help her before someone gets turned into a bug."

As Audrey hurried away, Gideon turned to me. "I tried Logan, but it keeps going to voicemail. As for the numbers, I looked into them. They're coordinates for a cemetery. We should go over there now and check it out."

Great, a cemetery visit at night. *Because nothing says fun like a late-night stroll through a graveyard.* The last time I had the pleasure of being in one after dark was on Halloween when I was fifteen, during a game of Truth or Dare with my friends. The dare? To spend ten minutes alone in a cemetery. I'd been rigid with terror as I stood among the graves, the biting wind tearing through the darkness, punctuated by the hooting of an owl and the eerie silver mist clinging to the ground. The memory sent shivers down my back.

Gideon reached into his jacket and pulled out my gloves. "Put them back on. The cemetery manager shouldn't be there, but if we happen to run into him, it's best he doesn't see the dark magic on your hand."

"Why? Is he a demon?" I asked.

"No, but let's just say he has a strong aversion to dark magic and tends to be suspicious of anyone associated with it," he answered as I slipped on the gloves.

Ten minutes later, we were driving to the cemetery on Gideon's bike, which he'd retrieved from the abandoned factory. When we got there, we jumped over the low, brick wall of the cemetery. No one was around. The cold breeze brushed against my body, making me tighten my coat as we walked through the cemetery by the silver illumination of the moon.

I turned on the flashlight Gideon had given me. "What are we looking for?"

"I don't know yet. Maybe the symbol from the dead witch's message will be engraved on one of the tombstones," he replied.

We made our way along the path, shadows dancing around us like creepy creatures. A crow flew down and landed on a decrepit headstone, cawing. My neck and arms prickled with fear. I swallowed loudly. As I did, Gideon stopped and looked at me.

"Don't be afraid," he said in a calm and reassuring voice. After all the crap I'd been through since Cole had kidnapped me, I felt ridiculous for being so jumpy in a graveyard.

Pride wouldn't allow me to admit my fear, and I said, "What? No, I'm not scared. I've survived Ice Prison, crazy warrior vampires, and demons trying to kill me. I think I can handle an old"—and seriously creepy—"cemetery."

As soon as the words left my mouth, a loud growl pierced the night air behind us. I spun around, adrenaline coursing through my veins as I whipped out my dagger, my flashlight clattering to the ground. When I saw the threat, my heart pounded in my chest. I froze. A massive black jaguar emerged from the darkness and prowled toward us, its golden eyes gleaming with predatory intent.

"Sweet. Baby. Jesus," I muttered under my breath, dropping my tough-girl act. "You meant the jaguar..."

A short, amused sound escaped Gideon before his expression hardened as he met the animal's eyes.

"We're not looking for trouble," he said to it.

I snapped my head to Gideon. Was he seriously trying to reason with a massive, lethal cat as if it was a rational being? "You think telling a hungry jaguar we're not looking for trouble will stop him from making a meal out of us?"

"Visiting hours are over. The cemetery is closed, and you are trespassing," a deep male voice echoed in my head, almost making me jump out of my skin.

What the hell?

My eyes darted around, searching for any sign of another person as my grip on my dagger tightened. We were alone. The terrifying animal bared its white teeth at us. A flicker of understanding crossed its gaze, and it dawned on me with a jolt—the jaguar was communicating with us telepathically.

"We apologize for trespassing," Gideon said.

"Why are you here?" the voice growled in my head.

"We're investigating the death of a witch named Ivy, and a lead brought us here," Gideon replied.

The jaguar locked eyes with us, its amber gaze intense and unwavering. Then, its fur began to recede, melting into skin. Bones shifted and twisted until a naked man stood before us, all his muscles and glory on display. He was about the same height as Gideon, with a wrestler's build, and his skin was a rich, earthy brown. Dark stubble framed his square jaw.

His hair was pulled back into a man bun, and both sides of his head were shaved, giving him a wild and intimidating look. The man walked with the grace of a predator to a backpack leaning against a nearby tree and pulled out a pair of jeans, a long-sleeved shirt, and sneakers.

Puzzled, I whispered to Gideon, "What creature is he?"

"He used to be a vampire," Gideon answered.

"A vampire?" I echoed in surprise.

The man, now dressed, sauntered back to us and looked at Gideon. "I see you know my story."

"Well, there aren't many ex-convicts walking around in our world after spending twenty years in Ice Prison," Gideon said. The mere mention of that hellish place made my stomach churn.

"Forty years," the man corrected.

Unlike Gideon, who seemed at ease, I was on high alert. My time in Ice Prison had taught me the vampires roaming there were far from your typical vampire; they were more vicious, evil, and downright savage.

I gripped the hilt of my dagger. "What landed you in Ice Prison?"

A ghost of a smile spread across his face. "Is that your roundabout way of asking if I am a sadistic killer?"

Meeting his gaze, I lifted one brow. "Are you?"

"He was found guilty of distributing a book of dark magic spells and sentenced to eternal imprisonment in Ice Prison," Gideon revealed, his tone suggesting the man was not a dangerous criminal. The tension seeped out of my body, allowing me to retrieve my flashlight and sheath my weapon.

"Wrongfully convicted," the man growled, his eyes blazing with anger. "I was framed. My brother cleared my name. He found the evidence that proved my innocence."

His story intrigued me. This man had endured four decades in the Jungle, the section of Ice Prison reserved for vampires. Anything more than a decade in there was usually deadly for his kind. They succumbed to a gradual transformation, losing their memories as they turned into animals. Yet, he seemed to be able to shape-shift and also to have kept his memories intact. How had he retained them?

The man's phone rang, and he took it out of his jeans pocket. He answered it, keeping his eyes on us.

I looked at Gideon. "How does he remember his life before Ice Prison?" My voice was quiet.

"When a prisoner is exonerated, the Watchers are duty bound to release them, and if necessary, restore any lost memories, as in Emilio's case." Gideon nodded at the man, then added, "Memory restoration is a brutal process, however, and the chances of survival are slim."

"How is he able to change his physical form?" I asked.

"The ability to shape-shift occurs when the Watchers fail, for some reason, to fully fix the DNA of the released prisoner," he answered.

"Are those prisoners still vampires when they're not in their animal form?" I asked just as Emilio ended his call.

"No," Emilio answered me, his voice carrying a hint of sadness. "My DNA has been permanently altered, and the Watchers weren't able to repair it. The beast will always be a part of me. I can never return to what I once was, a vampire." After a moment of tense silence, Emilio directed his gaze at Gideon. "Tell me about your connection with the dead witch. Are you related to her Newborn lover, Logan?" My eyebrows shot up. How did he know about him?

"No, but we're looking for him. He might be able to help us understand some things," Gideon answered, then told him about the message Ivy had left in my ex's head.

"Do you know Logan? Do you have any idea where we can find him?" I asked.

Emilio was quiet for so long I thought he might not answer at all, but then he broke his silence with a single command, "Follow me."

As he led us deeper into the cemetery, I stayed razor-focused, alert for any sign of danger lurking in the shadows. The air grew thick with the scent of decaying leaves and damp earth. We walked past row after row of tombstones until we stopped at an old stone crypt. Vines crept up the walls like bony fingers. Ivy's name was carved above the door in an elegant, looping script.

Emilio gestured toward the crypt with a wave of his hand. "It's been in Ivy's family for generations."

Gideon looked at the three letters carved into the stone and said, "They're spelled with magic."

"Yes," Emilio confirmed. "The name carries strong magic. The letters on the door have changed five times since I first saw the crypt. Once, they read Doris, then Joan, Patricia, Nicole, Stephanie, and now Ivy."

Desperate for answers, I asked him, "What can you tell me about Ivy and her family?"

"Not much," he said. "I know that Doris was Ivy's mother, and Joan, Patricia, Nicole, and Stephanie were her sisters. They were all victims of brutal murder." Unease twisted in my stomach. Why would Ivy want me here?

I turned to Emilio. "Who's buried in this crypt?"

Gideon crouched down to examine something on the door and said, "Looks like it wasn't meant for burying the dead." I drew closer, shining my flashlight on the crypt to get a better look. The symbol Jared had drawn was carved into the base of the door.

Gideon straightened, his eyes meeting mine. "There must be something more valuable than bones inside. The symbol from Ivy's message is a powerful magical lock. You don't seal a structure with magic for a mere corpse."

"My thoughts exactly," Emilio said. "I only saw Ivy once when I was showing a burial plot to a human client. I spotted the witch whispering words of magic as the symbol on the crypt glowed. I don't mind witches using magic in the cemetery, as long as it's not dark magic. That could draw unwanted attention from the Watchers, and after my wrongful imprisonment, I'm not taking any chances. I won't give anyone the opportunity to pin false charges on me a second time. So, to ensure that no suspicious activities, such as the casting of dark spells, were taking place on the property under my care, I kept a watchful eye on her family's crypt.

"Sometime after I saw Ivy, Logan, a Newborn vampire, came to the same crypt. He stood there with a glow coming from his chest. I suspected something was wrong. When I got closer, I noticed a glowing pendant hanging from his neck. The symbol etched on that pendant was identical to the one on the crypt door. I demanded answers for his actions because I wanted to make sure the pendant wasn't connected to anything illegal.

"The Newborn looked like a scared rabbit, spilling everything without hesitation. He began by giving his name and mentioning that his lover was a witch. I asked for more details about her appearance and name. He answered, and it quickly became apparent that his witch was the same I'd seen performing magic. The Newborn claimed he'd found her on the floor of her living room, barely alive before he came here. Clenched in her hand was a necklace with a pendant bearing a symbol.

"In her dying moments, she told him she'd been murdered and instructed him to give the necklace to someone named Sydney Newbern." His eyes locked with mine. "Is that you, by any chance?" I gave a nod and he continued, "The Newborn remembered seeing the symbol on the pendant before, on the crypt, and came here.

"As he approached the stone, he noticed the name above the door had changed to Ivy, and the pendant began to pulsate with a white light, adding to his confusion. I told him to reach out to one of Ivy's witch friends to shed some light on the reason for the pendant's glow, but he shot down the idea. He didn't trust anyone in Ivy's inner circle when it came to the necklace.

"Since the crypt is under my supervision, I needed answers as much as he did. I dialed some contacts and found a witch who might be able to help. After placing her hands on the mystical pendant, she revealed it to be a key to the crypt, accessible to only one person." Both Gideon and Emilio shifted their gazes to me.

I sighed. "And I suppose that person would be me."

"It sure looks like it," Emilio said.

"Where is the necklace now?" Gideon asked him.

"I let the Newborn hang on to it as the necklace is useless, just a piece of jewelry without the person it's intended for. I gave him my number and told him to contact me if he ever found this person. He left, and two nights later, this happened."

He approached and pulled up his security camera feed on his phone, then showed us footage of Logan walking toward the cemetery gates. Three vampires jumped him before throwing him into a black van with a hidden license plate and driving off.

"It was Cassian's men," Emilio said, tucking his phone back into his jeans. "A wealthy, notorious collector from Pennsylvania."

"Yeah, I've heard of him. And his infamous cursed mansion," Gideon said.

"Cursed mansion?" I echoed, my eyebrows knitting together.

"Cassian has three properties in Pennsylvania," Gideon told me. "One of them is called the Cursed Mansion. Rumors have circulated about that place for years, with tales of satanic forces lurking within its walls and other unexplained occurrences."

"Both mortals and immortals avoid it like the plague. Even Cassian himself has not set foot in that mansion in decades," Emilio added.

My eyes widened. "Wow, sounds like a delightful place. That Cassian dude must be real bummed about his property value tanking." Shifting the focus back to Logan, I asked Emilio, "Do you know why Cassian would want to kidnap Logan?"

"Digging a bit, I found out the Newborn had stolen something quite valuable from his collection. His henchmen were sent to retrieve it and deliver Logan to their boss," Emilio answered and added, "If you're keen on tracking down the Newborn and the pendant, going to Pennsylvania to meet Cassian might be a promising start."

"Pennsylvania, huh?" I said, then turned to Gideon. "Looks like we're going to the Keystone State."

"You had better move fast. Cassian doesn't deal in forgiveness. You should hope he hasn't killed the Newborn yet," Emilio said.

"Thanks for the information," Gideon told him. "If Logan's still alive, we'll be back soon with the necklace to unlock the crypt."

Outside the cemetery, as Gideon booked our plane tickets to Pennsylvania, I remembered I had a morning shift the next day. Uncertain about the length of our trip, I called Veronica and asked if she could cover my shifts for the next few days. With her agreement secured, I hopped on Gideon's bike.

As we drove away, a strong sense of foreboding crept up on me. Since trouble seemed to have a knack for finding its way to my doorstep, I wouldn't be surprised if Gideon and I ended up in the back of a black van ourselves. It seemed like life had a way of testing my limits at every turn lately.

# Chapter 15

On the flight to Pennsylvania, curious about the Cursed Mansion, I asked Gideon for more details. Apparently, Cassian had been living outside of Pennsylvania when he bought it as a summer home in 1920. It wasn't until sixteen years later that the crazy stuff started happening. In the winter of 1936, Cassian received a letter informing him that the exterior walls, doors, and windows of the mansion had turned black overnight, leading him to suspect witchcraft.

Rather than seeking out experts in the field, such as witches, Cassian sent his own son to investigate. *After all, what father wouldn't want his own flesh and blood wandering around a creepy place with walls that have mysteriously darkened to black?* When his son didn't return, Cassian, ever the picture of paternal concern, ordered his men to search the mansion for him, but surprise, surprise, they also vanished without a trace.

It'd only taken Cassian losing his son and an entire search party to finally realize that maybe he should call in some real professionals. With two powerful witches at his side, he went to the Cursed Mansion. When the trio arrived, the vampire was stunned to find that not only were the windows sealed shut, but all the plants around the mansion had withered away.

The witches sensed powerful magic emanating from the obsidian walls and warned of a dangerous force that had taken root in his mansion. Despite their warning, Cassian was determined to uncover the source of the dark forces plaguing his property and ordered the witches to go inside, but they were too afraid. Being the douche that he was, Cassian threatened to withhold payment if they refused to enter the house. Reluctantly, they stepped through the front door, while he, of course, remained outside like a coward. For a while, nothing but the wind dared speak, until a scream, spine-chilling and raw, tore through the night's silence.

When the witches didn't emerge, he returned the next night, dragging a batch of kidnapped humans to throw in. He also managed to lure all sorts of supernatural creatures into the mansion on several occasions. None ever came out, so the mystery remained unsolved. However, Cassian had made an interesting discovery: only witches screamed within the mansion's walls. In time, the place had gained notoriety and became the subject of countless rumors and tales.

Cassian offered a tantalizing reward of two million dollars to anyone brave enough to enter the ominous mansion and successfully escape its clutches. Over the years, vampires, witches, demons, and humans alike had tried their luck, but each attempt ended in failure, and they were all presumed dead. The Cursed Mansion remained a mystery, shrouded in layers of the unknown and fear.

"So, what's the deal with that house?" I asked Gideon when we landed. "Is it really cursed, or is it some portal to another dimension?"

"If I had the keys to those questions, I'd be two million dollars richer," he said, flashing me a playful grin. When we reached arrivals, he looked to our right, alert and watchful.

I followed his gaze and spotted a man striding toward us. "Who's that?"

"Probably Cassian's driver."

Perplexed, I asked, "Cassian's driver? Why would his driver be here?"

"Before we left New York, I got Cassian's phone number and left him a message, pretending to be Logan's guardian. I offered to pay for any mess he might have made."

Vampire laws stated that an official guardian must be assigned to a Newborn vampire. Guardians were responsible for keeping their Newborns out of trouble and teaching them everything about their new existence as vampires.

"Why lie? Why not just ask Cassian for a meeting?" I asked.

"Ancient vampires like Cassian don't grant meetings to just anyone. The lie got me what I needed—his attention."

"How does Cassian's driver know what you look like?" I said.

"Cassian has our flight details, and I was the only vampire on that flight."

The driver stopped in front of us, dressed in a black suit that hugged his large frame, towering over us.

After a glance in my direction, he focused on Gideon. "Mr. Williams is expecting you at his estate. Follow me, please. Leave the Donor here." As the driver turned to walk away, Gideon stood resolute. The man stopped and gave him a questioning look.

"She's coming too." Gideon's tone brooked no argument. "Or you can count me out. I doubt Mr. Williams would be pleased to hear why he didn't get the money he was expecting tonight."

The driver's eyes narrowed, but he kept his tone even. "Fine. You may bring the human." We followed him to a BMW. Gideon and I slid into the back seat, and the car revved up and drove to Cassian's estate.

After a ride that felt endless, we arrived at a magnificent mansion, its driveway curving in a perfect circle. A cold drizzle dampened my hair as we trailed the driver to the imposing front doors. A uniformed guard stationed at the entrance ordered us to surrender our weapons before entering.

I hesitated, feeling exposed without my daggers. A reassuring nod from Gideon spurred me on, and we handed over our weapons. Once inside, the driver led us to the double-swept staircase covered in fine velvet carpeting. The vampire staff we passed on the second floor eyed me like I was a walking buffet, their gazes lingering on the curve of my neck.

*Yeah, keep dreaming, assholes.*

The driver stopped at a heavy wooden door and knocked.

"Come in," a deep male voice said from the other side, and the driver pushed the door open, revealing a lavish study with dark, rich mahogany wood paneling and elegant oil paintings in gold frames. The warm glow that flooded the room accentuated its luxurious details. A leather chair sat in front of a large desk that dominated the center of the room. Behind it sat a man, Cassian, I assumed, wearing a suit and a gold ring with a large, flashy ruby stone on his little finger.

"The thief's guardian is here, sir," the driver said as Gideon and I stepped inside. Cassian dismissed him with a wave, and the doors closed behind us.

The Ancient vampire looked at me and then at Gideon, a smile spreading across his lips. "You brought a treat. How thoughtful. But, make no mistake, one human will hardly make a dent in what you owe me, Mr. Hawthorne. Which is a lot of money. That Newborn of yours has been nothing but a headache. He stole a precious stone from me and refuses to give it back."

His voice was soft as silk, not a trace of an accent. Contrary to my expectations, he lacked the stereotypical appearance of an intimidating vampire lord. Cassian was slim, his long brown hair tied back tightly, his skin immaculately white and youthful, his features disarming in their warmth. But when it came to vampires, I knew better than to believe appearances; they could be deceiving. So, I kept my mouth shut and let Gideon do the talking.

"I apologize if I gave you the wrong impression about my Donor." Gideon spoke in a calm but deadly tone. "She's not a gift. And to be clear, if you so much as lay a finger on her, I'll make sure you regret it." He punctuated his threat with a smile that fell short of his eyes. "Now about my Newborn, Logan, and the stone he stole from you." The ruby on Cassian's finger suddenly flashed a bright blue. Gideon paused, his eyes flicking to the ring, while Cassian's gaze, gleaming with interest, settled on me.

After a moment, Cassian shifted his focus back to Gideon. "Ignore the ring; it does that sometimes. Please, continue."

"I am, of course, willing to pay for the stolen stone," Gideon said, "but before we proceed with any money transaction, I need to know what you've done with Logan."

"He's locked up in my basement, safe as can be for the time being." Cassian's appraising gaze swept over Gideon's clothes and watch. "Fortunately for him, it doesn't look like you'll have a problem covering the value of the stone he stole." With a smooth motion, Cassian slid open a drawer in his desk and pulled out a small glass box containing three shimmering red stones.

"The Witch's Protector," Gideon remarked.

"Indeed. Aren't they something?" Cassian sounded pleased and proud.

"And rare. I take it Logan pilfered the fourth?" Gideon asked.

Cassian nodded. "I explained to him how precious the stones were to me. It took me years to collect them at immense cost and effort. Your Newborn refuses to return it. So now you owe me half a million dollars. How will you transfer the money?"

Cassian's behavior didn't sit right with me. He thought Gideon was Logan's guardian, an authoritative and important figure to a Newborn. The very idea of lying to them or disobeying their orders was unthinkable to a newly turned vampire, as such defiance would result in severe punishment. If the Witch's Protector held such significance for Cassian, why didn't he urge Gideon to force Logan to reveal where he'd hidden the stolen stone? It looked like the Ancient vampire was more concerned with enriching himself with Gideon's money than with recovering his precious lost possession.

Echoing my thoughts, Gideon said, "Funny, I would've expected you to demand that I ask my Newborn to return the stone, especially since you claim he's still alive and the stone is so important to you."

Any semblance of affability vanished from Cassian's expression. He was ready to argue, but Gideon raised a hand to stop him. "Save it. It's obvious your stone has been returned. If even one was still missing from the box set, you'd be more focused on getting it back than haggling over money. Honestly, I don't care about that. My only concern is Logan. I'll pay whatever price you ask to get him back—assuming, of course, he's still alive, like you said. But if he's not... well, then we have a problem."

An uneasy silence filled the room until Cassian spoke. "Yes, your Newborn returned my stone." His nostrils flared. "The fool thought he could steal from me without consequences."

"Is he dead?" Gideon demanded.

Cassian leaned back in his leather chair. "Might as well be. I threw him in my cursed mansion two nights ago. You've heard the stories, I'm sure. Those who go in never come out. Are they all dead? I believe they are, but some think they've become evil spirits that haunt the place."

He pushed a button on his desk, and four large vampires in suits entered. I tensed. Cassian's eyes glowed jade green as his compulsion began to claw at my mind. When I blocked him out, a slight look of surprise settled on his face.

Gideon looked at the newcomers, then back at Cassian. "I guess the meeting's over, then."

When I tried to move, I felt like glue under my feet was holding me in place.

"Something's wrong," I said, noticing that Gideon was also struggling to move his legs, stuck to the carpet. Cassian laughed at my distress and twirled the heavy gold ring on his little finger.

"This beauty was made in 1455 for a human nobleman who longed for magical powers. His obsession with magic led him to a powerful illusionist who forged this ring for him. With it on your finger, you can cast simple spells and control anyone trapped within a sigil circle. You're standing in one right now, hidden under the carpet."

Confused, I didn't understand why he had bothered to trap us in the magic circle. Why not just order his vamps to kill us? He got up and walked around his desk then leaned against it as he stopped in front of us. A knot of tension formed in my stomach. My heart thundered in my ears, and my gloved palms were damp with sweat.

"Ordinarily, I'd be fit to be tied up over such a waste of my precious time," he said, "but it seems fate has given me something more valuable than money." His gaze fell on my left hand, quickening my pulse. Then his eyes returned to Gideon. "Your human is no ordinary Donor, is she?" A mean smile appeared on his face. "When the ring glowed earlier, it revealed that something dark and rare was hidden beneath her glove." He muttered a few words, and the glove on my left hand began to twitch. Before I could react, an unseen force yanked it off in one swift motion, and the glove fell to the floor, revealing my tattoo.

At the sight of it, his eyes widened in admiration as he continued, "I've come across some mighty rare things in my time, but the dark magic on her? That's something else."

"The tattoo you're drooling over is more trouble than it's worth," Gideon told him. "The Watchers are on the hunt for the witch behind the tattoo and everything connected to it, including the human." He gestured at me, his words a lie clearly intended to discourage Cassian's interest in my tattoo. "Unfortunately for me," he continued. "I was a bystander, swept into this mess while minding my own business. The witch who cast the tattoo put a spell that forced me to protect the human, and now I'm stuck playing her bodyguard. You'd be wise to stay away from the tattoo and the human. Just let me go with her. There will be no hard feelings about my Newborn; consider it water under the bridge."

"I'm not going to let your human go, but I have no intention of keeping her here. Although the idea of adding her to my collection has its appeal, I have other, far better, plans for her," Cassian said.

"Plans? What kind of plans?" I demanded, dreading his answer.

Cassian's eyes gleamed with malice. "Throughout the years, beings of many kinds—witches, demons, vampires—have ventured into my cursed mansion. But none have possessed the powerful, rare dark magic that graces your hand. I wonder if it might be the key to breaking the curse that haunts one of my houses."

"You can't be serious. Do you really think a human is the solution to your mansion problem? Let her go and throw me in there instead. I'll get you the answers you so desperately seek, and I won't ask for the reward," Gideon said.

I jerked my head to Gideon. "What are you doing?"

"Your human is getting inside my cursed mansion. If you wish to join her, be my guest. The more, the merrier, right?" Cassian's gaze went to his vampires. "Inject him with the silver-like serum." Looking back at Gideon, he explained, "This serum will temporarily paralyze you and make you sick like silver does, but it won't kill you. It's just a precaution in case you consider something foolish like fighting my men to escape. I must avoid that, for humans are so fragile; a single physical altercation could prove fatal."

Two vampires approached us. With our feet glued to the floor, we tried to resist them. Despite our best efforts, one vampire managed to grab my arms and forcefully tie them behind my back while the other overpowered Gideon and injected him with the serum. Alarm shot through me as Gideon's skin grew paler, his expression trying to reassure me despite our dire situation. When it was clear Gideon was in no condition to defend himself, Cassian barked an order to his men, instructing them to transport Gideon to the Cursed Mansion and wait for him outside.

After they took him away, I was hoisted over a vampire's shoulder and carried outside to the driveway. Helpless and restrained, I was chucked into the back seat of a white Cadillac with tinted windows while Cassian took the front seat next to his driver. As we hurtled down the highway, fear gnawed at my insides and dark thoughts raced through my mind, each more terrifying than the last.

When the car came to a stop, the back door flung open, exposing me to the cold night air. Shivering, I scrambled out. Outside the car, I found myself on a large, flat circle of barren grass surrounded by a dense forest. The moon cast an eerie glow over a massive, three-story mansion. Black as pitch and ominous as death, it loomed in the center of the clearing, its blackened windows and doors giving no hint of what lay within.

The black stone structure gave off a malevolent aura, as if waiting for its next victim. The air crackled with a sense of foreboding that turned my blood to ice. I looked at the Audi Gideon was in, parked next to the Cadillac, and then at Cassian standing in front of me.

"I'm the one you want inside. You don't need the vampire too," I told him.

"Take him out," Cassian barked at the driver of the Audi, ignoring me.

Gideon was pulled from the car, and my heart lurched at the sight of him. His eyes were half open, and he appeared to be paralyzed. Two vampires were holding up his limp body.

I glared at Cassian. "You bastard!" I wanted to rip his heart out.

Looking amused by my outburst, Cassian instructed the vamps holding Gideon, "Throw him in."

"No!" I cried as they dragged him to the front door. They opened it, and beyond the door was nothing but impenetrable darkness. With a brutal shove, they sent Gideon hurtling into the abysmal void.

"Now the human," Cassian said to the vampire next to me. In an instant, I was thrown over his shoulder again, and just as quickly, we were at the massive front door. He set me down, and my pulse spiked as terror shot through me like an electric current. My gut clenched, and a horrifying possibility snaked into my mind. Could the insidious mansion have already killed Gideon?

With that bleak thought, Cassian's goon shoved me through the door and into the darkness.

# Chapter 16

Inside the mansion, the pitch-black void vanished in a puff of smoke, giving way to the faint glow of a tarnished brass chandelier hanging above me. The dim light cast eerie shadows on the peeling damask wallpaper that covered the walls. Not far in front of me, double doors stood open, revealing an ornate foyer that bore the scars of time, with a dilapidated staircase leading to the upper levels of the mansion.

"Gideon? Where are you?" I called.

I caught movement from a dark corner, and then the sound of a heavy door slamming echoed behind me. I jumped and turned to find a solid wall where the door I'd been thrown through should have been.

"Your heart's racing." I heard Gideon say, his voice ragged. I felt him tear the cuffs from my wrists, and I pivoted toward him. At the sight of him alive, albeit frail and battered, relief crashed over me. The serum had wreaked havoc on his body. His face was gaunt, accentuating the hollows under his faded eyes and the sharpness of his cheekbones. His hands trembled, his veins snaking like rivers beneath his translucent flesh. He could barely hold himself up, but at least he was no longer paralyzed.

"I'm scared. I don't know how we're gonna get out of here. I'm also worried about you," I said, then rolled up my sleeve and offered him my forearm. "Drink."

"No, it won't speed up my healing because of the serum."

I dropped my hand. "Then what will?"

"Time. Soon the serum will be gone from my body, and my full strength will return. Then we'll find a way out of here," he said.

He surveyed our surroundings while I examined the tattoo. The number remained the same. The dark magic didn't seem to affect the house, nor did the house affect it, at least not yet. I prayed it was a good sign and reached for my cell phone, hoping against hope for a signal.

"Doubt it'll work in here," Gideon said.

I tried to turn it on without success. "Yeah, it's dead." I cursed and put the phone away. Fear tingled along my nerves. "It's so quiet. Do you think we're alone in here?"

"I don't know. We better be on our guard for any surprises."

"Yeah, and also wait until the serum has flushed out of your system before we venture deeper into the mansion to find a way out, like an open window or something." I moved to a patch of floor that seemed less rotten than the rest and sat down, motioning for him to join me. With an unsteady gait, he made his way over and sat down beside me.

"I don't know how long we'll be trapped here," he said, "and demons may roam this house. Without BFB, your soul won't be protected. So if we run into demons, close your eyes while I take care of them." I hated the idea of standing by and doing nothing as he fought, but he was right. The moment the BFB had left my system, my soul became a demon charcuterie board.

Gideon's complete recovery had taken about fifteen minutes, during which time his gaze remained locked on the wide-open double doors leading to the foyer. I didn't let my guard down either, afraid that someone—or something—sinister might attack us. Luckily, it hadn't happened.

As we walked toward the foyer, the worn floor groaned under our feet, and the temperature grew colder, the smell of mold heavy in the air. A layer of dust covered every surface, and cobwebs claimed every nook and cranny. The black-aged walls were lavished with oil paintings framed in gold, their grandeur contrasting with the decaying surroundings. Above them, the ceiling featured intricate crown molding, adding a touch of faded elegance.

The grand staircase, constructed of dark oak, had a carved banister, a testament to the mansion's former splendor. Footsteps echoed from one of the corridors to our left, setting me on edge. Four figures emerged from the shadows: a blonde vampire with a duffel bag slung over her shoulder, two armed men, and a girl about my age with red, puffy eyes.

"Are any of them demons?" I whispered.

"No," he answered in a low voice. "The two men are human, and the girl is a Daywalker."

"We've got some people here," one of the guys said.

"They don't seem to be carrying any weapons," the one next to him told him, and the blonde vamp glided toward us. Gideon's fangs snapped in a warning.

She stopped in front of us and raised a hand. "Okay, now let's just take it easy. No need for fangs or fighting." She offered a strained smile. "I'm a very trusting soul by nature, so I'll give you the benefit of the doubt and assume you mean us no harm." The corners of her mouth fell, and her lips tightened into a straight line. "But if you prove me wrong, you'll get to know my not-so-nice side."

"We don't want to hurt you," I said. "We're just trying to find a way out of this house, and I guess you are too. Has anyone seen any windows in here?" From the outside, the mansion seemed to have windows in all the expected places, but inside, I'd seen nothing but solid walls where openings should have been. The four shook their heads, and the vampire's eyes fell on my tattoo.

Faint lines formed on her forehead as her eyebrows shot up. "Dark magic. How'd you get the number on your palm? Did something in the house do that to you?"

"No, and we'll leave it at that," I told her.

The vampire studied me for a moment before nodding. "Very well, I'll respect your wish to not discuss it," she said, then introduced herself, "I'm Sheila, and the girl here is my daughter, Rya. We've been trapped in the Cursed Mansion for some time. Rya and her friend thought it'd impress their sorority sisters if they snuck in here and told their story afterward." Sheila gave her daughter a scowl. "When I heard of their foolishness, I entered the mansion to find them."

Rya's eyes glistened with tears. "Mom, I've already said I'm sorry like a million times. It was a stupid thing to do. I didn't think the rumors about the cursed house were true."

Gideon scanned the group with piercing eyes. "And where is the friend now?"

One of the men spoke. "Dead. Me and my buddy here, John," he jerked his head to the other guy, "were upstairs when we heard screams. We sprinted down a hallway and saw the Daywalker and her friend with a kid downstairs.

Something was off about him. He had this scary grin on his face, like a wolf sizing up its prey. His eyes, man, they were hollowed out, burning with some dark shit."

"Yeah, he was like the worst kid ever! A total psycho!" Rya said.

"Honey, tell them what happened before you met the boy," Sheila told her.

Rya nodded. "After Ella, my sorority sister, and I entered the mansion, this strange fatigue just hit us out of nowhere. As soon as we closed our eyes, we fell into a deep sleep. It was super weird. When we woke up, there was this kid standing by the stairs who looked about fifteen.

"We went up to him. He seemed okay at first, even friendly, said his name was Walter. Then, boom, he started laughing like a maniac and threw some liquid on Ella, saying she'd die soon." She sniffed and wiped away a tear. "While Ella was screaming at him, these two guys came down from upstairs, and my mom suddenly showed up." Rya's tears choked her, and Sheila came over to comfort her.

"Yeah, when we heard the screams, Keith and I rushed downstairs," the other guy said. "The creep saw us and ran off down that hallway over there." He pointed to the dimly lit hallway the four of them had come from. "We chased after him, but he disappeared. We all spent about an hour searching for that kid, but not even the vampire could find him.

"Then the girl's friend collapsed dead in the hallway. A few seconds later, her body vanished before our eyes." The guy turned to Keith. "Why the fuck did you bring me to this crazy Addams Family place, man? You said it was gonna be easy, that we were gonna waltz in here with our guns, snap a few pics to prove we were inside, and make two million bucks. Instead, we've been stuck here a whole day and up to our necks in supernatural shit with no way out."

"Jesus, John. I already said I was wrong," Keith told him. "It was a mistake to come here, okay? I thought it was gonna be a piece of cake. We'd run into some bloodsuckers, take them out with our guns, and get the hell out of here to collect the reward."

Breaking the short silence that followed, I asked, "Have any of you seen a vampire here named Logan?"

They shook their heads, and Sheila looked at Gideon and me. "What possessed you to enter the Cursed Mansion? The reward? How long have you been here?"

"We were forced in by the owner, not long ago," I replied.

"Not surprising, considering the stories I've heard of his cruelty," Sheila said. Her eyes swept the room before settling on Gideon. "Any idea what we're up against?"

"Not yet. Are there others in the mansion besides the boy?" Gideon asked.

"Keith and I arrived yesterday," John said. "We didn't see a soul until we reached the second floor and stepped into a hallway. At its end stood this hot chick, who looked human and seductive. She waved us over with a sexy smile, and we were more than happy to oblige.

"You know, naturally, we thought we were in for a good time, but after we followed her into a room, the bitch slammed the door in our faces and locked us in. We spent hours in a small fucking room. When the door finally opened, we left the room and heard screams, then saw the girls and the boy. The rest you already know."

After John finished, I looked around the foyer. Despite the many people who had entered the mansion over time, there were no remains to be seen, not a single bone. What had become of them? Had their bodies vanished like Rya's friend? Or were they still here somewhere? And who were the boy and the woman who had imprisoned the men?

"That woman sounds like she could be trouble," Sheila said.

A shadow of worry passed over John's face. "It's not just her we gotta watch out for." His gaze moved to Gideon and Sheila. "You two are full-blown bloodsuckers. Soon your hunger will kick in, and the humans here will start to look like a nice, juicy meal to you."

"I came prepared with blood reserves that I'm willing to share," Sheila said, looking at Gideon.

"Whoa, what the..." Keith's voice crackled with panic.

We all turned our heads to see what had alarmed him. A thick blanket of white smoke drifted low to the ground and down the grand staircase toward us.

"What is that?" Rya asked.

"Could be poisonous," Gideon warned. His eyes darted around the room until he said, "This way, quick." We followed him to a door leading into a wide hallway, went through, and he quickly closed it behind us then stuffed his jacket under the gap to seal it. My heart pounding, I inspected the long, empty hallway that surrounded us for other threats.

It curved out of sight, lined with battered doors. The running rug on the floor was faded and threadbare, its paisley pattern barely recognizable, the walls covered with ornately carved wooden panels. The wavering flames of candles in the sconces provided the only light.

"Holy shit, this place is freaking me out," Rya said as she started moving down the hallway.

Sheila hurried after her and grabbed her arm. "Stay by my side. This house is dangerous, and you don't have vampire strength yet."

Rya was about to argue when a nearby door in the hallway opened. An old woman stepped out, and we all shrank back except for Gideon. As if compelled by the woman, he followed her inside. I hurried to stop him, but before I could reach him, the door slammed shut and all efforts to open it failed.

I looked at Sheila. "What in the world was that? Was she some kind of witch?"

Sheila shrugged as she shook her head. "I don't know. I couldn't sense what she was."

Keith approached with his gun drawn. "Maybe this room has a connecting door to the one your vamp is in," he said before opening the door next to where I was standing. That turned out to be a big mistake. An enormous black mass, the size of an elephant, crawled out. My jaw dropped as I blinked at the giant spider.

Sweet Baby Jesus. Could this freaking house get any weirder?

"Oh no, this is not good," Sheila said. "My daughter is absolutely terrified of spiders." As the monstrous thing drew closer to us, Rya's face contorted in sheer horror. A piercing scream escaped her.

"That's one ugly motherfucker!" Keith exclaimed.

"Let's shoot the fucker!" John bellowed, looking at his friend, and both unleashed a hail of bullets. However, the creature seemed impervious, its hairy exoskeleton deflecting the onslaught without so much as a scratch.

"Stop shooting! It's not doing anything. Just run!" I shouted over the deafening gunfire. Eight terrifying jet-black eyes turned toward me, and a thick, milky rope of web shot in my direction, arcing through the air like a lasso. It snagged, cold and clammy, around my ankles, pinning them together and sending me crashing to the ground.

The spider used the extended strand of web that was coiled around my ankles to drag me across the floor toward the room it'd come from. I tried to free myself by clawing at the web, which didn't do any good as the damn thing was too strong, too tight. Sheila flashed to my side, but even her vampiric strength couldn't rip through the spider's web.

"We need a knife to cut the strands," I told Sheila.

"I left my weapon in the foyer," she said.

"I think I have a knife here somewhere..." John put down his gun and fumbled in his pockets as the spider reached its lair with me in tow.

The air in the room he'd come from was thick with the pungent smell of decay and mold, the light cast by a small, rusty chandelier. On the other side of the room stood an empty acrylic glass box, its door flanked by handles and gaping open. The spider crawled into the big box, pulling me inside. I thrashed and writhed, trying to tear at the web, my nerves exploding with fear and panic. A pocketknife in his hand, John rushed in with Keith.

"Throw me the knife!" My voice cracked with urgency as I looked at John. The creature hissed, and before John had a chance to act, the door of the glass box closed on its own. The spider's attention returned to me, and it spat more webs. Within seconds, a silken shroud enveloped me from neck to toe. Lying on my back, I couldn't move my arms and legs. When the creature stepped out of the box, the door closed behind it on its own and gunfire exploded. The spider skittered toward the entrance of the room, ignoring John and Keith as they fired at it.

As soon as the creature left the room, I was hit with an acrid smell that filled the box, burning my lungs and making me cough. I raised my head to inspect the area and spotted a hole in the floor. It was right by my feet, and a sticky substance was oozing out of it. My heart sank. Oh, God, this was bad. Really bad.

Sheila and Rya entered the room, and the vampire rushed to the box.

"Don't worry, I'll get you out," Sheila told me, but just as her hand landed on the handle of the box door, her daughter's voice stopped her.

"Mom, no! Don't go inside! It's too dangerous! That stuff in there could be lethal, just like the thing that killed Ella."

"Honey, Ella was human. I'm not, I'm stronger. I have to try to help her, or she'll die."

"Please, don't," Rya begged. "Look inside the container. The liquid is everywhere. It'll kill you."

John chimed in, "I'd listen to your daughter. That girl in there is coughing up a lung. The stuff is highly toxic. I wouldn't let it touch me." Though doubt flickered in Sheila's eyes, her hand remained on the handle.

"You step in that box, and it's your own funeral," Keith warned. Sheila looked at me, then at her daughter. She made her decision and removed her hand from the handle.

"I'm sorry," she told me. "They're right. Whatever's in there could kill me, and I have to think of my Rya. I can't leave her alone in this house." I gave her a weak nod of understanding.

My cough got worse as the substance continued to rise along with my panic. Time was running out, and I had no intention of finding out if fate or Oberon, or whatever it'd been, would grant me another miraculous resurrection. I began to crawl toward the door. Opening it while tied up seemed impossible. Still, it was the only chance I had. Just in time to watch me die again, Gideon appeared in the doorway. His face tightened with alarm when he saw me.

"Hey, how'd you get away from that old woman?" Keith asked him. Ignoring his question, Gideon reached the box in a flurry of motion.

Sheila grabbed his upper arm. "Don't open the door! You can't save your human. It's too late for her." He shook off her hand.

"She's right," I croaked. Each word was with an effort, my throat burning with pain. "You could die."

"You open the door and that thing will spill out and might kill us all," Sheila told him.

"The idiot's deaf to reason. Screw that, I'm outta here," Keith declared, bolting from the room. John, Sheila, and Rya followed suit.

Gideon pulled on the door handle, but the door wouldn't open. His muscles strained as he applied more force and tried again; however, nothing happened. Deep lines of worry etching his face, he slammed his shoulder against the door. Once, twice, three times he rammed into it, each impact sending tremors through the glass but failing to break it. Even forceful kicks proved useless. He scanned the room, seeming to look for something to smash the glass with. I kept dragging myself toward the box entrance, praying the door handle would open from the inside.

When I reached the door, my vision began to blur at the edges, each breath a painful dagger piercing my lungs. With the last of my strength, coughing hard, I maneuvered myself to position my feet over the door handle. I pushed down, but it wouldn't budge. The spider web around my body made every movement agonizingly slow, a cold sweat breaking out on my forehead. A second, more forceful attempt was also unsuccessful.

I refused to give up and let this house kill me. Anger raged through me, pumping adrenaline into my veins. With a burst of determination, I kicked my feet downward, hitting the door handle with full force. The blow sent a jolt of pain up my legs, and I winced, tears stinging my eyes. The pain was worth it, though, as this time, the handle clicked and the door swung open. The sudden rush of fresh air was invigorating. The substance in the box poured out, soaking Gideon's boots before he approached me.

"No, keep your distance," I rasped, my voice barely audible.

Ignoring my warning, he scooped me into his arms, and in a heartbeat, we were in the hallway outside the room. After Gideon laid me down, he managed to rip through the intricate webbing wrapped around me, peeling away the clinging silk. The searing pain that had consumed my lungs and throat began to ease, as did the relentless coughing. Free of the sticky strands, I fell into Gideon's embrace. A rush of relief coursed through me as he kissed the top of my head.

"Hey fang boy, I asked you a question earlier that went unanswered," Keith said. "How'd you get away from that old woman?"

I pulled away and looked at Gideon. "What happened to you? Were you under a spell?"

Gideon's brows furrowed. "I'm not sure. I know she wasn't a witch; I'd have sensed it if she was. Yet I was still under some kind of magic. She led me into a room, and her form shifted. Her features rearranged until she bore an uncanny resemblance to you."

"To me?" My voice leaped up.

He nodded. "Your double then tried to drive a silver knife into my heart. I had no choice but to fight her until..." His shoulder tensed, and he closed his eyes for a moment, as if the memory pained him. When he opened them, his voice shook a bit. "You..." He paused again before correcting himself. "She... she died in my arms. Then the spell's hold on me wore off, and I was able to leave the room. That's when I heard the commotion and saw you in the glass box."

"This is all so strange," I said, and something over my shoulder caught his attention. Glancing back, I noticed two oak T-back chairs lined up against the wall. "Those weren't there before." I got up to approach them.

"Look closely at the carved wood panel above the first chair," he told me, getting to his feet as well.

I examined the intricate carving. "Yeah, I see it. The letter *T* is carved into it."

"Yes," Gideon said. "Seems like someone has intentionally added it to the carving design. They're probably responsible for the chairs too."

My brows knitted. "But why would they—"

"Hey, check this out!" John shouted, bending down near a door not far from us. "There's something glowing on the floor over here!" He picked up a piece of jewelry, and when he came over to show it to us, I gasped, recognizing the necklace. It'd belonged to Mayet and contained the Tara Stone, which she'd used to track down Gifted humans.

"That's impossible," I breathed, then looked at Gideon. "How did Mayet's necklace get here?"

Gideon was about to respond when Sheila's scream tore through the air.

"No! Don't!" Her warning was directed at Keith, who had his hand on the door handle of a closed room.

"Why not?" he shot back. "That spider might come back, and we need to find a safe place to hide."

Before any of us could stop him and prevent another potential threat from coming out, he flung open the door. The color drained from his face as his gaze fell on the nightmarish sight that had emerged—a grotesque creature with the head and torso of a wolf, but lobster claws for hands and goat-like legs.

If I thought I'd seen true horror before, I'd just been proven wrong.

# Chapter 17

"Oh my God! What is that thing?" Rya screamed.

"It's th-th-the m-m-monster from my nightmares," Keith stammered. John lunged forward and yanked his friend away from the door. The creature bared its sharp teeth at them, then unleashed a roar that shook the floor. As they both backed away, John stumbled on his feet and fell. The necklace slipped from his grasp and flew through the air, landing several feet away.

The creature, fast and strong, pounced on its prey and tore into John and Keith with savage precision. Bones shattered with sickening snaps, each crack echoing through the hallway like a morbid symphony. Their blood splattered the walls and floor. They were dead before we could do anything to help them.

"Holy shit! Holy shit! Holy shit!" Rya shouted hysterically. The monster's head jerked toward her, strings of blood dripping from its teeth. Sheila lunged at the beast with a primal cry, desperate to protect her daughter. As Gideon joined the attack, leaping at it from the side, I scanned the room for a gun or improvised weapon. My eyes landed on the wooden chairs. I sprinted over, grabbed one by the legs, and turned just as a bone-chilling wail rent the air.

"No! Mom!" Rya yelled as the beast ripped Sheila's head off and crushed it with its claws. I rushed to Rya and tried to stop her from running to her mother's mutilated body, but she tore herself from my grip. Gideon's attempt to hold her back also failed; the creature tossed him aside like a rag doll, and he crashed into the wall. The monster's jaws wrapped around Rya's waist, lifting her up and slamming her to the ground with enough force to pulverize bone.

Gideon got back to his feet and jumped onto the creature's back. He kicked and punched at its sides, but the creature continued its unyielding attack on Rya, tearing at her skin and clothing. Blood spurted from her body like a sprinkler.

"Hey, you! Over here!" I bellowed at the beast, trying to draw its attention away from Rya. But the thing didn't even spare me a glance, consumed by its brutal assault. I hurled the chairs at it. The wood shattered against its hulking frame, yet the beast barely missed a beat in its relentless assault on Rya. Her screams had faded to wet, choking gurgles as her life rapidly ebbed away.

"She's dead! There's nothing more you can do for her! Run or it'll come for you next!" Gideon roared before the creature threw him back against the wall with a resounding thud. My eyes found John's discarded gun lying amid the carnage.

"No. I have a plan," I shouted to Gideon. Then I maneuvered my way through the mutilated bodies, grabbed the gun, and unleashed a barrage of bullets into the beast's back. The creature turned and looked at me. *About damn time!* I finally had its attention. Fury burned in its gaze, and I ceased my fire. Its eyes narrowed as it stalked toward me.

I backed away slowly, leading it into the room with the glass box. Gideon followed the beast. The air was thick with fumes from the sticky substance that coated the floor. Coughing, I moved to the open door of the glass box and stopped. The creature crept closer, ready to rip into my flesh, and I could have sworn I saw a smile on its face.

"Kick its back—hard," I told Gideon, who was standing behind the beast.

"Watch out," he warned before his powerful kick propelled the creature forward. I dove to the side just in time as the beast hurtled past me and into the glass box. I then quickly closed the door. The creature stood up and slammed its claws against the walls in a frenzy, roaring.

We fled the room and closed the door behind us. Back in the hallway, I let out a shaky breath. As the adrenaline drained from my system, I noticed that everything had disappeared—all the blood, the bodies. Only the broken chairs remained scattered about.

"Where did it all go?" I asked.

"The Tara necklace, it's still here." There was a note of surprise in Gideon's voice. It was lying on the floor down the hallway, about thirty-five feet from us. We stepped to it, and something caught my eye. A letter *T* was etched into one of the doors to our left.

I nudged Gideon and pointed. "Look at that."

He pocketed the necklace and examined the mark. "It seems like someone is beckoning us inside."

I eyed the door warily. "Could be an axe murderer or something."

"Yeah, probably," he said, and his eyes went over my shoulder. "But I say we take our chances with whoever's behind that door over the alternative."

I was about to ask what alternative, but when I turned around, I had my answer. The nightmarish wolfcrab, for lack of a better word, was standing outside the room we'd put him in, snarling at us.

Oh, crap!

"Yep, inside the room it is," I said, praying that this creepy house wouldn't conjure up something more terrifying than a wolfcrab or a giant spider. The beast charged down the hallway at an alarming speed when Gideon opened the marked door. We dove in before he slammed it behind us.

As he pressed his weight against the door, bracing himself for the inevitable impact, I prepared myself for an ambush from inside the room. But to our surprise, neither the expected impact nor the ambush occurred. I glanced around the room, looking for something to barricade the door. The windowless room was warmer and less gloomy, yet still bore the marks of neglect and decay.

Faded floral wallpaper peeled away in patches, revealing cracked plaster beneath. Dusty Victorian furniture, including a threadbare love seat and a pair of chairs, sat faded and stained in the center. The wooden floor was scratched and scarred, warped by the weight of countless years, and from the ceiling, an old Victorian pendant gave off a pale, flickering light. I was about to walk over to a chair and use it as a block when a cheerful voice stopped me.

"Yes! You've seen the *T*'s."

Gideon flashed his fangs at a girl who approached us from a dark corner. She was tall, maybe a year or two older than me. Her black sweater clung to her slender frame, and faded jeans disappeared into boots. Her chestnut hair fell over her shoulder in a thick braid. Her eyes were a vivid emerald, and her white skin didn't hint at anything vampiric.

"Come any closer, witch, and you'll wish you hadn't," Gideon warned.

She halted, raising her hands defensively. "Whoa, take it easy, tough guy. I'm not a threat, okay? You're safe here. The room is warded. Don't worry, nothing can get in." Her eyes dropped to Gideon's jeans pocket, and she seemed relieved. "Oh, good, you have the Tara Stone necklace with you. I can sense it."

"Was it you who brought it into the house?" Gideon asked, but she was distracted by my tattoo.

Her mouth opened as her eyes rounded. "Dark magic... How in the world—"

"The tattoo is none of your business," Gideon said, his tone harsh.

She exhaled, a hint of frustration evident. "Still don't trust me, huh?"

"And why the hell should we?" I asked. "We have no idea who you are or how you got here."

"Fair enough," she said. "I'm gonna tell you everything you need to know about me, so you'll see that I'm not a threat to you." She went to settle into a faded chair, then motioned us to the love seat across from her. After exchanging glances, Gideon and I walked over and sat down, still on guard.

"Okay, I'll start with my name. I'm Taissa."

"So those mysterious *T*'s in the hallway and on the door were the first letter of your name?" I asked.

"Yes, I was trying to get your attention to come into the room," she answered.

"Why not just open the door and talk to us?" I said.

"Did a spell trap you in here?" Gideon asked.

"Look, I know you want answers," she said. "I get that, but first, let me tell you why I entered the mansion and how I ended up in this room. Once you understand the whole story, I promise I'll answer any questions you have."

I looked at Gideon. He nodded, and I told her, "All right, we're listening."

She smiled and began, "When I was a kid, I used to hear all these crazy stories about this spooky black house out on the outskirts of town. One day, I asked my parents if the rumors about the mansion were true, fully expecting them to laugh it off as just another tall tale. They didn't, though.

"They confirmed that some of the stories were true and gave me my ancestor Mildred's journal. Mildred was close friends with a human woman named Mrs. Arden, who served as a housekeeper at the mansion, long before it became the infamous, eerie structure it is today. Mrs. Arden knew about the existence of the Hidden World, and that the owner was a vampire."

"Wasn't she afraid to work for a ruthless vampire?" I asked.

"Sure, a little, but Cassian had never hurt his mortal staff before, and she needed the money. Plus, let's not forget, she had Mildred for a friend, a total kickass illusionist," she replied, then continued the story, "Shortly after Mrs. Arden began working at the mansion, one of the young maids, Anna, got knocked up. Three months later, she gave birth to a healthy baby. And that was when the shit hit the fan."

I frowned. "Did you say three months?"

Taissa nodded. "Yep, this was no ordinary pregnancy. The baby's father was a demon, and the mother was a human."

"A demon-human hybrid? That's not possible," Gideon said. "Demons cannot father children with humans."

Her lips twitched into a smirk. "Oh, but they can. However, it's like finding a four-leaf clover in a field of dandelions—very rare but not entirely impossible." Gideon's expression remained skeptical, and she added, "I know it's hard to believe, but hybrids are real. I'm not making this up."

I looked at Taissa, puzzled. "Say it's true, why didn't the demon suck Anna's soul? Why did he let her live after sleeping with her? Aren't all demons pure evil?"

"Demons have sexual needs too. Anna was just lucky to meet a horny demon instead of a hungry one. Anyway, when Mrs. Arden told Mildred about the pregnant maid, she was as skeptical as you are," she turned her gaze to Gideon, "but after Mildred went to the mansion and put her hands on the maid's belly, she could sense through her magic that the fetus was a supernatural hybrid, part human, part demon.

"She consulted her magic books, hoping to find something about hybrids, but she came up with zilch. The next time she went to the mansion, it was to help deliver the baby. Though she was only three months pregnant, Anna was already in labor. Much to everyone's surprise, a perfectly healthy human baby boy emerged. There was no trace of anything demonic in him, despite what Mildred had sensed when the boy was in the womb.

"Mrs. Arden and Anna were relieved, and the mother named her baby Walter. However, Mildred had a nagging feeling that something wasn't right. She decided to keep her concerns to herself, not wanting to worry the young mother and Mrs. Arden. After that day, Mildred sought the opinions of five knowledgeable witches about the unusual pregnancy, but none believed a demon could've knocked up a human.

"Fast forward fifteen years, Mildred met a witch named Paul. He believed such a thing was possible because he'd had a similar experience. His adopted human daughter got mixed up with the wrong crowd and got pregnant by a demon. Like Anna, her baby was born after only three months and was fully human. At first, everything seemed normal with the baby girl, but when she hit eleven, things took a bad turn. She began to slowly change in appearance and behavior until she became a full-on demon.

"Paul freaked out and worried about everyone's safety. He and his daughter decided to lock the demon kid up and feed her only the souls of bad people. This messed-up routine continued until they received a visit from a vamp who called himself Edward Young. He'd heard about the hybrid kid and told them he ran a secret facility dedicated to helping children like her.

"He explained that the half-human, half-demon hybrids were born fully human. However, they also carried demon DNA. The demon DNA is undetectable, even to supernatural beings, and it behaves like the UV virus, remaining dormant until triggered. But unlike the virus, the demon DNA doesn't kill the hybrid when it's activated.

"Instead, it becomes sentient, develops a mind of its own, and gradually takes control of the hybrid's mind and body, transforming them into a demon. After that, there is no trace of humanity left in them, only darkness."

"What flips the switch on the demon DNA?" I asked, resting my elbow on the love seat's arm.

"Discovering they have demon DNA," she answered. "As long as they're unaware of it, thinking they're normal humans, their human side stays in charge. However, if they learn the truth, accidentally or not, it's game over. This is what happened to Paul's grandkid. She found out she was a half-breed, and it awakened her demon side.

"After hearing Paul's story, Mildred returned to the mansion to warn Anna never to tell Walter that his father was a demon. But, plot twist, her kid overheard the whole conversation, which woke his demon DNA. A few weeks later, Mrs. Arden asked for Mildred's help. Walter had become a demon and had eaten the souls of three maids.

"Mildred went back to the mansion, and to protect the people there, she locked Walter in a room on the second floor. What she didn't know was that as a hybrid, he had a special ability. The little devil could siphon the powers of others. Just as she turned to leave the room, she felt her own magic begin to fade, sucked right out of her. She grew weak and collapsed to the floor.

"As she struggled to reach the doorknob, she realized that Walter, empowered by her magic, was going to be one hell of a demon, a nightmare on steroids. Unwilling to let him become an unstoppable force of darkness, she mustered every ounce of her remaining magic and cast a kick-ass spell that sealed them both in that room. No one could get in or out.

"He was steaming mad. After he finished taking all of her powers, he tried to break her spell, but the little shithead failed and Mildred refused to help him, which made him even angrier. He tortured her by slowly eating her soul, enjoying her screams. Mrs. Arden, who was on the other side of the door, heard her friend's suffering and begged him to stop, but he didn't give a shit and killed Mildred.

"When Mildred's husband came looking for her, Mrs. Arden tried to get him to leave to save his life. However, he was dead set on finding his missing wife, and the demon kid ate his soul right through the door, leaving their children orphaned. Afraid the situation with Walter would get worse, Mrs. Arden contacted Mildred's sister Grace. Unfortunately, bad weather screwed up her arrival time, causing a two-week delay.

"By the time she made it to the mansion, the souls of everyone in the house had been eaten—all but Mrs. Arden. The housekeeper wasted no time in filling her in on the unholy mess and warning her about how powerful

Walter had become. Even behind a door, he could sense and eat souls anywhere in the mansion. No barrier could stop him from feeding on his victims, unlike an ordinary demon."

"He didn't kill the housekeeper, why?" I asked.

"After he offed everyone, he needed someone to be his personal food delivery service and his link to the outside world," she replied. "Mrs. Arden did whatever he asked just to live another day. Grace was also safe from Walter, despite her inability to undo the spell that locked him in the room. He kept her around because he'd gained new powers and needed a tutor. As a witch, she was just the person to help him navigate the new magical waters he found himself in.

"The housekeeper and Mildred's sister found themselves confined to the mansion. Both played puppets to Walter's whims in order to stay alive. Mrs. Arden lured poor people into the lion's den to satisfy his hunger while Grace taught him witchcraft through the door. Walter was an eager student, and Mildred's magic flourished in his demon body, making him a very powerful witch after three years of studying with Grace.

"However, he felt that his powers were being wasted as he was stuck in his room. He was frustrated that he couldn't use them to do more interesting things, like take over the world. So he thought, hey, why not turn this whole mansion into his private little kingdom, where he'd rule as king from his room. Mrs. Arden would bring more people into the mansion, and they would be at his mercy.

"He could play God, having total control over his victims, deciding whether to kill them or keep them alive just for his twisted pleasure. He also wanted to have eyes in every corner of his domain to see the raw fear on his victims' faces as they tried to escape his terror. So, he decided to do something drastic: use his powers to fuse his soul into the walls and floors of the mansion.

"After he did that, the whole place turned black. The walls, the floors, the doors, the ceilings—everything was him now. From that day on, no one who entered the mansion could leave. He gets his kicks playing with his victims before they die, boredom and sadism fueling his sick games. A powerful hybrid, he can peer into his victims' minds and uncover their darkest fears and nightmares, then bring those terrifying visions to life to kill them.

"Witches get special treatment from him 'cause he has a real hatred for us, thanks to the grudge he still holds against Mildred for what she did to him. Any witch who crosses the threshold of his mansion is burned alive on the spot."

When she stopped speaking, I leaned back in my seat and let the weight of her words sink in. I was surprised to learn the mystery that had shrouded the Cursed Mansion for years had all begun because of a mere teenager.

Now the question was, how could we escape him when so many before us had failed?

# Chapter 18

"Why didn't the housekeeper make a break for it when the demon let her out to get him food? And what about the witch? Did she try to escape?" Gideon asked Taissa.

She shook her head. "When Grace entered the mansion, Walter ate some of her soul to weaken her before she could even think of casting a spell against him. He also wanted to steal her magic, but there was a limit to how much power he could siphon. Anyway, since her soul was not whole, Grace was unable to harness enough magical energy to cast the complex spells she needed to defend herself and Mrs. Arden from him, or to escape.

"After making sure Grace wouldn't be a problem, he made her teach him two spells that sealed her and the housekeeper's fate. The first was to alert him if they ever tried to escape the mansion. The second was to force Mrs. Arden to return whenever she went out to get food. It also prevented her from seeking help of any kind."

"What happened to them in the end?" I asked.

"After three relentless years under the demon's reign of terror, they reached their breaking point and hatched a plan to get rid of him. One fateful night, Mrs. Arden ended a man's life while Walter fed on his soul. They figured if they could keep Walter from consuming the man's entire soul, he'd die like any other demon.

"But that shit didn't die 'cause he was no ordinary soul sucker. He survived their murder attempt and went into full vengeance mode. In his rage, he killed them both without considering the consequences, like who would care for and guide him now that they were gone."

"You seem to know an awful lot about the mansion's history after Mildred's death. Last time I checked, witches can't keep journals from beyond the grave." Gideon's cold tone conveyed suspicion.

"Before I stepped inside the mansion, all I knew about it came from Mildred's journal, which my parents had given me. The pages detailed her experiences within the mansion up until the day she disappeared," Taissa said. Then she reached into a big bag beside her chair and pulled out an old leather-bound book. "This is Grace's journal, written during her time here following Mildred's death. It wasn't just a personal chronicle. Unmarried and childless, she created it as an informative guide for her sister's descendants in case they ever found themselves in this hellhole, too.

"With what little magic she could muster, she wove a simple spell to ensure that if Mildred's bloodline ever found themselves in this mansion, they would come into possession of her journal. That's why the book literally popped into my hand when I entered the house. So, to answer your question, I know everything that happened here after Mildred's death because I've read Grace's journal. Twice."

I looked at her. "How'd you end up in the mansion? Did someone drag you here against your will? And how are you still breathing? I mean, you're a witch, and Walter is all about roasting your kind the moment they set foot here."

"Before her disappearance, Mildred wrote in her journal that she was going to the mansion to help the housekeeper deal with Walter, who had turned into a demon. After reading it, I suspected Walter had murdered Mildred and everyone who's ever gone into the mansion. Determined to stop him from hurting more people, I entered the mansion willingly. When I told my parents I planned to get inside the Cursed Mansion as soon as I mastered my magic, they tried to talk me out of it. Eventually, though, they came to terms with the fact that their rebellious daughter wasn't going to budge.

"Before I left for the Magic Academy, they gave me an ultimatum: either I agree to never set foot in the Cursed Mansion, or they'd kick me out of their lives. That was the last time I spoke to them. I graduated six years later, but I wasn't in a hurry to explore the Cursed Mansion. I knew that relying on my magic alone wouldn't be enough to survive in the house. Even powerful witches could be heard screaming after entering the place.

"So, I asked one of my professors at the Magic Academy for advice, and she said there might be something that could keep me safe in the mansion—the Tara Stone. I was like, seriously? Finding it seemed about as likely as sprouting wings and flying to the moon. My hope of stopping Walter crashed. Then one day, while browsing in a magic shop, I overheard something interesting.

"Two witches were gossiping about a pearl necklace rumored to contain a piece of the Tara Stone. According to them, it'd been brought all the way from Ice Prison and was going to be auctioned off in New York City. Though skeptical, I hopped on a plane to the Big Apple and found out they were right. Some witch friends helped me track down the necklace and steal it before it was sent to the auction house." A loud thud outside the door stopped her, and I glanced over in alarm. Was it the wolfcrab?

"Are we really safe in this room?" I asked her.

"Walter can't get to us here. I used the necklace to ward the room against him and his magic. The Tara Stone enhances the powers of witches. Without it, I would've been toast the second I stepped into the mansion," she said.

"A giant spider and a strange combination of wolf and crab attacked us. Where did they come from? Did Walter create them?" I asked.

Taissa grimaced. "A giant spider? Yikes. Yeah, that was Walter's doing all right. The creatures weren't illusions, though. They were real. Remember what I told you? He can get inside his victims' heads and dig up their worst fears or messed-up stuff from their past and bring it to life."

The pieces began to fall into place. Before Keith died, he'd identified the wolfcrab as the creature from his nightmares. Rya's arachnophobia was probably why a giant spider had appeared, and my nightmare experience with Brad must have been the reason I was dragged into a glass box. One of the horrible tests Brad, the human who had worked for Mayet, had put me and several other girls through involved being in a glass container filled with water while our hands and legs were tied up.

"We stumbled upon the Tara Stone necklace outside the door, in the hallway. How'd it wind up there?" Gideon asked Taissa.

"I had it with me when I entered the mansion two days ago. As I hit the foyer, an illusion of a kid climbed down the grand staircase. The hate in his eyes screamed Walter. I mean, who else despises witches like that?"

"Wait a minute," I interrupted. "You're saying he was an illusion, right?" She nodded and I continued, "But shouldn't you, as a witch, be immune to illusion magic? How'd he manage to make you see him, to see his illusion?"

"He's a demon, too," she explained, "so his magic doesn't work like other witches'. Because of that, he could mess with my head without breaking a sweat. And that's exactly what he did. After telling me his name and how much he hated witches, the little devil tried to use his magic to paralyze my body and lift me off the ground. He wanted me to feel completely powerless against him before roasting me alive with one of his spells. Thanks to the necklace, his efforts went up in smoke, and it drove him crazy that he was unable to control or kill me.

"Then he fell silent, and I felt this intense pressure in my mind. I couldn't block him out even with the necklace. He was on a hunt for my deepest fear, and he found it—rats." She winced in disgust. "I've been terrified of them since I was little. He used his magic to create a river of rats that flowed into the foyer. Even though I knew they couldn't hurt me because of the necklace, I was overcome with terror. I bolted into a nearby hallway with those repulsive things hot on my heels.

"As I was running down the hallway with my bag, I tripped and hit the floor. The necklace slipped from my grasp and skittered out of reach. There was no time to retrieve it. The rats were closing in fast, and without the necklace, they could make a meal of me. Searching for a safe spot in one of the rooms in the hallway was pointless as the shithead could get to me anywhere in the house. My only chance of survival was to cast a solid ward against his magic.

"The boost to my powers I'd received from the Tara Stone began to wane without the necklace. I had to act fast. Using the last of my enhanced magic, I cast a powerful ward on the first room I got in, which saved my ass. Walter has no access to this room, even though every wall in the mansion is connected to his soul. There is just one small problem with the ward, though.

"In my haste to seal the room against outside threats, I messed up the words for the warding spell. As a result, the door can only be opened from the outside. So, anything conjured by Walter's magic can swing it open. But at least his creatures can't step through." She sighed. "As you can imagine, I was in a bit of a pickle until you came. I couldn't open the door or fix the ward because it was too powerful. I need the necklace to do that."

"And what if we hadn't come with the necklace?" Gideon asked, his tone angry. "We'd be trapped in here too."

"I heard screams through the door," she replied evenly. "I assumed lives were in danger, so I sent you the *T*'s. Or would you rather be truly dead, vampire?"

"Speaking of *T*'s, I think it would've been nicer to get a message that actually contained something more substantial than a single, cryptic letter." Gideon's voice was gruff.

"I did try to send a more detailed message, but Walter's magic wouldn't let me. All I could manage to create outside the room were the chairs and the *T*'s. Figured it was better than nothing," she said defenselessly.

"All right, let's forget about that," I cut in. "What matters now is that we're here, and we have the necklace, which..." I squinted in confusion as I noticed two partial walls flanking a toilet seat in a dark corner. It looked out of place.

Taissa followed my gaze and explained, "Wasn't sure how long I'd be stuck in here, so I quickly conjured a working makeshift toilet before my enhanced powers ran out."

"Why did you need enhanced powers for that?" I asked.

"Creating such objects with magic takes a lot of energy and skill, and even if you have all that, it doesn't always work. The enhanced powers made it much easier for me."

A thought crossed my mind. "You mentioned a limit to Walter's power absorption. Is it possible that over time this limit has been lifted, and now he's able to siphon off your powers through the door?"

"No, because according to Grace's journal, he can only take the powers of one person, no matter how much time has passed," she replied.

Gideon looked at Taissa. "Grace and the housekeeper died a long time ago. Who has been feeding the demon since then?"

"I don't know," Taissa admitted. "My guess is that he's been feeding on the souls of the many people who have entered the mansion over the years. I can only hope we don't end up like them." She put Grace's journal back in her overstuffed bag. I caught a glimpse of the supplies she had packed: canned food, bottled water, and a handgun. She closed her bag, then took a pack of cigarettes and a lighter from her jeans pocket.

"Sorry, this whole situation has me on edge, and when I'm stressed, I gotta have a smoke." She flashed us an apologetic look before she lit a cigarette.

As she took a long drag on her cigarette, Gideon said, "We need to start planning our escape."

"Yeah, but how?" I asked. "The demon controls everything in the mansion. The house doesn't even have a front door to escape through, or windows."

"That's why we have to unlock the demon's door and kill him. It's our only way out of here," he said, then turned to Taissa. "With the Tara Stone, do you think you could break your ancestor's spell?"

"Yes," she answered and blew a stream of smoke into the air. "Here's what we're gonna do. I'll put a spell on the gun I brought, fix the ward, then take the gun and necklace and go upstairs to kill Walter while you stay in here."

"Why does the gun need to be spelled?" I asked.

"If what she says is true, and the demon has magic powers, he'll use them to deflect normal bullets away from him and his heart, making it difficult to kill him," Gideon explained. His gaze returned to Taissa with a stern expression. "We're coming with you. I don't trust you, so the necklace stays with us the whole time."

Taissa drew another lungful of smoke from her cigarette and let it trickle through her nostrils. "It's best if I wear the necklace this time, so I don't lose it again. Plus, a witch has to touch the stone to use its power. That's why it was useless to Walter when it was in the hallway.

"As for you coming with me, I'm not strong enough to protect two more people from Walter's magic, even with the stone." She dropped the cigarette on the floor and ground it with her heel, then put the cigarette pack and lighter in her bag before turning to Gideon. "Listen, I know we just met, but I'm still asking you to trust me. Hybrids do exist, and there is one locked up on the second floor.

"He's a real threat, using magic to scare and slaughter his victims. You're a vamp, she's a human. Neither of you stands a chance against him 'cause it takes a witch with the Tara Stone to take him down. Like it or not, right now I'm your only chance to get out of this shithole."

"She's got a point," I told Gideon. "We're not exactly swimming in options here. I wouldn't be surprised if that giant spider or the wolfcrab combo is still out there, just waiting for us."

Gideon was silent as he seemed to weigh our alternatives.

"How about this?" Taissa broke the silence. "I'll create a know-it-all mirror."

I raised an eyebrow. "A know-it-all mirror? What's that?"

Gideon explained, "It's a magical mirror that will allow us to see the witch in real time once she leaves the room."

"You won't be kept in the dark. You'll see and hear everything I do," she said. This seemed to sway Gideon. He fished the necklace from his pocket.

Before giving it to Taissa, he warned, "Betray us, and I will kill you."

"I won't," she promised.

She stood and with the necklace in her hand, she muttered incantations under her breath. A moment later, a large, full-length standing mirror popped into existence in the middle of the room.

"Wow," I breathed as I examined it.

"The ward's fixed. You're protected by strong magic in this room," she said.

"Think you can overcome your fear of the rats this time?" Gideon asked her.

"They scare the shit out of me, but yeah, I'll manage," she replied.

After she left, I looked at Gideon. "If she dies, we're up the creek without a paddle." His expression was stone cold as he kept his gaze fixed on the mirror.

"Let's hope she makes it," he said.

# Chapter 19

I fidgeted with my hands as we watched Taissa through the mirror. It showed her walking down the hallway outside the room and then entering the dilapidated foyer. She glanced around the empty room, her chest rising and falling rapidly. She stopped at the foot of the grand staircase, her face crinkled in anger at something unseen.

"You worthless demon. Today is your lucky day. I'm going to set you free, but don't celebrate yet. Because right after, I'm gonna kill you. Your reign of terror ends tonight," she said, clearly addressing the illusory Walter.

"Can you see him?" I asked Gideon.

He shook his head. "Walter's magic doesn't affect us because of the ward."

A sneer curled Taissa's upper lip. "What's so funny, demon?" Fear crept into her face as she looked to her right. She closed her eyes, took a deep breath, and when she reopened them, she appeared more composed. "Your rats don't scare me anymore, you little freak." She reached up to touch the necklace. "You see this? It protects me from them."

She climbed the stairs and reached the second floor, then walked down a decrepit hallway with Victorian wallpaper in a state of disintegration. Coming to a stop in front of a door on the right, she pointed her gun at it and chanted some words, the pearls around her neck glowing. When she finished the spell, a man appeared down the hallway.

"Oh, really?" he said as if Taissa had told him something. A storm of rage distorted his pale face as he focused on her. "You finally crawled out of your room? No more hiding behind your illusory tricks? You stupid asshole, you've just made a huge mistake by revealing this form of yours isn't an illusion—because now I can kill you!"

He reached Taissa in a second and knocked her down. Caught off guard, Taissa froze, unable to react or defend herself. His eyes turned silver, and fangs sprouted from his gums. Horrified, I watched as the vampire snapped Taissa's neck. Then shock hit me when I recognized him.

"Oh my God, it's Logan."

"Yes, looks like we found our Newborn, and he was just being played by the demon," Gideon said.

"I'm free. I'm free now! You don't control me anymore!" Logan shouted.

The door to the room Taissa had unsealed opened, and a teenage boy with fair skin and a mop of curly brown hair stepped out. His face and body were that of a fifteen-year-old, and his clothes were straight out of the early twentieth century. Despite being locked in a room for decades, they were in immaculate condition, leading me to believe they had been preserved by magical means.

Logan's gaze shifted to the demon, and his eyebrows drew together in utter bewilderment. "What the hell is going on? I-I-I just killed you... Who are you? The demon's identical twin?"

"Are you sure it was me you killed?" Walter asked. "Do you even know how to kill creatures of my nature? Such a task requires a gun, you imbecile. Oh, gracious Lord, sometimes it amazes me how effortlessly one can deceive novice vampires. Your senses are as feeble as those of humans. You wonder who I am? Not an illusion, I can assure you. I'm Walter." A cruel smile curled his lips. There was a brief silence before the vampire's face lit up with realization. Logan stared at Taissa's lifeless body for a moment then slowly shook his head.

"No, what have I done?" He fell to his knees next to Taissa. "Oh, God, I'm sorry, I'm so sorry. The illusion spell... I thought you were him in the flesh. That's what he told me. I never meant to..." His words dissolved into sobs as crimson tears streamed down his cheeks. He buried his face in his hands.

Walter rolled his eyes at Logan's agony, and then something caught his attention. He walked over to Taissa's body and took off her necklace. The demon examined it.

"Fascinating, the necklace holds great power. The witch spoke the truth," he murmured to himself. Logan's focus went back to Walter, his eyes blazing with hate as he sprang to his feet. He lunged at him, but the demon flicked his wrist, sending Logan flying. He hit the floor with a heavy thud then tried to get up but couldn't. Magic had pinned him to the floorboard.

"She wasn't lying; the demon does have magic powers," Gideon said in astonishment.

"Yeah… and we're royally screwed; the only person who could've helped us kill him is dead," I said. *Soon we will be too*, I thought.

Walter's eyes sparkled as he smiled. "What say you, Logan? Shall I bring an end to your immortal being in this very moment?"

"Let me go, you psycho!" Logan screamed.

Walter continued talking, ignoring his rage. "I have not yet determined if you shall prove useful to me in the days to come. However, I'm in a cheerful disposition, so I'll let you live for the time being."

As a string of curses flew out of Logan's mouth, the demon moved to the wall near him. He pressed a hand against it and grinned.

"At last, our shackles have been removed. Freedom is ours now. And I can step out into the open air," he said to the wall. Dropping his hand, he moved back to where Taissa's body was and stared down.

"Whoa, it's like he's looking right at us. Can he see us?" I asked.

"No, but he can sense the witch's spell. He knows we're watching him," Gideon replied.

Walter grinned as he spoke to us. "Hello and welcome to my home. As I reckon you already know, I'm your gracious host. I must say it is not very nice of you to hide in that warded room. Makes it a hassle for me to have fun and kill you. I should rightfully be discontented, but at the moment, I'm in high spirits and feeling generous. I'm willing to offer you a quick death. No pain.

"However, should you continue cowering in that room, my pleasant demeanor and patience will dissolve. I'll be very upset, and you'll suffer the full weight of my wrath. As a punishment, I'll lock you in the warded room with a spell.

"And when you, vampire, eventually grow famished, you'll slay the hapless mortal, who will have nowhere to run. Then, as the sands of time trickle away, starvation will take its agonizing toll on you, and you shall meet your own gruesome demise." The demon put the necklace in his vest pocket. "You have five minutes to decide your fate. In the meantime, I shall be waiting outside your room for your decision. Choose wisely."

He turned and walked away, leaving Logan twisting and screaming. Taissa's spell didn't follow the demon, and we watched his back as he walked down the hallway toward the grand stairs. Then with a snap of his fingers, the mirror became a regular one.

"Damn it!" I said, running my hands through my hair.

Gideon rushed to Taissa's bag and rifled through it frantically until he found a silver dagger. Relief washed over his features. He bent down and slipped the weapon into his ankle holster.

"What are you doing? You know a silver dagger won't do the job. He's a demon. Don't we need Taissa's gun to kill him?"

"It's not for the demon, it's for me. If we can't find a way out of here, the hunger will inevitably drive me to the edge. The moment I become a threat to you, this knife will go straight into my heart." His voice was solemn.

I shook my head. "No, that's not an option. You're gonna feed on my blood so you don't get all fangy and out of control."

"I can't drink your blood every day if you don't eat properly, and there isn't much food in the witch's bag. Without enough vitamins and minerals in your body, your blood won't nourish me. And as a result, my saliva won't be able to heal you. You'll quickly become anemic, and after a day or two, you'll die," he said.

Desperation clawed at my chest as I slumped into the love seat with a heavy sigh. What the hell were we going to do?

Gideon took a seat beside me and stroked my cheek. "It's going to be okay."

"How? We can't kill him, and we're trapped here." Frustration leaked from my voice.

Our situation seemed hopeless, and he knew it too. But somehow, he managed to remain optimistic.

"We'll get through this," he said.

The five minutes Walter had given us were up, and we heard his voice through the closed door.

"I reckon you have made your decision. Very well, from this moment, my magic will not allow you to enter the hallway outside of your room. I

shall take pleasure in the anguished cries of the mortal as she meets her end."
Gideon looked at the door and glared, his eyes glowing gold. Yeah, I wanted
to kill the bastard too.

In the hours that followed, Gideon paced the room like a caged animal,
lost in his thoughts. I, too, racked my brain for an escape plan, but my mind
drew a blank, and despair began to set in. I was scared, tired, hungry. Gideon
must have heard my stomach because he grabbed a bottle of water and food
from Taissa's bag and went to sit beside me on the love seat.

Once the food was down the hatch, my eyelids played the heavy game.
Our lives were hanging by a thread. Sleep was the last thing I needed to do,
but no matter how hard I fought the exhaustion, I quickly lost the battle.

# Chapter 20

For a few days, Walter had been outside the door, letting us know of his presence with his taunts. As time ticked away, we kept looking for ways to free ourselves, but so far we had come up with nothing. Rationing the supplies from Taissa's bag, I survived on limited food and water. Gideon, on the other hand, had been fasting and was growing weaker by the day.

He refused to take even a sip of my blood for fear of losing his grip and draining me. The thought of him losing control and turning into a bloodthirsty maniac had terrified me to my core. I felt powerless. His condition had been getting worse and worse, and he wouldn't let me near him.

But tonight, as I slept on the love seat, I stirred from my slumber to find him hovering over me. Close. His expression was flat, his ice-blue eyes impassive. He looked paler than usual, with chapped lips and dark circles under his eyes. I carefully maneuvered my body into a sitting position, putting some distance between us.

"Gideon?" I said. Fear clutched at my throat. Was he still himself?

His eyes moved to the hollow of my neck. Flecks of gold began to shine in his irises. I jumped to my feet and darted across the room. In a flash, he appeared in front of me, blocking my way. His fangs snapped as he growled at me. I stepped back, but he grabbed my arm and slammed me against a wall.

I kicked and punched him before I was neutralized within seconds. Even though he hadn't eaten for days, he was incredibly strong. His body pinned mine against the wall, leaving me immobile and vulnerable. There was a gleam of madness in his piercing golden eyes as his lips approached my exposed neck.

"Please, Gideon, don't," I said, struggling to hold back the tears that were welling up. "Fight your way back to me." My voice trembled with emotion.

"I know you're still in there." His mouth came close to my neck, his fangs grazing my skin. Tears slipped down my cheeks as I whispered, "I love you."

He froze. A long, frightening moment passed before he raised his head to meet my gaze. The animal frenzy in his eyes faded, replaced by the familiar blue. His fangs retracted, and he recoiled from me as if I was a deadly poison.

"Oh, God, Sydney... I..." His face was blank with shock.

"It's okay," I said, my voice steady despite the turmoil raging inside me.

He shook his head. "No, it's not. I almost killed you. I thought I had more time before I might harm you. It's too soon for me to lose control like this. It must be the magic of the dead witch, her ward. It's affecting me negatively, causing me to lose self-control."

He sat down in a chair and reached into his ankle holster, pulling out Taissa's dagger.

"No, no, no, don't you dare." I moved toward him.

He stopped my advance with a raised hand. "Stay back. I can barely restrain myself."

My heart clenched. I wiped away the tears streaming down my face. "I won't watch you die."

"I'm sorry, love. It has to be done. You're not safe around me." His hands shook.

"I don't care. You are not killing yourself." I was about to take the knife from him, or at least try to, when Walter spoke through the door.

"I wonder something, human. The vampire is ready to meet his maker, and here you are, wishing to pry the silver knife from his trembling hand? Why in tarnation would you want to keep sharing a room with a bloodthirsty vampire? Has love gone and addled your sense of self-preservation? Well, isn't that something? I don't recall being such a witless soul in my mortal days."

A sudden thought struck me as I looked at the door. It was closed, so how did he know Gideon was holding a knife and his hands were shaking? My confusion lifted as Taissa's words flashed through my mind, and I remembered Walter had become one with the mansion.

Noticing the change in my expression, Gideon asked, "What's on your mind?"

"I just had a light-bulb moment," I said. "The ward keeps Walter from entering the room or using his magic against us while we're in here. But that doesn't mean he's cut off from the room itself. The prick has a front-row seat to what goes on in here, even with the door closed. He can see everything we do because the walls, the ceiling, the floor—they are all him. Which made me wonder; what if he can physically feel every knock and thud on the floor or walls as if they were one of his organs?"

Gideon's dry lips formed a soft smile. "Let's give your theory a whirl." There was a sliver of hope in his voice. He drove the dagger straight into the wooden floor, burying the point in it.

Walter hissed, then laughed. "Fools, I do not care about a little pain. Stab or shoot the walls and floors all you want. It is but a minor annoyance." I went to Taissa's bag and sifted through its contents until I found a lighter.

I took it out and smirked. "And what about fire? Burning this damn house to the ground—just a minor annoyance, too?"

A loud bang on the door reverberated through the room. "No! You wouldn't dare!" The demon's voice quivered with a mixture of anger and fear.

"I wouldn't? Why not?" I taunted, playing with the lighter, flicking it on and blowing it out. Of course, I was just putting on a show. Walter's spell had created an invisible barrier at the entrance of our room, trapping Gideon and me inside. With nowhere to escape, a fire would be very bad for us, too.

Walter voiced my thoughts. "You cannot leave the warded room. If you ignite a fire, both you and the vampire will face dire consequences."

"You're right," I told him. "I can't leave the room. What have we got to lose, though? We're going to die anyway. But you... Oh, you have much at stake, like your home. If I set fire to the mansion, you'll be in so much pain I doubt you'll be able to douse the flames with magic in time. You know, fires tend to spread quickly."

"No, not my house. Don't harm it," Walter pleaded, his tone almost desperate. A grin spread across Gideon's face, reflecting my own satisfaction. It looked like I'd found our bargaining chip—the mansion. The demon had an emotional attachment to it, and judging by his reaction, preserving the place meant more to him than the prospect of being charred to a crisp.

Strangely, I could understand why. His essence had been in these walls, ceilings, and floors for a century. Every crack and nook had become a part of who he was. Losing the house would be like ripping out a piece of his soul that no magic could ever repair.

I clucked my tongue in disapproval. "You're not telling me what I wanna hear, Walter, and that's making me all butterfingers. Things," I flickered the lighter, "could slip outta my hands and scorch the floor."

"No! Don't! I will grant you whatever you desire," Walter said. He mumbled something through the door, then said, "I have reversed my spell. You and the vampire are free to leave the room and my house. I will not cause you any harm."

I smiled. "Ah, now we're talking. But we still have a problem. You see, you're a demon, so your word is worth nothing."

"I will cast a spell of truth upon myself," Walter said.

"Good. And the Newborn vampire, what have you done with him?" I asked.

"The young vampire is currently fastened by chains in a room with bags of blood," Walter replied.

"Take us to him, then cut him loose and let him go too," I said, and Walter didn't argue. I exhaled in disbelief. Were we really going to get out of here? Was this damn nightmare going to end? Gideon opened the door, and Walter cast a truth spell on himself. The demon's eyes turned pitch black.

"How can we be sure he cast a truth spell on himself?" I asked Gideon.

"He's not putting on an act. I can see the magic in his eyes, the truth spell. However, we'll take extra precautions just in case," he replied and instructed the demon to create handcuffs that would temporarily neutralize his magic and prevent him from devouring my soul.

Enraged, Walter refused. I pressed the button on the lighter, and a bright red flame burst from the top, a reminder of the consequences of his refusal. Reluctantly, the demon did as he'd been told. Once the cuffs were on, we asked him if they worked. Forced to tell the truth, Walter replied that they'd be effective for the next few hours. Content with his answer, we left the room to free Logan. Walter took us to the second floor.

As we walked down the hallway where Taissa had died, I asked the demon, "What do you do with the bodies of all the people you kill? Why do they disappear?"

"A spell I cast transforms the bodies of the deceased into a painting or a piece of furniture, and they are now scattered throughout my lovely house. When it grows overly crowded, the enchantment causes some of them to vanish. The witch, in case you were wondering, now graces my living room as a fine painting," the demon answered with a smile. I sneered at him as I shook my head in disgust.

Gideon picked up Taissa's gun. "Which room is the Newborn being kept in?"

"It's two doors down from here," the demon answered him, guiding us into a large, dirty room with no furniture. Logan was sitting on the floor across from us, shackled to the wall by his right ankle. Plastic blood bags littered the floorboard, three empty, four full. Beside Logan was a black bag I recognized as Sheila's.

Logan's eyes landed on Walter first, fear flickering across the vamp's face. Confusion followed as he noticed Walter's bound hands and our presence beside him.

"What's going on?" Logan asked.

Gideon's irises gave way to gold at the sight of the blood in the packets. He snatched a full bag, ripped the top off with his teeth, and chugged down the red liquid. In a matter of seconds, he had polished off four bags, his complexion improving as his skin returned to its normal color.

"You're free. We're getting you out of here," Gideon then said to Logan, breaking the shackle around his ankle in two. Logan seemed too overwhelmed with joy and relief to ask questions. But when we reached the foyer, he stopped us, looking as if he'd realized something.

"Wait, wait." He glared at Walter. "Is this just another illusion?"

The truth spell prevented Walter from lying when he spoke, but it didn't compel him to answer questions. So, he just gave Logan a smile that said, "You caught me," letting him believe our escape was not real. The bastard took pleasure in watching Logan's face as his hope was shattered. I cleared my throat, producing the lighter from my pocket. That wiped the grin off Walter's face.

He pursed his lips at me then said to Logan, "You can trust your own eyes, vampire; there is no magic at play here." Logan opened and closed his mouth several times.

When he finally spoke, he looked at Gideon and me. "Is it true? Am I free?" I nodded, and he ran his fingers through his hair in relief. Then, his mood shifted, his eyes turning silver as he glared at Walter with a snarl. "I'm gonna kill you!"

Gideon stepped in front of him and put a hand on his chest, stopping him. "No, we might need him."

Breaking the tension, I interjected, "Let's just get out of here, okay?" Logan was silent for a moment. He seemed to be trying to regain his composure before nodding.

My heart pounded as we walked through the double doors that led to the vestibule of the mansion. At the sight of the front door, the tightness in my chest eased, and I exhaled slowly. Was it really over?

"See if it's locked," Gideon said, holding Walter's arm above his elbow.

I went to check. The door was unlocked, and I swung it open. A refreshing gust of cold night air brushed against my skin. I took a deep breath as I watched the tall trees outside sway and rustle. Tears of joy filled my eyes.

Freedom. Sweet, sweet freedom.

I turned to Gideon. "We made it. We're free, and it's night outside; it's safe for you and Logan to step out." He gave a quick nod, then pulled out Taissa's gun and pointed it at Walter.

The demon's obsidian eyes widened. "Hold on, we struck an agreement."

"No, actually, we didn't," Gideon told him. With a firm squeeze of the trigger, the bullet tore through Walter's chest. The demon's face froze with his mouth open as his body fell to the floor and he died.

"Hell yeah! He's dead!" Logan cheered and gave the demon's lifeless form a solid kick.

A wave of triumph went through me as I looked at the monster lying dead on the floor, and I wondered what his spell would turn him into. I hoped it was a toilet bowl. I wasn't going to stick around to find out, though. Not wanting to spend another second in this damn place, I walked out with Logan and Gideon, who had taken Mayet's necklace from Walter's vest.

"Why'd you two bother to save me? Who are you?" Logan asked as Gideon and I watched the walls of the mansion slowly return to their original color.

I shifted my focus to him. I had so many questions about Ivy, her murder, her family, and my ex's mysterious connection to all of it. But first, I needed to know if he still had the pendant.

"I'm Sydney, the one Ivy asked you to give the necklace to before she died. Do you still have it?"

Logan's eyebrows reached for his hairline. "So you're Sydney." His gaze swept over me. "I don't get it. You're only human, not some powerful witch. Why would she want you to have access to her crypt? Were you friends?"

"No, I didn't know her, but for some reason, someone used compulsion on me, and I was forced to go to her apartment where I found her dead in the living room," I said.

His eyes narrowed. "How would you know about Ivy's necklace or me if you weren't friends?"

"Because usually, after someone has been compelled to an apartment with a dead witch in it, the natural follow-up would be to start investigating. That's how I found out about the necklace and you," I answered.

"Ah, right. That makes sense," he said.

"The pendant—where is it?" Gideon demanded.

"I don't have it with me. It's in New York. You'll need to come with me so I can give it to you," Logan replied.

"Before we go with you, can you tell us what led to Ivy's death? Did she fall in with the wrong crowd? Do you know who killed her and her family?" I asked, wanting to hear his side of the story.

"I wish I could point a finger at who might have wanted them dead, but the sad truth is I have no idea because Ivy never really let me into her world." His face reflected a mixture of anger and emotional pain. "She was the queen of secrets, keeping so many things to herself, especially about her family. She hid me from them, afraid they'd judge her for dating a vampire. It was frustrating as hell. Any other girl, and I would have walked away, but Ivy was different.

"I fell hard for her the moment we met in a coffee shop. She was with her close friends, both witches, Piper and Tyler. Tyler wasn't my biggest fan, but Piper and I clicked right off the bat. The three of us were tight until Ivy's sister was murdered. Things got worse between Ivy and me then. I wanted to be there for her in her grief, you know. I thought she'd finally let me in and tell her family about us. I couldn't have been more wrong. Instead, she pushed me further away, leaving me even more on the outside. It was infuriating.

"She ignored my calls and made up excuses to avoid seeing me. I tried to give her space, thinking she wanted some time to grieve her sister's death alone. But then Piper called with shocking news—another of Ivy's sisters had been murdered. I was angry; how could Ivy not tell me? Her boyfriend, the one who would do anything for her. The next night, I went to her place, ready to confront her for keeping me in the dark. When I saw her face, though, my anger faded.

"Her eyes were all swollen and red from crying. I felt like shit for thinking only about myself. She had just lost two of her sisters, and here I was coming to her apartment to give her a hard time. I wanted to hug her, but she pushed me away. She told me to stay away from her because it wasn't safe for me to be in her life anymore. She didn't explain anything, just ended our relationship right then and there. I still had feelings for her and was worried about her. I tried to think of reasons why someone would want her sisters dead.

"I wondered if it had anything to do with the murder of her parents, a tragedy that had happened not long before we met. Then I remembered something. Piper had once mentioned rumors in the witch community that Ivy's family wasn't your average bunch of witches. They were special. Maybe that was why they were murdered. I don't know.

"After the breakup, another one of Ivy's sisters was killed. I felt so hopeless because there was nothing I could do to protect her from a killer who was obviously targeting her family. Then one night, Piper knocked on my door looking worried. She said Ivy had called her and asked for help finding rare and exotic ingredients for a spell.

"Although Ivy refused to explain what the spell was for, Piper agreed to help rather than have Ivy turn to the black market. After they managed to gather the ingredients legally, Piper opened the spell books and did some research. She found out what kind of spell required these special ingredients. It was for a complicated spell that intended to summon a supernatural being."

"Who did she want to summon?" Gideon asked.

He shrugged. "No idea. Piper called her and then went to her apartment to find out, but she couldn't reach her. After that, she came by my place and clued me in on the whole situation with the summoning spell. She was worried Ivy might try to summon the person who had murdered her sisters. I told Piper that if Ivy didn't want our help, there wasn't much we could do about it. After Piper's visit, I found a new job, since I hated the previous one, and went on with my life, doing my best not to think about Ivy.

"Then one night at work, I checked my phone during my break and saw many missed calls from Ivy. I dropped everything and raced over to her apartment. I knocked, but there was no answer. Her front door was unlocked, and I walked in.

"I heard a faint heartbeat and shallow breathing, and there was Ivy, just lying there, barely hanging on. Recent magical activity was evident as various objects were floating around the room. I rushed to her side and started to call for help, but she stopped me, saying it was too late for her, that she'd been poisoned, and it'd spread too deep into her body. I refused to accept there was nothing that could save her. I was about to call Piper when a necklace with a pendant slipped from her grasp.

"She asked me to give the pendant to a girl named Sydney Newbern. It looked like she had more to say, but then she... she died." His voice broke on the last word and he looked away, beyond the mansion's dilapidated porch and into the darkness. A long moment later, he let out a shaky breath and continued, "There was something else. A piece of paper on the coffee table. It struck me as odd, given Ivy's usual diligence in keeping her coffee table clear of anything that wasn't a plant pot and a TV remote.

"It had a name written on it in Ivy's handwriting, and on the other side, she'd written down an address along with the day of the week and the time. I called the witch police and reported Ivy's murder anonymously. I then went to Piper and told her what had happened. When she saw the piece of paper, she had a pretty good idea why Ivy would have written down an address and a time. The advanced summoning spell Piper was afraid Ivy was going to cast demanded consistency."

"Consistency?" I repeated.

"Yes. Say you do a spell that requires consistency and a few days later you decide to cast it again, you have to perform it at the exact same time and place, with no wiggle room."

"So what Ivy wrote down was the time and place she cast the summoning spell?" I asked.

"Yeah, it looks that way," Logan answered.

"What was the name Ivy wrote down?" Gideon asked.

"Jared Coleman," he said. My ex? Why on earth had she written his name? "Piper and I did some detective work and located him at a bar called Hell's Happy Hour. I was ready to march right up to him and grill him about Ivy, but Piper was afraid he'd refuse to talk and things would get ugly. Since she's not good with spells that force information out of humans, she suggested I go inside and pay some smoking-hot girl to work her charms on him and extract the details of his connection to Ivy."

Gideon shifted his gaze to me. "Summer."

Logan's eyebrows rose. "You know her?"

"We've talked," I said, then asked, "Does Piper know you paid Summer with her favorite earrings?"

"Of course she does," he answered, sounding insulted. "I didn't steal them from her if that's what you're getting at. Piper felt something was wrong with her earrings after one of her meetings with Tyler. She suspected he'd tampered with them somehow. He was always good at hiding his spells, so she took the earrings to a powerful witch to have them checked.

"After her suspicions were confirmed, she was really pissed at Tyler and wanted to throw them away, but I told her I'd take the earrings. The jewelry was expensive, and I was gonna sell them to solve some of my money problems. But I ended up giving them to Summer as payment."

"Is that why you stole from a vampire like Cassian? Because you needed money?" I asked.

"Yeah, money was tight, so I stole from him. It was months ago, and I thought I could get away with it. Dumb move, I'll admit, but I was desperate for some cash to cover rent and stuff." He rubbed his neck, looking like something was bothering him. "I'm curious, who told you I had Ivy's necklace? That's one piece of information I'd rather keep under wraps. If the pendant played a role in Ivy's murder, I don't want to be the killer's next target because of it."

"The manager of the cemetery where Ivy's crypt is located saw you with it. He said there was a symbol engraved on the pendant," I told him.

"Oh, that symbol." There was a hint of unease in his voice. "It scared the hell out of me when it suddenly started glowing. When the necklace slipped from Ivy's hand, the symbol looked familiar. Then it hit me—I'd seen it before. There was a time I suspected she was cheating on me because of her secretive behavior. So, I followed her one night and saw her go to a cemetery. She was visiting her mother's crypt, and the same strange symbol was carved on it.

"After Ivy died, I went there to examine the symbol. I was shocked to see the name carved into the stone was now Ivy's. The pendant began to glow like crazy, and that guy, the cemetery manager, suddenly appeared, looking suspicious. I have no idea what he is, but I can tell you he is definitely not human. He thought there was some shady illegal stuff going on, like dark magic, and demanded I tell him what I was doing.

"He terrified me, and I had to lay it all out: why I was there and my connection to Ivy. He seemed to believe my story and asked if there was a witch I knew who could explain the glowing necklace. I told him I didn't trust anyone. As much as I love Piper, she has a bad case of verbal diarrhea, and I didn't want the whole witch community to know about the necklace and the fact that I had it. But the manager of the cemetery wouldn't let it go.

"He called a witch to check the necklace. At my request, she promised to be discreet about the whole thing. When she came and touched the pendant, she said it was a key to Ivy's crypt and only one person could use it. She also told me the symbol on the crypt was actually a magical lock that can be opened by the pendant.

"After the manager, who seemed relieved there wasn't any dark magic going on in the cemetery, left with the witch, I secretly buried the necklace not far from Ivy's crypt. I can just imagine the manager flipping if he finds out the necklace is still in the cemetery. That guy was seriously off the charts with his paranoia."

"Burying the pendant in a graveyard seems like an odd choice. Why not keep it somewhere secure at your place?" I asked.

"I thought the cemetery would be a good temporary hiding place until I bought a small safe. When I got one, I returned to the cemetery to retrieve the necklace, but I was kidnapped by Cassian's men."

As I had no more questions for Logan, Gideon walked over to the empty car parked in front of the mansion, and we followed him. He opened the unlocked driver's side door and found a wallet inside.

He checked it. "It's Sheila's."

I looked at him. "Well, considering she's no longer with us, I don't think she'll need her car anytime soon."

He put the wallet back in the car and got behind the wheel. Then he squeezed under the dashboard to hot-wire the ignition. After getting the engine running, he sat back behind the wheel and motioned for Logan and me to get in. Before we did, I used the lighter to burn the Cursed Mansion to the ground, reducing it to ashes. The nightmare house was no more—never again would another soul die in it.

It was three in the morning when we arrived at the cemetery in New York and met Emilio again. Logan led us to where he'd hidden the necklace and apologized to Emilio, who was furious he'd left it at the cemetery. After digging up the necklace, Logan held it out to me. At my touch, the pendant pulsed with silver light for a few seconds, sending shivers through me.

"I have this strange, intense urge to go to Ivy's crypt," I said.

"Compulsion," Gideon told me.

I grimaced, trying to resist. "Yes, it's the same feeling I had when I was forced into Ivy's apartment... I can't fight the compulsion anymore," I said, and we all started toward Ivy's crypt.

When we reached it, I stopped before its door. The pendant emitted a beam of bright blue light that touched the symbol on the crypt, causing the door to swing open. An overwhelming urge compelled me to enter.

"Sydney, stop! Don't go in there!" Gideon warned.

I turned around, puzzled to see the three of them standing about fifteen feet back.

"Why aren't you coming closer?"

"Powerful magic prevents us from approaching," Gideon explained, his brow furrowed with worry. "If you go in, you'll be alone in there. I won't be able to help if things go wrong."

"Don't waste your energy. Nothing can stop her now. The magic is too powerful," Emilio said to Gideon, and he was right. Despite every instinct screaming against it, I stepped into the crypt.

"No!" I heard Gideon yell as the door closed behind me.

# Chapter 21

Deep darkness enveloped me, and a damp and musty smell permeated the air. Two candles on sconces near the door lit. Their flickering flames cast a soft glow that pushed the darkness back a few feet, small creatures scurrying away from the light. As I moved forward, brushing aside cobwebs, more candles lit my way. I went down a staircase that led to an octagonal room. The light from the candle bathed the interior of the crypt in yellow.

I inched deeper inside. There were no coffins, just an empty, cold room with moss-draped walls. Suddenly, a ball of bright light popped into existence in the center of the room, startling me. I jumped back, scrunching up my face to shield my eyes from the blinding light.

As it faded, my vision cleared to reveal a sight that left me breathless with astonishment. Facing me was Ivy, her eyes hollow and shadowed. Her complexion was pale, and her damp hair clung to her skin. She was wearing the same clothes as the night I'd found her in her apartment.

Her gaze was focused on my forehead, as if she didn't really see me. I waved a hand in front of her face, but her vacant eyes remained distant and unresponsive. She must have been some sort of 3D hologram. I reached out to confirm my suspicion and watched as my fingers passed through her incorporeal form.

The hologram began to speak. "Sydney, hi, my name is"—a short pause, then a correction—"was. My name was Ivy. By the time you see this message, I'll be dead. I wish we could've met when I was alive. I would've explained everything, but I was just poisoned, and I don't have much time before I die. You're going to find my body, and you'll be shocked, confused, scared.

"I mean, who wouldn't be, right?" A rueful laugh escaped her pale lips. "I'm sure you're wondering why you've been forced to drink mysterious potions in a stranger's apartment. Well, the answer lies in the Dragon Blood Curse, something you've probably never heard of before.

"The story of the curse began with Elizabeth, my great-great-great-grandmother, who was a formidable witch. She was known as the person to go to if you had a problem and was used to witches and humans coming to her for advice. Vampires and demons, though, had never been on her regular list of advice seekers, so imagine her surprise when a vampire showed up on her doorstep one night, seeking her expertise to solve his predicament.

"His daughter had contracted the UV virus, a death sentence for vampires. He offered Elizabeth a great deal of money to save his child from her grim fate. Elizabeth felt sorry for him, but she wasn't a miracle worker. There was no cure for the disease. Undeterred, he fell to his knees and begged her to at least try to find a cure. Her heart broke for him, and she agreed to help with no promises.

"Elizabeth worked nonstop in her study, experimenting with potion after potion in the hopes of finding a cure, but as she'd expected, none of her concoctions proved effective. Becoming attached to the sick girl, Elizabeth was determined to cure her. Desperate, she considered the unthinkable: tapping into the forbidden dark magic outlawed in our world. She knew the Watchers, a sort of police force, would sense when she cast dark spells, and she was looking for a solution to that problem.

"After scouring the magic books, she discovered references in the ancient texts to a potion that could hide the use of dark magic from the Watchers for a short period of time. The key element of the potion lay in acquiring a single strand of a Watcher's hair. Although obtaining such a thing had proven impossible to others, Elizabeth wasn't too worried. If anyone possessed the skill to steal the unattainable, it was Edwin, the vampire she was helping."

The name rang a bell from Mayet's story about him in Ice Prison. A vampire Ruler had tricked him, falsely promising a cure for his sick daughter in exchange for dragon blood.

"Once Elizabeth had all the necessary ingredients for the potion," Ivy's hologram went on, "She told Edwin it'd be best if he didn't come back for a while as she needed undivided attention to make the elaborate potion, which required spell work. After she finished with the potent concoction, she drank it. It didn't take her long to realize the Watcher's hair was altering her magic and amplifying her abilities. Yet, despite her increased powers and the use of dark magic, she still couldn't find a cure.

"When Elizabeth arrived at Edwin's home to break the bad news, she found him furious. While she'd been busy with the potion, a vampire Ruler had taken advantage of Edwin's emotional state and tricked him into stealing dragon blood by lying about a cure for his daughter. Since dragon blood is indestructible, Edwin asked Elizabeth to use her magic to hide the vial containing the dragon blood. He wanted to make sure nobody drank from it again.

"Elizabeth agreed and returned to her study to concoct another powerful potion. She gathered the ingredients needed to make the blood-filled vial invisible so that no one could get their hands on it. Carefully, she combined the ingredients in a bowl. Then, she added two drops of her own blood to bind herself to the potion, ensuring that she and only she could see the vial.

"As she intoned the incantation, weaving the words of the spell that would create the potion, she heard a loud noise from outside the study. Despite the distraction, she couldn't stop because these spells have their own strict rules. Once you start, you have to see it through to the end or risk consequences as severe as the death of your loved ones.

"Elizabeth hastened the spell as the sound of approaching footsteps grew louder. Then, the door flew open to reveal Serena, the same demon who would later be imprisoned in Ice Prison and try to steal your body there."

The name sent a shiver down my spine and took me back to that horrible place. How did Ivy know about what had happened to me in Ice Prison?

Ivy's voice cut through my thoughts. "When the demon's eyes locked on the vial near the bowl, Elizabeth realized Serena knew about the existence of the stolen dragon blood. Elizabeth couldn't use her magic to get the demon out of her house because she was still in the middle of the spell. Seizing the opportunity, Serena rushed to steal the vial. While chanting the spell words, Elizabeth pulled a knife from a drawer and attacked Serena with her eyes closed to protect her soul.

"During the struggle, Serena's blood fell into the potion, along with the vial, contaminating it. A thick cloud of black smoke rose from the bowl, and the Dragon Blood Curse was born. Shocked by the terrible turn of events, Elizabeth said the last words of the spell and then cast another to force the demon to talk. Elizabeth discovered that the demon king, Damon, had heard a rumor that Edwin had a vial of dragon blood.

"So, he sent Serena to steal it from him. Serena lurked outside Edwin's house, spying on him as he handed the dragon blood to Elizabeth. When Elizabeth trotted back to her house, Serena followed her and broke in to take the vial. When the demon finished talking, a rancid stench wafted from the potion bowl. Elizabeth hurried over and used her magic to find out what Serena's interference with the spell had done. It was bad. The demon's blood had twisted the result of the spell, and it went haywire.

"It created a curse that locked Elizabeth and Serena and all their descendants in an unbreakable bond. The thoughts, feelings, and pain of one would forever echo in the mind of the other. As if that weren't enough, they were also magically bound to the dragon blood in the vial, making them the only ones who could see it. This connection has a devastating effect—an all-consuming obsession with the dragon blood in the vial that inevitably culminates in madness.

"It's a really crappy curse to be born with." She paused and coughed for a moment, then wiped a bead of sweat from her brow. "Sorry about that. Where were we? Oh, right, the damage Serena's blood had done. Already starting to feel the obsession with the dragon blood, Elizabeth rushed to her collection of magic books. Unfortunately, there was no spell to break the curse, but she did find a potion that could temporarily stop any kind of obsession.

"After she finished making this potion, she moved on to the next problem: how to keep the stolen dragon blood from falling into the wrong hands. With the demon king aware of the vial, it was only a matter of time before others came looking for it. Elizabeth planned to hide the invisible vial somewhere safe, then come back to kill Serena. Her ability to see the vial made her an asset to the demon king or anyone else seeking the dragon blood as she could lead them to it.

"After gluing the demon to the floor with a spell, Elizabeth hid the vial in her husband's crypt, the same one you're in now. She figured no one would ever suspect it was there. When she returned home to kill Serena, she found her trembling witch neighbor instead. The girl, a young witch, said she'd heard screams coming from her house and knocked on the door. There had been no answer, so she walked in and followed the loud noise to the study, where she saw a raging demon.

"The demon had threatened to suck her soul if she didn't release her. Terrified, she'd used magic to free Serena. Elizabeth had to figure out a way to stop the demon from finding the vial for Damon. Calling in favors, she managed to frame Serena for helping a witch cast a dangerous dark spell. Imprisoned in Ice Prison, Serena lost her body and was locked in a box.

"But there was one more thing Elizabeth had to take care of. Since the dragon blood curse was hereditary, her descendants were in danger of being targeted by those seeking the vial as only the cursed could see it. To protect her bloodline, she cast a spell to keep the Dragon Blood Curse secret from as many people as possible.

"If you're not infected with the curse, and you happen to learn about it, the spell will prevent you from revealing its existence to anyone who is unaware of the curse, without exception. That's why those who are looking for the vial usually don't know it's invisible or that there's a curse. They have no idea they need someone like us to find the stolen dragon blood. Yes, us. Sydney, you have the curse as well."

# Chapter 22

I blinked in shock at the hologram of Ivy. I had the Dragon Blood Curse? No, she must have been mistaken. It couldn't be true.

"When Serena entered your body," Ivy explained, "the curse was passed on to you, creating an unbreakable magical bond between us. Even though you were in another dimension, it woke me up in the middle of the night. I saw Ice Prison through your eyes, felt your fear, your pain, and then Serena's death. The curse linked us on a deep level, though unequally since you're human.

"I can access some of your memories through dreams and compel you to do whatever I want. However, the compulsion part requires that I know your full name. You, on the other hand, are powerless to do the same, or feel our connection because you're human. With Serena, it was a different story. She had powers that protected her from my family, so we couldn't control her and vice versa.

"God, I despised the cursed bond I had with her. My mother never told my father about the curse, so he was unaware of the struggles his wife and children faced. Day in and day out, we rode the emotional roller coaster that mirrored Serena's feelings in Ice Prison—loneliness, anger, hunger, and despair. It was truly draining. My sister and I were so happy when we felt her death.

"Until we realized the curse had been passed on to an innocent human. We began to search for your identity, even though we had nothing to go on. Aside from feeling what you felt, we didn't know anything about you, not your full name, what you looked like, or where you lived. But we had to try to find you because you were in great danger.

"Since you're not a supernatural creature, your obsession with dragon blood will not only drive you insane, it will eventually kill you. I gotta say, the fact that you're a human raised some questions in my head, like how did you get involved in all of this? How'd you find out about the Hidden World?

"And how on earth did you end up in another dimension like Ice Prison with Serena trying to take over your body?" She sighed. "Well, whatever your story is, I guess I'll never know. Soon I'll be dead, leaving you the only one with the Dragon Blood Curse since Serena had no children and my entire family was murdered.

"You must be wondering about the terrible fate of my family. My parents were the first to die. Although my mother had extraordinary powers as a witch from Elizabeth's bloodline, the attacker managed to kill both her and my father, who was also a formidable witch. Whoever killed them couldn't have been human. The witch police investigated. They failed to find the killer, and just a few months later, my older sister was also murdered.

"This made me suspect someone was out to get my family. I didn't trust anyone, not even our police. Afraid that the killer might target someone close to me, I had to make the difficult decision to end things with my boyfriend, Logan." She paused, her expression softening, and her eyes drifting off into the distance, as if remembering the moments they had once shared. "I feel awful that I had to feed him so many lies.

"I wanted to tell him about the curse, and why I had to visit my family's crypt every month to drink a potion that preserved my sanity. But I had to keep the curse a secret, even from Logan, to protect my sisters. The fewer people who knew, the better." A tear ran down her cheek, and she coughed, sounding bad. "I better hurry up as I don't have much time left. There are a few more things you need to know.

"After my sisters died, I was so scared that I went to a fortune teller to see if I was next, but she was too nosy, asking personal questions I didn't want to answer, so I left before she could give me a reading. Then, I quit my job. Living off my savings, I stayed in my apartment, going out only when absolutely necessary. I spent my time trying to find out who the killer was. I also tried to discover your identity.

"I made a potion to induce dreams that could provide useful information about you, and not just random recollections from your past. It took some time, but the potion eventually worked. Yesterday, I had a dream in which I lived through one of your memories and saw it from your perspective. I was you, sitting on a bed with a friend. I think you were in your bedroom. Your friend was chattering about her mom's new boyfriend until there was a knock on your door and your sister came in.

"I learned your first name when she called you Sydney and said Jared had called her to say he was on his way over, which made you excited. Your friend then wondered why Jared had contacted your sister instead of you, his girlfriend. You speculated it was likely because your phone was on silent, so your friend asked you to check your cell.

"You reached for your phone on the nightstand and saw a missed call from Jared Coleman. When you tapped on his name to call him back, a full-screen picture of him appeared. I planned to use this information to track him down and then you."

So that was why Ivy had thought Jared and I were still together. She'd assumed this memory had happened recently.

"After I woke up from the dream," Ivy's hologram went on, "I searched my mother's books for a spell that required only the full name and physical description of the person I was trying to locate, rather than relying on their personal effect. This evening, I finally found one. To do the spell, I wrote your boyfriend's full name on a piece of paper, then described his physical appearance aloud and read the spell words.

"While tracking spells are not always accurate, to my surprise, this one was. It pinpointed your boyfriend's exact location, a downtown bar. I was afraid to leave my warded apartment because of the killer, but I had to find you. I couldn't just let you die from the curse. With pepper spray in my purse, I went to the bar. I ordered a drink, needing something to calm my nerves.

"As I drank while sitting at the bar, I scanned the crowd until I recognized your boyfriend. He was sitting alone in a booth. I went over and introduced myself, then got right to the point and told him I was looking for you. He seemed confused, and I realized I should've provided some background. He asked if I meant you by your full name.

"I was about to answer when my vision suddenly blurred and pain spread through my body. My magic detected a deadly poison coursing through my veins that would kill me within the next hour and a half. Someone had slipped the poison into my drink, most likely while I was distracted, looking for Jared in the crowd. My hands started to shake, and Jared asked me what was wrong.

"He gave me this look like I was some kind of nutjob, but I didn't have time to convince him otherwise or answer his questions. My main concern was to hurry back to my apartment and find a potion that would stop the poison and heal me. However, with the looming possibility that I'd fail and die, I also needed to make sure you knew where my family's crypt was since that's where the vial with the dragon blood is. And that you had the key to unlock the crypt.

"Using magic, I tried to plant in Jared's head the location of this cemetery along with brief explanations about the meaning of the numbers, the magical symbol that locked my crypt, and the Dragon Blood Curse. But the alcohol in his blood had dulled his mind, limiting my spell. The only part of my message that stuck in his unfocused brain was the coordinates of the cemetery and a description of the symbol engraved on my crypt.

"Unfortunately, there wasn't much I could do about his drunken state. However, I trusted that if I died, you'd be able to decipher the numbers on your own. As for the key, I planned to compel you to my apartment to take it with you. Then you could enter my crypt and see the message—this message—I intended to leave for you if I failed to save myself.

"Before I left the bar, I did one more thing. Given Jared's intoxicated state of mind, the spell I'd cast on him could easily backfire. To avoid any potential issues, I set the spell to only activate when Jared heard the voice or saw the face of the person he had romantic feelings for. I had to rely on Jared's emotions and feelings rather than objective identifiers like your full name.

"After I reached my apartment, and my desperate search for a life-saving spell or potion failed, I focused my energy on you, the one who still had a chance to be saved. In addition to the key, you also needed to drink some potions. Before the trembling in my hands got worse, I hurried to prepare them for you. The first one was designed for protection. I had to use powerful dark magic to make it, which is why I couldn't brew the same potion for my sister and myself.

"Though, now I don't have that problem. What are the Watchers gonna do? Arrest a dead witch?" She chuckled, which made her cough. When she stopped, she wiped her sweaty brow and continued, "My theory is that the killer is searching for the stolen dragon blood, mistakenly believing that murdering everyone with the Dragon Blood Curse will make the vial visible again. That's why I think they took the lives of my family—all of us had the curse, except for my father, who was just in the wrong place at the wrong time. If I'm right, you may be the killer's next target. Once you drink this dark-magic potion, they won't be able to see, hear, or touch you for five months."

I sucked in air, my heart skipping a beat. Cole! He couldn't see, hear, or touch me at the witch convention.

Sweet Baby Jesus. He was the killer!

Ivy's voice brought my attention back to her. "The second potion, made from Elizabeth's recipe, temporarily stops the obsession with the dragon blood in the vial. My family kept Elizabeth's potion in the crypt, but after my sisters died, I kept it in my apartment. There is something important you need to know about this potion. Its formula has been passed down through generations of witches in my bloodline; it's meant to be consumed by supernatural creatures—not humans."

Her expression fell into grave lines as she paused. Great, it seemed like whatever she was about to say was going to add to my long list of problems. So, what would the liquid from one of the bottles I'd drunk do? Turn me into an ugly toad?

"Your human body can handle a single dose of this potion, with side effects of fatigue and loss of appetite, but if you take it again, you will die a very painful and slow death," she warned.

Crap. Suddenly the idea of turning into an ugly toad didn't sound so bad.

"But that doesn't mean your fate is sealed," she continued. "You can't lift the Dragon Blood Curse, but there is a way to free yourself from the obsession with dragon blood in the vial for good. Though it won't be easy."

I sighed. *Yeah, as if it ever is.* "You'll have to steal an artifact from Heather, a.k.a. the demon princess, or as some call her, the bitch from hell. My family never tried it because we had Elizabeth's potion. But for you, it's worth the risk.

"The artifact was created sometime in the nineteenth century. There was a wealthy human lord who sought eternal youth and beauty from an old witch. When she refused to help him, he insulted her. In retaliation, she cursed him with an endless, tormenting obsession with youth and beauty until death, plunging him into misery.

"An illusionist learned of the cursed lord and offered to help, for a price. Though skeptical, he paid her a fortune to remove his tormenting obsession. Using a rare, ancient book of magic, she was able to create an amber sphere imbued with the power to undo any obsession born of a curse. If touched for three hours straight, the obsession would be gone forever.

"After the human lord died, a demon swiped the precious amber sphere and gave it to the demon king. Years later, he used it to cure Serena's obsession with the stolen dragon blood before she was imprisoned in Ice Prison. According to some credible people I've spoken to, the artifact is now in Heather's vault at her house.

"Stealing the amber sphere won't be easy, but don't be discouraged. You survived Ice Prison, which is remarkable, so I trust you'll be able to do it. Elizabeth's potion will give you two months before the obsession with dragon blood begins to consume you. That's enough time to plan your break-in."

Ivy paused, her face contorted in agony, her complexion draining of color as sweat kept dripping down her forehead. "Sorry, it's the poison... Anyway, after I was done with the potions, I used your full name to cast a spell that would force you to come to my apartment. Our special connection allowed me to bypass your compulsion immunity.

"I can sense that you are far from my neighborhood. Chances are I'll be dead before you get here, as I only have about ten minutes left to live." She let out a deep sigh. "There is something I'd like you to do for me. Just before I started recording this message, I called Logan, my ex. I needed to say goodbye and tell him how sorry I was for everything, and that I still loved him. To my disappointment, he didn't pick up, even after three tries. I don't know if he's mad at me or just busy. I'd really appreciate it if you could talk to him and let him know I never meant to hurt him, and that my love was wholehearted and sincere."

After she gave me his phone number, she coughed again, and fear burned in her eyes. The prospect of imminent death must have been terrifying, and my heart ached for her. From her pants pocket, she pulled out a necklace with a pendant bearing a symbol identical to the one that adorned the crypt door.

"I better wrap this message up and cast a spell to place it inside the pendant—which is the key. When you touch it, it'll recognize you because of the curse and the strong connection we have. The pendant will lead you to the crypt and open its door by connecting with the symbol on it. You're the only one who can enter the crypt.

"After the symbol opens the door for you for the first time, the crypt's name will eventually change to yours, which it'll learn from this message. When that happens, you'll become the crypt's owner and gain access to the vial with the stolen dragon blood. Sounds creepy having your name on a crypt, I know, but it's been a tradition in my family for generations. Whoever has their name above the stone door is entrusted with the responsibility of keeping the location of the vial secret and ensuring it stays there.

"As you're not a member of my family and human, I can't predict when your name will appear on the crypt. But when it does, you'll feel it. Then whenever you want to access the vial, simply place your hand on the wall facing the entrance. A drawer containing the vial will pop out of the wall and remain open for five minutes before returning to its secret location."

Her holographic image distorted and flickered as she leaned forward, her face tense with effort. I figured she must have grabbed her cell phone from a nearby table because the device appeared in her trembling hand as she straightened.

"While making the potions, my cell accidentally took some water damage. I managed to save it, but it doesn't look too good. I'm pretty sure it's living on borrowed time. Anyway, before it finally dies"—a sardonic laugh escaped her—"yeah, like me, I'll make one last attempt to reach Logan. I doubt he'll answer, but what have I got to lose, right?" she said with a bitter smile, struggling to maintain her cell phone steady. "Before I finish, I just want to stress again how important it is to keep the dragon blood hidden. If it gets discovered by demons or bad people, the world could be plunged into chaos." She sighed. "I wish you better luck than I had. Remember, there is a powerful, vicious killer out there. Watch your back."

Ivy's hologram disappeared, and I was left alone in the crypt, surrounded by an unsettling silence and a whirlwind of questions swirling in my head.

# Chapter 23

My brain went into overdrive, processing everything Ivy had told me. I felt like the universe was playing a cruel joke on me. As if a countdown tattoo wasn't enough, now I had a curse thanks to Serena! And to top it off, I had to steal a powerful artifact from none other than Heather, the demon everyone had warned me not to mess with because she was super dangerous and more evil than Satan himself.

I shook my head in frustration. Then another thought rushed into my mind—why had the man responsible for the tattoo on my hand killed Ivy's family? Was it really because of the curse? What was Cole after? Was I next on his list, now that I had the curse? A small creature scuttled past my feet, squeaking loudly as it moved toward the wall where the dragon blood was hidden.

My mind turned to the vial that so many were hunting for, including Eric. He'd claimed to be able to remove the ink from my hand, and from what Lily had said, he might be telling the truth. If I gave him the vial, I could finally be free of the tattoo. No more living in constant fear of what would happen when the countdown reached zero, and no more dark magic in my body.

I let out a heavy sigh. The temptation to give Eric the dragon blood to get rid of the tattoo was strong. Yet, I couldn't bring myself to do it. Despite Eric's previous help and assurances that he only wanted the blood to hurt his family, he was still a demon. Trusting a demon—a royal one—with dragon blood that could upset the balance of good and evil in the world would be nothing short of foolish.

I had two choices regarding the dragon blood: either follow in the footsteps of Ivy's long line of kin and keep the vial hidden in the crypt, or destroy it. Elizabeth and her descendants seemed to think the dragon blood was indestructible, but I knew better. I intended to give the vial to Gideon once I had access to it, so his witch could destroy the blood.

After deciding what to do with the vial, I wondered about the effects of the third potion I'd drunk. Ivy had explained the first two but said nothing about the third. Why hadn't she mentioned it? What was its purpose? She had also neglected to tell me about the summoning spell she'd cast. Who was the supernatural being she'd wanted to see?

I was lost in thought when I remembered I'd left Gideon waiting for me outside the crypt and he must be worried sick. I hurried back to the entrance. At the door, the candles blew out without a trace of wind, and darkness fell on the room. I opened the door and walked over to Gideon.

"Thank God!" he broke out, his voice heavy with relief. He pulled me into a hug so tight he seemed to forget vampire strength wasn't contagious.

Struggling for air, I managed to rasp out, "Can't... breathe." He quickly released me, a mumbled apology escaping his lips before he began firing off a rapid-fire stream of questions.

"I'll answer all your questions, but I need to talk to Logan first," I said to him and turned to Logan. "Before Ivy died, she left me a message magically placed in the pendant, and it opened in the crypt. The night she died, she called your cell but couldn't reach you. She wanted me to tell you she loved you and she never meant to hurt you."

"She actually said she loved me?" There was a hint of surprise in his tone, as if he thought she'd fallen out of love with him.

I nodded. "She never stopped loving you."

"What else did she say? Did she know who killed her? And why did she want you to have the key to her family's crypt?" he asked.

I had no intention of revealing details about the curse or the vial to him and Emilio, nor did I plan to tell them the identity of the killer. They would undoubtedly question how I'd come to know who the murderer was. Since I couldn't explain it or Cole's possible motive for his murders without mentioning the curse and the vial, I lied.

"I have no idea who killed her, or why she entrusted me with the key to the crypt. She recorded the message in her final moments, so it was brief and left me with many unanswered questions."

I shifted my gaze to Emilio before Logan could respond. "You don't have to worry about the Watchers snooping around your cemetery. There will be no illegal activity involving this crypt. Ivy and her family are dead, and now I'm the sole owner of it. Since I'm human with no magical powers, you can be sure I won't dabble in dark magic or attract the attention of the Watchers."

Thank God for the gloves that hid the ink on my hand.

Emilio was silent, his gaze narrowing in my direction. Unlike Logan, he clearly knew I was withholding details about Ivy, though I didn't expect him to push for answers. From what I could tell, all he cared about was keeping dark magic out of his cemetery to avoid any entanglement with the Watchers. Ivy's story didn't matter to him.

"All right," he said at last. "Just make sure nothing illegal comes anywhere near this property." Before turning and walking away, he added, "The main gate will remain open for the next ten minutes. I don't want to see any of you here after that."

Logan shot me a suspicious look after Emilio left. "That guy had a 'You're so full of it' look on his face when you said Ivy didn't share much in the message. How come you're the only one with access to Ivy's crypt? What's going on—what aren't you telling me?"

"Nothing," I answered. "The man is just paranoid, as you said yourself. I wish Ivy had more time to clarify things, but she used the last of her strength to express how much she loved you. Trust me, I didn't get the answers I was hoping for either. Maybe the person Ivy summoned will have answers for us. I need to talk to Piper about the spell to find them. Can you arrange a meeting with her?"

"Yeah, okay," Logan said, seeming to trust me again. "I left my cell phone at my place before I got thrown in that twisted mansion. I'll call her tomorrow night."

Gideon glanced up at the brightening sky before turning to Logan. "Sun's coming up soon. Let's exchange phone numbers and get out of here. Call us after you talk to the witch. Then, my advice to you is to get on with your life. Forget the crypt, forget the Cursed Mansion, forget everything, hard as it may be."

I thought Logan would reject the idea of moving on, but instead, he ran his hands over his tired face and nodded in agreement.

"Yeah, man, you're right. I tried, I really tried to help Ivy when she was alive and to catch the killer after her death, but I failed. Ivy is gone and there is nothing I can do to change that. I'll talk to Piper for you and set up the meeting, but then I'm done. I have to move on. This whole thing, it's just too much for me."

After the three of us left the cemetery, Gideon and I headed back to his penthouse. Like Emilio, Gideon could tell I'd lied. Feeling famished, I needed to eat before sharing Ivy's revelations with him. After I'd polished off a large sandwich, I told him everything. I figured he'd want to talk about the invisibility of the vial, the Dragon Blood Curse, and the fact that Cole was the killer. I also expected him to be excited that he finally knew where the dragon blood was. But he did none of that. Instead, he pulled out his phone with a solemn look on his face.

"What're you doing?" I asked as he tapped on his glowing screen.

"Texting Evelyn," he answered, his eyes on his phone. Then he looked up and filled in the missing pieces. "She's one of Heather's minions, and she despises her as much as Robin does."

"Okay and how can she help us?" I asked.

"Your life is in danger because of the curse; we must get that artifact for you—fast. Evelyn will have no problem sharing valuable information about her master, for money, of course. Before we break into Heather's house, I'll need the scoop on stuff like Heather's schedule, when she's usually out of her house, and most importantly, where she keeps her safe. Evelyn will give us all that."

"How can you be sure this demon won't feed you false info?" I asked.

"I'm not gonna bank on her intel alone. I'll tail Heather for the next week to confirm everything. Then there's Eric. Now we know why he really came to you; he's obviously aware Serena passed the curse on to you, which gave you the ability to see the vial. As long as he doesn't have the dragon blood, he's no threat to you. You're way more valuable to him breathing than dead.

"Eric's sadistic with no regard for others, but with you, he plays nice to gain your trust. We're gonna use that to our advantage. As Heather's brother, he may have some useful info about her that could help us. Text him to meet at his bar tomorrow night for a chat. When you see him, fish for as much information as you can about Heather's daily routine."

I grinned. "Yeah, I like the idea of playing Eric. I'll lie to him that I don't have the dragon blood and make him believe I'll give it to him once I find it. That way we can always manipulate him for our purposes."

Gideon shook his head. "No. We need him to remove the dark magic from your hand. We will have to give him the vial after we steal the artifact and cure you of the obsession."

I stared at him as my eyebrow shot up. "What! You cannot be serious. The dragon blood has to be destroyed."

"Not if it means there's a chance you'll die when the number reaches zero." He moved closer to me, his intense blue eyes piercing mine. "I will not lose you. We'll deal with the consequences of Eric having dragon blood after the dark magic is gone from your body."

I held his gaze. "Eric is a demon. Giving him the vial can only lead to disaster. I'm not gonna jeopardize the delicate balance of good and evil in our world, where everyone I care about lives, just to save myself. Besides, the end of the countdown does not necessarily mean my death. The decision to have Eric remove my tattoo in exchange for the dragon blood is mine alone, and you're just gonna have to accept it."

He bent his head, closed his eyes, and rubbed them with his thumb and forefinger. He knew he couldn't change my mind and seemed worried.

When he looked at me again, I said, "We'll find another way to remove the tattoo before it reaches zero." Standing on my toes, I planted a brief kiss on his lips and his expression thawed. Behind him, the white custom-fit blinds came down over the floor-to-ceiling windows, hiding the sunrise and keeping its light at bay. Soft, dim ceiling lights flickered to life, casting a warm yellow glow across the large living room. I let out a tired sigh.

He cupped my cheeks and said, "Let's go to bed and get some rest. We need it after all we went through at the mansion. We can talk about Eric and the dragon blood later."

I nodded, exhaustion tugging at every fiber of my being. Yeah, I desperately needed sleep.

# Chapter 24

It was six p.m. when Gideon woke me with a kiss.

"Hey," he whispered, sitting on the bed, wearing fresh clothes: black jeans and a tight long-sleeved shirt. The scent of clean soap from his damp hair filled my nostrils. He brushed a strand of hair from my cheek, and I sat up. After a satisfying, restful sleep, I felt new energy surging through my body. I was now fully prepared to face the challenges ahead, including stealing an artifact from the demon princess's house.

"Have you heard from the demon Evelyn?" I asked.

"Yeah, she agreed to meet. She's expecting me downtown in half an hour, so I better get going." He leaned down to give me a long kiss, then got up from the bed and grabbed his black leather jacket off a chair. "I'll come back when I'm done with the demon. Don't forget to text Eric to set up a meeting."

I nodded, and after he left the apartment, I checked my phone. One text, two missed calls, and one voicemail. I punched in the code and listened to the message.

"Hey, this is Logan. Just got off the phone with Piper. I told her the whole story about the black mansion, Ivy's crypt, and you. I'm sorry, Sydney, but she doesn't trust strangers, and I couldn't convince her you were okay. Anyways, the bottom line is, don't count on her talking to you.

"I did bring up Ivy's summoning spell, though, and she told me she's been trying to find out who Ivy summoned. A friend had pointed her to a book with instructions on how to recreate a witch's spell. Piper followed the instructions and now plans to cast Ivy's summoning spell on the exact day, time, and place of the original spell.

"She believes whoever Ivy summoned will reappear. She asked me to come with her, but I declined because I'm done with all this. I guess you and Gideon will want to be there to see who shows up. The spell will be performed in a public place. You can watch it without Piper knowing you are there, as she wouldn't approve. I'll text you the necessary details and a picture of Piper."

The voicemail ended, and I opened Logan's message. As promised, he'd sent me Piper's picture and the time and place she was going to recreate Ivy's spell. If she succeeded, the identity of the person Ivy had summoned would be revealed. I crossed my fingers for the spell to work. My focus then shifted to Eric, and I texted him to ask if we could meet. He replied a short time later.

"What a surprise, if it isn't the human I dislike the least. Swing by my bar in an hour. I'll see you there," the message read.

When I arrived at Hell's Happy Hour, the place was buzzing with activity but not jam-packed. I caught sight of Eric on the other side of the room. A smug look spread across his face when he noticed me, as if he thought I'd come to tell him I accepted his offer to give him the dragon blood. He sauntered over to me, and I followed him across the room then down a narrow hallway that led to his office.

The room didn't contain much, furnished with a desk, two chairs facing it, and a low couch along the left wall. He gestured for me to take a seat on the couch. As I made my way over, my eyes fell on the pair of books on his desk. One was called *Two Hundred Creative and Fun Ways to Torture*; the other was *Pride and Prejudice and Zombies*.

I nodded my head at the books as I sat down. "Quite an intriguing choice of reading material."

He joined me on the couch. "You mean *Pride and Prejudice and Zombies*? Go ahead, make fun of my literary tastes. But I won't apologize for what I love, or for having a soft spot for romance novels. I'm not ashamed to say this dashing demon is a sucker for a good love story." His tone was devoid of sarcasm or playfulness, carrying a weight of sincerity.

"You do realize it's a parody, right?" I pointed out.

He sighed audibly, as if my lack of appreciation for a good book was disappointing. "You say parody, I say epic love story." I rolled my eyes, to which he responded with a smile, then asked, "So what's the deal? Why'd you wanna meet up?"

Before I tried to uncover his sister's daily routine, I needed to ask him a few questions.

"I found out about the Dragon Blood Curse," I said.

He looked both surprised and pleased. "Oh, that's nice."

"You already knew I was cursed and could see the invisible vial, didn't you?" I accused.

He gave a nonchalant shrug. "Well, of course, why else would I bother to be nice to a human? Elizabeth's spell kept me from revealing the real reason I came to you. Had to feed you some line about you being oh-so-special and succeeding where others crashed and burned to explain why I'd offer a deal to a mere human. Gotta hand it to you, though, you surprised me. Wasn't sure you'd ever find out about the curse, not that it matters. Whether you know about it or not, it won't hinder you from getting the vial."

"Here's what I don't get: if the existence of the curse is a closely guarded secret, protected by an old spell, how'd you get wind of it?" I asked.

He relaxed on the couch. "Daddy Dearest has never been one to let me in on his shady schemes. So, when I noticed him spending countless hours trying to figure out how to free Serena from Ice Prison, I saw no point in asking him about it. I mean, why waste my time with him when I could just torture a few of his minions and get the juicy deets. At the time, I had no idea who the hell Serena was, which made me wonder why she was getting all of the demon king's attention.

"After a little digging and some severed minion fingers, I discovered Serena had these sick, badass abilities. I figured that was why the old man was so eager to get her out of Ice Prison, but I was wrong. One night, I happened to overhear an interesting conversation between my old man and my queen-bitch sister. They were discussing Serena and a secret curse."

"The Dragon Blood Curse," I said.

He nodded. "That's how I got the 411 on the curse and its backstory."

"How'd the spell allow your father to talk about it when someone was listening? And how did he and Heather even know about the curse?" I asked.

"Before Serena's ass was thrown into Ice Prison, she told my father about what had happened with Elizabeth. He learned that those who know about the Dragon Blood Curse can only discuss it with others who share the same knowledge of its existence. Also, you can't put anything about the curse in writing. This privilege is reserved only for the cursed. This is why, at my dad's request, Serena wrote the whole story down, like the good little obedient demon she was.

"He put the parchment in a secret safe that is magically protected. The parchment allows him to sidestep Elizabeth's spell by showing it to anyone he thinks should know about the curse, like Heather. As for why Elizabeth's spell didn't trigger when I eavesdropped on their conversation, it's because eavesdropping is apparently a loophole in her spell.

"Silly Elizabeth didn't take into account all the ways the existence of the curse could be revealed. Gotta love loopholes, right?" The corner of his lips quirked up. "Without 'em, I'd have no idea why Serena, who could see the invisible vial, was Daddy's golden ticket to getting the precious dragon blood."

"Like I am to you," I said.

His mouth pulled back in a smile. "Indeed you are, and I must admit, much to my surprise, you have not proven to be as useless as the rest of your kind."

I returned his grin. "I wish I could say the same, but no surprises here; I got exactly what I expected—a thoroughly psychopathic, evil jerk."

His smile widened, deepening his dimples and revealing a set of white teeth. "Awww, that's sweet of you. It's almost enough to make a guy blush. Although, I can't help but notice you forgot to include 'devastatingly handsome' in that charming list of descriptors."

I rolled my eyes at him and changed the subject to something more important. "Does your father know the curse was passed on to me?"

"Give me some credit. Do I seem like the kind of guy who doesn't look out for his own interests? Keeping your existence a secret from my old man is in my best interest. I don't want him to get the dragon blood. And he can't use you, by force or otherwise, to get it if he doesn't know there's another like Serena out there, now can he? He knows there was a human who passed the tests and was thrown into Ice Prison to free Serena, but he doesn't have a clue what you look like, and I've made sure to keep your identity from him.

"And how have I managed that, you may ask? Well, I killed everyone who could've told him about you, his witch, and the illusionist I sent to spy on you in Ice Prison. As far as my old man is concerned, Serena, the Ancient vampire, Mayet, and you were all killed by a gargoyle in Ice Prison. He thinks his brilliant plan to break Serena out went up in flames."

He chuckled with satisfaction before he went on, "You know, Oberon taking out Serena is a real head-scratcher. I mean, it's not like he's in the habit of saving humans. Or maybe it's just you. Could it be that he's taken an interest in that pretty dark magic tattoo on your hand?" He seemed to be asking these questions more to himself than actually expecting me to have the answers.

A thought occurred to me, and I redirected the conversation. "After Serena died, why didn't your father force Elizabeth's descendants to bring him the dragon blood? For that matter, why didn't you?"

"Stupidity doesn't run in my family. Going after a witch like Elizabeth or her descendants? Yeah, that would've been downright foolish. They're not your run-of-the-mill witches. Elizabeth possessed a trace of a Watcher's power, and her bloodline inherited it. My old man never bothered to track down those cursed witches. He pinned his hopes on Serena to lead him to the dragon blood. Now that she's gone, he can kiss that plan goodbye." A devilish smile appeared on his lips.

He glanced at the clock on the wall, and I remembered why I'd come here.

I turned the topic to his sister. "What about Heather? Is she working with your father to find the vial? What does she do all day anyway?"

"She helped him, yeah, but she's got her mind on something else right now, a side project that has landed her in another dimension. Which means my annoying sis is currently on a temporary vacation. But hey, at least I get a break from the torture of her presence for a while."

"Another dimension? Are you talking about Ice Prison?" I asked, fishing for more information.

"Heather in Ice Prison? Now that's a pleasant thought. All alone in there, miserable, suffering..." His eyes took on a distant look as he savored the idea. Then, a sigh passed his lips. "Ah, well, we all have our little moments of wishful thinking. Unfortunately, no, she's not rotting in Ice Prison. There's another world created by the big-shot royal fae Herit.

"It's in another dimension, and the only thing I—or anyone else in the Hidden World, for that matter—can tell you about it is that it exists. Where exactly is it? Why was it created? What secrets does Herit hold within it? Your guess is as good as mine, but not Heather's. According to my dad, she discovered its location, and one of her witches found the spell that can open a portal to this world."

"How'd she manage to do that?" I asked.

He let out a sneer. "The demon king and queen would probably say it's because she's some kind of genius, but let's face it, it's just a matter of luck. She got lucky, that's all there is to it. This dimension? Pff, it's probably some empty space with nothing of value in it. And when she comes back with her tail between her legs, empty-handed, I'm gonna grab me some popcorn and watch a show called 'Heather Gets Humiliated.'"

"Why didn't your father join her?" I said.

"The spell only allows one person to pass through the portal and can only be cast every fifteen years," he answered.

"Any idea when she'll be back?" I asked the important question.

"Well, it's not like I can just pull out my super awesome cosmic phone and call her. Cell reception isn't really a thing in other dimensions, I'm afraid. So, no, I have no idea when sis will be back." He narrowed his eyes. "You seem awfully interested in Heather today. Is that why you wanted to meet?"

He hadn't mentioned the obsession that came with the curse, which made me wonder whether he was aware of it. If I brought it up, I was certain he'd offer to help Gideon and me steal the artifact from Heather's house, as he needed me alive. I chose to remain silent on the matter, however. I didn't trust him, not for a second, to share anything that could give him power over me. My life would be in his hands if for some reason he decided to steal the artifact for himself and use it to extort whatever he wanted from me.

I feigned an exaggerated offended look. "Are you accusing me of something? I was just curious, that's all."

He gave me a lingering stare that kept me on edge. His silence lasted a beat too long, making me wonder if he believed me.

Then, with a mischievous twinkle in his eye, he said, "Okay, if you say so."

Before I could inquire further, a sudden knock at the door made us both turn to it. A woman poked her head in, her expression apologetic.

"Sorry, boss, we got some leech trouble out back that needs your attention."

"Be right there," he told her. The woman bobbed her head and closed the door. His gaze returned to mine. "Looks like our meeting will have to be cut short. Rain check on the rest of the Q&A?"

As I got up to leave, I said, "Go handle your business. I'll be in touch if I manage to find the dragon blood." Of course, I wasn't going to give the vial to a demon, but I wanted him to think he had a chance of getting it from me. A royal demon ally could come in handy down the road.

After I left the bar, I received a call from Audrey. The fiasco with the witch and her botched spell had finally been resolved. And now that the magic convention was over, Audrey was back home. I brought her up to speed on recent events, and she expressed disbelief that we'd made it out of that nightmare at the Cursed Mansion in one piece.

Trusting her discretion, I then confided in her about Ivy, the Dragon Blood Curse, and the artifact I needed to steal from Heather. She was also surprised to hear about that. She promised to keep it all to herself and to call me if she happened to find a spell in the next week that could stop obsession in humans. That way Gideon and I wouldn't have to break into Heather's house.

Before we hung up, I had one more thing on my mind. I asked her if there was any chance the potion that made me invisible to Cole had somehow magically linked me to him as an unintended side effect. The idea sounded far-fetched, but I had to ask, especially since magic and potions sometimes had surprising and unpredictable results. If such a connection between Cole and me existed, maybe there was a spell that could exploit it to track him down.

Audrey didn't have an answer for me, though, because Ivy had used a dark spell to make the potion, and Audrey's knowledge of that kind of magic was limited. Instead, she gave me Lily's number, suggesting I reach out to her since she was much more familiar with the subject. After thanking her, I called Lily and was glad when she didn't dismiss my idea. She assured me she'd look into it and get back to me soon. After expressing my appreciation and ending the call, I met Gideon in his penthouse.

The demon he'd talked to confirmed what Eric had told me: Heather was in some secret world created by Herit. According to the demon, Heather was searching for some powerful artifact that could help her in her mission, the details of which were known to only a few.

"Did your mother ever mention this mysterious dimension?" I asked him.

He shook his head. "She never said anything about it. I don't know what Heather's after, but that's not our main concern right now. What matters is that with her gone, it just got easier to get into her house to steal the sphere. I have no doubt Heather's place is magically protected, though. I'm gonna hire two witch pros, one specializing in magical home security systems, the other in cracking enchanted safes. I'll also put together a team to watch her house around the clock for the next few days," he said, then laid out the entire operation to break into Heather's house.

After he finished, I briefed him on the spell Piper intended to cast. Since it wasn't scheduled for this week, he said we should focus on it after we got the artifact, to which I agreed. Our only concern now should be preparing for the break-in.

When you were stealing from a demon as powerful as Heather, there was no room for error.

# Chapter 25

Over the past week, Gideon had received daily updates on Heather's house and neighborhood from his hired team. They had given him important information such as whether her house was empty day and night, who lived nearby, which neighbors were human or not, and what their daily schedules were.

Despite Audrey's best efforts, she came up empty in her search for a spell to help me. Her lack of success meant Gideon and I had no choice but to go full steam ahead with our plan to steal the artifact. Once we had enough useful intel on Heather's residence, the two of us plotted how to pull off the heist with the help of a couple hired witches, Mark and Harper.

When the big night arrived, they met us in front of Heather's home. And boy, what a fancy place it was! The luxurious red-brick house looked magnificent, a black-paneled front door with carved stonework around it, framed windows, cast-iron railings, and planters of chrysanthemums on the lower levels. There was nothing to suggest evil incarnate lived there.

Gideon surveyed Heather's house, then looked at Harper, the witch who was to take down Heather's magical security system. "Your rep's got a good track record, but I need to know: can you handle this? The entire perimeter's sealed up with heavy-duty magic."

She seemed offended. "Please, breaking through this ward will be a cakewalk." Harper exuded confidence, and I had to admit, it put my mind at ease. The other witch, our safecracker, was carrying a black briefcase. He seemed to be in his fifties and impatient.

"Let's get on with it. We ain't got time to waste," he told Harper, then walked up the elegant stairs to Heather's front door. Harper, with a backpack on her back, followed him and pulled a pair of black gloves from her bag. As she put them on, her eyes went completely white and her mouth moved, but no sound came out. We waited, watching her do her thing, until Heather's house security was disarmed and we could enter.

When we walked in, the smell of lemon-scented wood polish filled the air. Gideon switched the lights on. They dispelled the darkness on the parlor level, revealing twelve-foot ceilings and beautiful herringbone oak floors. Off the foyer was a huge living room with a white marble fireplace and a pair of large windows overlooking the street.

As I took a step toward the living room, an unexpected wave of weakness swept over my body. Gideon's strong hands took hold of me and steadied me.

He looked at the witches. "What's happening to her?" His voice carried a note of alarm.

"The demon who lives here seems to have someone cast a human-repelling spell that makes any human who enters the house feel sick," Harper explained.

"And the farther you go into the house, the worse you'll feel," the other witch added.

"He's right. You need to decide if you still want to come with us," Harper said.

Another wave of dizziness and nausea hit me, and I clutched my stomach in pain. I looked over at Gideon. "I'll wait for you outside."

He nodded in understanding. "We won't be long."

I walked out of the house and doubled over, my hands on my knees, taking a deep, cleansing breath. The weakness slowly left my body as I stepped down the steps but was replaced by a chill of unease as I reached the sidewalk. I had an eerie feeling someone was watching me.

The street was empty, with only the occasional car driving by. As I made my way to a nearby tree to lean against while I waited for Gideon, I heard footsteps. I paused, my hand instinctively reaching for the dagger hidden in my jacket as I turned.

The tension in my muscles relaxed when I saw two teenage girls. They walked away, and I continued toward the tree until I heard breathing behind me. Whirling with a blade poised for action, I steeled myself. A shock of surprise rushed through me as I faced the mysterious woman I'd seen watching me from a distance on the street.

"You..." I whispered.

She was wearing the same white coat as the last time I'd seen her. She reached out and grabbed my left hand. I tried to pull away but couldn't. She was strong. As I struggled to free myself from her grip, I realized she meant me no harm. Her eyes weren't filled with malice or hostility, and even though her grip was firm, she wasn't trying to overpower me.

I stopped resisting. "Who are you? What do you want from me?" Bafflement laced my words. She gestured to her throat and shook her head, seeming to indicate she couldn't use her voice.

"You can't talk?" I asked, seeking clarification.

She nodded. She then moved her gaze down to the hand she was holding and turned it up. As she touched my tattoo, I was suddenly transported back to Heather's house and found myself standing in the foyer.

What the hell was happening?

I started for the front door, eager to avoid another bout of nausea, but then I heard voices coming from the living room. I turned around and saw a girl in her early twenties sitting on the couch with two men standing in front of her looking scared. Sunlight filled the room even though it should have been nighttime. My confusion grew. What was going on? Who were these people? Demons? Why did they seem so afraid? And why didn't I feel sick?

The front door swung open, and a man dressed in casual clothes, carrying a brown shopping bag, stepped inside. To my shock, he walked right through me as if I was a ghost. This, along with the daylight and my lack of nausea, made me realize I wasn't physically present in Heather's house. It looked like the mysterious woman was a witch and she was showing me something. Was I in one of her memories?

I glanced around, but she wasn't in the foyer or the living room. Could she have been watching this scene from a hiding place? Or maybe she hadn't been in Heather's house at all, but had cast a strong spell that had the power to reveal what had happened in there?

I followed the man who had just entered the house and went into the living room. My attention was captivated by the girl on the couch, who I presumed was Heather. She exuded an aura of power and confidence. Her eyes were forest green, and she had a resting bitch face.

She sat with her legs crossed, her feet clad in black stilettos, a spill of wavy, flame-red hair over her shoulders. Her white porcelain skin was smooth, and the tight black pantsuit with a deep V-cut on her chest fit her body perfectly.

The man I had followed bowed his head to her. "Mistress, please forgive my interruption, but the matter is urgent."

She regarded him with annoyance, the top leg bouncing up and down impatiently. "What is it, Rufus?"

He raised his gaze to meet hers. "Before I begin, mistress, I have the ice cream you requested."

She snapped her fingers and pointed at the man standing in a corner of the room. "You there, take the bag and put the ice cream in the freezer." As the bag changed hands, her attention swung back to Rufus. "All right, let's have it. What's so important?"

"I have reason to believe this meeting is being watched by a secret coven of witches who wish to destroy you. They're using powerful magic to monitor your every move," Rufus said.

She rolled her eyes at him. "You idiot, I am Heather. A princess. What kind of incompetent witch would even consider using their magic against me?" She let out a derisive laugh. "No one in their right mind would dare spy on me. Where on earth did you get this ridiculous idea?"

"Mistress, the queen shares the same concerns," Rufus told her.

Heather scoffed. "Oh, please. Don't even get me started on that pathetic excuse for a queen. She's weak and useless. Just because she found out the gift the king's witch gave her is a magical ring that records her every move doesn't mean I'm being watched. As if anyone would dare do that to me."

She released an annoyed huff of breath. "Now, before you came, these maggots," she nodded in the direction of the two men in front of her, "were about to answer if they failed me or—" A coughing fit gripped one of them, who nearly choked on his own saliva as unmistakable terror drained the color from his face.

The loud sound interrupted her flow of words. She paused and turned her gaze to the coughing man. "Rude. Can't you see I'm trying to talk here?"

In response, the man dropped his eyes to the floor, his voice trembling. "P-p-please forgive my rudeness, mistress."

Disregarding his apology, she held out her hand at arm's length to examine her long, red-painted nails. "Flawless, utterly beautiful." She lowered her hand, her gaze shifting to the two frightened men before her. "You know what would seriously piss me off right now?" Both men shook their heads, and she continued, "Ruining my fresh new manicure by beating the crap out of you two cockroaches." Her plump lips twisted into a sneer. "So, I sincerely hope you're about to tell me you didn't screw up and you managed to locate that bottom feeder for me."

One of them spoke up, his words hesitant. "Mistress, we've acquired the human's name, but it's proving to be a challenge. We need more time—"

Heather's deadly stare cut through his words. "More time?" She shook her head with a furious chuckle. "You need more time?" Her voice rose. "How hard is it to track down one filthy human? Huh?" She moved her head to look at Rufus. "I really want to make those idiots suffer, but I'm not going to ruin my immaculate manicure. Be a doll and take care of this for me, will you? Rip their hearts out, nice and slow. Make them suffer. And take it outside. I don't want their disgusting blood staining my exquisite rug. That would be even worse than having humans in my beautiful home."

Rufus bowed and led the two men away. They made no protest, seemingly resigned to their fate. Heather stayed on the couch while Rufus left. When he returned, a short time later, he once again lowered his head.

"Mistress, it is done."

Her jaw set. "Send more demons—competent ones this time—to track down that bottom feeder, Sydney Newbern."

A bolt of shock slammed into me. Why was she looking for me? Could she have been behind my abduction? Was she working with Cole?

"I'll have my best men track down the girl," Rufus said. "If I may advise, mistress, recruiting a more powerful witch to aid our efforts would greatly hasten the search."

"I'll speak to the king and compile a list of the most powerful illusionists he knows. You'll have a new witch by the end of the week. Anything else?"

He hesitated. "Yes, mistress. The current witch has a concern she feels you should be made aware of."

Heather heaved an impatient sigh. "Fine, let's hear it. But make it quick, I haven't got all day to listen to some witch's concerns."

"She says there are some humans who like to have their fortunes read. Sydney Newbern might be one of them," he told her.

She raised an eyebrow. "Do I look like I care about this trivial information? You better hope I start showing some interest soon because right now, I'm at a loss as to why you would waste my time with such nonsense. I don't give a shit if that human consults a fortune teller or not."

"I apologize for upsetting you, mistress. As your faithful servant, I thought you'd be interested to know there is a possibility the girl could receive a warning of abduction in the future from a Gifted human, such as a fortune teller. This could cause the girl to go into hiding, which would complicate our efforts to locate her."

He got her attention. She nibbled her lower lip for a moment before saying, "Yeah, I see your point. We'll have to take measures to prevent that. I'll have the new witch use dark magic. If a fortune teller sees me or a future abduction during a reading, a dark spell will prevent them from saying my name or anything about an abduction."

A pulse of shock went through me as the words of Madam Florence echoed in my mind.

*I have seen the face of unspeakable evil. You must be careful, for when the countdown ends, someone with evil intentions will come to you... A strong spell binds my tongue. It doesn't allow me to reveal any more details about this individual.*

Oh my God, the person she'd talked about was Heather! The demon princess would be the one standing next to me when the tattoo reached zero. She was responsible for everything that had happened to me. But why me? What was she after?

"Using dark magic? The Watchers could catch us, mistress. It's too dangerous," Rufus told her.

"No, they won't. Leave the Watchers to me. You're dismissed." She motioned for him to leave with a wave of her hand. When he didn't, she quirked an eyebrow in question. "Something else on your mind?"

He cleared his throat. "One other thing. The witch also mentioned most humans lack warrior skills and physical strength. I assume the human girl is not strong or skilled in fighting."

"I am well aware of that, Rufus. I'll take care of this problem when the time comes," she told him. He dipped his head, then headed for the front door.

When he left, the scene around me began to change. Heather's living room shifted into a long, white hallway with clean walls, a polished tile floor, bright lights above, and many closed metal doors lining both sides. As I looked around, fear wrapped its icy fingers around my heart. Oh, God, no. I was in the hallway outside the room where I'd been held by Cole. There was no mistaking it. This nightmarish place had been seared into my memory.

I buried my face in my hands. *You're not really here, you're not really here, you're not really here*, I chanted in my head, trying to control my heavy breathing. Then I looked up at the sound of Heather's voice. She was standing in front of me, a few feet away, near a closed metal door.

Dressed in black pants, a white shirt, and heavy boots, a man stood beside her, about six feet tall, all muscle with black skin, dark hair, and brown eyes. He didn't look like the type to smile much. His face was cold and impassive as he listened to her.

"This is where I keep my collection of rare creatures. I call this facility Eden," she explained. It was obvious the man wasn't one of her subordinates, judging by his demeanor and the way he held himself. He was someone important, maybe a royal demon. The sound of a woman protesting and screaming filled the hallway, interrupting Heather.

"What is the meaning of this?" Heather demanded of the man approaching her from the end of the hallway. He was dragging a woman by her upper arm as she struggled in vain.

The woman's captor reached Heather and bowed. "Mistress."

Heather's lips thinned into a tight line as she turned her gaze on the man. "Give me one good reason why I shouldn't have your head for interrupting me while I'm with Edmund."

"Mistress, please forgive me. I found this woman trying to sneak into the facility and free her daughter. I thought you would want me to bring her to you."

Edmund's eyes grew saucer-like as he stared at the woman. "But your kind is extinct." Heather's anger disappeared, and she smiled, looking pleased with Edmund's reaction.

"There are still a few Goldeneyes out there," she said. "In fact, I was just about to tell you I caught one"— her eyes flicked to the woman—"well, now two."

The mother pleaded with Heather, "I'm begging you, please release my daughter."

The demon princess snickered. "And why would I do that?"

"I have twenty thousand dollars in my bank account. If you release my daughter, the money's all yours," the woman promised.

Heather barked a cruel laugh. "Do you realize how ridiculous you sound? Look at me." She waved at her fitted business dress and heels. Then she appraised the woman's clothes. "My outfit alone probably costs more than you earn in a month. I don't need your money, you moron; it's the unique, powerful tears of your kind that I want."

"Then take me instead of my daughter. Use my golden tears," the woman said.

Could she be the mother of the girl who had been locked in the room next to mine? The girl with the golden tears?

Heather's crimson lips broke into a sadistic smile as she seemed to enjoy the woman's suffering. "Looks like someone here left their brain at home today. Allow me to connect the dots for you. Before your stupid attempt to break in, I had the pleasure of having only one of your extraordinary kind in my possession.

"Now, with you and your daughter, I have a pair. And two is better than one. I've been searching for your kind for years. Did you really think I was going to let either of you go?" She looked at her minion. "Lock her up. And make sure she's far away from her daughter's cell."

The man nodded and dragged the woman along with him as he walked down the hallway. The whole place started to fade away until I was back on Heather's street. The witch, or whatever she was, was still holding my hand.

I stared at her in shock. "What did I just see? Do you know what Heather wants from me? Or who Cole is?"

The barrage of questions stopped when her index finger touched the number on my open palm, demanding my attention. Her intense gaze held mine.

"I'm sorry. I'm not sure what you're trying to say," I told her.

She drummed on the tattoo with her finger. I looked at the numbers, then back at her finger tapping the ink, desperately searching for meaning in her silent gesture. Then I remembered that witches who came in contact with the tattoo always uttered the same two enigmatic words.

"Eternal gods?" I asked. "Is that what you're trying to tell me?" Her finger stilled. Yes, that was it. "What about eternal gods? What does it mean?" My words were charged with a mixture of anticipation and urgency.

Her face contorted with effort as she mouthed, 'No.'

"No? No what?"

She tapped the tattoo again and then shook her head.

"No eternal gods?" My tone held uncertainty. I expected another head shake, but instead, her head bobbed up and down a few times. What the hell was *No eternal gods* supposed to mean?

A sudden noise from Heather's house made the woman turn her head to it. When her gaze returned to mine, frustration clouded her features. She let go of my hand and hurried off.

"No, wait, please! Don't go," I called after her, but she disappeared into the darkness.

Gideon and the two witches emerged from Heather's house and walked down the front steps. Mark handed him a bag before he and Harper crossed the street to a car parked at the curb. When Gideon's eyes caught mine, he approached me with the bag slung over his shoulder.

"I have the artifact. We have to get out of here before Heather's neighbors—" His brow furrowed as he took in my shaken demeanor. "What's wrong? You look rattled."

I told him about the time I'd caught that woman watching me, then said, "She was just here, only moments ago." At his alarmed reaction, I added, "I'm fine. She didn't hurt me."

A passerby came our way, and I fell silent, watching the elderly man eye Gideon's bag suspiciously.

After the man moved out of earshot, Gideon said, "Tell me all about it when we get home."

# Chapter 26

Keeping my hands on the artifact for three hours straight was a challenge, to say the least, but by the end of the third hour, I literally felt a huge weight lift off me. I was pretty sure that meant the obsessive part of the dragon blood curse had been removed from my body. When it was over, I was so relieved. One less thing on my ever-growing list of threats that could kill me.

After Gideon put the artifact in his safe and returned to the living room, I told him what the woman had shown me. However, due to the weird ice-cream spell I was under, I had to leave out the part about the begging mother and her daughter, who were a rare species that cried golden tears.

"Heather? Are you sure it was Heather? Flaming ginger hair, green eyes?" Gideon asked when I finished.

"Yes. It was her. And for some reason, she decided to destroy my life. I can't figure out why me. Sure, I'm Gifted, but I'm still just an ordinary human with no unique powers." My blood seethed as I thought about how she and Cole had taken everything from me. I wouldn't rest until they both paid for what they'd done to me.

Gideon's voice pulled me back to the moment. "We need to learn the identity of the woman who showed you what Heather did. It looks like she has the answers."

"Yeah, I just wish it was easy to find her." I sighed, then asked, "If Heather hired Cole to kidnap me, do you think she knows I escaped?"

He shook his head. "I doubt that. According to Evelyn's timeline, Heather went to Herit's world before Oberon freed you. No one could have informed her you'd escaped."

"What about the demon I saw with Heather, Edmund. Have you heard of him?" I asked.

"He's Damon's right-hand man and a very dangerous demon. Royal blood. He's also someone who might know what Heather's up to. When'd you say Piper was going to recreate Ivy's spell?"

"Tomorrow at seven in the evening. Why do you ask?" I said.

"Two days ago, Edmund landed in a small, remote town in Mexico, where there are no demon territories. That makes it the perfect place for me to corner him and force some answers out of him about Heather. I'm not sure how long he plans to stay there, so I need to get to Mexico tonight before he leaves. Otherwise, I might miss an excellent opportunity for a not-so-friendly tête-à-tête with him to get answers."

"If you leave tonight, you won't be back in time for Piper's spell," I said.

"No, unfortunately, I won't."

"You got the play-by-play on where Edmund is. How?"

"I make it a point to keep track of where high-level demons are, self-preservation and all," he answered, and his gaze went to the number on my hand, a hint of concern on his face. "If Heather was the mastermind behind your abduction, we could figure out how to get her to remove the tattoo so you don't have to give Eric the dragon blood. I'm counting on Edmund to know when she plans to return. Let's just hope it's before the number hits zero."

I told him about the fortune teller's reading and said, "So we can be sure she'll be back in four hundred ninety-two days, standing by my side. Unless, of course, I manage to change my future by either stopping the countdown or getting rid of the tattoo."

Gideon fell silent, his expression turning contemplative.

"The number doesn't always go down by one every twenty-four hours," he said, breaking the silence. "There have been times it dropped within seconds, like when you died or got sick. With that in mind, it's plausible to assume Heather can't accurately monitor the tattoo's countdown. However, based on the fortune teller's insight, we know Heather will show up right when the number reaches zero. That's a hell of a coincidence, so I'm willing to bet Cole came up with a spell that will alert her before the countdown ends."

"Whatever Heather's plan is," I said, "it must be something evil. She'll probably want to kill me when I'm no longer useful to her, after the tattoo ends the countdown." Fear slipped into my voice. I knew I'd have to face her in person to get my revenge, but the thought of it stirred terror in my stomach.

Eric was different from Heather. Yes, he was a demon, but there was something in his eyes, something that wasn't completely evil. Heather, however, radiated nothing but malice, her gaze a window to a cold, merciless nature. She was a stone-cold psychopath, empty of any compassion or emotion. I now understood why everyone called her the bitch from hell.

Gideon reached out and placed his hands on either side of my face, fixing me with his eyes. "I will never let her hurt you. Ever. And I am not easy to take out." His ocean-blue gaze bored into mine, a silence filling the room as time seemed to stand still. A flicker of gold danced around the edges of his irises as he resumed speaking. "Do you have any idea how much I love you? Do you understand the meaning of my love? I will kill anyone who thinks of harming you. I will die before I let anything bad happen to you."

The deep sincerity in his tone made it clear his heart was in every word. I closed my eyes and felt his touch on my face.

When I opened them and met his gaze, I said, "I love you, too."

His eyes heated and swirled with passion, gold coloring his entire iris. He leaned in and covered my mouth with his. I felt my body respond to his deep, slow kiss. Our tongues intertwined as he eased me backward until I was lying on my back on the couch. One hand tangled in my hair, the other reached down to unzip my pants and slide inside.

He pushed my underwear aside and stroked my sensitive nub with the pad of his finger, then rubbed it in small circles. Arousal seared through me. His lips left my mouth and traveled down my neck. Sweet tension built inside me, and I moaned. As his thumb massaged the sensitive spot, he plunged a finger inside me, then another, stroking in and out, in and out, pushing me to the edge and beyond, and my body exploded in sheer ecstasy.

Before I could catch my breath, he whipped my pants and underwear down and off in one swift motion. Then he drew me up and onto his lap. I straddled him as he sat on the couch, pulling my top over my head to remove my shirt and bra. He leaned in, and his mouth closed over my breast, teasing my nipple. He unfastened his pants as he kissed my other breast. His hard length sprung out.

"Ride me," he rasped. I rose slightly and lowered myself down on him. He let out a low growl of satisfaction and pulled my head toward him to kiss me. Pleasure roared through my body as I rocked up and back. Breaking the kiss, he grabbed my ass with both hands and shoved up into me, plunging me up and down on him harder and faster.

I threw my head back, my hands behind me on his thighs. The pressure inside me grew and grew until a second orgasm ripped through me. Digging my fingernails into his thighs, I cried out. A minute later, he came with a low, guttural groan, and I collapsed against his chest.

We stayed in silence for a while as his thumb traced slow, soothing circles down my back. A pang of sadness welled up inside me as I thought about him leaving for Mexico that night. I knew it was necessary to uncover Heather's plans, but that didn't make the thought of separation any less painful.

After we showered, he dressed in a black ensemble and went to his armory room where he packed a bag of weapons. He didn't know when he'd be back, but before he left, he promised to keep me updated.

In the morning, I returned to work with a look of gratitude as Veronica brushed off how long she'd covered my shifts. Citing a "family crisis" to explain my extended absence seemed to satisfy her and the boss. Piper's spell occupied my thoughts for the entire shift, possibilities and theories about who it would summon swirling in my head. After punching out, I went back to my apartment with three hours to spare before Piper started the spell. I took a shower, changed into fresh clothes, and was about to fix myself something to eat when Lily called with exciting news. She'd discovered that dark, protective potions like the one that cloaked me from Cole had a unique property.

She explained that when I'd phased through Cole, the potion's intended target, it captured a fragment of his energy. This allowed the potion to analyze and study Cole's magical abilities in order to increase its effectiveness in future encounters with him. Lily proposed using Cole's energy fragment as a personal item to cast a locator spell on him. She warned that we'd have to do this quickly since we had limited time. According to her calculations, the potion would complete its analysis of Cole's energy and get rid of it within a day or two. Without wasting any time, I dropped everything and hurried to her apartment.

Her living room seemed ready for the spell. On her Persian rug was a circle of smooth, polished stones of various sizes and colors. Candles were scattered around them, creating a flickering glow, their exotic fruit scents mingling in the air. Small bowls of herbs and powders sat among the candles. Lily guided me into the stone circle and started the locator spell, her voice steady as she recited incantations from a thick book.

After she finished, she closed her eyes, then opened them. She smiled at me.

"It worked; we have Cole's location."

I gasped, my hand flying to my open mouth. I couldn't believe it! Revenge was no longer a distant dream!

"He's in the city, and I have the exact address," Lily said. "Now justice can be served. I'll contact the Watchers and have them arrest him." She stepped over to the coffee table and picked up her cell phone.

"No." I stopped her. She knitted her brows, and I added, "I mean, not now."

"Then when?"

"After I talk to Cole alone," I answered. She looked like she was about to argue, so I continued, "Lily, that man kidnapped me and branded my body with dark magic. I deserve the opportunity to confront him about his motives. If the Watchers take him and throw him in Ice Prison, I may never get the answers I need to find closure and move on with my life. All I ask is for a brief moment alone with him before you notify the Watchers."

There were a few things I planned to do when I saw Cole; turning him over to the Watchers was not one of them. I intended to uncover the reasons behind his actions, force him to remove the tattoo from my hand, and ensure he called off the men watching my family. Then I'd use my dagger, which could touch his body as it wasn't under the influence of Ivy's potion, and kill him. Yes, justice would be served, but not in the way Lily had in mind.

"How are you going to talk to him? He can't hear or see you," Lily pointed out.

"That won't be a problem; I'll write my questions down so he can see them. I just need to know if you can keep him from disappearing like he did before."

"He's very powerful, but so am I. I'll cast a magical field around the house that will prevent anyone inside from teleporting. It'll take a lot of energy from me, but it'll give you some time with him so you can have your closure. You deserve it."

I thanked her, and we drove to the address the spell locator had provided us. As Lily parked in front of a house nestled in a middle-class neighborhood, a whirlwind of emotions hit me. My heart was pounding with a mixture of anticipation and adrenaline. I could hardly believe I was only a few steps away from finally getting answers—and my revenge.

Standing in front of the house where Cole was supposed to be, Lily muttered the spell that would keep him from disappearing into thin air. Her body shook with effort, and just as her knees buckled, I caught her arm and eased her down onto the porch steps.

"Go talk to him. I'll be fine," she said.

"Are you sure you're okay? Your whole body is trembling."

"Yes, it'll pass, now go inside," she insisted. I nodded as I straightened.

The front door was unlocked. When I entered the house, my jaw slackened at the sight that greeted me. What the hell? The place was completely empty—no furniture, belongings, or even a trace of recent occupancy. My footsteps echoed through the bare rooms as I searched for Cole. He was nowhere to be found. My fingers clenched into fists while frustration consumed me. Where was he? As I turned to leave to inform Lily of Cole's absence, the front door swung open, and she stepped inside.

"He's not here," I told her.

"I know." She extended her hand to show me a piece of paper. "This appeared in my hand just a moment ago. It's from him, sent through his magic." I took the note and read it.

*Lily, I suppose you were hoping to have me arrested by the Watchers, but you underestimated me. You foolishly thought I wouldn't sense your locator spell. My powers are far beyond your comprehension, so I suggest you give up your fruitless search. You will never find me.*

*As for the human you used for your spell, tell her that while I can't see or hear her, my men, who know what she looks like, are watching her family closely. Any attempt to contact her parents or sister will result in their death. I can only imagine how much she misses them. But I did warn her that if she escaped, she would be all alone.*

Lily slowly shook her head, as if trying to make sense of the situation. "I knew he wasn't an ordinary witch, but in all my years, I've never encountered anyone powerful enough to detect a locator spell. A witch like him needs to be locked away in Ice Prison before he can harm another innocent soul. Coming here was a reckless mistake. If he had been in the house and felt threatened, who knows what havoc he might've wreaked. We must let the Watchers handle this, not us."

I understood Lily's concern. Cole was very dangerous, but I wasn't going to give up on my search for him. Arguing with her would be pointless; her resolute expression told me her mind was made up, so I just nodded in agreement. My eyes then swept the empty living room. Was this his permanent residence or a temporary one? Either way, it was possible the people who lived nearby might know something useful that could help me track him down. With Lily with me, though, now wasn't the time to talk to his neighbors. I glanced at my watch. Besides, I had to hurry to where Piper was going to do Ivy's spell.

After Lily dropped me off near a subway station, I took the train to the address Logan had given me. When I got there, I found Piper sitting on a bench across the street. She was nervously rubbing her hands along her thighs. Next to her on the bench was an open notebook. She took a few deep breaths before grabbing it and standing up. Her eyes fell on the pages while she fiddled with the strap of a cross-body shoulder bag. Then she read aloud Ivy's summoning spell from the notebook.

I stayed where I was, watching her. People and cars passed by as I waited, my mind twirling with anticipation. Who would show up? Who had Ivy wanted to talk to? The questions in my mind stopped when I noticed Piper had finished the spell. I darted my eyes around the street, watching for the person who had been summoned to approach Piper. Until I felt a presence behind me.

I spun around. My breath caught in my throat at the sight of the huge man standing before me—a mountain of flesh covered in muscle. His frame, well over six feet, towered over mine. The long-sleeved white shirt he wore barely contained his barrel chest, his bulky legs wrapped in well-worn blue jeans. His skin was smooth and black, his jaw like a chunk of granite, his intense, dark green eyes boring into mine.

God, I really hoped this muscles-on-muscles man was not a demon or some crazy person about to attack me. Even with my new physical strength from the dark magic on my hand, I knew I couldn't take him on. I started to plan my escape when his lips stretched into a warm smile. I let my guard down a bit. I mean, someone with ass-kicking intentions doesn't usually serve up a smile that could melt the polar ice caps, right? But who was this dude? And what did he want? I gave him a confused look, and the man's smile widened.

"Hello, little human," he said.

My eyes grew larger. Only once before had I been called little human, and that was by a massive blue dragon who had broken the rule of his kind to save my life from the gargoyles in Ice Prison.

I gasped. "Vakan? Is that you?"

The wind ruffled his black, shaggy, curly hair. "Yes, in my two-legged form." His voice was rich and deep.

All I could do at that moment was stare at him, rendered speechless by the tidal wave of shock that had crashed into me.

# Chapter 27

"Wh-why are you here?" I stammered when the ability to form words returned. Then, my stomach lurched with dread. His job was to keep the balance of good and evil by killing those on his list. Basically, his kind was like the Grim Reaper, and one of them was standing in front of me.

"Oh, no, I'm on your list," I whispered, taking a step back.

He raised his hand in a gesture of reassurance. "You need not worry about your soul, little human. My presence here is due to a summoning spell, not my list."

I blinked at his words. Why had Ivy summoned the blue dragon? I turned to look at Piper across the street. Her face was filled with disappointment, a clear indication she believed the spell had failed. As she stepped to the curb and shot out a hand for a cab, I looked back at Vakan.

He extended his hand to me. "Would you join me in a quieter setting?"

I wondered why he needed to hold my hand to go somewhere else, but I took it anyway. He'd saved my life in Ice Prison, which earned him my trust. The moment our skin touched, everything around me started to blur. The city street slowly gave way to high mountains and lush, green trees. The sounds of traffic and people were replaced by the soothing symphony of water running over stones, birds chirping, and wind blowing through the leaves. Moonlight filtered through the branches of the trees.

I pulled my coat tighter against the cold. "Where are we?"

"In Austria. I used my teleportation ability, which I only possess when I am in my two-legged form, to bring us here. I find the natural environment of Austria to be exceptionally serene and tranquil. Worry not, little human, I will return you to your original location once we have finished."

"Austria..." I murmured, my gaze wandering around my new surroundings in complete amazement until my eyes fell back on Vakan. I had never expected to see the blue dragon again after Ice Prison, let alone in his human form. I'd often wondered what had become of him. What punishment he'd suffered for saving me.

"The last time I saw you, you were flying off to be judged for helping me. Please tell me your punishment wasn't too severe," I said.

"For violating the laws of my kind, I am forced to carry the burden of human emotions for eternity."

His unexpected answer puzzled me. "A burden? Why? Isn't the ability to experience emotions considered a good thing to have?"

"Taking souls from living beings becomes a difficult task when one is susceptible to emotional influence. The sorrow I experience each time I reap an innocent young soul is deep and lasting," he answered. The guilt of being the cause of his punishment must have been written all over my face because his next words were, "Do not hold yourself responsible, little human. As a self-governing entity, I acted of my own volition when I saved you, and I willingly accepted full responsibility for my actions."

"Still, I feel bad you were punished because of me," I said, then frowned. "It's not fair. You don't deserve to suffer like that."

"There is no need for you to inconvenience yourself on my account." He paused for a moment then said, "I wish to speak with you about another matter, a magic wielder named Ivy."

"Yes, we definitely need to talk about her. I have so many questions."

"I thought as much. First, allow me to recount how I came to meet her," he began. "When I still lacked human emotions, I was unaffected by distractions and focused solely on my duties. However, in my new state, I found myself compelled by the feeling of curiosity when I sensed a spell being cast upon me.

"Although the magic of the Earth creatures has no effect on my kind, I chose to answer the summoning spell. Upon my arrival, I inquired of the magic wielder about the purpose of requesting my presence. She recounted her tale and expressed a desire to find the whereabouts of the human whose life I had saved. Her intention, as I came to understand, was to warn you of dark magic that bound you both."

"Dark magic?" I stopped him. "You mean the Dragon Blood Curse?"

"Curses are a form of dark magic," he answered. A drop of rain landed on my nose. I wiped it off and looked up at the night sky.

"We'd better find some cover," I said.

We moved under a large tree as the rain began to trickle down.

I closed my coat and told him, "All right, so Ivy cast the summoning spell to get you to bring her to me. Did she tell you how she knew you saved me in Ice Prison?"

"The curse, as you referred to it, sometimes causes the magic wielder to experience your memories in her dreams, one of which included the time I saved you. You and she share a connection," he answered.

"Shared," I corrected. "Past tense. She was murdered."

"Your revelation is unsurprising. The magic wielder claimed a dark soul had already taken her family from her. Fearing you might suffer the same fate, she sought to caution you against this dark soul. When she asked for my help in finding you, I explained that I lacked the ability to locate a soul who is not on my list."

A question came to me. "Ivy left me a message before she died. She talked about the curse, her struggle to survive, her fears—just about everything she'd been through. Except for one thing. You. Do you have any idea why she didn't say anything about summoning a dragon?"

"I did not wish for the magic wielder to retain any recollection of our encounter; therefore, I employed my magic to erase our meeting from her mind."

His words made me curious about something, and I asked, "She wrote down the date and time she'd cast the spell that summoned you on a piece of paper. Why didn't this information bring back her memory of meeting you?"

"Anything related to our encounter was erased from her mind. Consequently, the date and time written on the paper appeared blank to her eyes," he answered, and I remembered that Ivy also hadn't explained what the third potion had been.

"Ivy told me she'd compelled me to drink two potions, but I drank three. Interestingly, she made no mention of this mysterious third potion. Was that your doing too?"

"The magic wielder expressed concern for your safety, a sentiment I shared as well. The laws of my kind forbid me from interfering with the death process of beings who are not on my list. However, I was confident in my ability to evade detection for such wrongdoing if I saved you from death in a single instance.

"Before I departed from the magic wielder, I cast a spell to create a potion that could only be consumed by you. It served as a beacon to alert me if your soul ever entered the realm between life and death, where I can locate any soul I wish to. Unbeknownst to the magic wielder, I wove a magical link between my potion and her so that if she encountered you, the potion would manifest in your vicinity and compel you to partake of its contents. Upon discovering your soul had departed from your body, I took measures to return it."

"So when I died, it was you who opened the door to my parents' living room," I said.

"Yes, but you did not die. Your soul left your vessel. However, it still existed. I intervened and returned it before it was too late."

"Why didn't you say anything to me when you opened the door?" I asked.

"There is only a brief moment to reunite a soul with its vessel as it hovers in the realm between life and death, occasionally manifesting as a cherished memory. The urgency of the circumstance precluded any exchange of words. And after your soul rejoined its vessel, I once again was unable to locate you.

"When I felt the call of a summoning spell, cast by another magic wielder, my interest was piqued again. I was quite surprised to find you not far away. I had to seize the opportunity to have a proper conversation with you."

"I can't believe you stuck your neck out for me to save my life. Again. Wow... Thank you." Before I could think better of it, I hugged him. He stood still, looking as if he didn't know what to do with his hands. When I pulled away, he looked a little taken aback and confused. Apparently, hugs were unfamiliar territory for him, at least not in his human form.

"I'm sorry. I didn't mean to throw you off. I just wanted to show my appreciation. It's a human thing," I said.

His lips turned up in a smile. "You are most welcome, Sydney."

"I'm glad we talked. A lot of things make more sense now," I said. "But will you make me forget meeting you, like you did with Ivy?"

"No. It is imperative that you retain this memory, for I have to warn you of a serious matter," he answered.

My face screwed up. "Warn me about what?" The rain stopped, and the sound of flowing water filled the silence as his expression turned serious. My shoulders slumped as I exhaled. Crap. Whatever he had to say must be really bad.

His mouth set in a grim line. "I have seen the future of humanity. It was dark and bleak. The protectors of your realm, known as the Watchers, had been destroyed, and the strong species of your world ceased to hide their true nature from humans. They united to wage war against humanity and emerged victorious." Vakan's gaze hardened. "And they enslaved your kind."

"Are you saying there will be an apocalypse?" I asked.

"Allow me to reveal it to you," he said, extending his hand again. I accepted it, and we were transported to a hellish scene. I turned in a slow circle, a sense of dread rising in my throat as I surveyed the apocalyptic landscape.

Ashes fell like snowflakes from the gloomy gray sky. Everywhere I looked, there was destruction—concrete rubble, wrecked cars, fallen trees and branches, piles of debris of all kinds, burning tires, and half-destroyed buildings with smoke still seeping from embers. The damaged walls bore graffiti of both religious texts and gang symbols, and bodies lay scattered along the broken road and abandoned streets.

Horror crept through me as I shook my head in disbelief. "Is this really the future?"

"Yes," Vakan said.

I reached out and brushed my hand against the gray powder drifting in the air. "Why is it raining ashes?"

"Wars in which dark magic is rampant will inevitably lead to calamities such as ash falling from the sky and the occasional acid rain. To avoid this fate upon your world, you must find a way to prevent the annihilation of the Watchers."

"Aren't the Watchers indestructible?" I asked.

"They are beings of magic, and magic is not beyond destruction."

"What will happen to them? What will cause them to die?"

"I regret to say I lack the answers to these questions. When a pivotal shift for a world lies in its future, I catch glimpses of it. However, the intricate details of the unfolding events that lead to its future remain veiled from me," he answered.

"What about the date? Do you know when we are?" I asked.

"I am unable to pinpoint the precise moment of this event's occurrence, but I can say with a high degree of certainty it will not occur in the distant future, such as decades or centuries."

I glanced around me. "Your job is to maintain the balance between good and evil, right? So wouldn't a war against humans upset this balance? All I see here," I waved my hand at our grim surroundings, "is misery. So why would the dragons let this war happen?"

"Because the war will not upset the balance," he answered.

I thought about the dragon blood in Ivy's crypt. What if someone like Damon managed to steal it? Could his possession of the sought-after vial be the catalyst for the Watchers' downfall and the resulting apocalypse?

I looked at Vakan. "Suppose the balance between good and evil was disturbed beyond even your abilities to restore it. Could this indirectly lead to the elimination of the Watchers?"

"Such an imbalance would not cause the destruction of the Watchers; however, it would be devastating for your world. When a planet falls beyond the capacity of my kind to restore it to proper order, we initiate procedures for its termination," he answered. His words gave me another reason why I had to make sure the stolen dragon blood was destroyed. Vakan's eyes suddenly glowed with a bright green light. He closed them for a moment.

When they reopened, he said, "A new list has arrived that demands my attention. I must return to my duties."

He took my hand, and in an instant, we were transported back to the present and to the familiar streets of New York. I parted my lips to tell him about the stolen dragon blood and ask him to get rid of it, but before I could utter a word, he vanished into thin air.

As I stood in the middle of the street, my mind was consumed with thoughts of my family. If what Vakan had shown me was the near future, as he'd assumed, how could I protect them from it? The worry gnawed at me; I had no idea how to prevent the Watchers' destruction. A scream of rage, frustration, and utter despair bubbled up inside me, threatening to burst from the depths of my soul.

Then my phone buzzed. I pulled it out to find a text message from Ian. Oh, wow, I'd totally forgotten about him. I opened his text.

*Come by my office now. I've got answers for you about Oberon.*

Finally, a little break! I grabbed a cab and headed to his office.

# Chapter 28

Ian's office door was open when I arrived. Finding the reception room empty, I went in. He wasn't alone. He was sitting at his cluttered desk with a woman on his lap, her fingers tangled in his hair as he stroked her cheek. I cleared my throat to announce my presence, and they both looked at me.

"Sydney has arrived," Ian said to his companion as she rose from his lap and smoothed her knee-length skirt. The woman was strikingly beautiful, her brunette locks cascading down her back in a silken curtain. Her fine-boned face was framed by a delicate complexion, her skin smooth as velvet, a natural alabaster tone warmed by a subtle peach blush.

The woman's eyes popped open. "This is Sydney?"

I turned my attention to Ian, a hint of annoyance creeping into my tone. "Who is she?"

Ignoring my question, Ian said with equal irritation, "I did my job—without pay—and got the information you asked for. So tell Audrey we are square, no more unpaid cases."

Eager to hear what he'd uncovered, I asked, "What did you find out?"

The woman studied me and my ungloved left hand intently. "Is this really her?" Her voice was a combination of curiosity and disbelief. "She seems so... so... ordinary, despite the dark magic on her hand. Who cast it?" she asked me.

"None of your business," I replied, crossing my arms as I turned to Ian. "I wasn't aware there was going to be a guest at our meeting. Mind telling me who she is?"

"This is Orithia, my lovely common fae. I've been investigating your case with her assistance," Ian said. "While I focused on the details in our world, Orithia went back to the faerie realm and did some digging to uncover information for me there. Yesterday, we finally got to the bottom of why the king of the fae is interested in you. Orithia's reaction stems from her disappointment at seeing how human, weak, and unimpressive the future queen of the fae is."

"Future queen?" I echoed, not sure if I'd heard right or if they had lost their minds.

"Yes, you are Oberon's fated mate," he told me.

"What!" My voice shot up.

Ian glanced at the time, pulled off his tie, and tossed it on the desk. "I know, it shocked me too. Never before have I heard of a royal fae having a human mate."

Was he messing with me? Yeah, he probably was. I gave him a pissed-off look. "Listen, you jerk, if you couldn't find—"

"He's telling you the truth. You're Oberon's fated mate," Orithia said. I glanced back and forth between them, then realized they were deadly serious.

After a few minutes of processing this bombshell, I said, "Okay, say it's true; what does it mean to be someone's fated mate in the Hidden World, or the faerie world?"

"It means you and Oberon are destined to be together," Orithia explained.

I scoffed. "This is ridiculous. I don't even know the dude, and besides, I'm already in love with who I'm supposed to be with. Nothing's gonna change that."

"Except fate," Ian said.

"I don't believe in fate, and like I said, my heart already belongs to someone else," I told him.

"Have you chosen to love them?" Orithia asked me.

"You can't choose to love someone. It just happens," I told her.

"Exactly," Ian said. "The heart wants what it wants, and there is no point in fighting it. You won't be able to stop fate from making you fall in love with Oberon once you've spent some time with him."

Damn it! Ian's words had managed to plant seeds of doubt in my mind. He was right; when it came to love, free will took a back seat. I hadn't chosen to develop feelings for Gideon; in fact, I had resisted them for quite some time before finally accepting them.

I looked at Orithia and Ian. What if their detective work had been sloppy and they were wrong?

"How can you be so sure I'm meant to be with Oberon? Who told you that?" I asked.

Orithia walked to the door, closed it, and sat down in one of the two guest chairs facing the desk. She gestured for me to join her, and I sat down next to her.

"I was cast out by my family after I performed a forbidden spell against my father's warning," she said. "Banished from home, I chose to forge a new life in your world, where I met this sweet illusionist." She glanced at Ian and smiled before continuing. "When he asked for my help in solving your case, I agreed, intrigued by my king's interest in a human.

"The next day, I returned to my world and spent my time there gathering information. Until I overheard Oberon's advisor talking to another royal about our king's request to build a beautiful garden for his fated mate, a human named Sydney Newbern. And that's how I learned of your future role as the queen of the fae." At my disappointed expression, she gave me a sympathetic look. "I understand this is not what you wanted to hear, but I'm afraid you cannot escape or change this fate."

I needed to know more. "How did Oberon come to discover I was his fated mate?"

Ian offered a possible explanation. "It probably happened when he came to our world, on one of his rare visits. He must have felt an undeniable pull, a deep connection that told him his fated mate was here, and he searched for you."

"Well, I didn't feel anything. Is that because I'm human?" I said, feeling an annoying sense of déjà vu.

"Yes, your human nature has likely played a role," Orithia replied.

"How exactly does this whole fated mates thing work? Do all fae have fated mates?" I asked.

Orithia shook her head. "Oh, no, not at all."

"You need to understand something," Ian said. "What we call 'fate' is actually a powerful magic that can only be cast by the red dragon. Have you ever heard of the seven dragons?"

"Yes," I answered, and he continued.

"There are two ways in which dragons maintain the balance between good and evil in our world. One is through their list, and the other is through fated mates. On rare occasions, two souls are predestined to positively impact this balance. Only when these individuals are in love with their fated mate, and not necessarily at the same time, will their actions and choices help to ensure neither good nor evil exceeds the fixed ratio that must be maintained between them. The red dragon can sense when such a connection is made between two souls and will cast a powerful spell to cause them to fall in love."

"How can their actions affect the balance?" I asked.

"Let's say there's a mugger who's rotten to the core and has to die to keep the balance," he said. "Now, you have these two souls under the dragon's spell. The guy wakes up one morning and decides to buy an engagement ring for his fated mate. But on his way home, he ends up shooting that very mugger in self-defense after he violently tries to wrestle the ring from him, and there you have it, balance restored."

"Yeah, in our world, but Oberon doesn't live here," I pointed out.

Ian clarified, "Two fated souls don't necessarily have to be of the same species or even from the same world. However, I must admit a union between a royal fae and a human is unprecedented."

Hoping for a solution, I asked, "Is there any way to unravel the red dragon's spell?"

"No being can undo it except the dragon itself," Ian answered, then added, "You should know that since you're human, you'll need to look at Oberon—and not in a dream or illusion—before the spell starts to affect you. And unlike him, the effect on you will be gradual. As you spend more time together, affection will ignite in your heart until you find yourself in love with him."

I felt a sense of relief. "Great, because one look at Oberon and I'm dead, so that will never happen. Although it begs the question, why would the red dragon cast the spell on me if I can't even look at Oberon?"

"Perhaps that is the very reason your souls were destined to be together," Orithia replied. "In the faerie world, my king oversees a laboratory where a select team of his chosen scientists has been conducting cruel experiments on night creatures. He's interested in their Bounding liquid, a substance that stops the aging process in mortals.

"To make you immortal so you could look at him without dying, he's tasked his scientists with finding a way to enhance the liquid in the night creatures' fangs to grant immortality as well. So far, they have been unsuccessful, but they keep trying. Anyway, the night creatures in the lab were kidnapped from your world, and many of them died during the experiments. It's possible their deaths helped restore the balance of good and evil on Earth."

I sighed, then asked, "Let's consider a hypothetical scenario in which someone manages to resist the red dragon spell and doesn't end up with their fated mate. Could that upset the balance?"

"No, because the dragons' primary method of preserving it is through their list, not the red dragon's spell," Ian answered.

Then, a new question tugged at my mind. "How come Oberon didn't tell me I was his fated mate?"

"Revealing such significant information would cause you to ask him many questions," Orithia said. "He's probably waiting until you become immortal to have this conversation with you, so he doesn't have to worry about you accidentally catching a glimpse of him and dying."

Annoyance seeped through me. "Well, he can keep waiting. I have zero interest in becoming immortal or being with him. That's never going to happen. I'll find a way to fight the red dragon's spell."

Orithia looked at me as if I'd said something ridiculous. "You're a fool if you think the king of the fae is going to let you choose whether or not to be his queen. He'll do anything to make you his. He is ruthless, especially when it comes to getting what he wants. No one denies him."

Her words sent an eerie chill through my body, giving me goosebumps. Then I remembered what Gideon had told me, about how dark magic had once destroyed the faerie world.

"Isn't Oberon worried my tattoo might harm your world?" I asked Orithia.

"No. Even though the number is made of powerful dark magic, it poses no danger to our world in its current state as it's not an active spell," she said.

I thought about the place where I'd been held captive. Oberon had freed me from Heather's facility, so maybe someone in his court knew Heather's motives for imprisoning me.

I looked at Orithia. "Did you hear anything else about me during your investigation?"

"No, I didn't," she answered.

"Would you be willing to keep me informed about Oberon's progress with the Bounding liquid if I paid you?" I asked, hoping for a heads-up on when he'd pop into my life again.

She shook her head. "I'm sorry, but I can't. I'm afraid I'll arouse suspicion if I go back and keep asking questions about my king. I could be accused of treason, and the punishment for that is to have your wings clipped—a fate worse than death for a fae."

"What about sabotaging Oberon's team's experiments on the down-low?" I didn't really expect her to agree, but I had to try.

"Again, too risky," she answered. I let out a long breath as my shoulders hunched, and she said, "I know it's hard for you to accept the whole fated mate thing because you don't want to be Oberon's queen, but my advice to you? Don't fight your fate; you will never win."

A moment of silence fell over the room.

Leaning forward, Ian broke it by clasping his hands. "All right, I think we've covered everything. There's nothing more to discuss. This meeting is over." As I stood, he added, "Don't forget to tell Audrey there will be no more free services, particularly for her annoying human friends."

I shot him an exasperated glance before redirecting my attention to Orithia. "My advice to you? Don't waste your time on jerks. Trust me, there are far better guys out there than him." I turned and walked out of his office.

Outside, the night sky was cloudy, the crescent moon barely visible in the darkness. I walked to the subway, the draining effects of emotional exhaustion settling in my bones. When I reached my apartment, I flopped down on my bed with a heavy sigh and kicked off my boots.

In the silence of my apartment, my mind was a parade of thoughts, flooded with problems, questions, and emotions. Heather, the mysterious woman, the dragon blood, Eric, Cole, the end of the world, my family, the number on my hand. In the midst of my mental storm, Orithia's words filtered into my tired brain.

*Don't fight your fate; you will never win.*

Was she right? Was there no point in fighting? I didn't want to be Oberon's fated mate, but it didn't look like I had a choice. I closed my eyes and took a deep breath, trying to clear my head. When I opened them, I was filled with anger. I refused to accept that magic would decide my love life for me.

I didn't know what the future held for Gideon and me, especially since he was immortal and I wasn't. I loved being human and had no desire to become immortal. But I also loved Gideon. I wanted to be with him—and only him—despite the challenges of our different life spans and the uncertainty of what would happen between us after I got my revenge. Being with Gideon was my choice, and I would not let Oberon or a spell come between us.

I rose from the bed and went to open the window, needing some fresh air. As I looked down at the people below going about their normal lives, I felt a pang of envy. How I wished I could have that sense of normalcy, but my life had taken a hard left turn into chaos. I glanced at the tattoo on my hand, and dread trickled into me.

The number was a relentless reminder that the clock was ticking. What if I couldn't find a way to remove it and the number hit zero? What if Heather's plan was to destroy the Watchers, and the tattoo would somehow help accomplish that? What if I failed to prevent their destruction and the apocalypse began?

As the dark thoughts took over, I shook my head to push them out of my mind. I couldn't allow myself to lose hope—hope to get my life back, hope to be with my family again, hope to save the world. Tomorrow would be a new day, and with a fresh mind, I'd figure out ways to deal with the many challenges that lay ahead.

Yeah, it was a tall order. But hey, I was up for it.